PRAISE FOR JEANETTE WINDLE

"Windle is a top-notch storyteller."
PUBLISHERS WEEKLY

"Jeanette Windle's *Congo Dawn* brings home the profound truth that God's love and human suffering are not impossible contradictions, but a divine paradox those refined in the fires of adversity are best equipped to understand."

DR. BRUCE WILKINSON, internationally bestselling author of *The Prayer of Jabez*

"Jeanette Windle writes about the darkest corners of the world with absolute authority, using dogged research, an eye for detail, and her talents as a storyteller to make the reader feel absolutely *there*."

MINDY STARNS CLARK, bestselling author of *The Amish Midwife*

"*Congo Dawn* is a riveting story by Jeanette Windle, whose realism and attention to detail are second to none."

ANDRES SCHWARTZ, former US Navy SEAL

"Author Jeanette Windle paints a picture of the great Ituri Rainforest and its people that is so real I was whisked back to the Africa of my childhood. . . . An artistic triumph."

TAMAR MYERS, bestselling author of *The Witch Doctor's Wife*

"Jeanette Windle's portrayal of a female interpreter attached to Congo mercenaries creates a gripping story of forgiveness, hope, and love."

MARTHA MUNCE, vice president, Munce Group

"When it comes to international intrigue and the impact of Christ in hard settings, no one bests Jeanette Windle. *Congo Dawn* is another of her riveting stories."

GAYLE ROPER, bestselling author of *Autumn Dreams*

"Enthralling! Windle's masterful touch shines, [and] out of darkness and despair comes *Congo Dawn*, a gripping, heartbreaking tale that will infuse readers with a thirst for justice."

RONIE KENDIG, Christy Award–winning author of *Wolfsbane*

"*Congo Dawn* is that rare high-energy novel that doesn't just leave you breathless but with a good deal to think about once you close the book."

DON HOESEL, author of *Elisha's Bones* and *Serpent of Moses*

"A heart-pounding ride ripped from the headlines with an added punch of humanity that will tug at your heart and leave you looking at the world in a different light."

LISA HARRIS, author of Christy Award finalist *Blood Ransom* and 2011 *Romantic Times* best inspirational novel *Blood Covenant*

"I am really impressed with Jeanette's ability to transport readers to an unfamiliar environment. . . . It's obvious from the first pages that Jeanette really knows and cares about the Congo."

KAY MARSHALL STROM, award-winning author of the Grace in Africa series

"I loved this book. Jeanette Windle always delivers strong stories, characters you will fall in love with, and a spiritual theme that will either drive you to your Bible or to your knees. Once again, Jeanette delivers with another wonderful book that will keep you up late flipping the pages as fast as you can read."

WANDA DYSON, bestselling author of *Judgment Day* and *Shepherd's Fall*

"'Where is God in our darkest night?' The myriad story threads in *Congo Dawn* all do revolve around this question. Jeanette's genius is in how she weaves them all together, and in the flawed yet ultimately lovable characters she writes about."

WAMBURA KIMUNYU, author, publisher, and international board member, Media Associates International, Nairobi, Kenya

CONGO DAWN

THE SMALLEST FLAME
SHINES BRIGHTEST AGAINST
THE DARKEST NIGHT

CONGO DAWN

JEANETTE WINDLE

TYNDALE HOUSE PUBLISHERS INC.
CAROL STREAM, IL

Visit Tyndale online at www.tyndale.com.

Visit Jeanette Windle's website at www.jeanettewindle.com.

TYNDALE and Tyndale's quill logo are registered trademarks of Tyndale House Publishers, Inc.

Congo Dawn

Designed by Dean H. Renninger

Edited by Caleb Sjogren

Published in association with the literary agency of Stan Guthrie Communications, 1102 Dawes Ave., Wheaton, IL 60189.

Congo Dawn is a work of fiction. Where real people, events, establishments, organizations, or locales appear, they are used fictitiously. All other elements of the novel are drawn from the author's imagination.

Library of Congress Cataloging-in-Publication Data

Windle, Jeanette.
  Congo dawn / Jeanette Windle.
    p. cm.
  ISBN 978-1-4143-7158-0 (sc)
    1. Americans—Congo (Democratic Republic)—Fiction. 2. Suspense fiction.
3. Christian fiction. I. Title.
  PS3573.I5172C66 2013
  813'.54—dc23   2012036151

Printed in the United States of America

19   18   17   16   15   14   13
7   6   5   4   3   2   1

*To the medical personnel, mission pilots, and other volunteers
who courageously and selflessly continue to shine bright the
light of Yesu's (Jesus') love in the darkness that is today's Ituri
conflict zone, especially those who have contributed to this
story—you know who you are—I dedicate this book.*

While all events, characters, and the jungle mission clinic of Taraja
("Hope") itself are completely fictional, the story of *Congo Dawn*
was inspired in part by its true-life Ituri Rainforest counterparts,
Nebobongo and Nyankunde, targets of brutal massacres and
destruction by insurgent rebels during the 1964 and 2002
uprisings in northeastern Democratic Republic of the Congo.

PROLOGUE

Paradise Lost.

That translated piece of literature written by a long-ago foreign poet had been a favorite of Jesuit monks who'd taught a Congolese orphan boy his letters and their language many years ago. Perhaps because they'd felt just so at their exile to his own country.

"*Baba.* Father. Have you not understood what I said? With these we can now make a paradise out of our home."

Father and son stood on a stony outcropping that thrust skyward over the rainforest canopy, one of dozens of the strange rock formations that rose like termite mounds above the treetops, their stony composition bearing no apparent relation to the sandy soil or red clay that made up the jungle floor. Burial mounds of the Ancient Ones, tribal legends avowed before pale-skinned foreigners arrived to teach terms like *igneous* and *volcanic anomaly.*

"Baba, do you not see what a miracle this is? As great a miracle as finding you alive again. The Almighty at last has chosen to shower favor upon us. This place, our people, will never be the same again."

The tall, ebony-skinned youth was dressed incongruously for this place in collared shirt, slacks, and such shiny black shoes as his feet had never known during their growing years. But anxious, dark eyes and beaming smile were the same, though he now held out a handful of gray pebbles rather than the schoolwork of his boyhood. In years past, his father could have responded with unstinted praise, but now he shifted his own bare feet to look down over the cliff edge.

The clearing below stretched to the banks of a wide, lazy river, its water the dark tannin shade of tea, a drink the Jesuit monks had taught the older man to enjoy. Several dozen thatched mud-brick huts occupied the highest ground, beyond the reach of wet-season flooding. Women wrapped in the colorful lengths of homespun cloth called pagnes stooped among cultivations of cassava, maize, beans, yams, and peanuts. Others moved along a path from the riverbank, their graceful sway balancing pottery water jars on top of their heads.

Children too young for work or school scampered among banana plants, playing some game of running and hiding. On the river itself, a pair of hand-hewn wooden pirogues drifted lazily toward a bend where the watercourse disappeared back into untamed rainforest. Several village men, naked except for the same loincloth that was the older man's sole dress, stood precariously on the canoe rims to cast fishing nets woven of thin, supple lianas. Drawing the nets from the water, they removed a few catfish and eel, then cast the nets again.

Paradise Lost.

There was a time when such had been the older man's own opinion of this remote jungle locality. When this place had seemed to him an unjust and cruel exile.

Young then, younger than his last-born offspring now standing beside him, he'd been among his country's first high school graduates after their colonial masters at last packed up and left. By then a Congolese army officer named Mobutu had seized control in their place. Renaming his country Zaire, he'd promised that its vast natural wealth would no longer enrich foreigners but instead provide a grand new world of prosperity, justice, and peace for the Congolese people. The older man standing on the rock outcropping had been the first appointed administrator for the schoolhouse and health outpost their new government had pledged to build in every village.

Life here had not then been so isolated. There'd been a road. Just a dirt track carved through the rainforest but wide enough for motorized vehicles. The road's makers had not built it with any interest in the village. This region had none of the treasures its foreign masters had craved. No diamonds. No gold. No copper. Not even rich soil to be exploited for cotton, sugarcane, or other cash crops. It was simply a dot on the map. And though government tax collectors traveled the road, so did the army units who maintained a welcome stability.

Still, to a youth who'd known the amenities of a city, the taste of imported drink, the stimulation of books and travel, his appointment here had seemed more punishment than promotion. Unfortunately, he'd also been a kinless orphan without connections of blood or wealth to command better opportunities.

Why had he stayed? Especially since Mobutu's new name for an ancient land had proved to last far longer than his promises. Instead of schools and medical centers, Mobutu with his sycophants and endless greedy relatives had built for themselves palaces, parks, and places of entertainment. Betrayal in turn spawned revolt. Rebel militias of every stripe and tribal allegiance became as much a part of the Congolese landscape as crumbling bridges, abandoned rail stations, and beached riverboats.

Perhaps it was no more complicated than a village girl with the ebony roundness, graceful lift of head under her water jar, and strong limbs of true female beauty who'd by then caught his eye. Since the riverbank community was in essence a single intermarried tribal clan, he'd acquired along with a wife the extended family he'd never known in that Jesuit orphanage.

The older man standing now at the cliff edge had not left the Ituri Rainforest again. When the promised concrete school building never materialized, he'd used his own government salary to raise a mud-brick community center. There he'd taught classes and administered rudimentary health care until growing troubles outside the rainforest cut off even that meager stipend. As motorized vehicles stopped passing through, the road grew over with lianas and ferns. Market goods were reduced to what could be lashed to the frames of occasional bicycles that still wore a narrow track along the old road-bed. The community center's tin roofing gradually rusted away, to be replaced with the same thatch as the rest of the village.

By then the administrator had his own growing family. He'd kept them fed as other village families did by cultivating the soil, harvesting the abundance of rainforest and river. And he'd kept the school open, teaching each succeeding crop of boys and girls from the crumbling Swahili primers and Holy Scriptures that were the only books the village possessed. Though most considered squatting indoors over battered slates and mildewed pages a pointless exercise, there were a few with a hunger to learn who walked a full day down the overgrown road to where the foreign God-followers had healed the region's sick and offered a higher education to their children.

Including this youngest son standing before him.

The boy had not been gone long when news trickled into the village with the last of the bicycle merchants that the white foreigners had been driven from the rainforest, their hospital and secondary school burned to the ground by raiding rebels, the town's Congolese inhabitants massacred. To add terror were other rumors of villages wiped out by soldiers who were not rebels but wore the uniforms of government forces.

While war raged in the outside world, the village closed in upon itself. The bicycle trail was now a tangle of vegetation. Not in many seasons had their community received so much as a visitor from some other jungle village. For all they could know, they might be the only survivors left upon the planet.

Still, the schoolmaster, by now undisputedly acclaimed the village chief, continued to teach the children in faith that one day the road would open again to a wider world.

And the road had indeed opened to bring the return of a son he'd despaired still bore life. Leaning against a boulder down below was a small motorbike that had somehow pushed its way through the overgrown roadbed. The story his son told was not uncommon in the Congo. Among a few students evacuated with the white foreigners, he'd found himself in a refugee camp so far from home he could not have covered the distance in many days of walking. And other survivors had told him that every village in his Ituri district had been razed to the ground.

The boy's education soon secured him employment as a translator. Seeing potential in the young man, the foreign aid workers sponsored him for further education, eventually even outside the Congo itself. When he'd at last made his way back to this place, it hadn't been with any expectation of finding the village. But he'd been as delighted to discover his family still living as they were to receive him.

Not until he'd insisted his father climb this outcropping with him had he explained the real reason for his return. The older man shook his head now at the gray pebbles on his son's outstretched palm, not in negation, but perplexity.

"All know our country's very bones are filled with great treasure. But there have been foreigners here before to make their tests on these hills. Back when your oldest brother was still at his mother's breast. Graphite, they named this rock."

Plucking a chunk from his son's palm, he rubbed it across a nearby boulder. It left a dark streak. "See? These have proved useful enough to the children for forming their letters since we can no longer obtain pencils. But it is too common for the mining companies to come this far after it."

"Those who came before were wrong, Baba. This is what I have been studying since I left you. Geology. Remember this? The collection I made as a boy when you first taught us of the treasures a rock can hold?"

Yes, the older man recognized the small, lumpy bag crafted from sun-cured duiker hide. He remembered, too, the boy's disappointment that the glitter of a pyrite pebble was not in fact gold.

His son was still speaking. "Remember how angry I was that always it has been others—the foreigners, our own corrupt leaders—who reaped the benefit of such treasure and not the people under whose soil it was found? You taught me too not to hate or dwell on past injustices. To become a student and not a rebel. And as a student, I took my collection with me, even when I was running and in the refugee camp. I kept it because it was all I still had of this place. But when I found employment with a mining firm, I tested the rocks in their lab. And I found that those who came here long ago were wrong. That is not graphite you hold in your hand, but a treasure infinitely more valuable. A treasure not even known to exist in your childhood. Valuable enough to bring to this place employment and restored roads and electricity. Better schools and a hospital. All the goods and opportunities I have seen in the outside world that our people have so long been denied."

The youth trailed off, for the first time registering that his father did not reflect his own excitement. "Why are you not rejoicing, Baba? Is this not what you have prayed for? A better life for our people? For the children you have taught?"

The village administrator was too troubled now to hide it from his expression. Was it for this he'd sent his son from the rainforest to seek a higher education and better world? Such naiveté? Such foolishness?

Paradise Lost.

Strange that only now, as he contemplated its loss, did the village administrator recognize any similarities between this place to which he'd been so reluctantly exiled long decades ago and a Garden described in the Holy Scriptures. A Garden where the first man and woman had opened their eyes to the presence of a Creator God who walked with his children.

Had that first couple looked out as he did now over such endless, tossing, verdant waves? Had they marveled at orange, pink, and lilac flowering trees and rainbow-hued orchids spilling over branches and down tree trunks? Had they smiled or frowned at the chattering, chirping, croaking, cawing, and other noises that signaled the jungle's richly varied animal life? Black-and-white colobus monkeys. Cockatoos and macaws. That rarest of rainforest mammals, the okapi, an odd if beautiful hybrid of zebra and giraffe. The more abundant duikers and bongo antelopes kept in check by leopards.

And human predators as well, indication that this was not after all the original Paradise. Down below, a group of village men were just now emerging from the rainforest into an orchard of mango, citrus, papaya, and coconut palms. Among limp shapes slung across shoulders, the administrator could pick out antelope, boar, and a vine-tied clutch of pangolin, that tasty rainforest resident with the shape of an opossum and the shelled armor of an armadillo. Added to the catch of those fishermen in the pirogues, the village would eat well tonight.

Yes, if life here was simple, isolated, precarious of existence, bowing always to the vagaries of nature that could in an instant send flood, forest fire, or pestilence to sweep away the timid hold its small band of human inhabitants had carved out on the riverbank, it was perhaps not so ill as the older man had often thought it.

In a gesture that surprised him with its violence, he slapped the gray rock chunks from his son's hand. "As you said, Son, when have the people under whose soil such treasures have been found ever been permitted to profit from its wealth? Tell me now! Whom have you told of this treasure of yours?"

His son looked more bewildered and disappointed than angry at his father's reaction. "I saw no reason to keep it secret. On the contrary, it took much persuading before my employers were convinced that I was not wasting their time."

The younger man held up a small, plastic-shelled oblong. The administrator alone among the villagers would recognize its purpose. A cell phone.

"I have already let them know that I have confirmed a sufficient source to justify their interest. And why not? We will need help from the outside—much investment—to develop this treasure. The first step will be to open the old road."

He'd lost his father's attention. This rocky knoll had always been a handy lookout for forest fires. But not for enemies slipping up on the village. The jungle canopy was too impenetrable for that. This time, though, the height of the stony outcropping had provided advance notice of invasion. The older man was already scrambling downward toward the village as quickly as the steep slope permitted. As soon as he was within earshot, he raised his voice in an ululating cry.

It was too late. The roar of two helicopters swooping in low over the jungle had roused more curiosity than alarm. The villagers were hurrying into the open to stare upward as the helicopters hovered above a cassava field.

Shiny black shoes slipped and skidded on the rock behind the administrator as his son scrambled after him. "Baba, there is no need of fear. It is only our investors."

But the men jumping from the helicopters' open sides did not wear the suits or carry the briefcases of businessmen. These were predators. And not of animals, but of men. More ominously, neither did all have the dark skin or features of Congolese.

His son was now at the older man's side. "There has been some mistake. I will go speak to them."

But his father was shoving him into the cover of trees and lianas and brush with all the strength of rage and panic and despair. "No, I am chief here. I will speak for my people. You must escape. You must find help."

The screams had already begun. His youngest son had obeyed his orders and was no longer in view. As he strode into the open, the older man found himself in complete agreement on one point.

Life for his people, his village, this beautiful rainforest paradise, would never be the same.

CNN, Kinshasa, DRC—The Democratic Republic of the Congo made public today the latest discovery of this mineral-rich nation's exploitable natural resources in the northeastern province of Ituri. This vein of molybdenite, prime source of the rare metal molybdenum, already shows promise of surpassing the recent molybdenite finds in Mexico and Siberia combined.

Wall Street Journal, **New York—**Mining companies hoping to cash in on Ituri molybdenite were disappointed to learn that global consortium Earth Resources has already struck a deal with DRC's Ministry of Mines in Kinshasa for an exclusive mining concession in the aforementioned zone. Earth Resources CEO Trevor Mulroney and regional governor Jean Pierre Wamba in Ituri province's capital of Bunia jointly express their satisfaction that this project will bring badly needed economic stimulus and employment into this war-weary and poverty-stricken province.

Military Industry Today, **London—**News flash for the private defense industry. Prominent British entrepreneur Trevor Mulroney announces the recent acquisition by his consortium Earth Resources, Ltd, of a controlling interest in the private military corporation Ares Solutions. The original founder of Ares Solutions two decades ago, Mulroney expresses pleasure at this new alliance between Ares Solutions and Earth Resources along with expectations of continued rapid growth and profits for both entities and their shareholders.

Kinshasa Times, **Bunia, DRC—**Breaking an extended cease-fire, rebel forces are again threatening the peace of northeast Congo, using the cover of the Ituri Rainforest to strike villages and raid government installations. Daily reports of atrocities are pouring into UN peacekeeping headquarters in the Ituri capital of Bunia. Recent advancements in mineral development of the region have been threatened by attacks on the molybdenite mine and ore-transport convoys.

CHAPTER ONE

He could stop this with a word. A raised hand.

Instead he began the task for which he'd come as a band of armed men fanned out, kicking in bamboo doors, tossing torches onto thatched roofs, dragging residents still groggy with sleep into the open. A spattering of gunfire on the far side of the village signaled the first resistance.

He made no effort to interfere when the first woman was tossed down onto the red dirt of the clearing. Flames leaping high from burning huts now matched the red and orange streaks lightening a dawn sky above the jungle canopy. The gunfire had become a steady staccato. He closed his ears to its clatter. To the shouts, screams, moans. The terrified sobbing of a child.

But he could not so close his eyes. These images would never leave his mind.

By the time all fell silent, the rising sun had cleared the treetops. But its cheerful rays could not penetrate a black pall of smoke that drifted upward to cast its spreading shadow across the sky.

He turned his head as a hand touched his shoulder. His second-in-command stepped close to murmur urgently, "The searchers found nothing. Learned nothing. We must go before the smoke is spotted and others come."

But he shook off his subordinate's warning hand to stride out across the clearing. Stepping around prone shapes and viscous scarlet puddles, he peered through smoldering doorframes until the thunderous crash of a collapsing roof startled him into prudence. Only when he was satisfied nothing remained to be done did he lift a hand in signal. As he slipped noiselessly into the rainforest's camouflage of leaf and vine and root, a phalanx of phantoms melted into invisibility with him.

Behind them, all that remained of what had been a tranquil rainforest community were embers and dead bodies.

He did not permit himself to waste a heartbeat on pity.

After all, none had been granted him or his!

> > >

UGANDA-DRC BORDER

"The problem with these people, *bokkie*, isn't that they can't be bought. It's that they just won't *stay* bought!"

Robin Duncan had no illusion that the brawny, flaxen-blond South African mercenary was referencing their Congolese driver, who still sat unmoving behind the steering wheel of the ancient two-and-a-half-ton market truck, staring out a cracked windshield.

Nor a dozen equally brawny Caucasian males hunkered down on a pile of luggage in the truck bed.

Nor even the two border guards who'd waggled their heads and AK-47 assault rifles at the passports and stamped visa forms Robin offered through a rolled-down window.

No, Pieter Krueger's latest disgusted pronouncement was directed at the same person or persons responsible for Robin's own sour attitude and sore posterior. Cracked vinyl upholstery over broken wire springs was hardly adequate protection against twenty kilometers of jolting through deep ruts, untrimmed brush, and dry streambeds. Especially when she'd been awake and on the move for over twenty-four hours.

Robin straightened her spine to ease stiffened back muscles as she stepped away from the truck cab. Just beyond the truck's rusted hood, a metal pole extended across the dirt track. A round hut squatted in the shade of several large mango trees, its conical thatched roof giving the appearance of a witch's hat.

Black letters staggered drunkenly across the whitewash of the hut. *Services de l'immigration République démocratique du Congo.*

A touch of officialdom drooped from a second metal pole, this one vertical. The sky-blue banner with a diagonal red stripe banded in yellow and a yellow star in the upper-left corner—the DRC's most recent version of a country flag. A scattering of cinder-block shacks completed the hamlet. Shops, apparently, from the boxes of cigarettes, aluminum cookware, grain sacks, and mounds of fruit and vegetables that were identifiable even under a coating of red dust.

But if this Congolese strip mall existed to capitalize on transnational traffic, business was poor. The market truck was the only vehicle pulled up to the roadblock. Behind it, the dirt track snaking back through the no-man's-land held only a few trudging pedestrians balancing loads on their heads along with a rapidly approaching dust cloud. A motorcycle, judging by the size of the cloud and the distinct rumble. Beyond the roadblock where the road disappeared again into a dense tangle of green, not a motorized vehicle nor even a bicycle was in sight.

Which might account for the swarm of vendors already mobbing the truck with dusty glass bottles of Coca-Cola and Primus, the region's ubiquitous local beer, as well as plastic baggies filled with a cloudy liquid that could be palm wine or coconut water. And the bored indolence with which the two guards ambled around the truck to peer through the wooden slats at its cargo of passengers and luggage.

"So just what's the holdup?" A hand dropped onto Robin's shoulder. "Why are they not letting us through?"

"They say there's a problem with our papers. You'll have to go inside and speak to the com-mander." Robin inched away as Pieter Krueger's large frame loomed uncomfortably close. She'd been working a UN fact-finding mission as team linguist in Haiti when the private security company that held her contract, Ares Solutions, had contacted her. Two of the language skills listed on her résumé— French (excellent) and Swahili (passable)—were urgently needed for a brand-new security contract in eastern DRC. The hazard pay bonus offered was generous enough to suggest caution if Robin didn't need the money so badly. She'd been issued a replacement for Haiti and an e-ticket to Kenya by the time her duffel bag was packed.

In the Nairobi airport, Robin had joined up with some two dozen other Ares Solutions operatives. From their introductions, the group constituted a fairly stereotypical representation of their chosen career in more ways than just the inevitable safari-style clothing, Kevlar vests, wraparound sunglasses, and muscled builds. Two German commandos. Several Australian and New Zealander former paratroopers. A scattering of East European elite troopers whose Cold War training offered few employment opportunities at home these days but was a hot commodity in the private military market. Robin's only countrymen were a pair of Vietnam-era Green Berets, gray-haired and weather-beaten.

But by far the largest contingent were white Africans. South African commandos who'd gone freelance once their country fell under black rule. Rhodesians who'd fought as teenagers in Ian Smith's Bush War before that country became Zimbabwe. Angolan Portuguese. Three white Kenyans who'd served in the British Special Air Service. A pair of apartheid-era Afrikaner combat helicopter pilots.

All had that ineffable air—less arrogance than supreme self-confidence combined with somewhat-unkempt personal grooming—that suggested they'd knocked around the planet's sleazier underbelly long and successfully enough that they simply didn't care what any other human being might think of them. Dangerous men, definitely. For hire, perhaps. But still warriors and superlatively expert at their craft. English was the one language they'd all demonstrated in common. None spoke more than a few words of French or Swahili, not even the Kenyans, in whose country the latter was a primary language among its black majority population.

Well, that was why Robin was here.

The single other outlier on this mission was a third passenger now clambering down from the truck cab, pale-blue eyes blinking behind metal-rimmed glasses. His gaze shifted only fractionally from the reinforced screen of a tough-travel notebook computer to find his footing. Round-shouldered, brown hair untrimmed, Carl Jensen looked so much the image of Shaggy on *Scooby-Doo* that Robin had found herself instinctively glancing around for his canine companion.

"You mean *you'll* have to speak to this commander." White teeth flashed in chiseled, handsome features as Krueger stepped forward to reclaim the space Robin had inserted between them. "You did well enough in Arua. But border authorities in these parts are not so predictable, especially for a woman. Just stay close to me, speak only the words I give you, and you'll be safe enough."

An Afrikaner in his late thirties, Pieter Krueger had introduced himself in Nairobi as manager for Ares Solutions' African operations. He'd herded the group onto a C-130 four-engine military cargo plane chartered to ferry their team along with a full load of mission supplies from Nairobi to Bunia, in the DRC. But the pilot had announced midflight that their clearance into the Democratic Republic of the Congo had been inexplicably revoked.

They'd diverted instead to land in Arua, a Ugandan border town. While a handful of Ares Solutions operatives remained behind to mount guard over the plane's contents, Robin had used her halting Swahili to help Krueger negotiate ground transport just over the Congolese border, where arrangements had been made for an air pickup from Bunia.

"But we do not have much time. We still have a drive ahead to the airstrip, and our flight could be landing anytime now. You might as well learn now our new mutual employer has no patience for unpunctuality." Krueger's hand on Robin's shoulder slid down to the small of her back as though to steer her toward the border outpost. "I must say a female translator is still a surprise. I have served in the past with Trevor Mulroney, and he is not the sort to hire a woman for such a mission as this. Or at all. Not that I am complaining to have such a pretty young *bokkie* on the team."

Robin gritted her teeth at his appreciative leer and the warm pressure of his hand. Pieter Krueger had insisted Robin join him and Carl in the truck cab instead of crouching down against a whirlwind of red dust in the open truck bed. To facilitate communication with the driver had been his stated rationale. The South African mercenary was admittedly a striking male specimen whose rugged, blond good looks could have graced a Nazi-era poster for Aryan perfection. And single, he'd been quick to let Robin know.

But after the past hour of running commentary on corrupt African governance, unruly native populations, Krueger's exploits fighting in Africa's many wars, and the general worthlessness of the entire continent north of Johannesburg, Robin wasn't so sure she'd brokered the better deal. And if his Afrikaner slang was the endearment she guessed, Robin was going to have to set some hard boundaries before this contract progressed much further.

Not for the first time in the testosterone-dominated profession she'd chosen.

"So, anything cold to drink around this place?" Carl Jensen slammed shut his laptop to glance around.

"Cold, no. Wet, yes. Just don't buy anything that isn't factory bottled if you don't want to pay for it later." Gesturing to where her teammates were already trading coins for drinks, Robin used the interruption to step discreetly away so Pieter Krueger had to drop his hand. The South African threw her a sharp glance, white teeth disappearing into a frown. But without further comment, he strode toward the whitewashed hut. Robin followed, deliberately lagging two paces behind.

Overhead, a fierce sun marked the hour as close to noon. Breaking out a hand wipe from the knapsack she carried over one shoulder, Robin swabbed perspiring cheeks as she walked. It came away sodden with red mud. A breeze whistling through the mango trees brought with its cooling touch a scent of dust and green mangoes, manure, and fermenting palm sap, tapped all over Africa as an alcoholic beverage.

Drifting from inside one of the shops, the syncopated beat of a carved-wood drum accompanied a man's voice crooning a Swahili folk ballad. In a cultivated field beyond, a pair of zebras, mother and foal, munched contentedly on whatever crop was planted there.

Zebras! How long had it been since Robin had glimpsed a zebra outside a zoo?

There'd been a time in Robin's far-distant childhood when the sights, sounds, and smells of an African countryside roused only delight, a magical real-life version of Disney's *The Lion King*. The vast green horizons and bright-red earth like nothing else she'd seen on the planet. Those peculiar flat-topped trees for which she knew no name, dotting open pastures like inverted brooms. Clusters of thatched huts, round and square. The chaos and bright colors of an open-air market. Grinning dark faces and the staccato of bare feet pounding in dance for the latest community excuse of celebration.

But today Robin saw instead the rheumy, sunken eyes of several small children peering from an alley between shops, their naked bellies swollen from parasites and malnutrition. The angry desperation of vendors battling for a rare sale. Piles of rotting garbage that competed with the fragrance of fresh-picked fruit. The casual, even bored brutality with which the two guards were now using the butts of their weapons to beat back a few peddlers who persisted in hassling the new arrivals.

I am so tired of war and hunger and poverty. Of places and jobs like this. Of human misery and sheer human meanness that never seems to reach its limit! All the more reason to get through this checkpoint and this contract as quickly as possible.

Which did not prove so simple a matter as Robin had hoped.

The interior of the border outpost was a single large room open to the thatched roof. A metal filing cabinet, scattered plastic chairs, and the rickety wooden table that served as the immigration counter constituted its sole furnishings. Geckos scurried up walls where whitewashed plaster had crumbled to reveal mud brick beneath. Something unseen rustled in the dried palm fronds directly above Robin's head. The only lighting filtered through a pair of small windows.

"So you understand, your papers are no good here." A short but powerfully built man, the outpost commander had barely glanced at the stack of signed, stamped immigration forms before waving them away. On the table in front of him, empty Primus bottles crowded a manual typewriter. A sickly-sweet aroma of marijuana smoke suggested the lethargy and reddened, dilated glares of two more guards who'd jumped to their feet as the group entered were not after all due to boredom or interrupted slumber. "This means you cannot enter my country."

"I don't understand. How can these visas be no good?" Robin asked with a patience she did not feel. Even as she spoke, through the open door she took note of the motorcycle she'd heard earlier pulling up outside. Bundles lashed to its frame were piled so high she caught only a glimpse of blue jeans as a passenger dismounted. Robin pushed the stack of paperwork across the table. "These visas are issued by your own government. We received them just this morning in Nairobi."

"Then that is the problem. You have not crossed into the DRC from Kenya, but from Uganda. So that requires a separate visa. You cannot proceed without it."

But you rejected our visas before you even knew we'd originated in Kenya! Robin didn't dare introduce logic audibly into this proceeding. Recent years had taught her only too well the lessons of dealing with Third World bureaucracy. Never argue injustice. Never look a uniform in the eye. Grovel humbly and smilingly. Above all, let small-minded, petty officials, especially those carrying automatic weapons, feel as big and powerful and important as necessary to get the job done!

Behind Robin, Pieter Krueger's body language radiated impatience while others of the team were now jostling through the open door. Though Ugandan border control had required them to leave their weapons with the C-130, such a sizable group of large, muscled expatriates was attracting unfriendly glares from the commander's two bodyguards. Robin didn't care for the restless twitchiness with which they were fingering their AK-47s.

In her most conciliatory French, she pleaded, "But we have a plane waiting to pick us up. We won't have time to return to Uganda and come back. Surely there must be something we can do. Someone we can talk to. We have come to your country by direct invitation of the Ituri governor, Jean Pierre Wamba. See, here is his letter of authorization."

The commander's glance of incomprehension at the typed French and scrawled signature under an official letterhead confirmed Robin's suspicions of the man's illiteracy. "And what good is this? How am I to know it is not a forgery? No, you must return to Uganda and purchase new visas."

He wasn't going to budge. Her shoulders slumping in defeat, Robin murmured unhappily to Pieter Krueger, "I'm sorry, but I've tried everything I can, and I'm afraid we're just out of luck. He insists we have to go back to Arua and get new visas before we can cross. Can you radio our pickup and let them know we've got another delay on our hands?"

"You've got to be kidding! Mulroney swore he'd taken care of all the paperwork for this mission. Like I said, these people just won't stay bought."

It was as well Robin didn't understand Krueger's stream of low, furious Afrikaans. As the outpost commander's unyielding expression dissolved into a scowl, she braced herself to break into the South African's invective. But an amused voice, its accent unmistakably American, did it for her. "Hey, don't give up so fast. You should know Commander Patrice isn't really expecting you to go all the way back to Arua. Just to offer the proper incentive. As any half-baked briefing for travel in this region should have warned you. Here, maybe I can be of assistance."

Robin's peripheral vision identified a glimpse of blue denim as the motorcycle passenger. But it wasn't the welcome offer of help that whirled Robin around. She could actually feel blood draining from her face as her eyes widened in shock. No, she hadn't imagined she recognized that sardonic baritone. The motorcycle passenger appeared almost slight next to a huge Bulgarian mercenary who'd entered behind him until he strode forward enough to reveal he was several inches taller than Robin's own five feet eight inches. He looked thinner than Robin remembered, though no less muscled under a T-shirt so red with dust its original hue was a matter of dispute.

And older, deep grooves traced the stern edges of his mouth from high-bridged nose to firm chin. Nor did those tawny-brown eyes, fringed in long, dark lashes, hold any of the smiling warmth Robin had once known there. They were instead guarded and somber as though with unforgotten pain or grief. An always-deep tan was now burned to coppery bronze only a shade lighter than his close-cropped curls. All but for a single ridge of healed scar tissue that ran palely in a jagged line from below his left ear down his neck to disappear beneath the thin material of his T-shirt.

The sudden whitening of that scar, his change of expression to disbelief as Robin whirled around, made clear she, too, was amply recognizable despite the passage of years.

He'd approached so close now that she could make out her own wavery reflection in his stunned dark gaze. Tired oval features that never truly tanned, thanks to the same genetic makeup responsible for a red-gold mane currently tucked under a floppy brimmed hat. A straightforward blue-green gaze this man standing in front of her had once compared to the quiet beauty of the Himalayan mountain pool beside which they were bivouacked at the time.

His sharp inhalation of breath, the stiffening of his body in mid-stride, permitted Robin to release her words through unsteady lips first. "Michael Stewart! What—what are you doing here?"

He unfroze, finishing his stride so that he closed the gap between them. "What am I doing here? I at least belong here! What are you doing here? And with this bunch. You're the last person I'd have thought would ever trade in fatigues to go freelance."

Of course, Michael had grown up in sub-Saharan Africa, son of American medical missionaries, though Robin did not remember exactly where. Or her subconscious deliberately chose to forget. His stories of African rainforest life, as idyllic in their telling as Robin's own childhood memories, had contributed to the bond that once existed between them.

He broke off, his firm, straight mouth twisting suddenly, his glance sliding away from Robin before he added quietly, "I never got a chance to say . . . I've been wanting to tell you for a long time . . . I am so sorry about your brother. My deepest condolences."

After five years of waiting for those words, they were as unexpected, even unwelcome, as his appearance. Now it was Robin who froze. She was no longer in the muggy, dark confines of a Congo border outpost, but on a chill, high Himalayan mountain ridge. The dust in her nostrils no longer equatorial Africa's red soil, but the powdery, light dirt of Afghanistan. Dampness streaking her face no longer sweat, but tears. Explosions and the *rat-tat-tat* of automatic gunfire rang in her ears. Her bloodied hands frantically pressed back the crimson flood welling up through shattered body armor.

Then the roar of the evac helicopter hovered down, and this man's younger self was jumping out to push her aside. The last time she'd seen or heard from Michael Stewart, he'd been lifting Robin's groaning, semiconscious, but very much alive youngest sibling into the helicopter. Not just her sibling, but the incredible, talented, wonderful human being who'd been Robin's best friend in this world.

And this man's too.

Or so she'd believed.

CHAPTER TWO

"You're sorry! That's all you have to say? When you swore you'd save him? When you abandoned both of us? When it's your fault he died?"

Fists pounded against a hard chest. Fingernails scratched at tanned features. Boots lashed out to strike blue denim. Screamed-out invective, raw with anguish, released long-pent-up fury.

"Why are you telling me this now? Why didn't you come to me before? When it still mattered! When I'd still believe you! Don't you know how much I hate you more than I ever thought I cared about you? That I will never to the end of my days ever forgive you?"

The blood rushed back into Robin's head. A deeply drawn-in breath filled her gasping lungs, slowed her racing pulse. No, from Michael's unscratched features and the disinterested expressions all around her, Robin had disgraced neither herself nor her mission. Her tantrum, both verbal and physical, had remained where it belonged— only in her mind. A step backward placed her at a safe distance from her target. She did not, could not respond to his statement.

Instead, she demanded coolly, "You said you could help us? Just how, exactly?"

The outpost commander had shown no objection to Michael's interruption. On the contrary, he'd lost his scowl. Behind him, the two guards were actually lowering their weapons. It was Pieter Krueger who stepped up beside Robin to query suspiciously, "You know this man?"

"We served together in Afghanistan," Robin explained tersely. "This is—"

The new arrival was already stepping forward to offer a handshake. "—Dr. Michael Stewart, on assignment here with Médecins Sans Frontières." He rolled the pronunciation of the Switzerland-based humanitarian organization across his tongue like a native French speaker. "Zipped over to Uganda for some medical supplies needed ASAP at a mission hospital compound out in the Ituri Rainforest near Bunia. A delay at the pharmacy there cost me my seat on this morning's UN flight."

So since Robin last saw him, Michael had achieved his dream of becoming a surgeon in his father's footsteps. He held up a cell phone. "A UN colleague in Bunia just tipped me off they've scheduled an extra charter to pick up an expat security team stranded down here. Can I hope you're that team? And that I might hitch a ride back to Bunia?"

The South African's narrowed glance from Robin to the newcomer held neither welcome nor friendliness, but his broad shoulders hunched a grudging admission. "Yes, it is our charter. And if you can spring us through this minefield in time to make our flight, I'm sure we can arrange a tagalong."

Michael was already turning to the outpost commander, breaking into such a colloquial mix of Swahili and French that Robin had to strain her language skills to follow it. But there was no mistaking that the American surgeon was no stranger here. Or that he'd come prepared to negotiate his own passage. As Michael spoke, he unobtrusively deposited next to the empty Primus bottles three sizable plastic containers labeled *ibuprofen*. Now smiling broadly, the commander retreated with Michael to the rear of the hut for a brief murmured conversation. When they walked back, the commander scooped the ibuprofen out of sight into a file cabinet drawer while Michael swung around to address the Ares Solutions contingent.

"Now that Commander Patrice has heard the urgency and importance of your mission, and as a personal favor to this region's beloved leader, Governor Wamba, he has reconsidered his decision and will issue a special visa kept for just such emergency situations. But the forms and stamps needed for these special visas are very costly. The price will be one hundred US dollars or fifty euros each. Cash only."

Neither tone nor expression displayed any tinge of irony as Michael translated the outpost commander's words. Robin was less controlled at suppressing an outraged gasp. "But that's twice what we paid in Nairobi just this morning!"

Considering this country's meager living standard, it was also likely more than the outpost commander's entire monthly salary. "He can't be serious. If we have to pay an additional fee, fine. But don't tell me there's some special visa he's suddenly authorized to issue. This is nothing but a bribe and an outrageous one! I'm not sure I've even got that much cash still on me. And how did you get by with a few bottles of painkiller?"

An irate murmur rippled through the Ares Solutions group. In response, the Congolese guards abruptly raised AK-47s. Registering the angry expressions and aggressive body language on both sides, Robin could be thankful her own team had been forced to stow away weapons. The first major assignment she'd been given for this mission was not going well.

Michael's own expression had hardened to the same unyielding stone as the Congolese commander's. In a low voice, he said harshly to Robin, "Look, call it a bribe or what you want. But you can take it or leave it. Bottom line, the government here doesn't often bother paying these guys' salaries. So the only way they eat is by collecting their money elsewhere. You prefer they take it out of those dirt-poor villagers out there or some pack of wealthy foreigners wandering into their territory? Certainly none of you look like you've missed any meals. As for me, you do an emergency appendectomy on the guy's kid, and maybe he'll cut you a break too!"

From his girth, the outpost commander had missed no meals either. But Pieter Krueger was now speaking up impatiently. "Look, the doc's right! You're just wasting time and energy arguing with thugs like this, and we're sure not going to shoot our way out. So now we know what's needed, let's just get out of here. Anyone doesn't have the fee on them, I've got some cash I can advance. Whatever you spend will be reimbursed along with your other travel expenses, so dig into those pockets before we miss another flight."

Michael Stewart was already heading out the door. Commander Patrice took his time comparing the team's head count to a pile of dollars and euros before proceeding with his "special visa," a simple ink stamp on the forms they'd already handed over. By the time the group climbed back into the truck, the motorcycle with its high load was long gone. But when the market truck jounced several kilometers later onto another dirt airstrip, Robin spotted the bike at the end of the runway, its African chauffeur helping Michael unlash packages.

For all their haste, the airstrip itself was still empty. But just as the market truck drew up behind the motorcycle, Robin heard the drone of an approaching aircraft. By the time the Ares Solutions team had off-loaded their own luggage, a white and sky-blue twin turboprop plane with *United Nations* lettered in black along the fuselage was touching down. The plane taxied to their end of the runway, stirring up a fresh storm of red dust until the propellers slowed to a stop. A section of fuselage unfolded to become steps leading down.

Robin's teammates were already grabbing duffel bags and heading for the plane. As Robin hoisted her bag to her shoulder, Michael abandoned his packages to stride swiftly toward her. "Look, we have to talk."

"You've had five years for that." Robin didn't even glance his direction as she pushed by him. "I'm not interested."

A statement that was not true. There were many things Robin

wanted to ask Michael. *Where have you been all these years? Why did you never bother to so much as call or write? Was it guilt or indifference?*

Robin wasn't sure if she was relieved or disappointed when Michael didn't persist. Instead he turned back to count off some bills to the motorcycle driver. A tall, lean man had now emerged from the interior of the plane and was hurrying down the steps. His physical fitness belied an age Robin knew to be early fifties, a quarter-inch haircut too blond to detect any gray strands. Though she'd never met him personally, Earth Resources CEO Trevor Mulroney was no stranger to Robin; his corporation's recent acquisition of Ares Solutions had disseminated widely throughout the private military industry as well as international news coverage.

In press photos, Robin's new employer had always been styled in the tailored suits, Rolex, and handcrafted dress shoes expected of a billionaire entrepreneur. But the ease with which he'd shifted to the mercenary "uniform" of khaki clothing, body armor, combat boots, and Oakley sunglasses currently pushed up onto his head to reveal a piercing blue gaze was no real surprise. The news coverage had indicated that Trevor Mulroney was a decorated veteran of the British Special Air Service and on the short list at Buckingham Palace for a knighthood to reward both military and civilian contributions to the British Crown.

More startling was the machine pistol visible in a shoulder holster. This despite the red circle slashed by a line that was the planet's universal interdiction symbol interposed atop the outline of a machine gun just above the plane entrance. UN contract flights even in the planet's darker corners had a deep-seated bias against civilians toting weapons aboard. An indication of just how much clout her new boss wielded.

And for Trevor Mulroney to be supervising in person, this op must be higher profile than the simple security mission Robin had envisioned. The Earth Resources CEO took time to greet each arrival, checking them off a clipboard as they slung their luggage into an open cargo bay and boarded the plane. Until Robin arrived at the foot of the stairs.

Sweeping Robin with a head-to-toe survey, her new boss visibly blinked. "And just who in bloody blazes are you? Krueger only mentioned one extra passenger."

"Chris R. Duncan, sir, reporting for duty." Robin pointed to an unchecked name on his clipboard, giving the official appellation lettered across her Ares Solutions credentials. "Right there. I'm the team linguist contracted for this operation."

"But you're a woman!"

The statement was so obvious, this time it was Robin who blinked. Trevor Mulroney and Pieter Krueger had hardly been alone in this group to remark on her gender. An inevitable by-product of her career choice, the murmurs, sly glances, guffaws of laughter, and occasional crude pickup lines from her male companions had trailed Robin all the way from Nairobi. Which was precisely why Robin's own unisex beige slacks and button-up shirt were of sturdier material than this equatorial setting called for and deliberately on the baggy side, her oval features naked of cosmetics, red-gold hair scraped back into a bun tight enough for a Victorian spinster.

Or a female Marine on patrol. "Yes, of course I'm a—"

A forefinger stabbed at the clipboard. "I don't know what game you're playing, lady. But I hired a trained soldier with combat experience for this job. Maybe you didn't bother checking, but this is the Congo. And we're not headed to some neat little UN compound, but a war zone."

Trevor Mulroney shuffled aside his list to pull out a single-sheet computer printout. "I've got here a Chris R. Duncan, age twenty-seven, served as a lieutenant in the US Marine Corps before going freelance PMC. Specialty: languages. Conversant in six, including French and Swahili. Combat experience includes one tour of duty in Afghanistan. While there, received the Medal of Honor for conspicuous bravery under fire. Since I'm well aware the Americans don't permit women in combat units, that was a particularly careless mistake. Your next mistake is that I have long-term business ties in Nairobi, Kenya, and I recognize this name. A Colonel Christopher Robert Duncan commanded the US embassy Marine unit there back in '98 at the time of—"

"—the American embassy bombing," Robin finished quietly.

Trevor Mulroney stared at her. "That's right. This Chris R. Duncan must be the son. I assume that's where he picked up his Swahili. Whether or not you do speak the language, next time you're going for a fake résumé, I'd pick a less conspicuous family record to hijack."

Let's not leave out Grandpa Brigadier General Christopher Robert Duncan and Great-Granddaddy Major General Christopher Robert Duncan. If the blood had left Robin's face, it was not just the mention of Nairobi, but because she'd recognized the young, thin face under a Marine dress uniform cap stapled to the top right corner of the printout. Swallowing with difficulty, she shook her head.

"You have the bio right. You just have the wrong Chris R. Duncan in the picture. My younger brother, Christopher Robert Duncan, also served briefly in the Marines. Personnel was constantly mixing up our files. But Christopher was still a private when he was . . . when he lost his life in the line of duty in Afghanistan."

Robin didn't allow the sudden tightening of her throat to affect the evenness of her tone. "The rest of the bio is mine, I can assure you. You're right that the US military doesn't assign women to combat units. But lines get blurred in places like Afghanistan, and the Afghans don't take kindly to foreign males interacting with their womenfolk. I was part of what they called a 'female-engagement team,' attached to combat units as liaisons to the 50 percent of Afghans who happen to be women. The medal—I just happened to be in the wrong place at the wrong time."

A very wrong place at the absolute worst moment of her life.

Firmly, Robin went on. "I apologize if your fact-checkers mixed my military records with my brother's. But a quick check will confirm I am the actual former Marine lieutenant, Christina Robin Duncan, hired for the position of team linguist. Though in civilian life I prefer to go by Robin. As to being a woman, I make no apologies for that. I am very good at what I do. I've been freelancing as a linguist for any number of private security firms for the past four years. Including your own, most recently. Which is why I assume I was offered a generous incentive to transfer from the Haiti UN contract at a moment's notice. As requested, I took the first available flight to Nairobi to meet up with the rest of your team. They wouldn't be meeting this flight if I hadn't been along as translator." Perhaps a slight stretch of the truth.

Mulroney checked her name on the clipboard, signaling at least temporary surrender, but his nod was brusque. "Well, I can hardly leave you here, so get aboard. But believe me, I'll be contacting Ares Solutions HQ just as soon as we reach Bunia. Bottom line, I don't care if you're who you say. Rendezvousing with burqas in Afghanistan hardly qualifies as combat experience in my book. I don't know what idea you have about this op, but it's not some translation gig for a bunch of State Department tourists masquerading as a UN fact-finding detail. We're not looking at just a chance of fighting; it's a certainty. I simply can't afford to waste resources or transport for anyone who can't protect themselves, much less take the fight to the enemy."

"I can assure you I'm quite capable, not only of protecting myself, but of doing the task of a combat soldier if need be."

"And I can personally testify the lady has not exaggerated her language qualifications. Surely, old friend, for such a pretty little *bokkie*, you can make an exception here."

Robin's reaction to an arm suddenly wrapped around her shoulders was as unplanned as it was immediate and automatic. Bending abruptly forward, she twisted her body sharply. Even as she broke free from that uninvited embrace, a large male frame flipped head over heels to land with a thud that kicked up a cloud of red dirt. Before her assailant could move, Robin's knee was pinning down his breastbone, the razor-sharp blade of a knife she'd yanked from a certain discreet inner pocket of her right boot pressed against his Adam's apple.

Trevor Mulroney's reaction was as swift as Robin's, the Uzi machine pistol jumping to his grip as he ordered curtly, "Drop it!"

But Robin was already rising gracefully to her feet, her knife disappearing back into its hidden sheath. Gaping faces of her teammates crowded in the plane's doorway or pressed themselves to the portholes as Pieter Krueger scrambled to his own feet. Beyond him, Michael Stewart, still loading packages into the cargo hold, had straightened up to watch the exchange, his tawny gaze unreadable.

"So you can defend yourself." Trevor Mulroney slid his Uzi back into its holster. The Oakley sunglasses shifted toward Pieter Krueger. "Though you, Krueger, I remember as a whole lot faster. I certainly hope I haven't chosen the wrong man to handle combat operations on this mission."

Savage fury had wiped the smile from Krueger's good-looking features. He glared at Robin as he brushed red dust from his clothing. "She couldn't do that again with fair warning."

"That's rather the point, isn't it?" Robin responded sweetly. Here was the time to lay down those hard boundaries. "Don't ever touch me again without my permission!"

An unexpected smattering of applause greeted her ultimatum, and Robin registered expressions of approval and respect among her travel companions. The Ares Solutions operations manager could respond with anger or shrug it off as a joke. He chose the latter, hands spreading wide in capitulation, handsome features once again displaying an arrogant grin as he called out, "Okay, boys, she caught me fair and square. Now you know here's one *bokkie* who doesn't mess around, so watch your hands."

Trevor Mulroney's own smile was sardonic as he returned his gaze to Robin. "If you're as competent with your other duties, maybe I should reconsider requesting a replacement. Since language skills like yours are in short supply and Krueger here vouches for your credentials. Now if you two are finished, let's get this show on the road."

Pieter Krueger brushed past Robin up the steps and into the plane without glancing her way again. Retrieving her knapsack and tossing her duffel bag into the cargo bay, Robin followed. As Michael Stewart and Trevor Mulroney ducked through the door behind her, a man in the uniform of a UN contract pilot stepped out from the cockpit to tug up the steps. Russian or maybe Ukrainian by his coloring and features. A safe-enough guess since much of the UN air fleet was contracted from the former Soviet Union.

The aircraft cabin was narrow, just two seats on either side of the aisle, but with only their team aboard, there was ample room to spread out. Robin ignored renewed applause as she threaded past her teammates.

Not all were applauding.

Robin caught a cold and humorless blue gaze from Pieter Krueger, then a somber glance from Michael as he slid into an empty row. Settling into a window seat, Robin tamped down a hysterical giggle. Or was it a sob? She'd laid down the necessary boundaries, but she'd also clearly made an enemy. And was it just ghastly coincidence, deliberate manipulation, or some twisted cosmic sense of humor that had brought her together in this place with the one man on the planet she'd never wanted to see again?

I don't believe in coincidence. And I'm not important enough for God to waste humor on me. But I sure can't see Michael manipulating something like this either, since he can hardly want to see me any more than I want to see him. Especially after all these years. If I'd just remembered he came from anywhere near this part of the continent, I'd have turned down this contract, no matter how big the bonus.

No, you wouldn't! Robin released a pent-up breath as the plane's twin propellers roared back to life. It didn't matter. None of this mattered. Only the job she was here to do.

Robin had come to this place and time for one purpose only. And not to fight some war. She was here to save the life of the only person Robin still permitted to wrap warm fingers around her frozen heartstrings.

A precious redheaded four-year-old whose birth certificate bore her own name of Christina Robin Duncan.

CHAPTER THREE

Fortune favors the bold.

The axiom was one by which Trevor Mulroney had steered his life. Now only the boldest course would salvage the fortune to which that life had been dedicated.

Mulroney unhooked an intercom mike as the twin prop picked up speed down the airstrip. All over the plane cabin, bodies were slumped, seats tilted back in defiance of takeoff protocol, eyes closed, earbuds tucked in—the universal posture of off-duty warriors. His new team looked exactly like what he'd ordered. None, by their résumés, the squeamish sort. All with extensive freelance experience in fighting Africa's dirty wars.

Except the woman.

Whether Lt. Chris R. Duncan proved a problem or an asset, time would reveal. Since he had far more pressing problems to address, Trevor Mulroney simply made a mental note to roll a few heads in his latest acquisition's human resource department as he announced, "Welcome to the Congo. We'll be hitting the ground running in about ninety minutes, so make the most of your siesta. There should be drinks and snacks somewhere. Feel free to forage."

By the time Mulroney replaced the mike, his new employees were already mobbing the galley area normally graced by a flight attendant. Mulroney ignored the breach of airline protocol as he ducked into the cockpit. Any of this bunch who couldn't keep their feet during a flight takeoff might as well break a leg now and not waste a slot on his team.

The ground was now receding quickly. Dropping into the copilot's seat, the Earth Resources CEO connected a Bluetooth earpiece to his satellite phone's video feed and punched in a number. The UN pilot raised no objection to this fresh violation of procedure. Nor did Mulroney worry about eavesdropping. Communicating flight arrangements had already stretched the Russian's limited English, and from the rhythm with which the pilot jigged in his seat, his headset was currently broadcasting a Congolese soukous band, not flight data.

"Mulroney, you old son of a gun, good to hear from you. But what's so urgent to drag me from a Pentagon brunch before the coffee's poured? And what in seven shakes of a bull's tail are y'all doing over there in the DRC? Figured you'd be at Buckingham Palace getting gussied up for the queen. I'm told we'll be calling you Sir Trevor any day now. Congratulations."

Trevor Mulroney didn't ask how the gray-haired Caucasian male grinning up from his satphone screen had on tap Mulroney's current GPS coordinates from six time zones back across the Atlantic. Instead he bared porcelain caps in a smile that conveyed none of the mingled resentment and contempt he felt for his virtual companion. Resentment because this man on the screen had attained the pinnacle of multibillion, multinational power and wealth that was his own sole life ambition. Contempt because he had reached that pinnacle by sheer accident of birth, not scrabbling after it as Mulroney had by his own wits and courage and hard work.

"Since when did you start getting your news from the tabloids? Yes, it's true the nomination made the final cut. But nothing firm from Her Majesty yet."

In reality, whatever his passport indicated, Trevor Mulroney considered himself no more British than his virtual companion was the homegrown cowboy the man's exaggerated drawl affected. The Earth Resources CEO had reached his adult growth in Rhodesia back before its ungrateful black majority insisted on throwing off benevolent European rule. His ambition then had not extended beyond taking over his family's sizable tobacco holdings and enjoying a white man's life of privilege in Africa. To preserve that heritage, he'd fought bitterly like every other patriotic white Rhodesian in Prime Minister Ian Smith's Bush War.

Mulroney had still been in his teens when he first met the man on the satphone screen. A freshman diplomatic attaché at the US embassy in Rhodesia's capital city of Salisbury, now renamed Harare, Howard Marshall came from a family tree as close to aristocratic as his own democratic nation claimed. For generations, its members had walked the halls of power in Washington, DC, built business empires across their own country and abroad. The clan had spawned senators, ambassadors, national intelligence directors, and at least one president. A young Trevor Mulroney had supplied some usable intel to the freshman diplomat. The swiftness with which a certain troublesome native political activist disappeared had confirmed Mulroney's own suspicions that Howard Marshall was far from a simple attaché.

Ian Smith had in the end, of course, lost his war. Once Rhodesia abolished white rule in 1980, renaming itself Zimbabwe, the Mulroneys had joined an angry exodus back to their original citizenship country, Britain. With no professional training other than managing a vanished family estate, Trevor Mulroney had parlayed his bush-fighting experience into a career with the elite British Special Air Service. He'd served with enough distinction to earn a commendation for valor during the first Persian Gulf War before leaving the

SAS for what he still considered his true home, sub-Saharan Africa. With a motley assortment of South Africans, Rhodesians, Algerians, and other white mercenaries left disfranchised by black independence in their nations, he'd fought his way across Africa in conflicts from Angola and the Congo to Sierra Leone and Equatorial Guinea. Eventually he'd founded his own private military company, named unsubtly after the Greek god of war: Ares Solutions.

Meanwhile, Howard Marshall had followed the usual family track up the rungs of power. While eschewing elected office, he'd served in various State Department positions, including embassy appointments across sub-Saharan Africa, a region in which the Marshall clan had accumulated extensive oil and mining shareholdings. The two men had kept in touch, Marshall throwing Ares Solutions the occasional security contract bone while Mulroney handled several discreet operations for certain unnamed contacts of Marshall's. But by the 1990s, white mercenaries running Africa's civil wars had fallen from popularity.

Mulroney sold off Ares Solutions to a British SAS buddy just in time to miss the post–9/11 private security bonanza of Iraq and Afghanistan. Not that he'd suffered financially, because what his clients hadn't paid him in hard cash, he'd accepted in mineral options.

By the time his SAS buddy was racking up millions securing embassies and shepherding convoys, Trevor Mulroney had notched his first billion in diamonds, gold, and coltan and had sunk his first oil well off the Equatorial Guinea coast. Ranked now as one of Britain's ten wealthiest business tycoons, he'd long since shed his Rhodesian accent, and no one but the tabloids had the gumption to bring up his colonial origins or the dubious foundation of Earth Resources, Ltd.

When his former SAS buddy had decided to cash in and find a tropical beach to enjoy his new wealth, Trevor Mulroney had seized the opportunity to return the private military company to his own assets portfolio. Not out of personal nostalgia, either. Mulroney had his own vision for what a new and improved Ares Solutions could offer this planet.

And his own interests.

Howard Marshall was by this time firmly ensconced in his own nation's capital, where he'd served a stint as CIA director for one administration, ambassador to the UN for another. He currently chaired the Strategic Forum on Sub-Saharan Africa, a think tank dedicated to the profitable development of Africa's vast natural resources. All without neglecting the defense industry consortium that was a specialty of his own particular family branch.

Because one empire was never enough for such a man, Howard Marshall had also invested generously in the industry's newest mineral development consortium, Earth Resources, its own specialty the always-growing list of rare earth minerals so essential to twenty-first-century technology, including many of the Marshall clan's commercial ventures.

Trevor Mulroney would be happy enough with the single empire he possessed. He could only hope his virtual companion had not yet turned his intrusive nose to sniffing out just how shaky that dominion really was. Who could have anticipated the recent revolt that closed down Equatorial Guinea's oil production the same week Earth Resources sank its first well? And those ridiculous "conflict mineral" embargoes might have been designed to target a map of Mulroney's own mineral concessions.

He'd still have been on firm ground if the Ares Solutions acquisition hadn't cleaned out all his remaining cash flow. That his newest venture would not amply restore stripped accounts before the shareholders and corporate board, including its chairman, Howard Marshall, called for an overdue audit, was a gamble Trevor Mulroney had never dreamed he might lose. As a result, his corporation's current bank assets were not the healthy fiction both tabloids and Buckingham Palace assumed, but a desperate juggling act of shifting assets and credit lines.

A campaign setback that would not matter if today's operation went as planned.

"So what is it, Mulroney? Some problem with our new molybdenum concession? I'm assuming that's why you're in the Congo. I've been following the news on renewed insurgent unrest in the Ituri region. You led me to believe this was a zero-risk investment. That the LRA and other rebel groups had laid down arms and were eager to join in the political and economic process. Tell me you weren't wrong. That you aren't calling to inform me I've wasted a ten-million-dollar investment. Or is it Kinshasa putting on the screws again as to what constitutes 'exclusive development rights'? That I can do something about."

Trevor Mulroney maintained the affable show of porcelain caps. "You of all people should know there's no such thing as zero risk. The concession itself isn't an issue. Kinshasa charged an arm and a leg for granting us a jump on the molybdenite strike. But implicit in the hefty commission they pocketed was the assurance that all rebel groups were cooperating in the cease-fire. That the UN peacekeeping contingent had things under control. And that regional government forces could guarantee our security."

A comprehending grunt came from the screen. "You're talking about our good pal Jean Pierre Wamba."

In one of those regular ironies of Congolese politics, the current governor of Ituri province was the former warlord of the same rebel militia that had fought government forces in that region to a standstill, his present reign less a reward for coming to the peace table than acknowledgment that Kinshasa, two thousand kilometers to the west, had no real control in this part of the DRC.

"That's right. I'll admit things haven't gone too smoothly. I assume you've been following the renewed rebel unrest in the zone. Wamba's pocketed his own hefty commission in exchange for providing troops to secure the mine and transport convoys under one of his field commanders, Samuel Makuga."

"Ah, yes, I remember Makuga from the peace negotiations. Wamba's second-in-command, a capable fighter. Congolese father who's actually some kind of cousin to Wamba. These tribal clans always stick together. Ugandan mother with connections in Kampala that proved useful to Wamba. Wamba always was Uganda's candidate. They gave him sanctuary for years in return for access to minerals in his territories."

Again Mulroney raised no questions on how the man on the screen knew so much about his hirelings. "Makuga seems capable enough. But our operations here have been under attack since the beginning. At first it was simply annoyance. Cutting fences. Theft of company property. But the attacks have escalated in extent and sophistication over the months. Sabotaging a transport barge filled with ore. Land mines on the road. Assaults on supply convoys. I have, of course, approached MONUSCO command."

Mission de l'Organisation des Nations Unies pour la stabilisation en République démocratique du Congo, an unwieldy moniker commonly reduced to MONUSCO, was the United Nations stabilization mission. "They just mutter that their rules of engagement permit only defensive resistance against attacks on civilian populations. So what are we if not civilian?"

Howard Marshall made no effort to answer that particular question. "What I'd like to know is why I'm hearing these details for the first time. And why would the rebels be going after the molybdenite mine? It isn't as though molybdenum were your typical conflict min eral rebel militias can easily exploit. Shutting down our operation there simply means no profits for anyone."

If Trevor Mulroney was no geologist, he'd profited enough from such minerals to know exactly what Marshall meant. The so-termed "conflict minerals"—diamonds, gold, and more recently, coltan, a black, tar-like mineral essential to the production of cell phones, computer chips, and other microelectronic technology—all had the advantage of being extractable from their surrounding terrain with minimal technology, their high value making them profitable for smuggling even in small quantities and on foot.

Molybdenum, by contrast, was a processed mineral requiring heavy machinery, electricity, lots of water, and a large workforce to separate it from its parent rock. A metallic, silver-white element, its usefulness came from its high melting point, almost twice the melting point of steel. Which made it in high demand for steel alloys but neither uncommon nor outrageously expensive.

Not a line of questioning Trevor Mulroney wanted to pursue. Nor that the situation was somewhat worse than he'd just painted it.

"Who knows why they're doing it. Maybe the rebels have no interest in molybdenite at all, just in destabilizing the zone. What matters is that everything's under control. Which is why I hadn't bothered you or the board about it. In fact, I'm flying in as we speak with a team of our old Ares Solutions pals to handle restoration of security personally. Unfortunately, it looks like Wamba's decided to throw his own monkey wrench into the gears. And that's why I called you."

The Earth Resources CEO briefly summarized the morning's events. "I need my cargo plane ASAP. Your government's got more muscle here than mine. I was hoping you might call in some local markers to lean on Wamba. More than that, I'd appreciate it if you could unleash any eyes, ears, and noses you've got available locally to dig into what Wamba's up to these days. Find out if he's been playing footsie with any other multinationals. Maybe looking to sell us out on the molybdenum concession."

The request tacitly acknowledged Mulroney's awareness that the other man still maintained active fingers on the pulse of his nation's intelligence services. Fingers that could prove the salvation of Trevor Mulroney's shaky fortunes—or his complete undoing.

Agreement reached, the Earth Resources CEO disconnected his Bluetooth. Best-case scenario, Wamba was just flexing his sizable muscles and would listen to reason before it proved necessary to order that C-130 back to Nairobi.

And worst-case scenario?

Returning the satphone to a pocket of his Kevlar vest, Trevor

Mulroney shifted his gaze to the winged shadow flitting over the jungle canopy below. He didn't even want to think about the worst-case scenario. But it had to be considered. Someone somewhere had figured out the real reason Trevor Mulroney was back in Africa, personally commanding one last combat mission.

Or thought they had.

> > >

If he could not save, he could at least exact revenge.

The watcher inched forward on a branch no thicker than his own torso. Which left the rainforest floor terrifyingly far below. Sunshine dappling through the thick green foliage indicated a clearing ahead. He slid farther until the branch, now swaying slightly under his weight, thinned to the circumference of his thigh. Here he could see into the clearing.

Yes, they were coming—much later than expected, but heading directly toward him. The watcher inched no farther. The movement of a tree bough out of sync with its neighbors would draw even careless eyes.

And his enemies were not careless. The perimeter guard they'd set to herd their charges was too tight for any to slip away. The advance sentries had learned to be cautious, scanning the ground for trip wires and booby traps, slipping warily forward, vigilant for ambush.

But they did not look up.

At least not far enough. Proof that for all their fighting skills, these invaders were not rainforest natives. Even if their eyes had pierced the foliage above them, they would not have spotted the long, black shape of a man stretched prone. Instead dried smears of gray-yellow mud and red-brown clay created an illusion of mottled shadows. Hues deliberately selected to disappear against the tree bark. Tufts of grasses, leaves, and moss fastened to appendages with vines broke up any human silhouette. Just so had the village men in his childhood hunted the giant forest hog and the more dangerous but beautifully skinned Ituri leopard.

Below, the laborers had begun their work. Felling a giant hardwood in itself could take a day or more. But today's objective, a fine mahogany, had been cut down yesterday, the reason he'd chosen this vantage point. Workers were now sawing branches to manageable portions while others loaded wood onto a pair of carts.

The watcher allowed relief to whistle softly out between his teeth when he spotted among the work party the person he'd hoped to see. Would the laborer in turn recognize slashes into tree bark that had not been there when work broke off the night before? Slashes that might have been left randomly by saw and axe if one did not know the markings hunters of his village used to signal each other in the rainforest.

Wielding an axe to chop away leaves and twigs, the laborer worked his way gradually up the huge trunk toward the fallen tree's verdant crown. Two final slashes forming a rough V where a massive upper branch forked might also have been happenstance. Certainly a nearby guard displayed no interest when the laborer disappeared into the tangled vegetation. It was not long before the laborer emerged. A few intermittent axe strikes while hacking at twigs demolished that subtle downward arrow.

So he'd understood the message. Had he found the package?

The watcher settled again to wait. The laborer was now drifting over toward a cart. Abandoning his axe, he helped wrestle a stubborn log onto the load, then took his place with a dozen others pushing at poles that thrust out from either side. Was that a glimpse of palm-leaf wrapping thrust among the raw wood as the heavy cart began trundling across the clearing?

In any case, success or failure was now out of the watcher's hands. The cart reached an open gate. Sentries keeping watch along a perimeter fence did not pause in their bored pacing to glance toward the toiling laborers pushing their load of wood.

Then the cart was inside the gate. He'd done it. He'd penetrated his enemy's defenses.

But just as an inaudible sigh of satisfaction left his lungs, he saw one of the laborers lose his footing. The stumble threw off the plodding gait of his neighbors. Feet entangled, two went down, then another. The cart wobbled, then tipped, spilling the load of wood. The watcher tensed as guards rushed forward.

They did not approach the load, their distant shouts and gestures of their automatic weapons clearly ordering the laborers to repair their carelessness. One by one, the sawed chunks were wrestled back onto the cart. Whether his own contribution to that cargo remained undiscovered, the watcher could not tell, nor could he even distinguish from this distance the laborer who'd recovered the small package. But there was no swarm of unusual activity from the guards to indicate anything amiss.

Then once again the cart trundled forward. The guards returned to their sentry posts. The watcher let himself relax fractionally.

Now all he could do was once again wait.

Dare he pray?

CHAPTER FOUR

Robin had tried to follow her companions' example and catch up on some of the last twenty-four hours' missed slumber. But her racing mind would not shut down. Directly across the aisle, Carl Jensen already had his laptop powered up again, the screen showing some sort of schematic drawing, his fingers racing across the keyboard. Grabbing her knapsack, Robin dug out the iPad that had only recently replaced a laptop for her international travels, its military-grade protective sheath purportedly adequate against disasters ranging from dust and raging floodwaters to a four-story drop, while its smaller bulk was infinitely more convenient for tucking into hand luggage.

This trip had been so sudden, there hadn't been time for Robin's usual thorough research of her destination. But she'd utilized airport Internet during an Amsterdam layover to download an array of web files. For her own reasons, Robin kept a Google alert set for Africa's regional news. But of the continent's fifty-plus sovereign nations, the

Democratic Republic of the Congo was not among those she'd visited before, nor had she paid much attention till now to its backstory.

Robin returned to the detailed history she'd started reading on an earlier flight. The DRC's time line differed little from much of sub-Saharan Africa. Warring tribes. The arrival of white colonialists. Armed insurgency. Independence. Black dictators replacing white colonial masters. Back to armed insurgency and warring tribes. An occasional glimmer of budding democracy and cessation of hostilities.

If the DRC offered any difference, it was only a matter of extremes—and the bizarre historical footnote of its original colonial master, King Leopold of Belgium, who'd claimed the Congo back in the 1880s not in the name of his country, but as his own personal bank account, the largest chunk of personally owned planetary real estate in human history. His business model of forced labor and community quotas was implemented by a mercenary army, the infamous Force Publique, whose disciplinary measures included the *chicotte*, a metal-studded whip, along with hostage taking, chopping off hands, and execution for obdurate workers.

Africa's "heart of darkness" was how classic novelist Joseph Conrad had dubbed the Congo in his fictionalized memoir chronicling Leopold's reign of horror. Whether the title referenced the black savages he'd met in its jungles or the white savages raping its resources was never quite clear. But the country's course hadn't truly changed even with later independence, which brought only three decades of rule under dictator Joseph-Desiré Mobutu, who matched Leopold's excess and avarice. And the rebel militias who finally overthrew Mobutu in 1996 seemed to have lifted their playbook directly from Leopold's Force Publique, raping, pillaging, cutting off hands, using hostage slave labor to mine conflict minerals. Even in the present day, the Congo seemed a microcosm of just what a dark, cruel place humanity had managed to make of the beautiful planet they'd been handed, each excessive atrocity giving emphasis to just how evil evil could be.

Even its victims seemed more passive and long-suffering in their patient endurance. Why did they not just curl up and refuse to survive such adverse conditions? Or rebel as one voice and raised clenched fist against such injustices as were daily visited upon them? Instead the Congolese population continued limping through one day after another with astonishing resilience until a bullet or machete or one of war's other killers, hunger or sickness, finally offered respite.

Not that Robin had any particular interest in finding answers to such questions. She was no humanitarian like Michael, but a hired professional here to earn the fair market price she'd contracted for her services. One month, they'd told her. Thirty days. Thirty thousand dollars. A thousand dollars a day might seem a lot to those who'd never worked in a conflict zone. Broken down to 24-7 constant duty, it didn't add up to such an excessive hourly rate. But it was enough to make a difference between life and death.

If only a month didn't prove too long.

This family will not lose another Chris R. Duncan. I won't let it happen.

The words on Robin's iPad screen suddenly blurred. Slipping it back into her knapsack, she closed her eyes. But Robin could no longer shut out the unwelcome flood of memories that had been battering against her carefully erected emotional defenses since she'd glimpsed on Trevor Mulroney's clipboard that red-gold crew cut and masculine version of her own features under a Marine dress uniform cap.

If Michael Stewart's heritage could claim three generations of medical mission service in the Congo, just so Robin's own family tree was synonymous with the United States Marine Corps. At least in the Duncan telling of history. While the halls of Montezuma might be hazy of proof, there'd definitely been a Christopher Robert Duncan on the shores of Tripoli. Certainly one had fought in the American Civil War. On the side of the Union, of course, since no Duncan ever fought a losing battle.

In each generation, there'd been a firstborn son to carry forward the name of Christopher Robert Duncan, all of them bred for command. Though Robin's own father had never advanced beyond a colonel's rank. And his eldest child was the only firstborn female documented in family annals.

Therefore, of course, not eligible for the name every Duncan firstborn had inherited for generations.

To give Colonel Duncan credit, he'd shown no ill will to Robin's older sister for her missing Y chromosome. Kelli was all a proper Duncan daughter should be—pretty, beguiling, the Duncan red-gold hair and pale features on her imbued somehow with a femininity Robin lacked. Her interests were what Duncan males expected of their female family members: domestic affairs, parties, makeup, hair, clothes, and finding a good-looking, well-situated husband.

Preferably a Marine.

To give her father credit again, something Robin was loath to do, Colonel Christopher Robert Duncan hadn't been so harsh while his wife was still alive. Christina O'Boyle had grown up in Kenya, only child of American missionaries who'd taught at the Christian university in Nairobi. She was back in the US for college when her parents lost their lives in a plane crash. Robin could forgive much when she remembered how her mother's face had softened every time she told the story of the handsome Marine captain who'd invited her to dance at the Marine Corps Birthday Ball. How he'd proposed on their third date. Robin could understand why. Her mother was as pretty, charming, and feminine as her firstborn daughter.

Christina's second pregnancy three years later had been difficult. Enough that the Navy obstetrician who oversaw her delivery warned the couple they were unlikely to conceive another child. Which was why Christina had insisted on giving a version of the Duncan family name to their second daughter: Christina Robin Duncan.

But the obstetrician proved mistaken. The delivery of a son just eleven months later almost cost Christina O'Boyle Duncan her life. This time the Navy doctors insisted on making sure there'd be no further baby Duncans. Her husband made no objection now that he had his own Christopher Robert Duncan.

No, that wasn't fair. Colonel Duncan had genuinely loved his sweet, pretty wife, and her health had undoubtedly been a top priority. Their middle child was young enough not to protest becoming Robin while her younger brother went by the unabridged Christopher until he reached an age to shorten it to Chris outside the immediate family.

"My Christopher Robin," their mother termed the pair whimsically. And indeed the two had grown up more as twins than mere siblings. Especially since Robin had been the proverbial tomboy, leading the way into every outdoor sport, adventure, and mischief available to herself and Chris.

Which might have been where the trouble started.

Christina O'Boyle Duncan had not forgotten her aspirations of returning to Africa. Robin could admit her father had requested assignment to the US embassy's Marine detail in Nairobi as much to make his wife happy as because it was an excellent career move. Those years the Duncans had spent in Africa, first in Kenya, then on assignment in Tanzania, followed by a tour of duty back on US soil, then a second tour at the Nairobi embassy, were as perfect a childhood as any little girl could want. Once her youngest was old enough to start classes at the international school, Christina had returned to work as an attaché in the embassy's consular division. And if Colonel Duncan was by nature reserved and always busy, he still knew in those days how to smile.

A change in the twin props' rhythm brought Robin back to the present. The plane had now reached cruising altitude. From the sun's position and a map included in her country overview, their flight path followed a slightly southwest trajectory to Bunia. Directly below, the winged shadow was now flitting across tall, rocky peaks of the Blue Mountains that divided the DRC from Uganda. Off to Robin's left, a sparkle of water was Lake Albert, famed as the backdrop for Humphrey Bogart and Katharine Hepburn's World War II standoff with the Germans in the film classic *The African Queen*. Through a porthole across the aisle, open savannah and rolling green hills stretched to a darker green stain on the far horizon.

The perimeter of the Ituri Rainforest.

From this height, it was all as beautiful and serene as the Paradise of legend, with no hint of the wars and blood that had stained its red soil. Undoubtedly Robin's memories were also rose tinted by the halcyon veil of childhood. Certainly she'd had no knowledge of the darker issues facing Africa and its people. Her memories were rather of the throat-catching beauty of Kenya's Rift Valley. The thunderous noise and rising mist of Victoria Falls. The white-capped majesty of Mount Kilimanjaro. Open-air markets and thatched huts and Masai herdsmen with their cattle. School days, sleepovers, and field trips with her friends at the international school.

Perhaps all images one might expect from a privileged, sheltered expatriate child. But there were wonderful memories, too, of her mother's many African friends and their children, from whom Robin had learned her first Swahili. While in Nairobi, Christina O'Boyle Duncan had insisted they attend services at the Kenyan church her father helped found, its toe-tapping music and warm exuberance a far cry from the Episcopalian liturgy that was the Duncan clan's concession to religious observance.

Yes, up to Friday, August 7, 1998, Robin's memories offered no reason for bitterness. The three Duncan offspring had been at a school friend's pool party when Robin felt the blast, enough to wonder if there'd been an earthquake before diving back into the water. Hours passed before adults interrupted with a terrible story of explosive-laden trucks detonating outside the US embassies in Nairobi and Dar es Salaam, Tanzania. Among the American dead was embassy attaché Christina O'Boyle Duncan. Later investigations would tie the bombings to an Islamic fundamentalist group named al-Qaeda, placing its leader, Osama bin Laden, on the Most Wanted Terrorists list.

For Robin it was the end of innocence. Of childhood. Of eyes that saw only beauty in her world. Of possessing a father who smiled or spoke as though to a daughter instead of a raw Marine recruit.

With what seemed indecent haste, the three Duncan children were repatriated stateside to live with Colonel Duncan's sister, unmarried with no children of her own. Looking back with the eyes of an adult, Robin could admit it likely wasn't easy for Colonel Duncan to pick up the parenting pieces with three grieving, sullen offspring on his rare visits stateside. She could understand her father's preference for his pretty oldest daughter, so like his deceased wife. She could even understand, if not accept, his disapproval of Robin's own rebellion against the proper conduct of any Duncan female.

What Robin could not, would not, ever accept or forgive was Colonel Duncan's treatment of the wonderful young man whom destiny had fated to be the last Christopher Robert Duncan.

CHAPTER FIVE

"Touchdown in ten minutes. Let's lock and load, boys."

At Trevor Mulroney's terse announcement over the intercom, Robin sat up with a jerk. She must have dozed off after all because the mountain peaks and blue glitter of Lake Albert had both disappeared beyond her window. Instead rolling, tree-cloaked hills were giving way to a flat, arid plain. As the twin prop dropped in altitude, Robin located on the horizon a haze of smog and dust.

Bunia, regional capital of Ituri province.

Somewhere behind Robin, the creak of a folding door panel was followed by a Serbian operative hurrying past her up the aisle. A reminder that the rear of this plane presumably held the first functioning restroom since their C-130 had touched down in Arua. Unbuckling her seat belt, Robin pushed to her feet. She was not alone. All along the cabin, sprawled bodies were now heaving to upright positions, adjusting wraparound sunglasses, stowing electronics and other belongings in knapsacks.

Not quite all.

"Dr. Michael Stewart, did I remember that right?" The accordion folds of a travel map blocked the view of a nearby row's two occupants as Robin slid out into the aisle, but Pieter Krueger's self-assured South African inflection was impossible to mistake. "I really appreciated the helping hand getting our team across the border back there. Didn't you say something then about working for Doctors Without Borders? That you're stationed at some medical compound in the rainforest near Bunia? It sounded like you know this part of the Congo well. I was hoping you might give me some input on this map before we land."

"My pleasure." The quiet reply confirmed the long, brown fingers holding the porthole side of the map as belonging to Michael. "And I really appreciate this lift to Bunia."

"It's this northeast quadrant that I'm interested in." There was a rustle as the map was folded into a more manageable rectangle. "By the way, I couldn't help noticing you're acquainted with our new team translator. A small world. Or are you the reason our pretty little *bokkie* took a contract in such a nasty back alley of Africa?"

Robin could have slapped that suggestive bark of laughter. But Michael responded dispassionately. "Actually, it was quite a surprise. I haven't seen or heard from Robin Duncan in years. Not since we served together in Afghanistan when I was a Navy medic assigned to the Marines there."

Conversation broke off abruptly as brown and blue eyes with remarkably similar cool expressions flickered her way, and Robin suddenly realized she was only too obviously standing stationary in the aisle, eavesdropping. Her face warmed as she whirled around to push in on the restroom's folding door.

The plane restroom was not only functional but had running water to wipe away red dust from face and arms. Much refreshed, Robin eased open the folding door with a silence that acknowledged deliberate intent to eavesdrop.

"Yes, I grew up in Taraja and know that area well," Michael's quiet tones were explaining civilly. "My grandparents actually founded the hospital and school there. Back then it was an easy day's drive from Bunia with a pretty decent road.

"Beyond Taraja is where you get into real deep rainforest. There is still the occasional scattered village, but no roads, just bike trails and footpaths. And even when I lived out there as a kid, the road from Bunia to Taraja was so deteriorated, we basically kept to mission planes for transporting personnel, supplies, and more urgent medical cases back and forth from Bunia. I assume you're aware Taraja was razed to the ground like every other settlement in the area when the worst of the fighting swept through there a decade ago. My parents were among the casualties, and without medical staff, the place remained abandoned for years."

Taraja. The childhood home of which Michael had told Robin so many stories back when they'd been on speaking terms. *Taraja* was the Swahili word for *hope*. An appropriate enough name for Christian missionaries to choose for their home. Michael had never mentioned the compound's destruction or his parents' deaths. But then Robin had never told him the less happy portions of her own life history. Perhaps because Afghanistan contained too much misery of its own to introduce past griefs.

"Taraja actually reopened about six months ago, thanks to some new mining operation that cleared the road, making it possible to get out there and patch up the airstrip and clinic. But from what I've heard, that mining operation closed as quick as it opened. I've only been back in the Congo three months myself, and I've always traveled out to Taraja by plane. So I couldn't really tell you whether or not you could move any sizable operational force over that road. What I can tell you is that it would take more time than you might care to invest."

"That's all I needed to know."

"My pleasure. And again, thanks for the lift."

As a rustle indicated the map was being refolded, Robin quickly slipped out of the bathroom and into her own seat. There was no reason why her hands should be trembling as she made sure her own belongings were all safely tucked away in her knapsack. Straight ahead now on the plateau, a grid of red-dirt streets, corrugated metal roofs, thatched shacks, and occasional clusters of taller concrete and brick buildings was rapidly expanding. The twin prop dropped again, abruptly enough for Robin's stomach to rise into her throat. But neither that discomfort nor their fast-approaching destination kept her mind from returning her thoughts again to the past. This time to a less distant past.

A difficult birth and sickly infancy might explain why Christina O'Boyle Duncan's only male contribution to the family tree was slight and small for his age, but not his preference for sketch pad and paintbrush over a football or gun. In their childhood, Robin had instinctively sought to deflect Colonel Duncan's disapproval by pulling Christopher into her own athletic interests. But that couldn't last forever. Her brother was simply too gifted an artist, his quiet, contemplative personality as stubborn in its own way as his father's.

Which didn't keep Colonel Duncan from striving to change his son. When home on leave, he'd done his best to interest Christopher in his Duncan heritage, dragging him to firing ranges and exercise grounds. But by the time Robin's younger brother reached adolescence, his father simply despised him.

The irony was that Robin would have given all her possessions to step into her brother's shoes. Fiercely proud of her family heritage, she wanted nothing more than to follow in the Marine footsteps of her father and grandfather and the long line of warrior Duncans before them. When Colonel Duncan dropped in long enough to enroll Christopher in the military academy where male Duncans had attended for generations, Robin had pleaded to join her brother.

That was a mistake.

While said academy had long since opened its doors to gender equality, Robin wasn't ignorant of her father's opinions on females in the military. Even worse, their invasion of that bastion of unadulterated testosterone, the United States Marine Corps. A Duncan female so staining the family honor was a more offensive moral lapse than a son who preferred paintbrush to assault rifle. Why couldn't Robin model herself on her older sister? Was her father to have only one child who wasn't a complete disappointment?

Since Robin knew too well whence she'd inherited her own stubbornness, she didn't even try to change her father's mind. Instead she charted her own course, joining the ROTC, then enlisting immediately upon graduation in the Marine Corps. Finishing top of her boot camp class, she'd been accepted to Officer Candidates School with a specialty in languages, adding Spanish, Arabic, and Pashto to her Swahili and the French she'd studied in school. When three years later she received her second lieutenant commission, Colonel Duncan hadn't bothered coming to the ceremony, though Kelli and her aunt were there to applaud.

But not Chris.

As much as her father disapproved of Robin's career choice, he'd raved furiously when Chris graduated with honors from the military academy only to announce he was enrolling in art school. Colonel Duncan had called Chris ugly names, accusing him of things that had no basis outside his own stereotypes and prejudices, then given him twenty-four hours to report to Marine boot camp. Instead Chris had moved out, bouncing back and forth for the next year between friends' couches and dead-end jobs.

Robin remembered vividly the day Chris called to let her know he'd just arrived at the Marine Corps Recruit Depot on Parris Island, South Carolina.

"I'm not enlisting to please Dad. Or even to get him off my back. It's just the only way I'll ever get the funds for any serious art school. I'll do one tour of duty, then use the benefits for a decent college art program, maybe even Paris. Besides, maybe there's enough Duncan blood in me. I'd like to prove I'm capable of being a good Marine before choosing to be a good artist."

Chris had proved it so well that Colonel Duncan consented to join his two daughters for his namesake's boot camp graduation. By the time Chris shipped out to Afghanistan, Kelli had fulfilled her own family expectations by marrying a tall, good-looking Marine armed combat instructor. Robin's own deployment to Afghanistan had come six months later, her language skills and officer's commission coinciding with a new program that embedded female Marines in combat units to help engage with Afghan women.

A bonus was being reunited with her younger brother. Robin had no doubt her brother was on-site from the moment she walked into the Kandahar base and spotted delicate but powerful black-and-white ink drawings tacked up on the walls.

Drawings that exquisitely captured not just a soldier's daily life but the stark southern Afghanistan landscape, the worry and defiance on a village elder's face, the grime and grin of a small boy toting an AK-47.

If still slight of build and quiet of speech, Chris had earned his own respect and even popularity among his Marine peers. Both for the sharp perception so evident in his art and for being a soldier who could be counted on to do his job competently, unstintingly, and under fire. His superiors had even proposed publishing his portfolio of a Marine's life in Afghanistan.

Robin had been so proud of Chris—not just of his accomplishments, but of the intelligent, thoughtful human being he'd become. Would their father ever have come to see that a Duncan son could be both artist and man of honor?

She would never find out because within the year both were gone.

As was his closest friend, United States Navy Petty Officer First Class Michael Stewart.

CHAPTER SIX

Just down the aisle, Pieter Krueger had gotten to his feet and was heading back to his own seat. Robin caught Michael's gaze on her and quickly turned her head to the window. But it wasn't the plateau rushing up toward the plane Robin saw there.

By the time combat medic Michael Stewart had deployed to Afghanistan, he'd already tucked under his belt a bachelor of science and the classroom half of a general medical degree. If he spent little time in the horseplay and joviality of off-duty Marines, it was because he'd laid out a clear and pressing goal for himself. Attain a Navy scholarship to finish his medical training. Put in the necessary years to reimburse the Navy for its investment. Then return to Africa where he'd grown up as the son of medical missionaries.

Robin hadn't been in the same Marine platoon as her brother and Michael. But the three spent every available off-duty moment together, their similar expatriate African childhoods a common bond.

Robin was not quite sure at first just what she found so attractive in her brother's friend. Maybe Michael's easy acceptance of his friend's sister that let Robin be for once nothing more or less than herself. The spell of his childhood stories and descriptions of an African rainforest that reminded Robin of happier times. His determination to serve not just his country but his fellow man.

Or perhaps it was the simplicity of his faith that carried Robin back to her mother as nothing had in years. When on base, the three friends attended the same contemporary Christian Sunday service. On several occasions when the chaplain was absent, Michael had taken his place. For all his family background, Michael was no hammer-over-the-head preacher, but calmly matter-of-fact as though a loving Creator God was such an incontestable no-brainer that despite all this planet's stark contradictions of ugliness and darkness, the subject needed no debate.

Perhaps because of a similar missionary heritage, Christina O'Boyle Duncan, too, had exuded just such warm, unquestioning faith, and sometimes when Michael's quiet baritone expounded a Bible passage, Robin could close her eyes and almost feel the gentle brush of her mother's hand over her hair and face instead of a scorching Kandahar breeze. That forgotten sense of security, love, and an almighty God still on his throne that had been life before August 7, 1998.

Yes, Robin had found herself liking Petty Officer First Class Michael Stewart very much.

Which only made Michael's ultimate betrayal far worse. If not for Colonel Duncan, Robin's brother would never have found himself in the wrong place at the wrong time on that sweltering Kandahar summer afternoon. But if not for Michael, he'd never have lost his life there.

Robin wasn't even supposed to be on that mission to a village rumored to be a Taliban arms depot. But the female engagement officer assigned to her brother's unit had a bad case of Kandahar's revenge, and Chris hadn't hesitated to recommend his sister's Pashto skills. Their Chinook transport helicopter had just disgorged the Marine unit when gunfire broke out. Robin's brother went down in the first volley. A rocket-propelled grenade tore through the propellers before the chopper could retreat off the ground.

While her companions fought back with a withering counter-fire, Robin worked frantically to stanch the blood flow spilling over her brother's body armor. She breathed relief when two helicopters drowned out the crackle of gunfire.

Apache combat aircraft circled around to strafe the area while a medivac chopper hovered down to retrieve the wounded. Spotting Michael's concerned tawny gaze and set jaw among the medics jumping down, Robin surrendered her brother's barely conscious form.

"Please, help him. You can't let him die. Don't let him die."

Michael had been reassuring. "It's not as bad as it looks, Robin. He's going to be okay. I won't let him die, I promise you."

The medivac helicopter was lifting off when the world exploded. Robin remembered only agonizing pain slicing through her back and legs before darkness mercifully closed in. When she opened her eyes again three days later, it was to discover she'd been airlifted to the hospital facility at Bagram Air Base outside Kabul. Another week passed before she'd recovered enough to be informed her brother hadn't made it back alive.

The official explanation was as senseless as unavoidable. An Apache missile fired into the compound had set off a buried drum of that rumored Taliban ammo. While several teammates caught exploding bullets, Robin's was the most serious injury, her right leg shattered in two places, another bullet narrowly missing her spinal column.

Robin was not particularly grateful for her survival. Not when her younger brother, her best friend, the person she loved most was dead, his gifts and talents wiped out as though he'd never existed. And where was Michael Stewart, who'd promised not to let him die? If he couldn't get leave for a Bagram visit, why not a phone call or even a written condolence? When Robin finally worked up enough nerve and outrage to initiate queries, she was told only that he'd been transferred stateside.

That Michael would leave Afghanistan without even contacting Robin seemed unbelievable. Unless he felt too guilty for his lapse of duty to face her. For the official mission report stated unequivocally that her brother's wound had not been initially life-threatening. He'd simply bled out before ever reaching base.

By the time Robin was stable enough to be relocated stateside for physical rehabilitation, the Duncan family was facing further calamity. The same week Colonel Duncan was diagnosed with fast-spreading pancreatic cancer, Kelli's perfect Marine officer husband had inexplicably walked out on both his marriage and the Marine Corps. Though neither Colonel Duncan nor Kelli proved willing to elucidate, Robin gathered that his disappearance involved something less than reputable. When he rammed his motorcycle into a freeway divider, his blood alcohol showed three times the legal limit. Since his death came after a dishonorable discharge, Kelli inherited no benefits. She'd changed her surname back to Duncan just in time to discover she was pregnant. And like her mother's, the pregnancy promised to be a difficult one.

With characteristic dramatic flair, Kelli begged Robin not to abandon the family in this hour of crisis. Colonel Duncan was more forthright about Robin's obligations. Her duty to the Marine Corps was brushed aside. Hadn't Robin's short-lived tour in Afghanistan proved the point that women didn't belong in a combat zone? Whatever strings Colonel Duncan pulled, Robin found herself with an honorable medical discharge without ever being quite sure how it had come about or even when she'd agreed.

As for Michael Stewart, however bewildered and hurt, Robin would have been open to any reasonable explanation. But he'd never again contacted her. When Robin managed to track down his military APO address, her letter had been returned with a cover notice that

Petty Officer First Class Michael Stewart was no longer enlisted in the United States Navy. Robin hadn't wasted further effort trying to locate him.

Especially since by the time Robin's namesake was born, Colonel Duncan had given up his own fight for survival. Not once in those months did her father bring up their mutual loss of his only son. Nor what was almost as great a loss to Robin, the sacrifice of her hard-won position in the United States Marine Corps.

Had she remained at his side because, despite everything, she still loved her father and longed for his approval?

Or did she hate him because despite all her hard work, effort, and sacrifice, in the end Colonel Duncan had won their bitterly fought personal war?

Robin's father clung to life long enough to see Christina Robin Duncan II enter the world six weeks before her due date. He'd died without ever learning how precarious his granddaughter's hold on life would turn out to be.

Robin could have walked away after her father's funeral. Rejoined her unit. Picked up the threads of her own life dream. But from the moment she'd lifted a five-pound Kristi into her arms, looked deeply into those blinking, sleepy little eyes, she'd known her father was right about one thing. You didn't walk away from family. Not if you were a Duncan. Not if you were a Marine. *Semper fidelis* wasn't just for the battlefield.

The post–9/11 private security boom was still exploding. Robin quickly discovered her language and combat skills could fetch a high price in the private sector, enough to pay the expensive health insurance willing to cover a high-risk child. In consequence Robin had bounced these last four years from Iraq to Kyrgyzstan, Sierra Leone, Nigeria, Kashmir, Sudan, Haiti, and now the Congo.

But her occasional week home was worth all the travel, dirt, poverty, and inconvenience. Even at age four, Kristi displayed not only the red-gold hair of the O'Boyles and stubborn resilience of the

Duncans, but all the precocious creativity and perceptive intelligence of the uncle she'd never met.

Robin had endured as Duncans always did. Done her duty to her employers. Been the responsible head of family. And sometimes even smiled. When her niece's small arms wrapped around her neck. When, in the middle of a war zone, the beauty of a flower or a sunset, the music of bird or brook tugged at her senses, offering the illusion that all was still right with this world.

But that smile hadn't curved Robin's mouth since a phone conference with Kristi's pediatrician two days ago confirmed that her niece would never reach age five without the experimental surgery some insurance adjuster had arbitrarily categorized as optional and high risk.

This mission pays twice the Haiti contract. Enough to secure a loan so Kelli can schedule the surgery. And a bonus for every day under a month in which we complete our primary mission, whatever that proves to be! The landing gear touching down on a tarmac strip forced Robin's thoughts back to the present. The aircraft taxied toward the cluster of small buildings and hangars that was the Bunia airport. Beyond this, a chain-link fence topped by concertina wire cordoned off a massive white complex trimmed in sky blue. The color combo that marked a United Nations mission anywhere in the world.

As the twin propellers whined down to silence, the UN charter pilot emerged from the cockpit to fold the door down into steps. Robin remained in her window seat as her teammates began deplaning. Across the tarmac, she could see a red-and-white four-passenger Cessna taxiing slowly from a hangar. Robin kept her gaze on the Cessna even as her peripheral vision caught a masculine shape turning back in her direction.

"Robin, my connecting flight's already overdue takeoff, so I've got to leave immediately. But I'd like to get in contact later if possible. We've clearly been talking at cross-purposes, and we need to set things straight."

The mature thing to do—that which she'd schooled herself to

do for five long years—was to look Michael straight in the eyes, sum up a cool, dismissive answer. But to Robin's horror, such a lump had risen to her throat at that quiet, familiar voice, she didn't dare turn her head. Seconds ticked on as she fought for composure. At last a soft sigh came from behind her.

"Okay, Robin, I really do have to go now. But God didn't drop you back into my life without a reason. We will talk before this is over, and that's a promise."

The inflexible determination in his tone was the Michael she'd once known. The one who did not break his promises. The Michael she'd learned painfully did not really exist. Robin had remained dry-eyed through her father's horrific death by cancer, the long years of shouldering responsibility for two other lives. So why was dampness now blurring her view?

Her peripheral vision confirmed Michael's retreat down the aisle. Directly below Robin, the UN pilot had the hold open, her team-mates already slinging out duffel bags.

Enough! You claim to be a Marine? Then stop your whining and get your boots in gear! The mental order was in her father's stern voice. Its effect was to straighten Robin's shoulders, wipe a hand across her eyes.

Which cleared her vision enough to offer an excellent view of the battle scene abruptly exploding on the tarmac outside.

CHAPTER SEVEN

A convoy was racing out from between two hangars with such speed that several Ares Solutions operatives stretching their legs beyond the plane's wings had to throw themselves out of the way. The first two vehicles were pickups. Each open bed held a large mounted machine gun. Khaki uniforms waving automatic weapons crammed every other inch, including running board and tailgate. The last vehicle was a cargo truck also filled with armed uniforms.

Most striking was the middle vehicle, a stretch Hummer polished to burnished bronze despite the red dust, its tinted windows with that extra thickness denoting bulletproof panes. A Congolese flag flapped from its hood ornament. As the convoy slammed to a stop, uniforms poured out of their vehicles, dispersing in a wide perimeter around the plane.

The UN pilot was scrambling back up the steps into the plane. The Ares Solutions team had reacted immediately, dropping behind the mound of unloaded cargo, rolling for cover under the fuselage, little retreat though either would offer from those powerful machine guns. Here was where the body armor and weapons left behind in Uganda would come in handy. Robin was already reaching for her knapsack. She'd made her own preparations before leaving the C-130. Reaching inside to detach a false bottom, she felt the comforting shape of a Glock 19's handgrip slide into her fingers.

"That's General Wamba's vehicle. What's he doing here?" Michael had paused partway down the aisle to follow the same scene outside. He glanced back at Robin, his mouth grim. "I'll check it out. You stay down out of sight. Wamba's men can be—well, let's say unpredictable."

"*Me* out of sight! I'm at least armed. You're the one who'd better stay down." The Glock was now out of concealment. Robin double-checked that the ammo clip was in place as she headed toward the hatch.

But Michael had already pushed past the pilot. By the time Robin scrambled to the better vantage of the open door, he was heading across the tarmac toward the convoy. The two mounted machine guns immediately swiveled to converge their trajectory on his position. Michael did not slow his stride, though he spread his hands wide in the universal gesture of goodwill.

Robin's fury at his imprudence battled with unwilling admiration. She'd spent her life among the toughest of tough males. Testosterone was measured by how well you fought, how straight you could shoot, the iron you could pump. Courage by keeping your head under fire, defending your fellow Marine. Competence by proficiency and speed in dispatching the enemy.

But whatever her personal conflict with this man, she could admit there was also a toughness and courage in walking out there alone, unarmed, exposed to those deadly gun barrels. Nearing the Hummer, Michael called out in French, "I'm Dr. Stewart with Médecins Sans Frontières. And this is a UN flight, not under Congolese jurisdiction. What is the difficulty here?"

A soldier stepped forward to open the passenger door of the stretch Hummer. Robin's pent-up breath escaped her teeth at the man now unfolding himself from inside. By the time he'd stretched to full height, he loomed above Michael, easily six and a half feet and massively built—not showing any visible fat, but powerfully muscled. His skin tone was one of the darkest Robin had ever seen, of a black so absolute it glistened almost blue in the sun. A heavy jaw protruded ahead of a full mouth, his nostrils so wide as to seem almost flat. A red beret tilted at a jaunty angle on a clean-shaven scalp, his khaki uniform—perfectly creased from recent pressing—glittering with medals. Though it was the arrogant lift of head, supreme confidence of posture, and a self-possessed chillness of gaze that marked the new arrival as a warrior and commander of men.

Even without a phalanx of machine guns and automatic weapons at his back, he would have been an intimidating figure. But Michael simply identified calmly, "Governor Wamba, a pleasure to meet you again. We conversed at the UN reception last month."

"Ah, yes, the new American doctor." The Bunia governor's French was deep, gravelly, proficient. "You gave me advice as to the pain in my kidneys. It proved most effective. But you are not who I was informed would be on this flight."

Trevor Mulroney was striding forward, calling as he did so, "They're friendlies, boys. You can come out. And where's our translator? Duncan!"

Robin tucked her Glock into the back of her slacks before hurrying down the plane steps. By the time her boots touched the tarmac, Robin's teammates were edging warily out of concealment. Robin could have smiled were it politic to do so; every one of them had rustled up a weapon—Glocks, Uzi machine pistols, even one collapsible-stock abbreviated M4 automatic rifle. So she wasn't the only one whose hand luggage hadn't quite matched that Arua customs declaration. Maybe her teammates really were as good as their boasting, mercenaries or not. Which augured well for the success of this mission.

As Robin reached Trevor Mulroney's side, Michael retreated an unobtrusive step or two, though he remained at Robin's back. Across the tarmac, Robin noted the red-and-white Cessna now taxied to a halt beyond the soldiers. A tall, lanky man in jeans and T-shirt had climbed down from the pilot's seat and was watching the unfolding drama.

Beside Robin, Trevor Mulroney had to tilt his head far back to meet the governor's chill eyes. But he looked less intimidated than annoyed as he demanded in furious English, "Governor Wamba. You want to explain just what my plane's doing sitting over in Arua right now? That wasn't what we negotiated!"

At the governor's blank stare, the Earth Resources CEO snapped irritated fingers toward Robin. "Do your job."

Robin hurriedly translated his demand into French. Around her, the Ares Solutions team stood easily among the scattered luggage, offering not so much as a twitch of limb that might convey aggression. In contrast, Wamba's men were as fidgety as cats about to pounce, even after following a shouted order to lower weapons to their sides. Despite the uniforms, these were no ordinary peacekeeping troops. Facial scars that might have been shrapnel or some bizarre tribal tattooing. Teeth filed to unnatural points. Missing fingers, eyes, even ears. Many looked barely past puberty, though a universal gauntness might have contributed to that impression. Wamba's troops evidently ate less well than their commander.

Their adornments were likewise hardly army issue. No shiny medals here, but fetishes of feathers, glass, and other unidentifiable objects attached with huge safety pins or tied around biceps. Garlands of threaded bullets, bone bits, and human teeth draped around necks and hung down gun belts.

And their eyes. Unblinking. Whites yellowed. Bloodshot with chronic disease, alcohol abuse, or both. Black pupils unnaturally distended despite the afternoon sun. Opium or hashish? Whatever the soldiers' ages, those eyes held no youth, only the dead, cold emptiness of practiced killers.

Robin's mouth felt suddenly dry as she awaited Wamba's response. So this was the infamous rebel commander who'd been named governor of Ituri province as his spoils of the peace process. And from the looks of his merry band, he'd simply integrated his ragtag militia into the official government forces. These were the local allies on whom the Ares Solutions team had been told they could depend?

Wamba's own cold, black stare did not shift from Trevor Mulroney as his huge shoulders rose and fell. "I have changed the arrangement. I know you *mzungus* too well."

Mzungu was not French, but Swahili slang for *white man*.

"You throw us here in the Congo a few coins while you make yourselves rich off this mine for which you fight. As you can see, I have many men for whom I am responsible. Their families too. They have not received payment for their services from Kinshasa as was promised when we swore peace. If they go hungry, how am I to hold them to the peace treaty? No, the payments you have made are not enough. I want a percentage of the ore that is brought out of the mine as well. The same that you are giving to Kinshasa."

As Robin translated in low, quick English, Trevor Mulroney waved an impatient hand. "Look, we can talk later about any changes in price negotiation. But bottom line is, right now and as long as the mine is shut down, any percentage of its profits is going to be exactly zero. So how about you help me get the mine reopened. Then we can chat about your fair share."

The governor's frown did not ease as Robin finished translating.

"That is not acceptable," he rumbled. "I will agree to negotiate later about percentages. But only if you pay another fifty thousand immediately—euros, not American dollars—to help meet the immediate needs of my men. And another fifty thousand on the day the mine reopens."

Trevor Mulroney's glance swept across the empty glares and unsmiling faces of Wamba's militia before he shrugged. "This is not what we agreed. But I'm willing to compromise. Fifty thousand, but only when all my equipment is delivered and on-site. And American dollars, not euros. And an equal bonus the day the first ore shipment makes it safely to Bunia."

From their lack of response, Robin guessed Wamba's militia was no more fluent in French than in English. Trevor Mulroney met Wamba's glare with an unflinching one of his own while Robin finished the translation. The silent duel seemed to go on for an eternity. But in the end, Governor Wamba broke off eye contact first, spreading large palms in acquiescence. To Robin's shock, when he spoke, it was in heavily accented but fluent English.

"Done. For now. But I must see the fifty thousand in cash before I will give orders to allow your cargo plane across the border."

Trevor Mulroney was smiling affably, but his own cold, blue gaze held no corresponding humor as he addressed Wamba directly. "So you speak English. Forgive me for having brought a translator for all our meetings to date. If I'd been aware—"

The lift of wide shoulders held no apology. "I was in exile for many years in Uganda and Kenya. A wise man does not neglect to learn the language of his hosts. But sometimes it is useful to listen to a person's words when he does not know they are understood."

From Mulroney's suddenly wooden expression, Robin knew he had to be wondering if he'd said anything in English he wouldn't have wanted Governor Wamba to understand. The militia commander's own stare shifted for the first time to Robin. A sudden display of strong, white teeth proved more fearsome than his frown. "Though since you will need her no longer, I will take your translator as my profit instead. I have never possessed a woman with hair like fire before."

Without warning, Wamba reached out to grasp a red-gold strand that had somehow escaped Robin's cap. It was not the first time such a thing had happened to Robin. In her childhood, the African villagers had been as fascinated by tresses the shade of sunset as she was by their own tight, black curls. But never then had she felt as violated as though the man had laid hands on her body. She dared not move, could barely force air into her lungs.

So far today she'd been infuriated by the border outpost

commander. Annoyed by Pieter Krueger's antics. Distressed at Michael's reappearance. But never frightened.

Robin was afraid now, this uniformed giant with his cold, dead eyes and rivers of blood on his hands without question the most terrifying, dangerous human being she'd ever encountered. Surprise tactics such as she'd used on Krueger would have no impact on that massive frame, and their small team could not begin to defy Wamba's combat force should the Congolese warlord choose to carry out his threat. There wasn't even any appeal. This man was the law here. The only law, accustomed to doing as he chose, taking what he wanted.

Which didn't keep rustles and angry murmurs from sweeping through the Ares Solutions team. Weapons went up immediately among Wamba's militia. The mounted machine guns swiveled. Shadows froze. All but one quick, hard step behind Robin. Michael Stewart. And though he alone here bore no weapon, there was something equally dangerous in the tautness of muscle, the coiled-spring tension of his body language, as he stated flatly, "No disrespect intended, Governor Wamba, but that isn't going to happen."

That fearsome smile did not waver. But to Robin's surprise, and her relief, the militia commander released her hair strand. "She is your woman, then, Doctor? You had only to say so. A doctor who can heal my kidneys is of greater worth to me than any woman."

"She's no one's woman," Trevor Mulroney interjected smoothly. "At least not here. But since your men don't speak English, I'm still going to need her services. In any case, you don't want this woman, however unique. I've seen her take one of my best fighters down with a knife to his throat." He jerked a thumb toward Pieter Krueger, behind him. "A man would be a fool to permit so dangerous a weapon near one's bed."

As Governor Wamba's smile abruptly left his face, Robin could almost hear a collectively suspended breath. Then the governor burst out laughing. "I possessed such a woman once. And you are right. Since I am no fool, I will leave you with your translator."

At Wamba's shout in Swahili, his troops broke formation and began piling back into their vehicles. Trevor Mulroney swung around on Robin. "Duncan, you're dismissed."

Still shaken, Robin retreated to the pile of unloaded bags. Michael did not follow but spun around on a heel to head across the tarmac toward the Cessna. Its pilot hurried forward to meet him, a folding dolly over his shoulder. Presumably the connecting flight Michael had mentioned. *MAF* was lettered on the Cessna's tail. Robin was well acquainted with Mission Aviation Fellowship, a Christian humanitarian organization. Since MAF's intrepid volunteer pilots were usually last out of a combat zone and first back in, Robin had recently accompanied UN fact-finding contracts on MAF flights in both Haiti and Sudan when commercial airlines were still refusing to resume service.

The Earth Resources CEO huddled in conversation with Governor Wamba only briefly before the huge warlord refolded himself into the Hummer. Mulroney's affable expression evaporated as he strode back toward the plane. "That was *not* in the mission plan! Once that C-130 arrives, let's make sure we're not caught again with our pants down."

When he turned to Robin, his tone was more censorious. "As for you, Duncan, this is precisely why I don't hire women for the field. I'm heading into town with Wamba. Got to scare up some cash and make some plans. I shouldn't be long. For the rest of you, the airport is closed since there are no further scheduled flights today. And you won't be here long enough to warrant troubling our neighbors for hospitality."

Mulroney nodded toward the huge white and sky-blue development they'd flown over upon landing. Down here on the tarmac, one could see the airport was actually two complexes. Chain-link and concertina wire fencing closed off a profusion of helicopters, personnel carriers, and a large cargo plane, all with the white and sky-blue markings that screamed *UN*. On the Congolese side, the only aircraft currently visible outside a small terminal and hangars was the MAF Cessna.

Mulroney had turned his frown from Robin to the UN complex.

"Especially since our peacekeeping buddies over there have been less than helpful to our mission thus far. And they have a certain—well, let's just say a negative attitude about gun-toting professionals coming into their territory who aren't under their command. We'd never have got this charter flight if I hadn't assured them it would be ferrying unarmed noncombatants."

His frown became a grin as a blue glance swept over the Ares Solutions team's mysteriously materialized hand weapons. "In any case, you'll have to make yourselves comfortable in that hangar over there until I make some arrangements. Duncan, you may need to translate if you run into a guard. Just watch yourself. Any more incidents like this and you're on the next plane out, no matter what your credentials. Oh, and deal with that hair. Paint it brown or something. Around here, it's a red flag to a bull."

The Earth Resources CEO's thin pun as he flapped a hand toward Robin's head brought chuckles from her teammates. Robin was not amused. *And Neanderthal attitudes like yours are why jobs like this get complicated. None of you have to hide who you are to do your job!*

But a fair universe was something Robin had long given up expecting. Instead she wordlessly tucked the offending strand under her cap as Mulroney strode back to the Hummer. The convoy was roaring away by the time she'd shouldered her duffel bag to trudge after her teammates toward the indicated hangar. The UN plane was now taxiing toward its own quarters. Robin's occasional glance as she crossed the tarmac followed Michael and his tall friend trundling the trolley piled high with packages toward the Cessna. But she caught neither man looking back, and just as the Ares Solutions team reached the hangar, a whine of propellers rose behind them.

Robin turned to watch a red-and-white bird shape speed down the tarmac. Lifting off, it banked west.

So Dr. Michael Stewart had exited her life as quickly and definitely as he'd reentered it.

CHAPTER EIGHT

The hangar proved to be a completely empty metallic shed resting on a concrete pad, the doors standing wide open at both ends, which permitted a clear view of the chain-link fence dividing the airport from the city of Bunia beyond. The only life Robin spotted beyond her own team was a handful of guards lounging in the shade of the terminal and hangars. A breeze whistling through the open doors offered scant relief to the equatorial heat beating down on the metal shell. Robin could be thankful for her foresight in seizing on the amenities of the UN plane. There was more than one disadvantage to being the only female on a field team.

But at least there was shade, and her teammates were already discarding their burdens and making themselves comfortable. Pieter Krueger had ignored Robin since their earlier run-in. But Robin remained leery enough to drift over next to the more innocuous Carl as she slid her own luggage to the concrete. Carl was looking patently miserable, narrow features behind metal-rimmed glasses pink from heat and sunburn, his unkempt hair and clothing dark with sweat. He'd deposited a wheeled travel bag on the concrete. But he kept his computer case hugged tightly to his chest as he wandered toward the rear of the hangar, where he could look out through the chain-link fence.

"Are we really locked up in here? I'm dying of thirst! And hungry! I never did manage to purchase anything back there at the border. It looks like there's shops over there. There's got to be a way we can get out there to buy some food and drinks."

Another indication the Shaggy clone had minimal field experience. Stepping up beside him, Robin dug into her own knapsack to pull out one of several water bottles she'd stowed there along with a trail mix bar. She handed both to Carl, then dug out another water bottle for herself. Rule of thumb on the road: always carry on your body enough basic survival supplies to endure at least forty-eight hours if caught by landslide, flood, canceled flight, political coup, hostage situation. Or just poor planning and careless hosts, as now.

"Hey, thanks!" Carl Jensen was already tearing into the trail mix bar, gulping the water.

Not yet opening her own bottle, Robin studied the dusty, sunlit panorama beyond the perimeter fence. The regional overview Robin had skimmed on the plane listed Bunia's sprawl as encompassing more than a quarter-million residents. But the airport complex was on the city fringe, and most of what she could see beyond the fence was open pasture, tilled fields, and scattered thatched huts. A dirt road led to a graveled parking area outside the exit end of the small terminal. Across the road a few buildings and market stalls presumably offered food and drink to deplaning passengers.

Or catered to the residents of the UN complex. A more sizable populace filling a nearby field behind more chain-link fence, concertina wire, and neat rows of tents would not have cash for such purchases. Robin had seen its replica recently enough in Haiti for instant identification.

A UN refugee camp.

A painted mural displaying diamonds and gold jewelry above one storefront explained Bunia's size, despite its virtual isolation except by air. According to that overview, the hills around this plateau were rich in gold, coltan, and other minerals. In more peaceful times, the city's mineral trade had been the bedrock of its economy. More recently, the region's natural resources were both target and financier of tribal militias, government forces, and neighboring occupiers alike. Chief among the latter were the Ugandans who had entered eastern Congo more than a decade back, ostensibly as peacekeepers, but accused of allying with various militias in return for mineral payments.

Including the eventual victor, Bunia's current governor, Jean Pierre Wamba.

Still, when international pressure finally ousted Ugandan forces from Bunia in 2003, the outcome had not been peace, but a bloodbath that ripped Ituri province apart. Hundreds of thousands more were left displaced from burned-out homes and fields. Many of them, all these years later, still occupying that UN refugee camp across the way.

Michael's own childhood home had been among the burned-out communities, by his brief comments. And his parents had been there during the attack. Did Michael have any living family left? Robin shook off that line of thought, refusing to allow memories of Michael to dog her.

The arrival of an unscheduled flight had inevitably attracted attention. Uneasy glances at a strolling airport guard did not keep a group of locals from drifting over to where they could peer through the fence into the open hangar. And not to pitch a sale. The moment the guard disappeared around a corner, a large woman in a bright-yellow pagne and matching turban broke away from the pack.

"Please, my daughter is blind. She has not eaten in days. I need money for medicine. Have mercy, for the love of God!" Though she spoke in French, her upward cupped palm, the bandage covering the eyes of a small child she thrust against the fence, needed no translation.

"Would you look at that poor kid!" From Robin's side, Carl Jensen left the shade of the hangar door. As he hurried toward the fence, he reached into his computer case. The handful of bills he pulled out were American dollars, almost as easily cashed in the DRC as Congolese francs.

Catching Carl's action, Robin started immediately after him. "Are you out of your mind? What do you think you're doing?"

But she was too late. Carl had already thrust the bills through the chain links toward the woman.

As though the action were a signal, the entire group surged forward. Unlike the perimeter defenses protecting the UN complex, the fencing here only reached Robin's shoulder. A host of hands grabbing at Carl's offering sent the bills flying. While some scrambled for the money, others were reaching through the chain links, between the barbed-wire strands. Their clutching grips pinned Carl against the fence as they snatched at his glasses, an iPod he'd tucked into a breast pocket, his computer bag.

Reaching the fence, Robin wrestled the computer bag away, then tugged urgently to free Carl himself. The man clearly had no skills in self-defense. What was he doing on this team?

A sharp burst of automatic gunfire brought Carl's abrupt release. Two airport guards raced forward, though it was not their weapons that had fired into the air. The commotion had drawn the entire Ares Solutions team to crowd the hangar's open rear doors. Glancing around, Robin caught the metallic sheen of an Uzi machine pistol disappearing back under the armpit of one of the gray-haired Vietnam vets.

Ernie Miller, if Robin remembered their introductions correctly. She mouthed a thanks as she urged Carl back toward the hangar.

The airport guards were now using the barrels of their rifles as battering rams against any remaining hands reaching through the fence. With shouts of pain and anger, the crowd fell back. The large woman who'd triggered the assault shook a furious fist toward the congregated Ares Solutions team, her broad, dark features under the bright-yellow turban twisted with hate. "You *mzungus*, you are all the same! You take and take and take and never give!"

Then she did something startling. The angry fist became a fore-finger sliding across her Adam's apple in an unmistakable gesture of a slit throat before she pointed that finger at Carl. Not even the guards' shouted threats stemmed her vituperation as the crowd drifted toward the marketplace.

As soon as they were at a safe distance, the Ares Solutions team headed into the hangar, and Robin rounded on her companion. "Well, that went nicely! So is this your first freelance out of the play-pen? Or are you just an all-weather idiot? Bottom line, you *never* give handouts to a beggar in a place like this! You don't look at them. You don't meet their eyes. Not unless you've got enough for everyone. Or a hankering to start a riot. You're just lucky you didn't get yourself killed out there. Or at best robbed blind!"

Though Carl's iPod was now gone, he'd managed to protect his glasses. Pale-blue eyes blinked rapidly as he adjusted the metal rims back in place. But sunburned features showed as little penitence as comprehension. "That's pretty harsh, Ms. Duncan. So excuse me for making an effort to help a blind kid! I wouldn't have pegged you of all people as so lacking in plain human compassion!"

Why, because I'm a woman and therefore a pushover? Robin wanted to scream in defense. *Do you know how long it took me not to care? To steel myself to walk past starving children and ignore a mother's pleading eyes? But you can't save everyone! And you'll just break your heart trying! The only way to survive out here is to keep your mind on your own job. Worry about your own family. Your own survival. Maybe that's how these people survive all this too. By focusing on their own lives. Their own next meal. Their own next breath.*

Carl was still speaking, aggrieved. "And why's that woman so angry? At me, anyway? I mean, I was the one trying to help. It was her own people who stole the money I gave her. We're the good guys here, trying to restore order to this godforsaken place. So why take it out on me?"

How did one disillusion such naiveté? Robin made an impatient gesture. "Just take a look at yourself."

Carl's iPod might be gone, but one wrist still bore an expensive diver's watch. A glint of gold chain was visible above a sweat-stained collar. His computer bag was of fine, burnished leather.

"You're carrying more on you, in that computer bag, in your luggage over there, than that woman's likely to own in a lifetime. The money you so casually doled out as charity is more than she'll see to feed her family for a month. Every day she watches rich foreigners walking off planes into her country to make their fortune off the backs of the Congolese. I mean, think about us. Sure, our op will hopefully restore some order. But let's not forget we were hired first and foremost to restore mine production for a British billionaire. And we'll be paid well for doing so. Nothing wrong with that. But from that woman's POV, why should she see us as saviors instead of exploiters? Or feel any particular gratitude for the occasional crumbs that get tossed her way?"

The other contractor could not have been far different in age from Robin herself. But at his change of expression, now bewildered and unhappy, Robin suddenly felt old enough to be his mother. More gently, she added, "Look, if it makes you feel any better, that woman wasn't the real thing. Or her kid."

Carl didn't appear convinced. "How would you know?"

"Easy, too much flesh on her bones. And the kid's. They've been eating well enough. And I saw the kid pull up her bandage to peek around when you were digging out money. No, they're pros hitting up foreign arrivals. A blind kid makes a good prop." Robin shouldered the knapsack she'd abandoned to run to Carl's rescue. Picked up the water bottle she'd let drop to the ground. "Nor does offering a temporary fix to the lucky few who can squeeze to the front of the begging line do any good in the long term. If you really want to help, you're better off donating to an aid agency and leaving the handouts to the professionals. Though if you do want to know how to distinguish genuine poverty, just check out that pair. Who, you'll notice, *aren't* asking for a handout!"

The mob's retreat now offered a clear view of the market area across the road. The pair Robin had indicated were a middle-aged man and a boy not far short of puberty. The latter looked so much a younger version of his companion that they were undoubtedly father and son. Both balanced on their heads huge bundles of the gnarled, twisted sticks and twigs commonly gathered in the countryside to be sold for cook fires. They wore only ragged shorts, which emphasized protruding ribs, the knobby joints of arms and legs so thin they didn't appear capable of supporting such a burden.

The pair's trudging pace had come abreast of a food stall piled high with small loaf shapes wrapped in banana leaves. *Kwanga* bread, shaped to imitate the French baguettes favored by the Congo's Belgian conquerors, but actually made of boiled cassava. Even as a child, Robin had found its slightly fermented taste unpalatable. But the boy's expression as he eyed the pile showed longing before he quickly looked away.

The father glanced down at his son, then suddenly stopped in front of the *kwanga* stall. After a brief conversation with the vendor, the older man pulled a sizable offering of sticks from his bundle. The vendor exchanged a single loaf for the firewood. Stripping the cassava bread of its banana leaves, the older man broke it in two, handing one part to the boy before biting into the other.

Robin was watching intently enough to catch the exact moment the boy glanced down to realize his father had given him most of the loaf. She didn't need to hear their conversation to understand the subsequent pantomime. The boy offering the loaf back. The older man shaking his head. The boy's teeth flashing white against dark features.

The entire exchange lasted only seconds before the two walked on, balancing their burdens with practiced ease as they crammed food into their mouths. But the boy's wide grin, the older man's answering smile, held such love, such an intimacy of parent and child, that Robin pulled her gaze away as hastily as though she'd inadvertently invaded the privacy of another's home.

So much love.

So much hate.

Which was the real Congo?

> > >

Hate roiled in his stomach, etched acid up his esophagus.

The watcher turned his head slowly, cautiously. A dozen meters away and slightly below his own elevation, a pair of eyes met his, a head nodded fractionally, the only indication in a tangle of leaves and vines interweaving one tall hardwood with another that other human beings shared this treetop eyrie. Below, the laborers were now finishing their task, the largest rounds that were the felled mahogany's trunk being rolled arduously across the clearing while the remaining chopped branches were loaded into the cart.

But the watcher simply settled himself more comfortably along the tree bough. Hours remained before night's dark cloak would permit the concealed onlookers to make their move. So he turned his head again cautiously to rest his chin against crossed arms. The action brought a strong whiff of human sweat and musk to his nostrils. Would his onetime colleagues ever recognize now the underfed, underclothed savage with a handcrafted bow tucked against his ribs instead of a briefcase, plotting destruction instead of ore-yield graphs?

The ease with which he'd shed hard-won trappings of civilization had proved almost as distressing as its necessity. Feet once softened by shoes were again so calloused they did not feel the roughness of tree bark and sharp stone beneath them. How quickly he'd adapted once more to the hunter's stealth that was every village boy's training for manhood. To eating what he could forage from the forest around him. The weapons he carried had been used by his forefathers long before the first *mzungu* penetrated the rainforest canopy. Arrows dipped in toxic toad venom. A spear whose hardwood point was as deadly sharp as tempered steel.

But if he had become once again as he was before, the boy who'd drawn his first breath in this rainforest, the same could not be said for his childhood home. The clearing below differed so completely from the lush, green panorama he'd looked across with his father what now seemed a lifetime past that only the position of that jagged, rocky knoll to his left confirmed this was indeed the place of his birth.

For one, the clearing had expanded enormously, the majestic hardwoods felled in a growing circumference around the base of the outcroppings. The fruit trees had gone first. Nor were there any longer thatched huts, vegetable beds, fruit orchards, banana plants, or corn patches. In their place was one vast field of churned-up reddish mud mounded with piles of gray shale that gave the appearance of some bloody, gangrenous canker eating away at the rainforest. The knoll itself was at least a third diminished as though a dinosaur's teeth had ripped huge, scattered bites out of it.

The devastation did not signify a lack of human denizens. At least ten dozen, maybe twice that, swarmed across the mud and over the outcropping's corroded face. Hacked with pickaxes at boulders loosened by explosives. Hauled heavy rocks in handbaskets and wheelbarrows. Crushed stone with sledgehammers. Sifted the broken rock through screens for uniform fineness. Passed water buckets in a chain from the river.

Nor were the toilers only male or even all adult.

In more civilized nations, a similar mining operation would have excavators and backhoes to dig out the ore-laden rock. Conveyor belts to move it. High-powered hoses and vats to pressure wash the ore, siphoning off the lighter slurry for processing into its final lucrative product.

And in this case a far greater treasure.

My dream for this place!

Anguish tightened the watcher's throat as he remembered the innocence of that dream, his naive assurance that he was bringing prosperity and a future to the people of this place. Was it because that dream had been so innocent, his love so naively sincere, that betrayal had cut so deep, the hate burning his insides so all-consuming? He'd loved his profession. Loved his people. Delighted in the rare opportunity a Creator God had given him to join together those two loves.

And now?

He strove to hold on to his fury, his hate. In them was strength. But grief shook him so strongly he buried his face in his arms, willing his body to stillness lest he draw spying eyes. If he could only go back to such loving innocence. Undo the last months. Become again the trusting youth who'd climbed that knoll, thinking only to offer his father the brave new world he'd discovered.

But his father had of course been right. All his love, his dreams, his trust in strangers—above all, in wealthy *mzungu* strangers—had been foolishness.

And now he himself had become a stranger his father would never recognize, never condone, perhaps never forgive.

The worst was that everything he'd accomplished thus far—what he did here today, all he could ever do—still would not touch his true enemy, sheltered safely, comfortably beyond any reach or real consequences. Like the watcher's forefathers who'd also fought *mzungu* invaders in this rainforest, he was simply too small, too weak against such wealth, such globe-spanning might.

But he could still fight on.

He could hate.

And even the sting of a small insect could prove painful.

The watcher lifted his head, renewed fury and resolve hardening his features to stone behind the mottled camouflage of dried mud and clay. Across the clearing, the last cart of branches was being unloaded onto a pile of lumber, the rest of the laborers now hard at work chopping the huge rounds of trunk into manageable sections. Another cart trundled away from the woodpile, but now it was mounded high with a shiny, black cargo. It headed for a noisy monster that reared its ugly, metallic head in the center of the clearing.

The huge machine was the reason for all this devastation. An ancient steam engine, its use of charcoal instead of processed petroleum fuels had circumvented every attempt to shut down the mining operation. Cut off the road, blockade the river, and the mine could continue processing and stockpiling ore as long as said monster supplied energy to those few operational pieces that could not be done by human hands. The final crushing of gravel to dust. The pumps separating slurry from shale. The electricity for a large Quonset hut where those who ran this place spent their days in relative comfort.

Because charcoal was created from wood. And the rainforest had plenty of that. A rough stone kiln beyond the gate that converted wood to pure, black carbon might have been a tower built to some insatiable pagan god, the smoke of its sacrifices never ceasing day or night. If left unchecked, that bloody, spreading canker below would swallow up not only his childhood home, but all this beautiful green paradise a Creator God had once crafted for man to enjoy.

But the monster was not today's objective.

The watcher was idly following the cart's progress past the gate area when he saw a sentry patrolling nearby halt in midstride. The guard stooped to pick up something near the toe of his boot. The size of a loaf of *kwanga* bread, it was thickly coated with the red mud in which it had lain, but a glint of black was visible as the guard turned it over. A chunk of charcoal, undoubtedly, fallen from some passing cart.

The guard had come to the same conclusion because he took a step toward the moving cart, tossing the muddy chunk onto its load. But even as he did so, the watcher's breathing stilled. Maybe he was wrong. Maybe the piece had tumbled from some other load.

He knew too well that exact shape and heft because he himself had crafted it. There'd been five such in the palm-leaf bundle. One must have dropped out and been trampled into the mud during that earlier spill.

No! Turn back! It's not time yet!

But the cart had now reached the steam engine. The watcher could only clench impotent fists as the laborers began shoveling its contents into the machine's fuel hopper. This could spoil days, even weeks of planning.

Or perhaps it was still possible to adjust his plans to this new turn of events. Taking out the mine's sole source of power could even prove an advantage. So long as the rest of his arrangements went forward.

Nothing in all his planning, his training, his experience prepared him for when it happened. The boom sent shock waves that swayed even the branch on which he lay, followed instantly by a thunder that was countless thousands of flapping wings as every feathered creature within hearing took flight. Flames and black smoke boiled up high above the jungle canopy. Then came another explosion and another.

There was no longer reason to linger. Across the way, a head shot up, eyes met his, then withdrew abruptly into the foliage. A rustle in the canopy around him signified the retreat of his other companions. He, too, needed to make his escape before the mine's security apparatus scrambled its inevitable response. But the watcher could not drag his eyes from the spreading inferno, close his eyes to the screams that were not only the harsh caws of fleeing birdlife.

It should have been satisfaction that gripped his soul. Instead he felt only unadulterated horror.

CHAPTER NINE

Ernie Miller, the Vietnam vet, had lingered as Robin and Carl Jensen reentered the hangar to tug shut the rear doors behind them. The guards outside offered no objection, and with prying eyes no longer able to peer inside, the crowded hangar now offered some semblance of privacy. Robin wasn't the only team member who'd traveled prepared. All over the hangar, trail mix bars and other refreshments, bottled water, even dusty Coca-Cola and Primus bottles from the border crossing were emerging from hand luggage. An iPod blaring South African pop officially kicked off a party.

Unsurprisingly, Carl headed to a rear corner and pulled out his laptop. Retreating to the opposite corner, Robin untwisted the top from her recovered water bottle, draining half its contents in one long gulp. She'd have given much for a restroom to change into fresh clothing from her duffel bag. Since none was available, she simply used the remaining water in her bottle to sponge face and arms again and slick back red-gold hair under her cap, tightly enough no strand would dare attempt escape.

But her thoughts were not so easily dominated. And why was that loving glance between father and son proving harder to banish from her mind than the large woman's screaming hate? What was it about this contract, this place, that was proving so disruptive to the protective shield Robin had so carefully erected around mind and heart over the last five years?

Or was it just the emotional upheaval of having Michael Stewart intrude into her life again?

Stuffing the empty plastic bottle into her knapsack, Robin dug out her cell phone. One of the few luxuries with which she'd indulged herself when she joined the private contracting world, liable to be dispatched anywhere on the planet at any time, was a global communications package that combined local cell usage with satellite coverage to permit calling home from virtually any GPS coordinate short of Antarctica. The cell phone screen read almost two hours past noon, and South Carolina was just six hours earlier, so Kelli and Kristi should be up and around.

Robin hit 1 on her speed dial, but there was no answer. Her sister and niece could be at an early medical appointment. Or Kelli wasn't near her cell phone. Or she just wasn't bothering to answer. Robin left a short voice message.

"Kelli, Kristi honey, just wanted to let you know I'm safe on the ground in Bunia, Congo. I'll try for a Skype video call just as soon as things are settled down. Love you!"

Exchanging the cell phone for her iPad, Robin ignored the noise to concentrate on her reading.

Another hour passed before Trevor Mulroney strode into the hangar. "Okay, boys, party's over. I do hope you haven't made yourselves too comfortable, because thanks to the kind intervention of our good friend Wamba—" Mulroney's mention of the Bunia governor dripped irony—"we're back on track again. With one slight change in plans. I had the administrator of our molybdenite processing facility here in Bunia cancel your reservations for tonight at one of Bunia's finer and only hotels. Unfortunately, to avoid any further—shall we say, misunderstandings?—the C-130 will *not* stop here in Bunia but will be flying directly to our forward operating base for unloading. Which means we need to be there to receive it. And since local air control has not been informed of the C-130's course change, I'd like to be out of here when they find out we've—uh, misinterpreted the scope of our instructions."

A few groans greeted the news that a comfortable bed, shower, and hot food were not on the immediate horizon. But expressions were philosophical. These men were soldiers, and part of that vocation was adapting to new variables at a moment's notice. Tacitly understood was the priority of placing the C-130's indispensable and expensive mission cargo beyond reach before a certain Bunia authority figure laid greedy eyes and sticky fingers on it.

"Our own ride should be here any minute. Willem, Marius, you ready to roll?"

Since these two were the Afrikaner helicopter pilots, Robin could guess just what their "ride" would be. But the Earth Resources CEO elaborated. "Kinshasa is being really sticky right now about freelance aircraft with military applications crossing their borders. Something about all those neighbors who've been supplying hardware to the various rebel factions. So we weren't able to bring in any of Ares Solutions' own birds. But the local military base here has a couple Mi-17s Wamba's been willing to let us contract."

The Russian-built Mi-17, a duo-prop transport and assault helicopter, was the workhorse of Third World conflicts, the Soviets having sold them by the ton to governments from Afghanistan to the Congo when the collapse of their empire left them short of spending cash.

"We will also have access for the duration to Earth Resources' own local executive helicopter. The choppers are on their way now over from Wamba's base. Which leaves a few minutes for a quick strategy meeting. Krueger, you want to show us that map?"

Bringing out the map Robin had earlier seen him showing Michael Stewart, the South African pushed aside duffel bags and food wrappers to spread it across a makeshift table. As the Ares Solutions team crowded in, Mulroney stabbed at the map with a forefinger. "Okay, this is where we are here in Bunia. This is the Ituri Rainforest. And here's our ultimate objective."

The spread-out map was no tourist guide, but a full-color, high-resolution satellite image. A dark-green mass marked where the plateau on which Bunia sat gave way to rainforest canopy, broken only sporadically by small clearings and the occasional snakelike meandering of streams. If there were trails or roads, they couldn't be made out through the thick foliage. But where Trevor Mulroney's forefinger tapped, a cluster of brownish-gray mounds rose above the canopy.

"If you've done your homework, you know these hills are an anomaly in the Ituri Rainforest no one's ever cared about until a few months back, when they were discovered to be solid lumps of molybdenite. Earth Resources snagged the concession. Unfortunately, some of the locals haven't been too happy about it, because the mine has come under attack practically since day one. Since enabling foreign investment is in everyone's best interests, Governor Wamba sent in a sizable contingent of his own troops. They were able to secure the mine well enough. But the insurgents simply melted back into the bush and turned their attention to keeping the processed ore from getting out. Other than by air, there's only two means of transport from the mine. A single road here—"

Mulroney's pen traced an invisible line across the mass of dark green, then pointed out a coiling snake.

"—or by barge when rainy season makes this river deep enough for passage. To date, there have been two major attempts to move stockpiled ore. The first was by barge. This hit an underground snag that had been booby-trapped with explosives. The barge was sunk, and in fact until it can be removed, the river route is impassable. The second attempt was a convoy protected by Wamba's troops. There was no frontal attack, just a tree fall across the road. But when the convoy stopped to clear away the tree, its removal triggered explosions along a quarter-kilometer section of road, taking out twelve trucks filled with ore. The worst was that investigation proved the explosives involved were stolen from one of our supply convoys. In all, at least a hundred tons of molybdenum ore were lost in each attack. Not to mention that without considerable reconstruction, which is hard to do under constant attack, the road is now useless as well.

"Leaving the mine completely cut off except by air. Which is, of course, where you all come in. Your mission will be to restore transport operations. First order of business, the Mi-17s will be dropping our team along with local reinforcements at the FOB to set up base camp before heading on to the mine for a supply dump. I will be taking our own chopper straight out to the mine for catch-up with Wamba's field commander, Samuel Makuga, and our mine administrator, Clyde Rhodes. The C-130 will leave Uganda once we've secured our base site. Any questions to this point?"

"You bet. I get my assignment." The speaker was one of the Afrikaner pilots, Marius. "Fly the chopper. Keep it operational. I assume you've allowed for spare parts and tools in that C-130 cargo. But I'm still not understanding exactly what our overall mission is here. Okay, so we help secure the mine, provide some air cover to reopen the road. But I've played this scenario way too many times before. Krueger said this was a short-term contract. One month. Those Mi-17s can pack some real firepower. But even if we blast everything that moves in the vicinity, all the insurgents have to do is fall back and wait until we leave. Look, Mulroney, I've fought long and hard with and for you over the years. I've never yet been on the losing side of a contract. But I'm not sure I see how this one's winnable. After all, Wamba's men have been fighting these rebels for months without any inroads. Unless you're planning on a long-term operation and a whole lot bigger than the team we've got here."

"Yes, and what is this other base camp you keep referring to?" This time it was Ernie Miller who spoke up. "I thought the mine was our FOB. Does this mean the mine's got no landing strip? If not, how the dickens are we going to get our gear into position to secure the place? No Mi-17's going to ferry what we've got on that C-130."

One stark difference that still surprised Robin between her former life and the private military world was the freedom with which subordinates could and did debate orders. Back talk that would have landed any Marine in lockup was not only accepted but expected. Of course out here a senior field commander on one contract might well be one's underling on the next. And since living to spend that generous hazard pay was a mercenary's ultimate goal, every private military contractor had a stake—and an opinion—in ensuring a profitable outcome.

"I wouldn't have you here if this wasn't a winnable mission," Trevor Mulroney responded calmly. "Nor is it our job to root out an entire insurgency. Or hold down long-term some major chunk of rainforest. On the contrary, you've got a very simple mission. Capture, dead or alive, one man."

The Earth Resources CEO tossed a computer printout on the table. The black-and-white photo had clearly been blown up from a much smaller size as it was fuzzy and extremely pixelated. The basic facial structure of an ebony-skinned African male in his late teens with strong-boned, elongated features and a prominent, high-bridged nose differed minimally to Robin's gaze from those of millions of other sub-Saharan young men. Other than, perhaps, the brilliance of the smile displaying strong, white teeth. Or the hopeful joy lighting large, dark eyes.

Trevor Mulroney's forefinger tapped the bright smile. "This is the man identified as the rebel leader. Not much to go on, I know, but it's the only positive ID we've got, his university application photo.

Which would help explain the sophistication of his attacks. The average rainforest villager doesn't know how to rig explosives or what to do with a detonator cap. Since even this picture is years old, our insurgent would be hard to pick out of a crowd except for one thing: he's got a large scar running down his left arm."

"What kind of scar?" Ernie Miller was scribbling on a notepad. "Knife? Gunshot? Lots of guys got scars."

"Burn," Trevor Mulroney elucidated laconically. "Shoulder all the way down to wrist. Not something you can miss. As to his identity, we don't know what his own people call him, but Wamba's men refer to him as Jini, or 'ghost' in Swahili, because he evaporates like smoke before anyone can get too close. For whatever reason, he's certainly made it a personal vendetta to keep any outside interests from his territory. The consensus is that if this Jini's taken out, any further insurgency will collapse of its own accord. As to just how we're going to manage that—"

Pulling a pen from a breast pocket, the Earth Resources CEO used it to draw a circle around the gray-brown mounds that marked the molybdenite mine. "Anyone here ever participated in a bush hunt?"

A number of Robin's teammates were already nodding in sudden enlightenment. Mulroney tapped the circle. "In a bush hunt, you don't fan out from a central location. You form a perimeter circle with nets and weapons around the area you want to hunt, then in coordination begin moving inward. Your prey naturally retreats from the hunters so that you have them penned within a smaller and smaller circle until they can no longer escape, when you take them out. You ask how we're going to manage that when Wamba's men haven't been able to get a whisper of the guy? Simply, air power combined with high tech Wamba didn't have. Our reconnaissance tech here—" Mulroney motioned toward Carl Jensen, who had closed his laptop at Mulroney's arrival to join the others—"has some toys, or will have once the C-130 touches down, that can practically do magic fitted into the executive chopper. Heat-sensor technology in the past has always been iffy when dealing with triple-canopy rainforest. Especially here on the equator, where air and body temperatures at ground level aren't so far apart. What we'll be using is the latest improvement that combines heat, motion, infrared, biometrics, and who knows what else to differentiate a guerrilla band from a herd of duiker antelope even underneath fifty meters of canopy foliage.

"With Jensen to pinpoint and track people movements, we'll be using the Mi-17s to drop in ground units along our initial bush hunt perimeter. The idea isn't to engage with Jini's forces or hide our presence in any way. Just offer enough resistance to discourage this Jini from engaging. Especially since with our aerial technology, he won't be able to pull the kind of ambush he's been getting away with. Our intel is that Jini can't have more than a couple hundred combatants, so he's going to retreat from any well-armed offensive line. The one place we'll be putting minimal defensive force, at least to all appearances, is at the mine itself. Which will push Jini that direction. Especially if it looks to him as though opposition forces are roaming his territory at random looking for him while leaving his principle target practically unguarded."

"Like cheese in a mousetrap," someone murmured with satisfaction.

"Exactly." Trevor Mulroney nodded. "Obviously we're going to need more than this team to carry out a bush hunt perimeter. Wamba has committed two thousand of his own men. This particular piece of rainforest may not be familiar to them, but they're all experienced militia fighters. Now I know we've got a communications problem. But Wamba still maintains strong ties with Uganda, especially now that a peace accord has been signed. He's arranged through his field commander Samuel Makuga, who has family connections in Kampala, a hundred Ugandan mercenaries. All former military who know this country from their peacekeeping days. Enough of them speak English as well as Swahili to serve as your liaisons with their men as well as our main boots on the ground."

Then why had Mulroney bothered hiring Lt. Chris R. Duncan? As for local allies, were they really to depend on former rebel insurgents and invading military—both groups as infamous for violence and human rights atrocities as this Jini?

The Earth Resources CEO answered her first question without need of asking. "Of course we don't want to be dependent on locals to give us accurate translation and intel. Which is why in doubt we have Ms. Duncan's ears and language skills to ensure we're not being spun a line. As to our FOB and the C-130, we've got that well covered. There's an airstrip about an hour's flight from here into the rainforest, but no more than ten minutes from the mine. Right on the edge of our operational perimeter, in fact. It's long enough to take the C-130, if barely, and has been recently repaired by some humanitarian operation that maintains a medical outpost there. A place called Taraja."

Mulroney tapped a clearing on the map not far from the gray-brown mounds. "We couldn't have designed a place that better meets our mission specs. Open space for setting up base camp. A local community for labor pool. Even medical support if necessary."

Taraja.

Michael's childhood home.

Robin's mind was churning. So this was the real reason Pieter Krueger had been pumping Michael for data on the plane, not help with his map! Did Michael even know about this? Surely he'd have given some indication if he'd expected to see Robin again in the very near future. This time Robin didn't hold back.

"Excuse me, Mr. Mulroney, but does Dr. Stewart . . . uh, the medical outpost personnel know we're coming? He never mentioned . . . I mean, well, humanitarian missions like Doctors Without Borders aren't usually so cooperative about getting mixed up with military ops. I'm just surprised they'd consent to something like this."

Trevor Mulroney made no effort to hide displeasure. "I never asked! This medical mission may use the airstrip for their own landing zone. May even have built it. But the land on which it's built and the local community happen to be under Bunia jurisdiction. Which means the only person we need permission from to set up operations there is Governor Wamba. But you bring up a good point. Prudence dictates establishing friendly contact with local expat agencies, especially since we just might need their services at some point. And since you, Duncan, would appear to be acquainted with this Stewart, that will be your first assignment."

A jangle interrupted Mulroney's terse order. He pulled out a satellite phone, the stab of a thumb silencing the ringtone. "Clyde? Yes, we'll be heading your way any minute. ETA another hour or so."

As the Earth Resources CEO listened, his jaw tightened in fury. Breaking off the connection, he spun back to the Ares Solutions team, piercing blue gaze now chips of ice. "Another change of plans, I'm afraid. We've got a situation at the mine. Seems our 'ghost' has decided not to wait for that bush hunt."

CHAPTER TEN

Me and my big mouth!

A beat of rotors flying in low over the hangar drowned out Trevor Mulroney's next words. Robin's thoughts were more occupied in any case with the Earth Resources CEO's final order. Whatever Michael's insistence, Robin had made her own determination never to see the American surgeon again. Seeking him out as advance scout of an uninvited invasion on his home base was hardly how she'd choose to thrust herself again onto his horizon.

The roar of aircraft receded enough to hear again what Mulroney was saying. "We don't know how bad this is yet. Or if it's an ongoing attack. But there are casualties, and site security is screaming for reinforcements. So we'll all be heading to the mine first as a show of force and to leave some of Wamba's men for perimeter control. Maybe a few of you as well if the situation warrants it. Everyone got that? Then let's roll."

Three helicopters had hovered down to the tarmac by the time the Ares Solutions team shouldered their baggage and headed outside. Bulkier than a US military Black Hawk and with a different contour of machine gun turrets and missile launchers, the two Russian Mi-17s couldn't be mistaken for anything but assault aircraft. Inside they'd been gutted of seats to permit more cargo weight. At the moment they were so packed with crates, sacks, and uniformed militia Robin would not have thought even those powerful rotors could lift the aircraft off the ground. As the South African combat pilots climbed into the cockpits, their Congolese counterparts clambered out and made for the airport exit.

Trevor Mulroney headed directly toward the third helicopter, much smaller and round of body. "Duncan. Jensen. You're with me."

Robin felt some compunction about settling herself into a padded seat with protective ear mufflers while her male teammates squeezed in among militia and cargo. The smaller helicopter took the lead lifting off, the two larger aircraft lumbering skyward at its tail like a pair of oversize dragonflies chasing a bumblebee. The Earth Resources pilot was a Ukrainian hire whose English proved adequate for a shouted consultation on where to install Carl Jensen's techno gear.

Which left Robin free to occupy herself with the unimpeded vista provided by the executive chopper's Plexiglas wraparound windshield. The shift from Bunia's savannah and rolling hills to the triple-canopy rainforest was as abrupt as crossing a line on a map. *So this is where Michael grew up. It's even more incredible than he claimed! How can anything this beautiful hold war and hate and death?*

From this height, the huge, rounded crowns of giant hardwoods looked like nothing so much as a vast field of broccoli ripe for picking. Here and there, flowering trees broke the monotony with splotches of orange, yellow, white, flame-red. Occasionally, a meandering brown zigzag of a river swept below the helicopter's runners. Even less occasionally, wattle-and-daub thatched huts dotted a clearing.

Once, the broccoli field broke away abruptly into a canyon so deep Robin could barely make out the silver ribbon that was a rushing river at the bottom. Tumbling out from beneath the rainforest canopy, another stream off to her left shot over the lip of a precipice to form a waterfall that disappeared in a white froth into the canyon's shadowed depths. As the helicopter crossed overhead, spray thrown off by the cascade caught the light to span the ravine below them with the delicate, multihued arc of a perfect rainbow. Robin could spot no other bridge across the canyon. The helicopter's bumblebee shadow flitting once again over green treetops might have been the first human presence to disturb this pristine landscape since its creation.

An illusion abruptly dispelled as the telltale markers of gray-brown mounds thrusting above the treetops gave way to a devastation that could only be of human derivation.

"ETA one minute," Trevor Mulroney announced abruptly, not to his fellow passengers, but into the radio mike of a copilot's headset. "Willem, Marius, site security says there's been no further hostilities. But be on the alert as you come in. You'll have to set down outside the fence. Krueger, set a perimeter guard on the choppers first thing."

Robin wasn't quite sure what she'd expected of a molybdenite mine. Underground shafts and diggings, perhaps. Some sort of organized infrastructure, definitely.

Instead this sprawling, ugly gash of red-brown mud and gray shale looked more stereotypical of the strip mines now largely outlawed in her own country. A high chain-link fence topped with concertina wire formed a meandering semicircle from the base of those gray-brown mounds to a nearby riverbank. Wooden observation platforms rose on either side of a metal-paneled gate and at intervals along the chain-link fence. Guards manning the watchtowers and patrolling inside the perimeter fence all wore the khaki uniforms of Wamba's militia.

But where were the buildings? The heavy machinery?

Nor at this moment did Robin see any human toilers.

The executive chopper hovered down inside the fence near a metallic octagonal bubble that was the enclosure's only real structure, a large Quonset hut. As Robin clambered down after her male companions, two large, muscled men, one who looked native Congolese in militia uniform, the other a Caucasian with sweat-stained safari clothing and a long ponytail, emerged from the Quonset hut. Nearby, smoke drifted skyward from a mass of twisted metal.

Outside the chain-link fence, the two Mi-17s settled on a muddy field separating mine and rainforest. As clam doors at the rear of the assault helicopters opened to spew out armed militia and foreign mercenaries, Trevor Mulroney stepped toward the two approaching men.

"Clyde, Makuga! What exactly is going on here? I thought you said the mine was under attack. And where are the workers? Why are mining operations shut down if hostilities are not ongoing?"

"Sorry, boss, but we've lost the steam engine." Trevor Mulroney's greeting had identified the ponytail as mine administrator Clyde Rhodes—South African, by his accent. "Which means pumps, electricity, everything. Not to mention the rock crusher and other equipment nearby when the steam engine blew up. It was bad enough once we couldn't transport. Still, we could at least stockpile your molybdenum so long as we could process the raw ore. Without that equipment, there's no point in having the workers keep excavating. As you can see, we've got way too much back pile already."

The man gestured first to the mass of twisted metal, then mounds of broken rock that lay everywhere in the clearing, tall as the Quonset hut. "Even if we could bring in another rock crusher and other equipment, there's no way to replace the steam engine. Not until the roads are open, anyway. It would be way too heavy to haul in by chopper. And that's if we can locate another. They're pretty obsolete even here in the Congo."

"But this is terrible!" The Ukrainian pilot had climbed down and was staring around in horror. "And I do not see the storage shed! Where are all the supplies I flew in this past week?"

"The shed went up right after the engine. We lost everything stored there. Which was anything too flammable to keep in the

Quonset hut. Kerosene for power tools and lighting. Gas cylinders for fridge and stove. Oil lubricant and processing chemicals. All the whiskey. Hence so much damage. We were thinking accident at first. That maybe the steam engine's boiler just blew. The thing's an antique piece of junk, after all. But it turned out to be an attack. Sabotage."

Rhodes held out what appeared to be partially burned charcoal. "You see that? Plastic explosive residue. A bomb, and a clever one. Someone hollowed out a piece of charcoal. Not from our kiln either. Maybe a chunk of burned tree from a forest fire. Clever! Somehow it got tucked into our charcoal supply. When it hit the furnace—boom! It wouldn't have been so devastating if the shed hadn't gone up too. At this point we're not actually sure if the shed explosion was another bomb or just a secondary detonation from flying shrapnel and sparks."

Trevor Mulroney lifted the fragment from the mine administrator's hand. "Any likelihood it was an inside job? One of the prisoners or a guard?"

"No way! Not the bomb, at least. We use explosives to loosen up the rock. But I'm the only one who handles the stuff. Nor would any of our workers have the know-how to put something like this together. We don't keep plastic explosives in the shed, fortunately, but under lock and key in the Quonset hut. Otherwise there'd be nothing but a crater here right now. Nor is any of our inventory missing. I already checked. No, this attack has Jini written all over it. My guess is the explosives came from the same hijacked load used on the barge and road. How he got inside to plant the bomb is the big mystery. Makuga's in charge of security, and his forces are all from his own clan, fiercely loyal to him; I can testify they keep this place buttoned up so tight a flea couldn't get through."

Rhodes indicated his companion. "One of the casualties was a nephew of Makuga's. Believe me, if he thought there was any way our workers could have made contact with this Jini, he'd have a confession sweated out of them by now."

That, Robin could well believe. The Congolese field commander looked enough like Governor Wamba to be a sibling or at least a distant cousin. Not just in powerful build and heavy, flat-nosed features, but the arrogance of posture and chillness of gaze. Not a man to cross without an army at your back.

Out here in the open air, Robin could see for herself that shattered machinery was far from the only damage. Sharp fumes of burning chemicals stung her sinuses. Shards of fuel drums and metal siding, puddles of melted plastic were scattered everywhere. Broken glass and charcoal fragments crunched underfoot.

And as warned, there were casualties.

Robin counted four badly burned and bloodied bodies heaped near a smoldering tower of roughly piled stones. One wore the uniform of a security guard. Mounds of processed black carbon identified the tower as a charcoal kiln. Now that helicopter rotors and engines had fallen silent, Robin could also hear groans, cries, whimpers of pain that made it clear this place wasn't as sparse of human inhabitants as it appeared.

Since her employer appeared in no immediate need of translation services, Robin followed the sounds to a huge pile of dried branches and foliage. This appeared at first to be discarded trimmings from charcoal production. But when Robin spotted an opening, she realized the piled-up brush actually formed a crude corral such as African herdsmen erected to protect cattle from marauders.

Though this corral imprisoned no animals. Pup tents of palm leaves lashed down over a latticework of branches provided meager living quarters. Still, a more careful survey showed Robin that this makeshift workers' barracks wasn't quite as pitiable as at first glance. A larger thatched roof shielded a fire pit where women prepared food. Grain sacks and reasonable flesh covering bones indicated this group ate as well as the average Congolese.

Which was no comfort to bloodied, fire-scorched human shapes laid out on straw mats like some bizarre hospital ward just inside the opening. Several were children. One, no more than three or four, a girl by the intricate hair braids, sat on a woman's lap, wailing. She displayed no burns, but a length of rubber tubing was knotted tourniquet-style above a gash that flayed her forearm open to the bone.

At the next mat, a white-haired African man bore down on a wad of cloth folded against an adolescent boy's upper thigh, forming a rudimentary pressure bandage. So at least one person here had some first aid training. But despite the old man's efforts, scarlet welled up around the bandage. The boy himself lolled unconscious against the mat, his dark, young features a peculiar gray shade that would have been deathly pale on lighter skin. Nearby lay a young woman, her face and upper body so badly burned that blackened flesh was sloughing away from exposed bones. She was only too unfortunately conscious, anguished moans and babbling attempts at speech issuing from mangled lips.

At those terrible sounds, horror and nausea boiled over into blinding rage inside Robin. Hardened into cold resolve. A man like this Jini who could so casually inflict such terrible pain and suffering on other human beings had to be stopped, whatever it took to do so.

Some protesting noise had left her own lips, because the elderly paramedic suddenly raised his head to call out in frantic French, "You there, *mademoiselle*, whoever you are! Please, you must help us! This boy is going to die! Please, we need a doctor, medicines!"

Robin started immediately forward, only to be stopped by two guards, who materialized from the shadows on either side of the corral opening to block her way with their automatic rifles. Whirling around, Robin raced instead back toward the executive helicopter. By now Pieter Krueger and several Ares Solutions operatives had joined Trevor Mulroney and the others. Out on the field, more of her teammates were coordinating the unloading of cargo by Wamba's militia.

"So, Clyde, I'll leave you half of our local contingent to bolster Makuga's security arrangements. We'll have to figure out how to get a generator and enough fuel out here at least to power the communications equipment. Make a list, and Ivan can arrange a cargo run from

Bunia first light tomorrow. I'll place the Mi-17s at your disposal for that. Should be able to fit a small generator in one of those."

Robin hesitated only briefly before thrusting her way into the group. "Mr. Mulroney, excuse me for interrupting. But we've got a more urgent need right now. There are civilian casualties here who need immediate medical attention. We've got to get them airlifted to a hospital! And if anyone on the team has some serious paramedic experience, we need that, too. And any available medical supplies!"

But Samuel Makuga was already shaking his head. "The criminals cannot be moved from here. They have their own doctor."

The heavy Ugandan accent of his English was guttural enough that Robin thought at first she'd misheard. "What do you mean, criminals? Are you referring to the mine workers? And I saw your 'doctor.' He doesn't even have first aid supplies in there!"

Robin swung around to face the Earth Resources CEO. "Mr. Mulroney, I'm not trying to cause trouble here. But I saw people in that corral over there who are going to die without immediate medical care. Kids! And what is this that the injured can't be airlifted out of here? Is this a mine or a prison camp?"

"Actually, it's a bit of both." Rhodes spoke up coolly. "As Mr. Mulroney here is well aware, if you aren't, lady. Look around you. That fence over there isn't just to keep insurgents out. It's to keep our workforce in. Eventually, if we can ever put Jini and his men out of business, we can bring in real equipment, build a modern mine out here. But right now this place is a hazard zone. And using prison labor for such is a common enough practice here in the Congo and elsewhere. Wamba has been generous enough to supply workers to get this venture off the ground. And before you get your nose out of joint, I run a clean operation here. Believe me, these people get treated and fed better than you'll find in any Kinshasa-run government mine."

Which was less approbation of this place than an indictment of the DRC's Ministry of Mines.

"As for the casualties," Rhodes went on, "as Makuga says, they've got their own shaman, healer, whatever you want to call him, and he's proved himself competent enough. Our medical supplies went up in smoke with everything else in that shed. But we've got some replacement first aid paraphernalia arriving right now."

His nod indicated a cartload of boxes and crates Wamba's militia had just trundled through the gate. Robin did not yield. "So does prison labor include women and children too? And first aid isn't going to cut it. Those people need a real doctor."

Trevor Mulroney raised a hand for silence. "Enough, Duncan. If you had appropriate experience, you'd be aware it's the custom here to let prisoners bring along family members with no other place to go. Or would you rather let them starve? The Congo doesn't have a lot of welfare handouts. As to your 'real doctor,' those aren't so easy to find around here. I'm sure this healer will do as well as some under-supplied, overcrowded government clinic back in Bunia."

"But that's not actually true. Finding a doctor, I mean." Robin squarely faced her employer, this time unabashedly pleading. "Mr. Mulroney, you told us we're just a few minutes' flight here from Taraja, where there happens to be a medical clinic and a surgeon. Dr. Michael Stewart, who flew with us to Bunia, remember? Didn't you say you wanted the locals' cooperation? How better than to show we're not just here to fight this Jini with guns and soldiers, but that we care enough to help his victims, too? I mean, General Wamba can hardly object to airlifting prisoners' family members. Or claim women and children are criminals to be locked up!"

Trevor Mulroney was silent longer than Robin could have wished. This was, after all, such an obvious call. He stepped aside to murmur briefly with Rhodes and Makuga before offering an abrupt nod.

"You really are a troublemaker, Duncan. But once again you make a good point. Rescuing survivors of this Jini's attacks will certainly score us some points with the natives. And considering the reputation of our local allies, we may need those points."

To Robin's relief, once the decision was made, Mulroney began immediately barking out orders. Within minutes, the executive heli-copter had hovered skyward and an Mi-17 settled into its place. Robin hurried back to the brush enclosure. To her displeasure, she found Samuel Makuga on her heels. At least his presence got her past the two guards. At Makuga's snapped orders in Swahili, four men lifted the mat with the badly burned young woman. The wailing little girl was carried out by her mother.

The security chief shook his head at a man and two women with lesser burns but permitted a badly burned young boy to be carried out. Meanwhile, the elderly medical worker had not left the side of the older boy nor stopped bearing down on his makeshift pressure bandage. Even in Robin's short absence, the boy looked grayer, the bandage more scarlet.

But Samuel Makuga again shook his head. "No, this one is not a child, but a man and a criminal. He cannot go."

All Robin's rage, the accumulation of twenty-four hours of sleep deprivation and emotional upheaval, suddenly reached a flash point. Her hands balled at her sides as she spun around. The Congolese field commander towered above her, but she met his glare squarely, hissing in her own poor but fluid Swahili, "The boy *will* go! If he does not, he will die. Is this what you wish? If you do not permit me to take him, I will inform Trevor Mulroney and Governor Wamba himself that you caused his death."

Whether her fury, her blatant name-dropping, or the unexpected-ness of her Swahili, the security chief looked briefly stunned. His glare bore down on Robin. Her own did not waver. Then Makuga's massive shoulders rose and fell. "The boy will go. But only under guard so that he cannot attempt escape. And do not think to contradict my orders, for they come from Governor Wamba and Mr. Mulroney."

It was a compromise Robin could live with. As Makuga strode from the enclosure, Robin turned to the boy's elderly attendant, switching back to French. "Bring this boy to the helicopter. We will take him to a doctor."

Now it was the attendant who shook his head. "They will not permit me to go. But the pressure bandage must be held in place, or he will bleed again. And he must have a doctor's care, even surgery very soon, or he will die."

His cultured French indicated far more education than some village schoolhouse. But there wasn't time to wonder. "I will hold the bandage in place and watch over him myself." Robin followed her promise with action. "And he will have a doctor's care very soon. We are not taking him far—to a place called Taraja where there is a surgeon, Dr. Stewart, who can help the boy."

This time it was the elderly medic who looked stunned. More than stunned. Robin had not realized the depth of hopelessness, despair, in the dark eyes until she saw hope, life, reborn there. "Dr. Charles Stewart? He has returned to Taraja?"

"Not Charles Stewart. Michael."

"Michael. The son. Then he too is a doctor now like his father? You know him? He is a friend of yours?"

"Yes, I know him." *Or at least I thought I did!*

"And will you give him a message? You who have shown yourself a friend to my people though you dress like a soldier and travel with Wamba's men?"

Samuel Makuga was striding into the enclosure again. This time there were other security guards at his heels. At his surly order, the men lifting the boy's mat started hurriedly forward, so that Robin had to move quickly too, in order to keep the pressure bandage in place. The elderly man kept step beside her for several paces, his urgent plea barely a whisper.

"Tell him—tell Michael Stewart—that all is not as it seems! Tell him . . . tell him the words of the Holy Book his father so often spoke. 'Woe to those who call evil good and good evil, who put darkness for light and light for darkness.' Tell him!"

CHAPTER ELEVEN

"All is not as it seems! 'Woe to those who call evil good and good evil.'"

What had the old man meant? The *woe* reference sounded scriptural and vaguely familiar. But to what did it refer? Or whom? And how did a criminal from a Bunia prison know Michael Stewart and his father? Where had he learned such educated French?

Well, those were questions Robin could pursue soon enough. But at the moment, more urgent issues occupied her thoughts and hands. The guards had pushed the old man away, forcing him back inside the brush enclosure, as Robin accompanied the straw-mat stretcher out to the Mi-17. She was too busy maintaining pressure on the boy's wound to look back.

Members of the Ares Solutions team were now helping lift straw mats through the clam doors at the rear of the helicopter. Samuel Makuga stood outside, checking each mat as it was lifted in. The teenage boy's mat was last, Robin keeping pace beside him, a hand holding the pressure bandage in place. At a snap of Makuga's fingers, two of the camp security guards clambered in after her, taking up positions on either side of the mat as though the prone youth might jump to his feet and attempt to flee.

No other accompanying attendants had been permitted into the helicopter, but with a total of six straw mats besides the little girl with the tourniquet, the interior of the Mi-17 was crowded enough. A half dozen of Robin's teammates rounded out the passenger load. Somehow, while Robin had been dealing with the injured, they'd all managed to provision themselves with the automatic rifles that Wamba's militia carried. As the helicopter rotors began to turn, Trevor Mulroney thrust his head through the open side door to address Marius at the throttle. "You have the coordinates? We shouldn't be long behind you. If the C-130 touches down before we do, you know what to do."

His piercing blue gaze shifted to Robin, kneeling beside the boy's mat. "Duncan, you requested this assignment. So I'm making you responsible for these people."

Side doors screeched shut. The Mi-17 climbed skyward. Hunkered down on a vibrating metal floor, Robin could no longer see the spectacular vista over which they were flying. Nor had ear mufflers been supplied here. If Robin found the noise horrendous, how frightening it must be for their new passengers, this flight in all probability an unfamiliar experience for them.

The little girl with the tourniquet had already grown hysterical when she was separated from her mother. Her wails grew to screams of terror until Ernie Miller lifted her onto his lap. Robin would not have thought that dour stranger's face, the weapon in his other hand, comforting to a small child. But after a few hiccups, the little girl fell silent against his Kevlar vest.

The noise at least helped drown out the badly burned young woman's garbled cries, the moans of pain and terror from the other victims. Robin's own patient, in contrast, showed no awareness of his surroundings, the rise and fall of his chest so slight Robin was terrified he might quit breathing altogether. For a dizzy moment, this was not the Congo, but the dusty mountains of Afghanistan; not an Mi-17, but a Black Hawk medivac helicopter; no young African boy, but a redheaded young man whose bloody wound she fought to stem.

The anguished screams, roar of rotors and engine, fumes of engine fuel, and sweetish, metallic scent of blood mixed with perspiration were pushing her over the edge. Robin's stomach rose into her mouth. Her vision swam. She could no longer breathe.

No, focus! You made a promise! This will not happen again! You will not fail this boy!

One hand on the pressure bandage, the other lightly on the boy's chest to monitor breathing, Robin closed her eyes, forcibly shutting out sight, sound, smell as she set herself to endure. And Trevor Mulroney's assessment of distance proved accurate enough because less than a quarter hour had passed when Robin felt the helicopter lose altitude. Then the jolt of runners touching ground.

The side doors screeched open before the rotors ground to a halt. Robin's teammates spilled out, weapons in hand, to take up defensive positions around the helicopter. All but the Vietnam vet with the little girl in his arms. Unbelievably, the child appeared asleep against his Kevlar vest. Squatting beside Robin, he slid his hand gently under hers to separate it from the pressure bandage. "I'll take over here. You go find that doctor pal of yours."

He raised his voice. "Frank, you want to lend the girl a hand?"

The other Vietnam vet strode over as Robin climbed stiffly from the helicopter. The Mi-17 had settled to the ground at the edge of a clearing much larger than the molybdenite mine. But in antithesis to that hideous eyesore, here the predominant color palette was green. Behind the helicopter, massive hardwoods rose to the height of twenty-story buildings. Straight ahead, a wide, straight ribbon of packed earth and stubble split the clearing like an arrow to disappear at the far end into a fresh tangle of brush and trees.

The airstrip.

On either side of the airstrip had clearly once existed cultivated fields and fruit orchards along with a neat grid of cinder-block and brick buildings. But all was now swallowed up by the tangle of nettles, vines, ferns, and palms that overtook any break in the rainforest canopy left unattended to a tropical sun. Broken-down walls and collapsed roofs showed black streaks of fire damage.

What exactly had Robin overheard Michael Stewart telling Pieter Krueger? Something about Taraja being razed to the ground a decade back. The mission school and clinic being closed. Its inhabitants killed or scattered.

But Michael had also mentioned a recent reopening of the Taraja clinic. Walking forward onto the airstrip, Robin spotted what she'd known had to be here. A path leading through undergrowth from the airstrip toward a collection of burned-out buildings off to her right. The glint of late-afternoon sun on unrusted metal roofing indicated at least some structural repairs. A scattering of thatched roofs was also visible above the tangle of foliage.

The airstrip itself showed no sign of the red-and-white Cessna, so either it had not yet arrived or had come and gone. Most probably the latter, considering the time lapse. Appearing at Robin's side, Frank Kowalski indicated the new roofing.

"I'm guessing you'll find your doctor pal up there. And from those shacks, there's got to be villagers around. They couldn't have missed our arrival. But I haven't spotted a living soul."

One could hardly blame any locals who'd heard the assault helicopter's approach for preferring to remain hidden from view. But time was running out for their injured passengers. "I'll go look for Dr. Stewart. If the other choppers get here before I'm back, please let Trevor Mulroney know where I've gone."

"Are you kidding?" The Vietnam vet had already started across the airstrip. "Ernie would have my head, and rightly so, if I let you go alone. First rule of hostile territory. Always travel with backup."

Robin didn't waste time arguing, breaking into a trot up the path with Frank close on her heels. They hadn't gone far when the underbrush opened into a cleared area. Mud-and-wattle huts dotted similar cultivations to those swallowed up by vegetation along the airstrip. Banana plants. Peanut beds. Vegetable gardens. Even a few surviving citrus, mango, and other fruit trees. Through the branches of the orchard, Robin caught a glimpse of brown water, signaling the lazy flow of a river, first prerequisite for any rainforest community.

Also scattered here and there were abandoned hoes. A basket of picked fruit spilled out onto a path. Pots bubbled unattended on outdoor cook fires. Several times Robin caught movement inside dark doorways. A glint of watching eyes. Still not a living soul ventured into the open.

The path threaded between several crumbled and blackened brick buildings. Then suddenly a sweep of trimmed lawn opened up in front of Robin. Beyond was the restored metal roofing she'd spotted from the runway.

Two buildings had been so repaired. The larger was a one-story brick building with a veranda running along the front. Here was the first human life Robin had spied, the veranda a mass of dark bodies, mostly children and women in bright pagnes. A young Congolese woman with a white lab coat and a clipboard was policing traffic through a screen door.

The reestablished clinic, she'd be willing to bet.

A side path off to Robin's left led to the second restored roof. It covered a square cinder-block structure, wide screen windows and unpainted metal door opening directly onto the lawn instead of a veranda. Unbelievably for this remote location, Robin could see the white parabolic disc of a satellite dish thrusting up its tall spike of an antenna at the high point of the roof. And were those tilted crystalline frames covering much of both roofs solar panels? Maybe this place wasn't quite as isolated as it appeared.

In the open area between cinder-block house and clinic, log pillars elevated a sizable thatched roof. Though empty at the moment, rough wooden benches indicated its use as community center, church, or both. Robin paused uncertainly under the camouflage of a patch of guava trees. The clinic was the most likely place to find Michael Stewart. But the sudden appearance there of two foreigners, one heavily armed, would inevitably provoke panic, especially considering Taraja's recent history.

But now another white lab coat was hurrying down the path in their direction. This one an African male perhaps a few years older than Robin's own twenty-seven. He was tall, above six feet, slimly muscled, with elongated, coffee-dark features and high-bridged nose. He stopped with a wary frown but no sign of fear when he spotted the newcomers ahead of him on the path.

"May I help you?" he demanded in sharp French. "We do not permit weapons here."

Robin tugged her cap from her head, letting her red-gold mane spill down. Here was one time when making her gender clear was to their advantage. "*Bonjour.* We're with the helicopter that just landed. I'm looking for Dr. Michael Stewart. I need to find him urgently."

The man shook his head. "He is in surgery. He cannot be interrupted."

"Then is there someone else in authority here I can speak to? Another doctor?" Robin suddenly remembered the elderly mine paramedic's mention of Michael's father. "Another family member perhaps? It's very urgent."

The man's gaze flickered from Robin to the large mercenary behind her, then indicated the smaller cinder-block building. "You will please accompany me."

Leading the way to the metal door, their guide did not bother with a knock before pushing it open. From inside, Robin heard a female voice call out in French, "Ephraim, there you are. Did you hear—?"

Their guide said something in Swahili too low and quick for Robin to follow but that had the immediate effect of cutting off the woman's speech. Then the door opened farther. The woman who stepped into view wore a typical Congolese pagne and turban, the material wrapping her from shoulder to ankle in a profusion of pink, orange, and yellow flowers. The toddler in her arms and an older child peering out from behind her skirts were both unmistakably African.

But the woman herself was Caucasian, about Robin's age. Brunette curls escaped the turban. Delicate features would have been strikingly beautiful but for a jagged, poorly healed slash above the right eyebrow that pulled that eye to a permanently distorted upward slant. Though any impression of disfigurement was banished by the warmth of the woman's smile, the amber friendliness of her gaze.

"So you are from the aircraft I heard landing." Her French held the same Congolese lilt as their white-coated guide's. "I am sorry there was no welcome. We weren't expecting another flight today. If we received radio notice and overlooked it, I apologize."

Robin shook her head. "No notice was sent. And I'm sorry to intrude. I was hoping to find Dr. Michael Stewart. Maybe you could help me instead."

But the woman's friendly gaze had now swept over Robin's own tousled red-gold mane and bedraggled safari clothing and widened apprehensively as it flickered toward the large, armed mercenary at her back before returning to rest on Robin's hot, perspiring features. She let out a sharp exclamation, her full mouth losing its generous curve, friendliness draining from her expression. And now the tall African man in the lab coat had stepped up close behind the woman, his body posture at once protective and menacing.

Robin hurried into a pacific explanation. "Look, I'm really sorry for the intrusion. My name is Robin Duncan. We just flew in from that new mine not far from here, and I'll be glad to explain more in depth just why we're here. But at the moment we've got a bit of an urgent situation."

And this is why I didn't want an armed escort. It's hard to get local cooperation when you start out by scaring them to death!

Or so Robin assumed was the reason for the sudden hostility facing her. Until the woman interrupted, this time flatly, coldly, and in English.

American English.

"I know who you are! You look just like your pictures. And Michael mentioned you'd arrived in the Congo. But if you've come here to offer some sort of apology, don't bother. You're five years too late!"

CHAPTER TWELVE

Now stripped of its cargo, the second Mi-17 lumbered skyward with the remaining Ares Solutions operatives and those Wamba militia not being retained for mine security. A snap of Makuga's fingers sent two of his new reinforcements to a large carton marked with the scarlet cross indicating first aid supplies, which they ferried over to the brush corral. Fine print on the cardboard identified the box as donated goods for the United Nations peacekeeping operation. As the remaining new supplies were draped with tarps in lieu of the destroyed storage shed, Trevor Mulroney revolved slowly on a boot heel to make a 360-degree survey.

"Now back to that attack. Clyde, Makuga, you both say it was this Jini, okay. But the man had to have inside help placing that bomb. Unless the guy really is a ghost. And I don't believe in ghosts."

"I don't see how," the mine administrator argued. "Even if this Jini has accomplices inside, he couldn't get close enough to pass off the bomb. You see the perimeter. I can tell you not a crow gets near the fence. The place is lit with security lamps at night. Even Makuga's men don't ever leave the security enclosure for fear of the 'ghost' picking them off."

"Actually, that's not true." Trevor Mulroney's Oakley sunglasses were now directed toward a dozen hardwood stumps at the far edge of the clearing beyond the perimeter fence. "You're forgetting just what powered our blown-up equipment."

"Well, yes, the logging parties," Rhodes conceded. "But they're well guarded. And the guards keep an eye on each other as well as the workers. Unless you think they're all in it, which is even less likely than ghosts. Makuga's clansmen aren't from this area and have nothing to gain by aiding a local insurgency."

"If you eliminate the impossible, the improbable is what remains." Mulroney tilted sunglasses upward to study a tangle of boughs and leaves and vines high above the stumps that interwove the separate treetops into a single labyrinth of foliage. He'd fought before in this kind of terrain. And while that fight had taught him to hate every humid, muddy, twisted, secretive square inch that made up a rain-forest habitat, he'd learned how to survive it.

And its natives.

"I know exactly how they did it because I know how I would do it. You've got to learn to think like a bushman. To look up and not just around. I'll bet our Jini was keeping watch somewhere up there while your logging party did its thing. Somehow he left a signal for his accomplice. And a package."

Mulroney raised a hand as a glowering Samuel Makuga spun around to shout orders. "No, there's no point in mounting a pursuit now. He—they—will be long gone. But I want this facility buttoned down tight. No one in or out, security or workers, until our ghost has been captured. Which shouldn't be an issue since further logging is now off the agenda. Meanwhile, maybe there was only one bomb, but let's not assume it. I want this place searched top to bottom. And

I want every person in that logging party interrogated, workers and security. Makuga, you've done this often enough before. Get on it."

As the Congolese field commander strode away with a surly scowl, Mulroney swiveled back to his remaining companion. "Now about getting the mining operation back on track. How much processed ore did you manage to sack before this happened?"

"Maybe ten tons since we lost the convoy last week." As a curse left Mulroney's lips, Rhodes spread apologetic hands. "Sorry, boss, but it's been slow as molasses doing all this without decent equipment. We've only managed this much by keeping that charcoal furnace running from sunup to sundown. And of course there's no way to continue now. Even if we airlift in a small generator, we'll be lucky to power the comm equipment and security lighting, not the kind of energy output needed to run the pumps and ore grinder. Not to mention, the cost of flying in fuel would be more than the profit margin on the molybdenum."

Even a small generator necessitated a regular flow of fuel. The incoming C-130 carried its own limited supply for the base camp setup. But splitting it two ways would run both dry quickly. Another major expenditure Mulroney didn't need right now.

"The truth is, boss, those hills aren't going anywhere. Certainly this Jini isn't going to cart them off. Wouldn't it be easier—and cheaper—to just pull out for now and come back once Wamba, Kinshasa, whoever, has restored order and reopened the roads?"

Clyde Rhodes kicked at the mangled, fire-scorched lump of metal that had been a steam engine as though a hard enough blow might somehow restore it to functionality. The geologist had worked for Mulroney since the early days of Earth Resources. He was the one who'd unearthed the obsolete equipment at a state copper mine his family had administered in South Africa for three generations before Nelson Mandela's rise to power resulted in a reshuffle in profitable government appointments. Even with Africa's minimal environmental regulations, the pollution of its charcoal-burning furnace was such that steam engines had long since been replaced by more efficient and cleaner electric- and petroleum-powered machinery. But it had served as backup on several Earth Resources concessions.

How much would he be removing from this place by now if he'd only been granted peace and stability enough to build up a modern infrastructure? One hundred tons a day? Two hundred tons?

Even the two hundred tons lost through the barge and convoy attacks would go far in solving Mulroney's immediate problems. The contents of that incoming C-130 had been available only because Mulroney had in essence hijacked an Ares Solutions contract ferrying supplies, weapons, and contract personnel to an American counterterrorism training operation in Yemen. Already both Yemeni and American authorities were screaming over the delay. If there were privileges to being the boss, even Trevor Mulroney could not put off for long the replacement of diverted resources.

The worst was that he was being squeezed by his local ally as much as by this Jini. Based on Mulroney's dealings to date with the warlord-turned-politician, today's shenanigans would not be Wamba's last attempt at a shakedown. In fact, if he had both his adversaries alone and at hand, he wasn't sure which head he'd remove from its offending body first.

Since he had neither, Mulroney knew now what he had to do. His next move was no longer a matter of choosing the best option, but of securing survival. "Well, get whatever ore you've got ready for loading. I'll send back one of the Mi-17s to haul it to our Bunia facility. As to pulling out, that isn't an option. If hand labor is all we have, we'll make do. Slow as molasses is still better than no production at all. Shift every worker and sledgehammer to breaking down those stockpiles. We'll fly in from Bunia what's necessary to complete the grinding and ore processing by hand."

Mulroney explained what he had in mind. "And, Clyde, if you don't have a minimum of twenty tons of ore ready by the end of the week, you're fired."

The Earth Resources CEO walked away before the mine administrator could make any response. His executive helicopter had lifted off earlier to make room for the medivac mission and was now settled down outside the perimeter fence. Instead of calling for its return, Mulroney signaled for the guards to open the gate. His strides across the muddy field afforded privacy to pull out his satellite phone. But he had not yet punched the speed dial when his phone jangled. An instant later, Howard Marshall's face appeared on the screen.

"I did the checking you asked. Wamba's had no communications with any of the multinationals bidding for the Ituri concession. Doesn't mean he couldn't be casting nets elsewhere. But I don't think so. Bottom line, he's hitched his star to you, and I'd say he's well aware he's not likely to get a better deal on that molybdenum from any of the runner-ups. Which doesn't mean he won't keep trying to get more out of you."

"Yes, well, that's what I was hoping to talk to you about." Mulroney explained the latest developments. "Unfortunately, our losses here at the mine and Wamba's shakedown have left me in just a bit of a cash-flow situation. Which is why I'm prepared to offer you an additional stake of my controlling interest in the Ituri concession. A modest ten million should tide things over until we can get security under control and the molybdenum operation running again at full speed. In fact, consider that ten million a short-term loan because you'll have it and your earlier investment back within three months guaranteed, with another 50 percent on top."

The Earth Resources CEO's measured tone gave no indication he'd just tossed his last chip into the game. Howard Marshall didn't answer immediately, but Mulroney recognized only too well that suddenly bland expression. So when the American did speak, his words held no surprises.

"And how do you figure making such a guarantee? Wamba isn't all the checking I've been doing. Why didn't you mention the Equatorial Guinea oil shutdown? Or the conflict mineral embargo from the

Central African Republic, where you've got your diamond concession? As to the Ituri concession, that's been a zero return to date. I've had my accounting department do the math. Earth Resources' claimed assets no longer seem to add up to its outstanding liabilities. And that was even before your bid on Ares Solutions. The other stockholders would not be too happy with the report I'm looking at. Some might even go so far as to talk fraud. For old times' sake, I can only hope you've got a good explanation. If only because I wouldn't give much for the odds of that knighthood if this same report reaches Buckingham Palace."

Trevor Mulroney would give even less. Nor would either palace or shareholders be pleased with what was a perfectly good explanation. But he didn't begin his defense immediately.

"Howard, have you ever considered that Earth Resources is now among dozens of multinational business enterprises—including your family's own Marshall Corp—with a gross annual product greater than half the member states of the United Nations? In fact, our two corporations alone have more power, wealth, and influence than the bulk of would-be empires throughout human history. People like us are the ones who make this planet work. We create the jobs. We bring need and supply together. We foster production, prosperity, and therefore peace among nations."

Mulroney could no longer keep bitter fury from raising his even tone. "Yet just because our power and influence don't fall within any single geographic or political territory, every backward, corrupt, bloodthirsty gang of thugs who manage to seize for ransom some chunk of the earth's surface area has more voice in global policy than we do. And can hold hostage our properties and investments to their own mismanagement, incompetence, and greed."

It wasn't necessary to explain which particular "gang of thugs" was currently affecting Mulroney's blood pressure. On the screen, Howard Marshall's eyebrows rose high. "It's the way the game's always been played. Mobutu. Wamba. Our distinguished new president in

Kinshasa. They come and go. We stay. Or walk away if the profit-risk margin gets too wide."

"Easy for you to say," Mulroney responded sourly. "How many generations has your family been buying up and deposing dictators for your own business interests?"

"For my country's interests," Howard Marshall corrected genially. "Business and national."

"Yeah, well, maybe you see a difference. The point is, there was a time when multinationals didn't put up with tinhorn despots and their shenanigans. When they ensured their own profit margins. Let's not forget India was forged from a bunch of quarreling warlords by a private merchant army backed by my own country's crown. Indonesia was similar. Britain's East India Company in India. The Dutch East India Company across Southeast Asia. King Leopold here in the Congo. They all protected their own interests. And in so doing built not only business empires, but political empires still friendly to the West."

His digression had brought sudden realization to his virtual companion's face. "Ares Solutions! So that's why you bid for it."

The Earth Resources CEO permitted a slight smile of admission. "9/11 has made mercenaries respectable again, as you should know, considering your country has shelled out the most in contracts. Instead of defending the thrones of Third World dictators, we're now the private enterprise arm of Western armies, embassies, corporations. Once again, a company like Ares Solutions has more firepower than the average UN member army.

"But if there's one thing those early multinationals knew, it's that sometimes you've got to make war to make peace. When I took back over Ares Solutions, I made an offer to the UN. A full-scale quick-deployment armored battalion, complete with air support, ground service, high-tech weapons that could put a fast end to any of the current conflicts requiring UN peacekeeping forces from the Congo to Haiti, Sudan, Kashmir. By taking the fight to the enemy instead of hunkering down behind barbed wire and electric fencing, we could save the lives of thousands, maybe even millions. Give these people a chance for a real life. And for a whole lot less than the billions our governments have contributed to decades of one futile peacekeeping operation after another. Including right here in Bunia."

Reaching the executive helicopter, Trevor Mulroney caught the interested eye of the Ukrainian pilot inside. He turned his back to the chopper as he finished scathingly, "They turned me down, of course. Doing something that actually makes sense instead of parading around in their pretty blue helmets would be just too easy."

Mulroney's intention might have been to set his business investor's mind at rest, but the expression showing on his phone screen had abruptly lost its blandness. Howard Marshall found voice to interrupt.

"Whoa, hold it there! Mulroney, are you out of your mind? You're proposing to invade the Congo with an armored battalion? Is that why you're there now? Do you really think Kinshasa would just stand by and cheer? Earth Resources may have the demographics of an entire country. But those geographic entities actually holding a seat in the United Nations don't usually appreciate a multinational usurping their function. Maybe in the eighteenth century, but not in the twenty-first. And for what—to reopen one mine?"

"Hey, let's not run ahead of ourselves," Trevor Mulroney cut in. "Of course I'm not proposing an invasion. You think I'm stupid?"

The American was wise enough not to respond.

"You don't use an RPG launcher to take out a wasp. But I do want to bump this operation up another notch. We now know this Jini was here at the mine within the last few hours. And he's on foot. Which means if I can get a perimeter in place, not within a week, but now within twenty-four hours, I've got him corralled. We can end this once and for all. But to do that, I need more resources. More boots on the ground. Transport to fly in Wamba's men instead of bringing them overland. As to cheering, let me assure you Kinshasa and Bunia both will jump at any helping hand that restores profits flowing into their own wallets. Especially when they don't have to pay out of pocket themselves."

"Yes, well, except it's my pocket, not yours, that you're suggesting gets picked."

"Your pocket can handle it. Marshall Corp's invested more than I'm asking in mineral exploration over the last year just in Africa." How he'd obtained those figures, Trevor Mulroney did not elucidate. It was enough to let his virtual companion know the Earth Resources CEO had his own intelligence sources. "The return here in goodwill alone will be worth your investment if a private corporation can claim credit for restoring peace to a war zone where people have been dying unnecessarily for years. Not to mention the precedent, should we pull this off, for the next time one of our assets is at risk in some Third World thug-controlled hole-in-the-wall."

"Goodwill doesn't pay shareholders, too many of whom happen to be my family members," Howard Marshall countered sharply. "Mulroney, I've never seen you like this. You've always known when to fold. When to walk away. This one almost seems—well, personal. Look, I don't like to lose an investment. And I'm truly sorry for your troubles. We've gone back a long ways together. But Marshall Corp is not a philanthropic organization. Nor is Earth Resources, however much sympathy one might feel for these villagers and miners hit by your rebels. For the ten million dollars you're asking, Marshall Corp can walk away from Ituri and begin again elsewhere. And molybdenum is hardly a rare metal. We've got a lead right now on a new molybdenum find in Chile seeking investors. Bottom line, one single mine in the middle of a Congolese war zone offers nothing worth pouring good money after bad. So may I suggest you cut your own losses and see what you can do to salvage your company."

"Ten million euros, not dollars," Trevor Mulroney corrected. "And actually, that's not quite the case. Which is why I'm prepared to offer you personally, not Marshall Corp, this once-in-a-lifetime investment opportunity."

"What is not the case?" Howard Marshall demanded. "The Chile discovery? Or that there's nothing special about this particular mine?"

"Both." Trevor Mulroney would have given much to go no further. His business partner would not be happy at what he'd already withheld. But he'd played his last chip and had no other moves left on this particular chessboard, if that wasn't a complete mix of metaphors.

And he knew his ally.

Simply, quietly, his even tone belying the fantastic import of his words, he explained.

CHAPTER THIRTEEN

Hot, angry phrases rose to Robin's mind, but before they reached her lips, a rapidly escalating roar pulled her gaze skyward. The unmistakable sound of a C-130 Hercules this time, not helicopter rotors.

It came into view directly overhead, massive, round-bellied, painted a steel gray, and unmistakably of military origins. The C-130 cargo plane, workhorse of the US Armed Forces, designed to take off and land on short runways under adverse conditions. And so inevitably the transport hire of choice for mercenary and humanitarian operations in any of the planet's wildest back corners.

Dropping in altitude, the C-130 circled left in a steep bank that would line it up with the grass airstrip down the path. And now the higher drone of rotors joined in. The second Mi-17 was arriving. Up the path on the hospital veranda, cries of alarm rose, fingers pointing at the sky. Patients who had hunkered down in the open now stampeded for the veranda. Those on the veranda were crowding and shoving at the clinic door, swallowing up the white lab coat with the clipboard.

This was exactly the panic Robin had been trying to avoid. Swinging back to the woman, she said urgently, "Look, if you know who I am, then I can't imagine how you could think I owe Michael any apologies. But that's not why I'm here. I have orders to fore-warn whoever's in charge here that your community is about to receive uninvited guests. A lot of them. But of first priority, we've got wounded down there on the runway. Evacs from an insurgent attack on a nearby mining facility. Among them women and children who are going to die without immediate medical attention. If Michael isn't available, is there some other doctor or even a nurse?"

The woman's coldness instantly dissolved into concern. From behind her, the tall, black man in the white lab coat stepped forward. "I am a doctor."

"Then please come with me. And hurry! There's one boy—" Robin looked at the woman. "I'll come back to explain about the airplane as soon as we can get the wounded to medical care. Just let your people know there's no reason to be afraid even if they see soldiers and guns."

As the woman let out a gasp of dismay, Robin spun around to leave. But her Vietnam vet bodyguard put an arm out to block her path. "I've got this one, Duncan. My pal and I have played field medic more years than you've been alive. We'll get the doc squared away. You stay here and carry out your orders."

"But if he doesn't speak English—"

The African doctor abruptly shifted languages. "I speak enough. Let us go!"

The two men were now racing down the path, the African shout-ing orders in Swahili even as he ran. The panic on the veranda sub-sided immediately. Several men separated from the crowd to follow the Vietnam vet and his companion toward the airstrip.

Leaving the two women to stare at each other. Now was the time to carry out Trevor Mulroney's command. Explain the logistics of two thousand armed combatants about to descend on this tranquil community. Make promises to soothe local ruffled feathers.

Instead Robin said abruptly, "Where could you possibly have seen pictures of me? And if you know so much about me, then you must know it is Michael who owes me an apology, not the other way around. Or didn't he tell you just why he left the Navy? Why I've heard not so much as an 'I regret your loss' in five years?"

Robin's glance fell suddenly on the woman's left arm cradling the sleeping toddler, a narrow silver ring visible on the fourth finger of her hand. "Are you—?" She cleared her throat to try again. "Are you Michael's wife?"

Genuine amazement banished the frown marring the other woman's gentle line of mouth. "No, of course not. I'm his sister, Miriam. I'm married to Ephraim, the doctor you just met. Did Michael never tell you about me?"

Yes, Robin could now see the resemblance. The dark-mahogany curls always cropped to a crew cut in Robin's memory. The width of forehead and shape of cheekbones where not marred by scarring. Eyes more amber than Michael's tawny-brown shade, but with the same thick, long fringe of lashes.

The roar of aircraft was starting to make conversation difficult. The C-130 had made its turn and was low over the treetops coming in for a landing. The second Mi-17 had retreated to a higher elevation and was circling directly overhead. Stepping back through the unpainted metal door, the woman raised her voice.

"Look, why don't you come on inside. Tell me whatever it is you came here to tell me. And it looks like we've both got some questions to ask. I'll answer yours if you'll answer mine. Over a cup of tea, maybe? Or would you prefer something cool to drink?"

The smile had not returned to the woman's face, but hostility had left her amber eyes. Robin stepped hesitantly forward through the doorway. Inside, large screen windows supplied light and a cooling breeze to a single open living area.

To Robin's right, one corner held a small gas stove. But the poured-concrete alcove intended for its propane cylinder was currently empty. Instead a slab of concrete beside the stove held a more typical Congolese cooking range: a raised cast-iron grill with firewood smoldering under a pair of sooty enamel pots. The smoke drifted upward toward a chimney opening overhead.

There was no refrigerator or sink. But a plastic basin sat on a wooden counter edged in colorful pagne material, and Robin counted two of the huge pottery jars that had been keeping water cool and clean in Africa's tropical climes for thousands of years. Shelving held plastic and enamel dishes while woven baskets hanging from rafters brimmed over with onions, cassava, carrots.

A wooden table and chairs completed the kitchen dining area. Across a concrete floor, wicker seats made a living room grouping around a bookshelf crammed with paperbacks. Beyond the bookshelf, Robin spotted the purpose for that high-tech array on the roof. A computer terminal hooked up to a headset as well as an ordinary phone receiver, along with a printer and other paraphernalia of twenty-first-century communication.

If simpler and smaller, the setup was not dissimilar to a mobile communications unit such as Ares Solutions used in the field. Why had Robin assumed that remote mission outposts were still relegated to the kerosene lanterns and ham radio roll call of her mother's childhood stories?

The left and rear walls were whitewashed wooden partitions. More pagne material curtained doorways. Through one curtain pushed to the side, Robin glimpsed army-style cots and an old steamer trunk.

In all, the home was simple and austere even by military base housing standards. But compared to Taraja's other mud-and-wattle homes, it was unexpectedly comfortable. Though wrought-iron bars outside the window screens and heavy wooden shutters currently open wide indicated how easily this place could be sealed into a fortress against storm or invaders.

Stepping through the open curtain, Robin's hostess eased her sleeping toddler onto an army cot while offering a small smile over her shoulder at Robin. "This is my daughter. Her name is Sarah, God's princess, if you know the biblical story. And this one's Michael, named after his uncle as well as the biblical archangel."

She pulled forward the child who'd been hiding behind her skirts, a boy, three to four years old. Raising her voice, Miriam switched suddenly to the swift Congolese-accented French she'd been speaking when Robin met her. "Benjamin, can you put on the tea water for our guest?"

Another boy, several years older, emerged through one of the other pagne curtains. He offered Robin a shy smile as he hurried to push a teakettle from the side of the cooking grill directly over the embers. It immediately began to steam.

As he drifted back over, Miriam pulled him close in a hug. "And this is my firstborn, son of my right hand, as the patriarch Jacob named his son. Though of course in the Bible, Benjamin was the youngest son, not the oldest."

Now that she knew the African doctor she'd met was their father, Robin could see Ephraim in the sleeping toddler and younger boy's long, narrow features and high-bridged noses. The oldest boy bore no resemblance that Robin could see to either parent, his features darker than his siblings' and round with the wider, flattened nose and out-thrust jaw more typical to Governor Wamba and his men's tribal affiliation.

But Robin's attention had been drawn away to a large corkboard nailed to the wooden partition. Along with scribbled notes and what looked to be flight schedules was tacked a profusion of photos. Some, dog-eared, even black-and-white, could have hung there for decades. There were aerial photos of what must have been Taraja before its destruction. Photos of Africans crowding around the same red-and-white Cessna Robin had seen in Bunia. Group photos of African children in school uniforms. Adults in lab coats.

From the school and hospital that had burned down?

Multiple photos showed two Caucasian couples at time periods and in clothing styles ranging over several decades. Michael's parents and grandparents? And photos of a young Michael with a small girl posing in front of what appeared to be this very house. Sitting in a classroom with African children. Playing on the grass airstrip. Smiling out from the pilot's seat of the Cessna.

"Was this your family's house? Michael never mentioned having a sister. Or much of anything about his family except how much he loved growing up in the rainforest."

"Yes, this is where we grew up. My grandparents built this house. And I guess I'm not so surprised Michael never mentioned me. Because that would mean bringing up everything else that happened," Miriam said cryptically.

Robin took a step away to look at a second collage of more recent computer printout photos tacked to the partition. Most were snapshots of Miriam's three children. But Robin stiffened. No wonder Miriam had recognized her!

"Michael e-mailed me that from Afghanistan." Stepping up behind Robin, Miriam gave a nod toward a photo whose backdrop Robin remembered only too well. It had been an off-duty field trip to the Band-e Amir lakes almost three thousand meters up into Afghanistan's Himalaya Mountains. The photo showed Robin, her brother, and Michael perched on a large boulder with the shimmering lapis lazuli of a mountain pool behind them, Chris with sketchbook in hand, Michael with an arm around Robin's shoulders and a smile curving his firm mouth, while Robin—had she ever really looked that happy?

He'd just told me my eyes were the exact shade of the water when one of the other Marines on that trip took that picture for him. When he asked me to walk with him down to the lake, I thought . . . No, I don't want to remember what I thought!

"That was the last picture Michael e-mailed us from Afghanistan just before . . . Well, to be honest, with the way things turned out, I'd have taken that down except that every picture it seems we've got of Michael over there has the same pair of redheads in it. He certainly wrote enough about you in his e-mails. And your brother. Said you were the best friends he'd made over there. The way he wrote about you in particular, I kind of got the idea that maybe he saw you as a little more than just a friend. I guess we were both wrong about that. When Michael told me he'd seen you earlier today right here in the Congo, I sure never figured I'd be meeting you for myself."

Robin turned to face Miriam. Across the room, her two sons were watching with solemn, dark eyes. The conversation had switched back to English. How much did they understand?

Looking at her older son, Miriam said gently, again in French, "Benjamin, take your brother outside. Don't go down to the airstrip, but perhaps you can watch the aircraft landing from the orchard."

As the two boys scampered out the door, the other woman straightened with a deeply inhaled breath, shifting back to English. "Look, I don't mean to be rude. But if you didn't come to make an apology, I hope you aren't planning to stay long enough to see my brother. The last thing Michael needs is for you to walk in upsetting his life now that he's finally managed to put it back together again."

Robin stared at Miriam. "You talk as though I somehow destroyed Michael's life. If you know so much about me, then you must know it's the other way around. Did Michael tell you how my brother, his so-called best friend, died? How Michael promised to save my brother, then just—"

"Don't even go there!" Miriam's interruption was fierce, her expression once again hostile and cold. "Let me make one thing clear. You couldn't destroy Michael if you tried. My brother's too good, too strong a person for that. He survived you as he's survived so much else he's suffered. And become a stronger, better person for it. A person with so much compassion and courage and endurance. But that doesn't mean as his sister I don't sometimes daydream of just what I'd like to do to you for hurting him.

"Yes, Michael did tell me what happened to your brother. And I understand your pain, of course. But how any intelligent, decent person could blame Michael—well, believe me, once you'd refused to see him, talk to him, even communicate by letter, we both got the point you felt Michael was somehow at fault for surviving when your brother didn't. To be honest, I was glad you chose to disappear from his life. If that's the kind of person you are, then the best thing for him was to forget whatever fantasy he had about you and move on with his life."

"Me choose to disappear!" Robin cried out as Miriam paused to draw a breath. "What are you talking about? And for your information, I didn't blame Michael for my brother's death. Not at first, anyway. I mean, mistakes happen. It was Michael's first evac under fire. I could forgive that."

Robin swallowed hard. *You will not shed tears in front of this woman!* But the hot moisture she'd bottled up for years was again threatening to spill over. "And maybe Michael was too embarrassed or it was too much of an inconvenience for him to attend his so-called best friend's funeral. Or offer his condolences in person. But a sympathy card at least might have been nice before he sailed off into the wild blue yonder. Or even the smallest explanation of exactly what did happen. That's what I can't forgive. Michael just disappearing like that without so much as a single expression of apology or grief."

This time it was Miriam who stared. "What are *you* talking about? Your brother was the first person Michael asked about when he came out of that coma and recovered enough to remember. You were the second, by the way. I should know. I was with him. When he learned what happened, he was so frantic I had to have his physician sedate him. He kept saying he had to speak to you. And he wouldn't believe he'd been in a coma so long without any word from you. What was between the two of you that would give him that idea, I don't know.

But I tracked down the information myself and sent you a letter to let you know how much Michael needed to hear from you. When you never responded, I thought maybe I had the wrong address. But when I called, and you made it clear you wouldn't so much as speak to him—"

The other woman broke off as Robin swayed and groped for a chair back, the blood draining from her face making her so dizzy she could barely keep to her feet. Robin managed to get words out through dry lips. "I . . . I don't understand. What coma? What happened to Michael?"

"Then you didn't know? But—how is that possible?" Again Miriam broke off. Grabbing Robin's arm, she tugged her down into a wicker chair. "You'd better sit before you fall down."

The teakettle had begun to whistle. Miriam hurried to the kitchen counter and pulled the kettle away from the fire, then poured liquid from a plastic jug into an enamel cup. Carrying it over, she thrust the cup into Robin's hands. "Here, drink this. Tea will be ready in a moment."

Robin's first sip proved to be a refreshing combination of tropical fruit juices. She waved a negative gesture as the other woman turned back toward the kitchen area. "No, please, this is all I need. Just—tell me about Michael."

Miriam sank into another chair. "I'd assumed you of all people would know the details. From the incident report the Navy sent me as Michael's next of kin, I understood there was some kind of explosion right when Michael's team was evacuating the wounded."

"Yes, an ammo depot." Robin managed a nod. "Some of those bullets caught me."

"Well, Michael caught two himself, both of them in the back because at the time he was bent over one of the wounded soldiers, trying to stabilize his bleeding.

"From what I learned later," Miriam went on, "the medivac chopper had already lifted off when the explosion happened. The other medic was busy with wounded. So he didn't realize immediately Michael had been hit. That medic did his best, but by the time they made it back to the base, your brother was gone and Michael was barely alive. One bullet was actually removed from the base of his brain, the other near his spine. Because of the severity of the brain trauma, he was airlifted directly to the naval hospital in Sicily instead of Bagram Air Base there in Afghanistan, then once he was stabilized, back stateside."

The woman's expression was accusing as she looked at Robin. "How could you not know all this, not even bother to find out, if you were such good friends as Michael made you out to be in his e-mails?"

"Because I was wounded myself," Robin whispered. "And by the time I could ask, I was told Michael had been transferred stateside. He was waiting for his transfer to medical school, so I assumed that was what they meant. And if there were any further official incident reports, I guess they went to my father as next of kin, not me. I looked up my brother's death report later, and it said his injuries weren't life-threatening. He'd just bled out. I sent a letter and e-mails to Michael's Navy unit but was told he'd been discharged. But Michael had my contact info. So when he never communicated, I finally assumed he'd chosen not to because he felt responsible for the circumstances of Chris's death. In five whole years, why wouldn't he have told me otherwise?"

"Well, for the first three months," Miriam answered dryly, "he couldn't because he was in a coma. When the news finally filtered its way out here to me as Michael's next of kin, I flew stateside. The doctors had removed the bullets, but they gave little hope he'd wake up from his coma or walk again. God was merciful—he did wake up, and though there was considerable nerve damage, he wasn't paralyzed. But that bullet in his brain had scrambled some nerve endings, and at first he thought he was back in college and there'd been an accident. We didn't want to tell him much while he was still so weak. When he finally did remember Afghanistan, his first thought was finding out about your brother and you.

"Michael still had difficulty speaking or writing. So I tracked you down for him. Found out you'd resigned from the Marines and were back living with your father, a Marine Colonel Christopher Duncan. I wrote you at the address I was given, asking you to come and see Michael—or at least call. When you never answered, I sent another letter certified mail. When that got no response, I tracked down Colonel Duncan's unlisted phone number through a Navy buddy of Michael's and called. Left a voice message."

A feeling of dread was rising in Robin as she shook her head. "I never got those letters or a phone call. I . . . I don't understand—"

Miriam's gentle mouth straightened into a firm line. "Look, I get you were going through your own trauma and grieving then. And I wish I'd known you were injured yourself when I was having all those dark thoughts about you. But at this point there's no reason not to be completely honest here. Or have you forgotten you called me back at the number I left? I was away from my phone, but you left a voice message, short but clear enough. You identified yourself as Chris's sister. Said your brother was dead, thanks to Michael. The rest of your family was moving forward with their lives. Michael was part of the past. And he was never to contact your family again."

Miriam's pretty, scarred features were suddenly bleak. "Letting Michael hear that message was the hardest thing I'd done for a while. But I knew he needed the closure. And he recognized your voice, so there's no point in denying it now. He never mentioned your name again, not until he came in this afternoon to say he'd run into you down at the border. But I knew my brother well enough to see he was devastated. Especially when it came on top of a medical discharge from the Navy after he'd worked so hard to qualify for their study program to finish medical school."

The dread was rising higher in Robin even as she whispered, "But I didn't call! I didn't."

Miriam was still talking. "You know, even after our parents died . . . after this—" the other woman's hand rose to touch the scar that pulled her right eyelid upward—"even when he had to drop out of medical school a couple years later because the scholarships ran dry, Michael could still always find a smile. Still urge me to hold on to God's love. But after that voice message, the smile never came back. I've been taught we're to forgive those who hurt us. And I thought I'd done pretty good at learning that lesson."

Again her hand brushed that scar. "But it's one thing to forgive those who've hurt me. Michael is the person I love most in this world besides Ephraim and my children. He's such a wonderful person, and he's done so much for me. Forgiving you for taking away that smile has been harder than forgiving anything that's ever happened to me."

The compressed line of Miriam's mouth relented slightly. "Even so, as I said, my big brother's the best, strongest, most courageous person I know excepting maybe my husband. He didn't give up. It took almost a year of rehab before Michael was fit enough to return to school. He used his benefits and a disability settlement from the Navy, then took out every loan he could to get through medical school anyway. By then I'd returned here to my family, of course. When Michael finished his surgical residency six months back, he accepted a grant from Médecins Sans Frontières. Surgeons willing to work in war zones and fluent in French and Swahili are hard to come by, so if he stays with them long enough, they'll help pay off his student loans. Being assigned to help us reopen Taraja is a bonus for both of us. All to say, I'm proud how far Michael's come these last years. So I hope you'll understand why I feel the last thing he needs is you of all people popping back into his life and turning it upside down again."

If Robin's every cell cried out to defend herself, she made no retort. How could she when proclaiming her own innocence meant pointing fingers inexorably elsewhere? The rising dread had now enveloped her. She had no doubt what had happened, however urgently she wanted to deny it. For the woman whose fierce amber gaze glared at her, Robin felt no corresponding hostility but rather a reluctant admiration, even kinship.

I once had a brother I loved like that! I fought for him like that! You think I don't understand? Agree completely?

But aloud she said stiffly, "Please believe I didn't come here to turn Michael's life upside down. And I can assure you I wasn't important enough to your brother to be the reason for him to stop smiling. As for that voice message, I know you have no reason to trust me, but all I can say is that it wasn't me who made that call. I . . . I think I know what happened, and I'm going to make it my business to find out. But that doesn't matter right now."

As Robin drew in a breath, the momentary silence confirmed what had penetrated her subconscious. The renewed beat of double helicopter rotors. The two Mi-17s were lifting off for their scheduled return to Bunia. As an escalation in noise indicated their close approach overhead, the front door slammed open with a metal clang. Miriam's two small sons raced in.

"*Maman*, did you see them!" the older boy called out in French. "Two helicopters! Big ones with soldiers!"

Robin pushed herself to her feet. "I need to get back to my team. I've interrupted your day far too long. But first please let me carry out my orders and pass on the intel that brought me here in the first place. Here's what you can expect within the next twenty-four hours, then over the next few weeks."

As she recapped Trevor Mulroney's earlier field briefing, Robin's head still whirled with the reshuffling of all she'd believed these last five years. For misjudging Michael, Robin could be glad to be wrong. But for Michael's sister to be telling the truth . . .

CHAPTER FOURTEEN

Men were carrying the makeshift stretchers into the clinic as Robin headed back down the path. She reached the airstrip to find the C-130 cargo plane's huge rear clam doors standing open, its cavernous interior already largely emptied. This was possible only because its cargo, a standard Ares Solutions field base package, had been preloaded for easy maneuvering on rolling pallets. While Wamba militiamen chopped halfheartedly to clear brush, Robin's teammates were erecting camp on an abandoned field directly across the airstrip from the clinic compound with the speed and expertise of a circus operation.

Which didn't keep Pieter Krueger from snapping at Robin as she stepped into his line of vision. "Where have you been, Duncan? We've got an FOB to secure before dark, and we've been having to make do with sign language for Wamba's men."

"Mr. Mulroney told me—"

"Mulroney isn't here," Krueger cut in curtly. "He's headed to

Bunia with the choppers and a load of ore. Won't be back till morning when Wamba's contingent starts flying in. Meanwhile you work for me. Starting with explaining to these lazy idiots how to dig a latrine."

Robin would have liked to follow up with the patients first. But in this equatorial zone, where the sun rose and fell every twelve hours year-round, nightfall was no longer far away, and Krueger was right that getting the forward operating base up and functioning before dark took first priority. If Miriam's husband was a doctor, he was far more capable than Robin of ensuring her charges' well-being. Robin's impulse to speed-dial 1 on her cell phone held even less priority.

Instead she followed on Pieter Krueger's heels, stretching her rusty Swahili to explain dimensions for a field latrine, then pitched in slashing pallets free from their plastic wrappings. The center of the forward operating base was a full-size trailer, winched into place by a four-wheel-drive jeep that had also been among the C-130's contents. This would serve as combination field office/communications center, and Carl Jensen headed straight for it to begin setting up his equipment.

A Quonset hut going up would serve as a supply depot while a smaller shed housed the generator that powered the base. By the time sleeping tents were pitched, latrines dug, and an electrified perimeter fence strung, the generator had purred to life and powerful security beams positioned atop the communications trailer had blinked on. The C-130 had long since lumbered skyward. The dozen-plus Wamba soldiers already on-site were now clearing brush for their own tents.

Outside the perimeter fencing, of course. First rule of thumb for a field mission. Nobody, but nobody, except Ares Solutions personnel set foot inside the FOB's safe zone. Two of Wamba's troops had already learned the hard way that Robin's warning about those red circles slashed with diagonal lines posted along the electric fencing was no fiction.

By now the setting sun had dropped below the rainforest canopy, leaving behind that oddly green paleness of a tropical twilight which would soon darken to full night with a swiftness unseen in latitudes more distant from the equator. So when a satellite dish unfurled on top of the trailer, Robin retrieved her knapsack from the small tent assigned exclusively to her as the team's only female and headed over.

Inside the trailer, packing boxes still littered the floor. But around the walls, viewing screens, computers, a satellite communications setup, and other office paraphernalia were already live and running. Carl Jensen scooted around the maze in a wheeled office chair, simultaneously talking into a Bluetooth headset, typing madly on a computer keyboard, and snatching up sheets of paper as they spit from a printer.

"Yes, the package came through intact. We'll have aerial surveillance gear ready to go up at first light. . . . Yes, I'll send a full report, no problem. Tomorrow then."

Walking over, Robin saw that the printouts were copies of the photo Trevor Mulroney had shown the team back in that Bunia hangar. Picking one up to study the young, dark features, she asked casually, "That Mr. Mulroney? If so, I should give him an update on the mine casualties."

Carl looked annoyed as he pulled off the Bluetooth headset. "Actually, if it's any of your business—which, of course, it isn't—that was my boss making sure our surveillance package made it safely."

So the Shaggy clone had forgiven Robin no more than had Pieter Krueger. Robin gave a mental sigh. At the rate she was managing to antagonize her teammates, this was going to be one long mission. "I didn't mean to be nosy. I just wanted to check if the satellite wireless system is up yet. I'd like to Skype stateside tonight if possible."

At her apology, annoyance ebbed fractionally from Carl's sunburned features. "Should be. You'll need your standard company access code. Just don't go too far from camp if you want a clear signal. While you're at it, take a few of those." Carl nodded toward the pile of printouts. "Mulroney wants us to get those out to the locals. See if anyone's seen our ghost. Maybe someone up at your doctor pal's hospital compound will recognize the guy."

Robin slid several prints into her knapsack and had her iPad out and powering up by the time she retreated down the trailer steps. As she threaded through tents and unpacked pallets toward the airstrip, she keyed in her Ares Solutions access code. A flexible mesh gating that, when closed, would complete the electrified perimeter, sealing off the team's FOB from the jungle night and any restless inhabitants, was still rolled open. An East European operative stood guard at the opening. Recognizing Robin, he stepped aside to let her through. Robin walked out onto the airstrip for privacy before punching through the Skype connection. This time her older sister appeared almost immediately on the iPad screen.

"Robin! I got your earlier voice message that you'd try to video Skype. Kristi and I were at the pediatrician's. Just walked in the door. Am I glad to catch you! I've got some news." Kelli broke off to wrinkle an exquisite nose. "Girl, what have you been doing with yourself? You look like you've been on field maneuvers. I thought this was a translation gig."

Robin glanced down. Setting up base had contributed a fresh coating of dirt and perspiration to already-bedraggled clothing. And was that a streak of blood from her medivac patient? "Kelli, I've been up for over twenty-four hours. I'm standing in the middle of a hot, muggy Congo rainforest. If I'd known you expected a salon visit before I called you, I'd have made an appointment."

"Don't be silly. I'm sure there's no salons in the jungle—"

"Auntie Robin!" A delighted squeal interrupted Robin's sister. Then a four-year-old version of Kelli's pretty face framed by Robin's own tousled red-gold curls squeezed into the video-cam image. "I heard you, I knew I did! Now I see you. When are you coming home? I was a good girl for Mommy at the doctor. And guess what— I can read more words now. *Cat. Hat. Sat. Rat.*"

The childish features on the screen were too thin and maybe

a little paler than normal even for Robin's niece, but alive with joy and excitement. "Kristi, how's my favorite princess in all the world? I don't know when I'll be home, but soon. I'll bring you something special. A surprise." If Bunia had no local souvenirs, there was always the airport gift shop. "And you are always a good girl for Mommy. And so smart. I'm sure I couldn't read so many words when I was four."

Robin forced herself to a full five minutes of untroubled listening before breaking gently into her niece's excited prattle. "Kristi, sweetheart, I need to talk to your mother a bit. Why don't you go play in your room for a few minutes, okay?"

"Okay! Bye, Auntie Robin!"

As Kristi's small face disappeared obediently from the iPad, Robin's older sister reappeared. "Good, because I needed to talk to you alone too. Brian—Dr. Peters, I mean, the pediatric specialist working with Kristi's case—thinks he can get the procedure scheduled within the month if we can swing the financing. He's been so wonderful with Kristi! He's even willing to waive all his own fees, so it will be just the surgeon and hospital stay. If it works—and Brian's pretty confident it will—Kristi will be completely normal and healthy for the first time in her life. Imagine, no more doctors, hospitals, being cooped up all the time with a sick kid. Not that I don't love Kristi so much it's been worth it!"

When Robin made no immediate response, Kelli leaned forward toward her own computer monitor's video cam, this time with a frown. Somewhere behind her, out of sight, Robin could hear tuneless childish singing, then a door slamming enthusiastically. "What is it, Robin? Is there a problem with your contract? Is the money not going to be here in time?"

"It's not the money." Robin scrutinized her sister's face. The flawlessly plucked eyebrows raised high in query. Perfectly applied makeup more appropriate for a dinner party than a doctor's appointment. The discontented droop of mouth. A childlike ingenuousness of expression that made Kelli seem years younger rather than older than Robin herself.

Robin steadied herself with a deep breath before seizing the bull by the horns. "Kelli, you won't believe who I've run into out here in the middle of the jungle. Do you remember Michael Stewart, who was such a good friend of Chris and me in Afghanistan?"

A startled gasp, a look of alarm before blue-green eyes opened to their fullest in wide-eyed innocence, confirming everything Robin had feared. Kelli's tongue marred the bright-red perfection of her upper lip before she asked with casual interest, "You mean that Navy medic you two were always mentioning in your e-mails? The one whose carelessness you said was responsible for Christopher's death? How awful for you! I hope it wasn't too horribly unpleasant."

"Actually, it was enlightening," Robin said. "You see, Michael isn't the only Stewart I ran into over here. Michael's got a sister, Miriam. She just described to me a certain voice message left on her phone by a female caller she and Michael assumed to be me. And since there's only one other person I know whose voice could be mistaken for mine—"

As Robin drew breath, Kelli's mouth opened and closed, but this time no words came out. Robin's tone turned stern. "Why did you do it, Kelli? How could you let Michael think it was me who called? And was it you or Dad who intercepted mail addressed to me?"

If Robin needed further confirmation, the suddenly crumpled expression on the screen, tears welling up, would have given it. Kelli wailed, "Robin, you don't understand. I . . . I wasn't thinking straight back then. I'd just lost Terry in that . . . that awful way! And found out I was pregnant. You were—well, you forget how bad it was for you. Then Dad's cancer diagnosis. And it wasn't me who intercepted the letters. I wouldn't do that. I found them one day in the stuff on Dad's desk after I'd moved in to help take care of you both those last months."

Don't you mean because you'd lost the roof over your head? But Robin didn't voice her correction aloud as Kelli went on defensively.

"When I found the letters, I really did want to tell you. But if Dad swiped them, he had his reasons. And you know how he was. He'd have been furious if I interfered. He was already so angry with me. The great Colonel Christopher Robert Duncan doesn't have a daughter who can't hold her man or makes a mess of her marriage. You couldn't possibly understand. I mean, you're the perfect Duncan daughter. I've got the lecture memorized. 'Why can't you be more like Robin? She always has it together. She never quits. She knows what she wants in life.' Dad was so proud of you, he could never stop talking about it."

Robin was stunned. "Are you kidding? Kelli Duncan, I love you. But I swear you've got rocks in your head. You've always been the favorite one. Feminine, popular, fun to be with. The one who behaves the way a proper Duncan daughter is supposed to act. As Dad never let me forget!"

"Really? Sounds like Dad played both of us." Kelli's expression lightened fractionally. "If that isn't a typical Duncan divide-and-conquer strategy! In any case, I had to agree with Dad that this Michael was bad news, whatever sob story his sister had written. You were barely getting back on your own feet. The last thing you needed was to get distracted over a man who'd already hurt you, hurt our family."

Kelli paused to chew at her lips, staining her front teeth with the lipstick. "Okay, maybe I was a bit afraid you'd fly right off to see him. I knew from your e-mails how much you'd liked the guy. And you're the forgiving type, whatever he'd done. I'm guessing that's why Dad didn't want to give you those letters. He knew you too. And we all needed you here. Me. Dad. Kristi."

"Maybe. But it should have been my decision, not yours," Robin said flatly. "And none of this explains why you'd make that phone call pretending to be me."

Robin's sister shook her head vehemently. "I wasn't pretending to be you. I only called so they wouldn't keep calling back. I just said I was Christopher's sister. Told them to leave our family alone. It didn't even occur to me they'd think I was you. Anything else I said—well, it was nothing more than I'd heard you say about the guy. Just because he now found himself in a hospital didn't change what he'd done to our family, to you especially. I really did think I was doing the right thing sparing you from having to talk to him."

"And I believe you really meant well. Except as it turns out, I was wrong. Michael wasn't responsible for Chris's death. As I'd have known five years ago instead of today if I'd ever gotten those letters and phone calls."

"Yes, well, I didn't know that part until—" Kelli broke off again, looking suddenly uncomfortable, guilty, even a little scared. And with reason if Robin's expression was anything as stormy as her feelings.

"Then you did know the truth about Michael, about how Chris really died! No more secrets, Kelli. When did you find out? How did you find out?"

Kelli's mouth made a moue. "Not until some months after Dad died. However incompetent he thought me, he'd still named his first-born executor of his estate. Maybe because there was no estate to execute. When I got around to sorting Dad's private archives, there it was. Not the sanitized write-up passed out to next of kin. But the full mission intel report. Trust Dad to have his inside sources. You'd taken your first overseas contract by then. So much time had gone by. You seemed to have forgotten the guy. And this Michael had clearly moved on. I mean, if the guy was serious about you, he'd hardly let one voice mail discourage him."

Her sister had a point. If Michael had really cared as much as Miriam hinted, wouldn't he have come after Robin once he was able? Whatever temporary hurt and misunderstanding he'd experienced, Michael had only too evidently put any memory of Robin and her brother behind him and gone on with his life. Some of Robin's anger dissolved as she saw the quiver of her sister's red-orange mouth, tears brimming over in her blue-green eyes.

Kelli ran a hand over her eyes, smearing her makeup. "That intel report wasn't all I found in those archives. Do you know why Terry left the Marines? Left me?"

Robin shook her head. "No, Dad never said. And you've never wanted to talk about it."

"I'd found out he was cheating on me. With a female Marine. Or so I was informed by a very reliable source—the female Marine. Terry denied it, of course. But how could I not believe it? I mean, look at me. Who could blame a man's man like Terry for wanting her, a strong, independent fellow Marine just like you, instead of me, the weaker, stupider, less capable Duncan edition? Okay, I was pregnant and maybe a little hysterical. Maybe we could have worked things out. Terry insisted he wanted to. But I made the mistake of telling Dad. Next thing I know, Terry's walking out my door and out of the Marines, dishonorable discharge for conduct unbecoming an officer. The female Marine too. Dad's files just confirmed who was really behind it all."

"Mommy, are you sad?"

At the childish query in the background, Kelli lowered her voice. "Whatever else, Terry was a good Marine. He didn't deserve that. I have to wonder if Terry would have crashed that motorcycle if—"

Kelli didn't finish the thought. "All these years I've wanted to tell you. But there seemed no point in stirring up the past. And . . . well, Kristi and I still needed you. I thought I was doing the right thing for all of us. But maybe I was just being selfish. Can you ever forgive me, Robin?"

Robin felt an unbearable weariness as she eyed her sister's anxious face in the screen. She'd no reservations that Kelli was telling the truth. Colonel Duncan would certainly have made it his business to obtain a full report on the combat incident resulting in his son's death. So he must have known about Michael's own injuries. If Robin truly had mentioned Michael more than she'd realized in e-mails home, then her father had been well aware Robin would want to fly directly to Michael's bedside. Could Colonel Duncan have possibly believed he was protecting his daughter from further pain? Or had he, like Kelli, feared Michael might pull Robin from where Colonel Duncan felt she belonged, caring for him on his deathbed, providing for Kelli in her pregnancy?

Of everything you've done, Dad, how can I possibly forgive this?

Still, other than alleviating hurt and misunderstanding, would things have been measurably different if Robin had received those letters? Robin could not have abandoned father or sister. And certainly not Kristi. Michael was committed to his own life path of medical school and a humanitarian career. In any case, there was no way to change the past.

"Hey, it's okay, Kelli. It really is. Of course I forgive you. And believe me, I wouldn't trade you and Kristi for any man on the planet. It's funny—I always thought Dad loved you best and disapproved of me and Chris. Maybe we were both wrong. Maybe Dad really did mean the good things he said about us to each other, even if he could never say them to either of us direct. But I've got to go now. A double kiss and hug to Kristi for me. And set things up with your Dr. Peters. If things go well here, maybe I'll even make it back in time for the procedure."

Disconnecting, Robin turned off her iPad. In the time lapse of her Skype call, the pale green of twilight had darkened to full night. Without the light of her iPad screen, the jungle sounds seemed louder and less friendly. A rustling in the brush could be wind or an unseen enemy. A soft grunting and chittering could be a band of monkeys settling down for the night or some strange predator. A staccato of drums in the distance could be Taraja's residents making music—or a call to war.

Only the yellow pool of illumination from the base security lighting offered sanctuary. Robin had taken a step in that direction when a crunch of footsteps on stubble spun her around. That she recognized instantly the outline of body, the tilt of head, even before a tall, lean frame approached within reach of the camp lighting said much.

"Robin! There you are! I couldn't believe it when Miriam told me you were here." Michael Stewart had changed clothes since Robin saw him last and had bathed recently, a floodlight glinting on still-damp hair, a whiff of soap and hospital antiseptic reaching Robin ahead of his swift strides so that she was suddenly conscious of her own disheveled appearance. But that didn't matter now. Only that she'd been given the opportunity to make things right. To straighten out five years of hurt and misunderstanding. *To set back the clock?*

But a more urgent consideration came first. Robin took a quick step forward to meet him. "Michael! I'm so glad to finally catch you. The casualties we brought in. Are they going to be okay?"

"They'll all live," Michael answered tersely, "though the burn victims will need to be airlifted out to a bigger facility for skin grafts and reconstructive surgery once they're stabilized."

Striding past Robin, Michael approached the base camp's fencing. The East European on guard strode forward. Then, as he identified the extra passenger from their earlier plane ride, he gave Michael a nod and retreated. Michael pivoted to face Robin.

"So you want to explain all this? I got the piece about an explosion at that new mine north of here. You said you'd hired on for a security op there. But when Miriam told me you were moving an entire army into Taraja, I was sure there had to be some mistake."

Now that he'd turned toward her, Robin could clearly see Michael's expression under the stark illumination of a floodlight, as cold and accusing as his tone.

"The Robin I knew wouldn't lie, so I sure hope you've got a good explanation how your so-called security op's become a full-blown invasion. Or why you let me rattle on this afternoon about trying to see you again if you knew you were coming here."

So much for apologies! Stiffly, Robin defended, "This *is* a security operation for the mine. But there doesn't happen to be an airstrip there. Which is why we're here. But I can assure you we've no intentions of disturbing your community."

But Michael interrupted with a sharp hand gesture. "Are you kidding? With a couple thousand of Wamba's goons flying in? Or did Miriam get her figures wrong? And all the high-tech gear you've got here? That's no security op. That's a war! And why Taraja? Don't you think these people here have seen enough guns and soldiers? They haven't even had a chance to rebuild from the last invasion. What kind of trauma do you think something like this is going to be to them? Whatever resentment you may harbor against me personally, I can't believe you'd lower yourself to take it out on innocent bystanders like this community. My home. My family."

Michael's tone hardened to what Robin could only read as condemnation. "Of course, a certain Marine lieutenant I once thought I knew would never have hired herself out to this type of gig. In case you've forgotten, I grew up in Africa. And if there's one thing this continent's long, dirty history of mercenary warfare has taught me, it's that when people like Trevor Mulroney and the rest of your pals show up, people like me end up with more bodies to sew back together. Or bury."

His words might as well have been a physical slap. Stung, Robin struck back. "Hey, maybe you've forgotten that the last time there were bodies to bury out here, Ares Solutions was nowhere around. If they had been, maybe things would have turned out differently. As to being responsible for us coming here, do you really think I'd ever deliberately set foot on the same continent as you again? You're the one who told Pieter Krueger all about the perfect place for a forward operating base. Blame yourself we're here."

However accurate her words, Robin regretted them the moment Michael's expression changed. How could she have forgotten just whose bodies had been among those who died in that prior attack? "I'm sorry. I didn't mean—"

"You don't need to apologize for the truth," Michael cut her off stiffly. "You're right. Ten years ago I failed to be here to protect my family and this community. And now I've failed them again dragging this mess down on top of them."

"Michael, you know that's not what I was implying." Robin halted before admitting more quietly, "And it's not really true you're the reason we're here. As you told Pieter, this is the only airstrip close enough to the mine to run this op. Believe me, I wasn't happy about it either. But our boss, Trevor Mulroney, says Wamba's got every right to authorize our being here. Is that true?"

Michael's expression passed through bitterness to resignation. "I guess so, technically. The government of Bunia and the DRC has never contributed a penny or an hour of work to make this place happen. But yes, I guess the airstrip would be considered public land. In my book, belonging to the people of Taraja. But in Wamba's book, I've no doubt he claims jurisdiction over this territory. So you're right. We've got neither legal recourse nor muscle to force your operation off our land. We can only hope that this time there's something of Taraja left standing when you and your hired killers get through here."

Robin abruptly lost her impulse to apologize. "That isn't fair! When we were in Afghanistan, how often did we fight alongside warlords we'd never bring home for dinner? Plenty of them with past blood on their hands too. But they were our allies at the time, and we fought for them and with them because the Taliban we were fighting were even worse. As to Ares Solutions, my team is hardly a bunch of rampaging mercenaries. Our own military and embassies would be the first to acknowledge private security companies like Ares Solutions do plenty of good around this planet. And this mission isn't just some for-hire operation to restore mining profits for a multinational or the Congolese government. You saw those casualties we brought in. There's a killer out there on the loose. A killer who needs to be stopped before he hurts more people, destroys more villages. I'd think you'd be happy someone was stepping up to stop him, even if it's hired mercenaries, as you put it."

Robin suddenly realized the East European guard a dozen feet away was watching their exchange with patent interest. Off to her left, the Congolese contingent pitching their own sleeping quarters had paused to curiously eye the new arrival. Throwing a glance that way, Michael stepped closer. But only to grip Robin by the elbow, steering her beyond the circle of light and onto the airstrip.

As Michael became once again only a tall, lean silhouette against the night, he lowered his voice, but not the cold forcefulness of his tone. "There's a big difference between Afghanistan and this. In Afghanistan we were fighting for our country. We were under the oversight of our military command. So were the private security contractors who worked with us. At worst, there were rules of engagement. Accountability to the American people, the Afghan government, the international community.

"Where's your accountability here? Your rules of engagement? How can you even be certain who are the good guys and the bad? And believe me, the line between the two around here isn't as clear cut as you want to think. Especially when you throw Wamba and his own band of bloodthirsty hired thugs into the mix. Are we now to the place where any enterprise with enough money can hire a private army to carry out their own little war in pursuit of their own for-profit interests? Whatever they're paying you, Robin, it's not worth this."

His hammering questions were ones Robin herself had raised earlier. But the accusing tone, her own doubts, the scene she'd witnessed earlier at the mine, roused her to angry retort. "Say what you like, but this is one mission I can believe in wholeheartedly. When we've taken this guy down and restored peace to this region, you can apologize. Meanwhile, just stay out of our way and let us do our jobs. And I'll do my best to make sure we stay out of yours."

"Maybe. We'll see." Michael released Robin's elbow but did not modify the hardness in his voice. "I'll concede you've got good intentions. But I also believe you're in way over your head. You don't know Wamba like I do. And you can't guarantee everyone hired on to your mission has the same good intentions. But enough said. As you point out, there's nothing I can do to stop what you're doing here. Which doesn't mean I won't be watching like a hawk. These people have suffered enough. My family has suffered enough. I wasn't here to stop it last time. But believe me, there is nothing I won't do to protect them this time around."

Even in the darkness, Michael's forward thrust of body line, tautness of muscle, and inflexible determination of tone were reminders that this man was no helpless civilian, but a soldier, a warrior, in his own right and way.

"You don't need to worry," Robin answered steadily. "Our orders are to stay well away from your medical facility and the local community. And those orders apply to Wamba's men too. You'll hardly know we're here."

"Good. Then we understand each other." He was turning away, walking off into the night.

No, we don't understand each other! All we've done is misunderstand! "Wait!" Robin called out.

The crunch on gravel stopped. A dark shape turned back.

Robin took a step forward. "I wanted to say . . . I—your sister told me . . . Well, it seems I owe you and your sister a big apology." She held up the dark rectangle of her iPad. "I just Skyped with my older sister, Kelli, and found out some things I should have learned five years ago. She's the one who called you. I . . . She had her own reasons. But I want you to know I never knew about the call or your letters."

When Michael didn't move, Robin stepped forward again, closing the gap between them. "I'm sorry for what I said to you earlier. I should have had more faith that there was a good reason I didn't hear from you. I should have had more faith in the person I knew you to be. And I had no right to blame you for my brother's death, even before I knew what really happened. I know you loved him like your own brother. I should have known you'd have done everything possible to save his life. I was just so . . . so confused and . . . and angry. And when I didn't hear from you—"

Robin broke off, wishing she could see the expression on Michael's face. If only he would speak. The silence dragged on so that Robin again took in the staccato of drums from the medical compound. A transistor radio playing at the militia campfire. A chorus of frogs that had taken up their night song in an overgrown field.

Then Robin heard the long, slow sigh of air escaping from lungs beside her. Michael's baritone above her head emerged into the night, quiet, resigned. "Apology accepted. I guess we both misjudged each other. But what's done is done. We can't undo the last five years. Maybe it was all for the best anyway. Now if you'll excuse me."

This time as Michael took a step away, there was no reason for Robin to stop him.

Yes, there was. Or was she simply grasping at excuses?

"I just remembered. I was asked to give you a message by an old man at the mine, one of the prisoners. Their healer, actually, the one who gave first aid to the casualties. It sounded like he knew you and your family. He asked me to tell the son of Charles Stewart—that's you, I assume—that things aren't as they seem. Then he quoted what I think might be a Bible verse. It didn't really make sense. 'Woe to those who call evil good and good evil, darkness light and light darkness.' Does that sound like someone you'd know?"

"A prisoner?" Michael had stopped, turned back. "So your well-intentioned corporate employer is using prison labor for his mine instead of offering employment to the locals? Why am I not surprised?"

"Only until the security situation is redressed, from what I understand," Robin defended. "Would you want them to expose local civilians to danger? Speaking of which—" she pulled out the sheaf of papers she'd stuffed into her knapsack—"one other thing. We've been asked to pass these around the local communities, including yours. See if anyone recognizes this man."

Digging out a penlight from her knapsack, Robin focused its thin beam on the top computer printout. "This is the insurgent leader we're after. The one responsible for all those casualties. Jini, they call him. The ghost. Maybe someone in your community knows him. And where to find him. Or—you grew up here. Do you recognize this picture? It's thought he might be a local. He can be identified by a massive scar running down his left arm. Bottom line, if you want us out of here quickly, help us catch him."

The thin beam of light cast Michael's shadowed features into sharp relief so that Robin caught the slightest narrowing of eyes, the tightening of a jawline, the compression of a firm mouth. But he shook his head definitively.

"The guy certainly has the look of the local Ituri tribal group. But he could be any one of a hundred I've met. As to the other, the 'woe' thing is a Bible verse my dad used to quote when he preached. So it sounds like your healer must have at least heard him preach at some point. But everyone in this region knew Dr. Charles Stewart. And my father and I both have been gone a lot of years. Certainly I can't think of anyone I'd know who'd have reason to be in a prison work camp. Maybe the man was just trying to convince you he's innocent and doesn't belong in prison. That's common enough for convicts in any country. Regardless, I'll be happy to show these around. Maybe someone will recognize the man."

Michael lifted the sheaf of papers from Robin's hand. This time Robin made no effort to deter his departure. She stared after the retreating shadow until Michael's silhouette melted into the dark shapes of bushes and trees on the far side of the airstrip. That Dr. Michael Stewart would out-and-out lie to her, Robin could not believe. Not unless he'd changed far more than he'd accused her of changing.

But that he hadn't spoken the full truth just now, she had not the smallest doubt.

Was it the picture or the old man's message that had given Michael pause?

And why would he conceal either from Robin?

CHAPTER FIFTEEN

How quickly Taraja became a bustling city, only to empty out just as quickly.

By sunrise the morning after the Ares Solutions team's arrival, the next C-130 flight was touching down on the runway, this time filled with Wamba's troops. Another plane arrived from the company's Nairobi depot with additional supplies and weapons. Tents rose. A field kitchen began offering alternative fare to MRE packets.

The three helicopters reappeared along with Trevor Mulroney. But by evening Mulroney had hopped a C-130 back to Nairobi's international airport. Not unexpected. The Earth Resources CEO undoubtedly had other responsibilities than the minutiae of a jungle security op.

Nor was he needed. The Ares Solutions team knew their job. As quickly as Congolese ground troops arrived, they were formed into units. Though Pieter Krueger was operations coordinator for the mission, Samuel Makuga had flown in from the mine to assume field command of Wamba's own troops. Now refitted with Carl Jensen's tech gear, the executive helicopter had begun its survey, reappearing every few hours for refueling. Satellite maps tacked all over the communications trailer walls were filling up with marked jungle communities and landing zones.

Robin herself roamed the FOB, translating a constant round of English, French, and Swahili between Ares Solutions operatives and Congolese unit leaders. With Makuga's arrival, Pieter Krueger no longer availed himself of her services. Clearly, Robin's assault on his ego, not to mention his body, was not an offense the South African mercenary forgave easily.

As she translated Ernie Miller's angry objection to the careless storing of fuel bladders, Robin's attention drifted across the airstrip to the break in the underbrush that marked a path to the Taraja community. How were the mine casualties doing? She'd hoped for a status report. But not a sound or human being had emerged from that green tangle since Michael had disappeared back into it. Nor had Robin's own responsibilities eased long enough to walk a kilometer or so, round trip, up to the clinic.

Glancing around at the base camp, Robin tried to imagine the scene from a villager's perspective. The growing swarm of hard-faced, armed Congolese troops. The tent city now swallowing up abandoned fields and burned houses. The periodic roar of a C-130 swooping in over the treetops. The circling down of choppers, their underbellies misshapen with the unmistakable outlines of rocket missiles and machine gun turrets.

I'd hide too. I'd be terrified to find myself alone with Wamba's goons, and they're on my side!

The Ugandan hires arrived on the second morning. One more irony of the region's political games was that elite troops blooded in one country's nasty civil war might be contracted as peacekeepers or mercenaries for another's. The Ugandans deplaning from the C-130 actually belonged to the same units currently supplying ground troops to the Bunia UN post.

What mattered was that they came from a former British colony where Swahili was the trade language but English the language of officialdom. Their arrival provided enough liaisons between the Ares Solutions operatives and their Congolese subordinates to alleviate Robin's own duties. Especially since the Ugandan arrival signaled the beginning of the perimeter deployment. Congolese units crammed into the Mi-17s, each headed by an Ares Solutions operative and a handful of Ugandans, then lifted off for one of the landing zones now marked out on the satellite maps.

By midafternoon, the base camp was virtually empty again except for a few units guarding the camp perimeter and supply depots. As Robin watched the final Mi-17 deployment lift off, Pieter Krueger strode over. "You there, Duncan. We're going to need some hand labor now that Wamba's men are gone. I need that field next to the fuel bladders cleared off for chopper landing so we can keep the air-strip free. If you've nothing better to do, trot on up to the clinic and see if your doctor pal, Stewart, can scare us up some locals with machetes."

For once, the South African's brusque order couldn't have co-incided better with Robin's own wishes. Stopping by her tent, Robin put on the cumbersome Kevlar vest that protocol required she wear under her khaki shirt any time she left base camp, then slid her Glock 19 handgun into a back holster. But she left behind the M4 assault rifle she'd been issued as well as her cap, tugging her red-gold hair loose from its tight knot before heading across the airstrip. She'd ap-proach the Taraja residents as a civilian, not an armed combatant.

Once far enough up the path that fruit trees hid the airstrip, Robin found the Taraja community less abandoned than she'd encountered it on her first trip. Adults and children had emerged from the scattered huts to chop at weeds and turn over soil in the vegetable gardens. Two women in bright pagnes stood in the shade of a mango tree, taking turns raising a heavy wooden pestle to drop into a hollowed-out mortar as tall as their waists. Grinding corn or cassava flour for the day's meal. Out on the river Robin glimpsed a canoe with fishermen.

Nor at this close range was there silence. The Taraja residents were singing as they worked. Softly, cautiously, but in a glorious rumble of harmony that swept Robin back to her childhood because the Swahili words and melody were among the first she'd learned in the Kenyan churches she'd attended.

"Yesu, nuru ya ulimwengu."

"Jesus, Light of the World."

Impatiently, Robin dismissed the jolt that once-familiar melody sent through her. *It's a mission compound. What do you expect?*

The cinder-block mission house was a logical starting place to fulfill Pieter Krueger's commission. But Robin headed instead farther up the path to the clinic. Its veranda was now empty of patients, the clinic door closed. But when Robin knocked, a female voice called out in Swahili, "We are closed for the day. The *docteur* is not here. Come back in the morning unless someone is badly hurt."

"Jambo!" Robin called the Swahili greeting through the door, then switched to French. "Forgive me for disturbing you. But I am with the security mission below. I'm here to check on the patients we flew in the other day."

The door opened. The young woman in the white lab coat whom Robin had seen on her first visit stepped out onto the veranda. *"Bonjour.* Come in. The doctor is not here now, but you may speak to the nurse in charge. She is with the new patients now."

Inside, the clinic was as starkly austere as it was spotlessly clean. A single long corridor ran from front to back, its floor smooth concrete, a row of doors on either side. An open door to the left revealed glass cabinets filled with medical supplies and a metal examining table. It currently held no patients but a pile of old cotton sheets. A pair of scissors lay on top of the heap. To the right, another open door revealed two rows of army cots, all filled, in an airy, whitewashed room. Large screen windows offered both light and breeze.

Robin didn't need to ask where her own charges could be found. She'd already spotted the armed guard standing outside a door at the far end of the corridor. The young woman had stepped into the examining room. Picking up the scissors, she began snipping a sheet into strips. Making bandages?

Robin headed up the corridor, passing a second patient ward before reaching the guard. Beyond him, the door stood open into a ward identical to the other two. On one cot, Robin spotted the boy with the severed artery. The small girl, her arm now cradled in a sling, sat cross-legged on the next cot, crying softly.

Closer still was the second guard Makuga had assigned to the mine casualties. While the first guard faced out into the corridor, the second was watching like a hawk an older woman in a lab coat who was dressing the young woman's terrible burns with gauze bandages.

If the guard recognized Robin from their mutual flight on the Mi-17, he gave no indication. This time Robin chose Swahili. "If you'll permit me to pass, I'd like to speak with the wounded we brought here, to ensure for myself they have all they need."

The guard did not shift his position blocking the doorway. "That is not permitted. My orders are that only the healers can enter to tend the prisoners. The prisoners are not allowed to speak."

"And my orders are to ensure the well-being of these patients," Robin responded sharply. "You were there when Mr. Mulroney placed these people in my charge."

A slight exaggeration perhaps. But stubbornness as well as genuine concern would not allow Robin to back down. Inside the ward, the little girl's sobs rose to a wail. The nurse had turned at the sound of voices, taking a step toward the door. She froze as the closest guard's assault rifle immediately rose. Across the ward, the teenage boy's thin body had tensed with the watchful caution of a deer poised to bolt from a hunter. Wide-spaced dark eyes, elongated, high-nosed features held neither fear nor anger but complete emptiness of expression. A boy that young should not know such wariness.

"I will not leave until I've satisfied myself personally as to the well-being of these people. So please step aside before I have to call Mr. Mulroney and let him know you are refusing to allow me to carry out my orders."

The first guard's reaction was unexpectedly swift and violent, his own rifle rising as he took a step forward to center its muzzle directly between Robin's eyes. "I do not know this Mulroney. My orders come from Makuga. And he does not permit disobedience to his commands."

Taking in a too-twitchy grip on the trigger mechanism, Robin could regret now abandoning that M4 back at camp. The guard's grin held vicious triumph, the pupils of his eyes too distended for the afternoon sun. How were Wamba's militia managing to feed their drug habit in the middle of the rainforest?

Something to bring up if she made it alive to the next team meeting. Robin's Glock was still tucked into its holster at the small of her back. But she was not about to instigate a shooting war with so many civilian bystanders. Instead she reached for the hand radio at her belt.

"Then you will explain to Makuga himself why you are refusing to allow me to carry out the orders of his employer and yours." Keying the mike frequency, Robin spoke into the radio. "Krueger, is Makuga still with you? I've got a problem up here with one of his goons."

"He's here."

A moment later, angry Swahili crackled from the hand radio's tiny speaker. "Who has disobeyed my orders to cause trouble? Their punishment will be painful!"

At the militia commander's unmistakable growl, the guard lost his grin and stepped hurriedly aside. Robin spoke into the radio in Swahili. "Never mind. It was a misunderstanding."

The other guard made no effort to deter Robin as she stepped into the ward. Nor did the nurse, who sidled past Robin and guards to scurry down the hall, her hands still filled with gauze. Stopping in the middle of the concrete floor, Robin checked off seven occupied cots. A match to the number of patients they'd ferried from the mine. The humid warmth of a jungle afternoon was such that none were covered by blanket or sheet. Which allowed Robin to see that the patients all looked clean, comfortable, their bandages fresh and white.

Most appeared to be sleeping or unconscious. But the little girl still wailed miserably. The older boy pulled himself to a sitting position to address her in a sharp, low murmur. Instantly the girl's wail subsided to a whimper. Robin walked over and spoke gently to her. "Can I help you? Are you in pain?"

"Mama! Baba!"

Robin sat on the edge of the cot and placed an arm around the little girl, taking care not to jostle the bandaged arm in its sling. "Your mama and baba could not be here. But we will soon have you back with them."

A promise Robin hoped she could keep. She caught the teenage boy's watchful stare from the next cot. Only the broad bandage wrapping his sutured thigh and the hollowed look of his wide-spaced eyes sunk deeply into their sockets by pain and exhaustion gave indication of the injury that had almost killed him. Now that he was no longer lying prone and unconscious, Robin could see that he was at that awkward stage of growth where childhood was just giving way to adolescence. Thirteen or fourteen years old at most. In Robin's homeland he would still be a child. Here in the Congo he was old enough to be counted a man and a criminal. Old enough to wage a war like so many of Wamba's youthful fighters.

Did he remember Robin's hand stemming the scarlet ebbing of his life force on the Mi-17? Robin returned the boy's gaze squarely as she wiped gently at tears staining the little girl's face. "Hello. I am so glad to see you are doing better. My name is Robin in my language. But you can call me *Chiriku*."

Chiriku—literally a sparrow or other small bird—had been her childhood nickname among Swahili-speaking friends to whom

Robin had been just nonsense syllables. "What is your name? And this little one's?"

Whether at Robin's atrocious Swahili accent or the image conjured by her nickname, the twitch of a smile touched the boy's lips. The tension of his muscles relaxed visibly, though his eyes slid toward the guards before he answered in the softest of murmurs, "Jacob. And she is Rachel."

Bible names, like Ephraim—indicators of the Christian missionary heritage among these people.

"Are you still in pain? Is there anything you need? Or Rachel? Anything I can bring you?"

But before the boy could respond again, a guard strode across the room and glared at him. "I said no speaking! Speak again, and it will be more than your next meal that is taken from you."

The unmoving tension had returned to the boy's thin frame. Robin found herself freezing in place as well. What was this, a prison camp instead of a mission clinic? The absurdity of it all would have been laughable were it not for that white-knuckle grip on the assault rifle, the furious flare of the guard's nostrils.

Robin could have persisted. There were countless questions she wanted to ask. To find out what had ever placed a boy so young behind high chain fence and barbed wire. But not at the risk of drawing down on him the guards' ire as soon as she was out of the room. Reluctantly, Robin detached herself from the little girl and rose to her feet.

Though Pieter Krueger is going to get an earful when I'm back at camp! This is hardly the treatment we agreed to when we let Makuga send guards. What does he think these people are going to do—jump out of their bandages and escape through the window?

The guard retreated to a less threatening distance as Robin headed back across the ward. Clearly, the Taraja staff were caring well for their patients, despite the oppressive presence of armed militia. She'd talk to Ephraim before leaving. See what contribution the Ares Solutions team might offer in return, at least in the way of medical and food supplies. But for now, she'd done all she could do here. Time to carry out her official commission.

Robin had almost reached the door when she felt a tug on her slacks, heard the tortured Swahili. "Jini . . . he is coming. . . . Save us. . . . Oh, it hurts . . . it hurts."

Turning swiftly around, Robin saw that the fingers clutching her slacks belonged to the female burn victim. She'd lain so still, Robin had assumed she was unconscious. But now she'd begun tossing so frenziedly on her cot, the newly adjusted bandages were in danger of being ripped off.

"Jini . . . coming . . . Jacob . . . find . . . husband . . . children . . . attack . . . men . . . guns . . . fire . . . Jini . . . save us. . . . Oh, it hurts!"

The low, moaning speech through mangled lips was so garbled as to be almost unintelligible. As Robin eased away to free herself, the fingers clutched more frantically. Robin's heart contracted in pity as she saw that those fingers were among the few parts of the woman's body not bound in gauze. Did she have a husband and children back at the mine? She must be frantic if she'd had no word of them.

No longer resisting the woman's grip, Robin stooped down to look into dark eyes rolling wildly in that white swaddling of bandage. "Just rest; don't move. Your family is safe. There have been no further attacks. And this Jini will not come near any of you again, I promise you. We will catch him."

But instead of calming the woman, Robin's words seemed to agitate her further, and as the woman's gaze darted back and forth, Robin realized the burn victim wasn't truly conscious. Though her babbled Swahili was so distorted Robin could make out only the occasional word, it sounded as though she was trying to explain what had happened at the mine. One word repeated again and again.

Jini.

Ghost.

Robin tried to hold the woman still as she thrashed. "Please, you must not move or speak. Jini won't harm you again. And your family is safe, I promise."

But now the guard was at Robin's side. Not to offer help, but to pull Robin away. "This woman must not speak. You will not stay here. You must go now!"

The guard sounded as frantic as though he'd be the one punished for his prisoner's infraction. This time Robin had no intentions of conceding. But her defiance proved unnecessary because the Taraja nurse was now rushing back into the room. Her hands no longer held the gauze bandages, but a syringe. "I am so sorry. I ran out of morphine with the others. Please, let me pass."

Even before the Congolese nurse plunged the syringe into the burn victim's flesh, the sound of her voice appeared to calm the woman. With a soft sigh, she relapsed into unconsciousness. Above the nurse, Robin caught a look of mixed fury and alarm on the guard's face.

Then, beyond him, she saw Jacob, his thin frame rigid, his gaze fixed on the chaotic bedside scene. The boy's elongated, high-nosed features and dark eyes were no longer empty of expression.

Robin could see no reason for the emotion that now filled them.

Stark, horrified terror.

CHAPTER
SIXTEEN

Robin offered no further resistance when a guard insisted on escorting her all the way to the veranda. *But I will be back—count on it!*

Heading down the path, Robin slowed her pace as she approached the cinder-block mission house. In carrying out her commission, should she seek out Michael as Pieter Krueger had ordered? Or simply leave a message with Michael's sister? Maybe even the Congolese doctor, Ephraim? The latter would be infinitely less distasteful. But also more cowardly.

The decision was taken from her as Robin recognized multiple voices floating from an open screen window. Glancing inside, she spotted all three of her contemplated targets. Miriam sat in front of the computer monitor, husband and brother leaning over her shoulders. The Skype video image on the screen was a fortyish Caucasian male. His voice crackled from the monitor's speaker. "We need confirmation of a clear airstrip, or we're going to have to reschedule the run."

"We're working on that now." The response came from Michael. "We'll let you know as soon as we have something concrete."

"Good. I'll talk to you then. Miriam and Ephraim, my wife wants to know when you're going to hop a flight over to Bunia. You haven't been out of Taraja since you left here."

"Tell her we miss her too," Miriam said. "And that air flight goes both ways."

"I'll tell her. But with the new baby, don't expect to see her out your way for a while. Over and out."

The speaker went dead just as Robin tapped hesitantly on the window screen. "Hello? Excuse me?"

The three at the computer swiveled immediately around. Miriam jumped to her feet. "Well, there you are. We were just talking of sending someone down to your camp to find you."

As Miriam hurried over to open the door, Robin stepped inside. "What is it? The patients? I was going to ask if there's anything we can arrange for their care. I know so many must be a real drain on your resources."

Ephraim's dark, handsome features lit up with the first smile Robin had seen on him. "That is most kind of you. It is of course our pleasure to care for these people." The Congolese doctor's English had a strong American accent. "But it is also true our resources are scarce. Anything you can supply, especially morphine and antibiotics, would be appreciated. And bandages."

"But that's not the issue at hand." Michael didn't look directly at Robin as he approached, nodding toward the computer terminal. "We've got a King Air fitted for medivac on standby to airlift the most critical patients to Bunia, where a Doctors Without Borders team is waiting to receive them. But the pilot can't take off without confirmation of a clear runway on this end. Is that C-130 still hogging our airstrip?"

Yes, the Ares Solutions operation had certainly impeded any local access to the airstrip during these last twenty-four hours. Robin pulled her hand radio from her belt. "I'll find out. I think the last cargo plane has taken off for the day. We can make arrangements to keep the choppers clear of the runway while you're using it."

"No, it's too late for today. We're talking a ninety-minute run from Bunia, and the King Air has to be back on the ground there before dark. The pilot says he can take off at dawn tomorrow morning. Which will put them here by the breakfast hour. Oh, and by the way—" Michael's tone hardened—"since you're volunteering your boss to shell out assistance, maybe you can let him know we'll have a bill for the medivac. King Airs don't come free, and Taraja prefers to use its budget for patients without a wealthy sponsor!"

Robin felt color rise in her cheeks. The cost to Taraja hadn't even occurred to her when she'd suggested evacuating the explosion casualties here. "I'm sure Mr. Mulroney will be happy to reimburse you for all your kindness to his employees. Just put a bill together for any patient costs. And I can check on that medivac right now."

Pieter Krueger answered her page. "Yes? You got those workers we need?"

"I'm dealing with that now. But the clinic's asking when the airstrip will be free for a medivac flight to move some of the mine casualties to Bunia."

"A medivac flight? For what? At your insistence, we evacuated these people to the Taraja facility. That should be the end of it. Makuga has made clear he expects them returned to the mine as soon as they are in condition to be moved, not elsewhere."

Reaching over, Michael lifted the radio from Robin's hand. "That you, Krueger? Dr. Michael Stewart here. Didn't expect when you asked me to read that map you had plans to move into my neighborhood. A heads-up would have been appreciated. And for your information, our regular medical supply run had to divert yesterday thanks to your preemption of our airstrip. Including pharmaceuticals urgently needed for our own patients as well as those you guys delivered here. You want to keep taking advantage of our facilities, you'd better clear us a landing. As to the medivac flight, some of your casualties are going to need serious long-term medical care. Moving them back to your mine facility is not an option."

"That's not up to you, Dr. Stewart." The radio speaker crackled. "Seems we already went over this. You have no jurisdiction here. Schedule your supply run if you want. But you do *not* have consent to transport prisoners without Governor Wamba's direct authorization."

Michael's tone lost any semblance of amiability. "This isn't a point of discussion, Krueger. You may control our airstrip. But you don't command Taraja or dictate our patient care. Nor do I think your employer's going to want to explain to the international media or the authorities in Kinshasa why his so-called security operation is impeding a globally known humanitarian organization from aiding victims of a guerrilla insurgency attack. Especially women and children. If those patients aren't permitted out tomorrow, Doctors Without Borders is going to want to know why—loudly and publicly."

The radio was silent. Robin had reached to take it back from Michael when it crackled again. "Fine. You're cleared from sunrise on tomorrow. Now let me speak to Duncan."

Robin lifted the radio to her mouth. "Yes?"

"Mulroney called. Teleconference in one hour. You can explain your latest fiasco. Just so you've got those workers here by then."

As the radio went dead again, Robin looked across at the other three. "Sorry about all that. I can't apologize enough for all the inconvenience we're causing you. And now to add one more. I've been tasked to inquire if Taraja may have some men free and willing to do some digging and clearing. They'd be paid well."

"But this is not an inconvenience," Ephraim spoke up immediately. "On the contrary. The people are afraid of your soldiers. But they also have needs for which cash wages will be welcome. If you guarantee their safe treatment, I will speak to the men and make arrangements."

"I'd appreciate that. Just send whoever you have available down to the camp. I will personally guarantee they're well treated. And now if you'll excuse me, I've taken enough of your time."

But Robin didn't head immediately toward the door. Taking care not to glance at Michael, she turned instead toward his sister. "Before I take my leave, I wanted to apologize too on my own behalf. When I left here the other day, I called stateside and discovered I've done you and your family a great wrong all these years. I don't expect you to forgive, but if I could explain—"

"Oh, Robin, you do not have to apologize or explain." Miriam took a swift step forward, and at the immediate shift to compassion in her amber eyes, Robin found herself swallowing a sudden lump in her throat. *She knows! He told her!*

"There's nothing to forgive either. Let's just put the past behind us, shall we?" Miriam shot a challenging glance toward her brother as she gave Robin a quick hug. Without answering, Michael headed across the living area to the computer.

"And please, don't even consider rushing off. I heard your colleague say you have an hour. Stay a bit and have some tea with us. It would mean a lot, really. It isn't often we get visitors from the outside, especially another woman. The MAF pilots come up sometimes for a meal, but they're all men. I'd like to hear what you've been doing since—well, since Afghanistan."

That Miriam wasn't simply being polite was evident in the shining honesty of her eyes, the smile that again radiated the warmth and friendliness with which she'd originally welcomed Robin. How long had it been since Robin had sat down for a chat with another woman? Since before the Haiti detail—Robin's teammates there had also been exclusively male.

Robin suddenly wanted very much to linger in this cozy room with the teakettle already steaming on the cooking range. To delay her return for at least a little while to a camp filled with hard-bitten mercenaries and Wamba's mangy militia, where she had to remain constantly on guard and watch everything she said and did. But she hesitated, her glance sliding sideways toward Michael.

Without lifting his eyes from the computer monitor, he hunched broad shoulders. "Hey, don't mind me. I'm heading back to the clinic as soon as I drop Sam an e-mail that his flight's a go. But do stay. We'd hate for you to think we're poor hosts here at Taraja."

As though taking Robin's acquiescence for granted, Miriam was already bustling around the kitchen area, whisking a red-checkered cloth over the table, setting out enamel mugs, shaking assorted store-bought cookies from a tin container onto a plate, pouring hot water into a porcelain teapot so old its flower-and-leaf pattern had almost worn away.

"Mama?" Miriam's small daughter appeared through the curtain of a doorway, rubbing her eyes as though just waking from a nap. Swinging the toddler into his arms, Ephraim carried her over to sit on his lap at the table. Robin's hand radio had remained silent, so when Miriam began pouring tea into mugs, Robin slid into a chair across from Ephraim.

Miriam handed Robin a cup of tea, then passed the plate of cookies. "So tell me what you've been doing since Michael saw you last. How did you ever find yourself in our rainforest? Such a small world!"

If the store-bought cookies were rather stale and crumbling from humidity, the tea was excellent. As Miriam asked one gentle, probing question after another, Robin found herself sharing far more of the last five years than she'd planned. But she carefully skimmed over her father's death. Kristi's health difficulties. Leaving the Marines for the private security world.

Across the room, Michael had switched off the computer. But if he had to get back to the clinic, he sure wasn't hurrying to leave. That he was listening closely, Robin could see. That her halting explanations were as much for him as Miriam, Robin was well aware.

Robin glossed even more carefully over the role Kelli and Colonel Duncan had played in the mix-up of five years ago. But Miriam didn't let it slide. "I don't understand. Your father was a Marine officer. Surely he at least would have received a full report about what really happened on that mission. Why would he not have told you?"

Robin went still. She saw Michael's back stiffen across the room. Both Miriam and Ephraim, even little Sarah, had their eyes fixed on her face, clearly expecting some explanation. Robin set her mug down on the table as she groped for words.

"I can't explain why my father did what he did. But you must understand he was a proud man. A proud Marine. From a proud and honorable line of Christopher Robert Duncans. And every one of his children had failed him. Once Chris was gone . . . well, my father was dealing with cancer, knowing he didn't have long and that his heritage, the Duncan family line, was now dead with him. I . . . I think it just—confused him."

As kind a description for it as any!

Robin hoped that was the end of it. But Michael spun around in his chair, exploding into speech. "What are you talking about, dead with him! Your father still had two live children, didn't he? This is the twenty-first century, isn't it? Let me tell you, from where I sit, it wasn't his kids who failed him. It was Colonel Christopher Robert Duncan who failed his kids. And if he isn't—wasn't—proud of the woman his daughter has become, that's his loss, not yours!"

The heated vehemence in his tone took Robin by surprise. Warmed her heart despite herself. Michael broke off, red suddenly staining his cheekbones. Jumping to his feet, he strode out the door without looking back.

> > >

The corridor guard had watched his comrade hurry forward to intervene. Once the other guard had escorted the intruder from the premises and returned to his post, the corridor guard stepped out the clinic's rear door. Here a lawn of cleared brush swept down to a patch of banana palms with the river visible beyond. Closing the door, the guard looked around to ensure no listening ears were close enough to overhear. Then he slid a small hand radio from a pocket.

The guard would have liked to ignore his standing instructions. Pretend this scene never happened. But somehow, as though by dark magic, the man to whom the frequency belonged would inevitably find out. And if the guard did not understand the purpose behind his orders, he knew too well the personal consequences of disobedience.

When the voice he feared crackled from the speaker, he summoned up instead what excuses he could muster. "There is a foreign woman here. The same female soldier who brought the prisoners. Because she works for the *mzungu* mine owner, I was not able to prevent her entrance."

"And? If you have disturbed me, she must have had speech with your charges. Have they disobeyed their orders?"

"Not the boy Jacob or the others. But there is a woman. She spoke aloud the name of Jini and much else. I do not know how much the foreign woman understood. But if she returns to speak again to this woman—"

"Set your mind at rest. She will not return. As to your incompetence in permitting the *mzungu* woman entrance, if you will do what must be done, perhaps it will be forgiven."

CHAPTER SEVENTEEN

Miriam looked thoughtfully from Robin to the empty doorway, but a small smile was curving her mouth. What wrong impression had Michael just sent running through her pretty head? Robin jumped into the silence.

"Hey, this is way too much about me. I'd love to hear more of your story. Do you have other siblings? Did you never return to the United States like Michael to study?"

Without intention, Robin's own glance slid to Ephraim. Miriam's smile became wry. "You're wondering how I ended up here married to Ephraim instead of settling down stateside with some nice American boy. No, that's okay." Miriam waved off Robin's instant protest. "Everyone wants to know. We don't mind talking about it, do we, Ephraim? It's a rather wonderful story."

Miriam's loving glance drew a flash of white teeth from her husband. The Congolese doctor rested a hand briefly on his daughter's tight curls as he spoke up. "Both Miriam's people and mine ask many questions. There are even those who disapprove of such a marriage between a *mzungu* and a Congolese. But Miriam and I know it was God who brought us together out of darkness and despair and made us one to serve the people of Taraja."

With a laugh, Miriam took pity on Robin's confusion and curiosity. "In brief, I *had* planned to return to the US for college, the usual path for missionary kids. Until the massacre intervened. Exactly ten years ago now, in fact. I'd just graduated from Rift Valley Academy over in Kenya."

Robin knew Rift Valley Academy, a boarding school run by missionaries outside Nairobi, because her own mother had attended there. Ten years ago would make Miriam a year older than Robin herself.

"Michael was back stateside. He was barely twenty but had already finished his bachelor of science degree thanks to AP classes and was on his way to medical school, planning to be a surgeon like our father. I was here packing up to follow his footsteps, except my plan was to specialize in pediatrics. There's always been unrest between the two major tribal groups in northeastern Congo. One was historically less prosperous than the other. They felt the white colonialists, then later Mobutu's government, favored the other. Gave them more land, better education, government appointments. Rather like the Hutu-Tutsi conflict that ripped apart Rwanda a few years back. And there might have been some truth to it. Certainly the dominant tribe held most of the power in Bunia.

"That's all changed, of course, since peace talks put the rebel leader Wamba into power. But in our part of the Ituri, the two groups have intermarried so much, I for one sure couldn't tell them apart. Ephraim's a good example, his mother from one tribe, his father the other. Certainly here at Taraja, we had both groups living side by side in peace. Attending the school. Receiving medical treatment. Because of that, even when fighting broke out again after years of relative peace, we felt safe. We were wrong."

Miriam's hand touched the scar pulling her right eyelid upward. Robin had been trying not to be obvious in studying the other woman's disfigurement, but she'd seen other such scars enough to recognize a machete slash and a deep one.

"It was the day before I was scheduled to fly out when an emergency call came in on the ham radio we had back then. A rebel militia involving thousands of fighters had attacked the main mission hospital compound to the west of us, not far from Bunia. Hundreds of townspeople were dead, the hospital compound burned and looted, the patients massacred. The militia leaders had agreed to permit an evacuation flight for the expatriate missionaries."

Miriam must have seen some change of expression on Robin's face because she added quickly, "I know that doesn't seem fair. But there wasn't much choice. The insurgents wouldn't permit airlifting the Congolese staff and townsfolk. I think they were just happy to get rid of the foreigners because they didn't want the international scrutiny killing missionaries would bring. But it still doesn't seem right."

"And I have told you that you cannot blame yourself," Ephraim interjected gently. "Or your people who were in the Ituri to serve the Congolese people and share with them the love of our heavenly Father. Those of the Ituri could at least hide in the jungle and among the villages. A *mzungu* would be quickly found and risk the lives of all."

"Maybe," Miriam conceded. "In any case, the rebel army was rumored to be headed next toward Taraja. So as a precaution, our headquarters chartered a UN C-130 to evacuate as many as could be squeezed aboard. Except my parents and I were away from Taraja, so we missed the flight. And before the plane could make a second run, the rebels hit. Taraja had over a thousand residents then. By the end of the attack, less than a hundred had escaped into the jungle, most of them eventually finding their way into the Bunia refugee camps. My parents were among those killed. I would have died too if Ephraim hadn't come looking for me."

Scooting her chair closer to Ephraim, Miriam rested a hand on her husband's arm. "I'd known Ephraim all my life. He was a local Taraja boy, a year older than Michael. He was Michael's friend, of course, not mine. I was just the little sister tagging through the rainforest at their heels. By the time I'd graduated from Rift Valley, Ephraim had graduated from Taraja's nursing program and was at the hospital training school in Bunia, working on his medical degree. In between, he was helping pastor a small church there. He was back in Taraja for the school holidays.

"Anyway, he found me after the attack. Tended to my injuries until a mission plane was able to fly in and evacuate the two of us along with a handful of other wounded still alive. Over the next months of my recovery, Ephraim and I came to recognize our love for each other. After we were married, we lived in Bunia while Ephraim finished his medical training. We came back here just six months ago to reopen Taraja."

The other woman's recitation was matter-of-fact and without drama. But the images of those burned-out homes and abandoned fields lining the airstrip allowed Robin to fill in the missing details only too vividly. She shook her head bemusedly. "I must say I couldn't imagine staying in the Congo after going through such an ordeal." As Robin in all her freelance contracts in Africa had adamantly refused to accept any postings in Kenya. "Much less coming back here to Taraja where it all happened. Even if you could forgive, how could you ever forget enough to feel comfortable here?"

Miriam responded with a smile. "You could ask the same of Ephraim. He too lost his family here. As to staying in the Congo, you don't understand. I may be pale of skin, but I am Congolese at heart. Michael would say the same. Though he at least feels equally at home in North America. In fact, he'll be heading back there within the next couple weeks for some more specialized training."

Her statement was a surprisingly unpleasant jolt. After all, Robin had hardly expected to see Michael again. Nor was she planning to be in Taraja any longer than necessary. So why did she care if Michael would be leaving here almost as soon as Robin herself arrived?

Miriam set down her tea. "Bottom line, though Michael loves Taraja, he could never live here permanently. His gifts are too unique, the opportunities to use them in such a small population too few. He's here now just to train our clinic personnel in basic battlefield trauma care such as he learned as a Navy medic. Broken bones. Machete cuts. Bullet wounds. Though we could wish otherwise, there's far more need of that kind of training than the brain surgery that is Michael's specialty."

Miriam smiled again at her husband. "But for me, the Ituri Rainforest is my home. Its people are my people. And my children are of course Congolese by blood as well as heart. For good or ill, I will never go back to my parents' country, unless perhaps to visit Michael and other family.

"As to forgiving, part of that comes with understanding. I cannot condone the rebels' actions. But I can understand their rage, even their hate against a *mzungu* like me. Did you know that when my grandparents first came here, black Congolese could not even walk in the 'white' parts of Kinshasa and other cities without a special pass giving them permission? And then only to do their jobs as servants to the foreigners. Servants in their own country where they could not hold any but the lowest positions of civil service or own land or businesses.

"I look back at my own childhood. We prided ourselves on living simply as missionaries. On sharing all we had with the Congolese. And yet our books and clothes and bikes, the special foods we flew in along with medical supplies, the generator for electricity and propane for cooking, houses of brick and cinder block instead of thatch, must have seemed unbelievable wealth to the villagers.

"Meanwhile, millions of Congolese were going hungry. No employment. No funds available for schoolteachers or health workers. But plenty for soldiers, who just happen to be of the dominant tribe, to guard the mines and roam the countryside. It's easy to understand why the rebels might feel they have a right to lash out, not just at their tribal rivals, but anyone with the same white skin as the foreigners who enslaved them for so long. My family—we happened to be the ones at hand when that anger exploded."

But Ephraim was now shaking his head. "No, my love, I have told you that you must not make excuses for our people. To understand, to forgive, is well. It is the way of Yesu. But no injustice past or present offers excuse for what happened here at Taraja. Not before God. Not before man."

The Congolese doctor looked at Robin. "My wife seeks always to think kindly of others. I too understand the rage that rises up in a people who feel oppressed. I have felt it myself. Even, may God forgive me, against *mzungu* I have met. Not such as the Stewarts. But others who did not treat a Congolese with such kindness and dignity as their own. Still, it has become too easy for us here in the Congo to point fingers at others for the blame of what has happened to our country. The *mzungu* who seized control of our land and its riches. Mobutu and his associates."

The toddler in Ephraim's arms had fallen back asleep. Ephraim shifted her to a more comfortable position as he went on quietly. "Except that it was not the *mzungu* who made Congolese turn on each other when independence came, every man grabbing what he could for himself instead of working together to make the Congo a great country. It was not Mobutu or the new government ruling now in Kinshasa who made Congolese pick up machetes to murder, maim, rape, and consume human flesh. Who pitted village against village only because they were of different tribes. That day ten years ago here in Taraja, it was not foreigners, but Congolese killing Congolese."

Remembered grief etched deep lines down the Congolese doctor's strong, handsome features. "What is most sad is that each of these tribes claims to be followers of Jesus Christ. You must understand that we here in the Congo have called ourselves a Christian nation for more than five hundred years since the Portuguese first brought Bibles as well as their slave whips to our land.

"So how is it that two peoples worshiping the same Creator, raising the same songs in worship, can even find within themselves such a desire to hate and hurt each other? We have a saying here in the Congo that is more true than I could wish to admit. It is that our Christianity is as wide as the Congo River at flood season, but also as shallow as a puddle under a hot sun in dry season. Perhaps you do not know such problems in your own country."

It had not been a question, but Robin answered wryly, "Shallow religion? Christians choosing to hate other Christians? I'm afraid my people can hardly plead innocent either."

"Yes, well, again, it is easy to point fingers. Under the *mzungu* colonialists, Congolese who adopted their faith, attended their schools and churches, and learned their ways had privileges pagan animists did not. So many became Christian, not of heart but self-interest. After independence this did not all change because once again it was Christian schools that offered the best education. Christian organizations that had the best job opportunities. Christian missionaries who brought aid and medical care. To work for such organizations is a prestigious career in a country where jobs are few outside the hard labor of the mines. To be pastor of a church built with foreign money and sustained by foreign donations has become too often a privileged livelihood passed down from father to son rather than a genuine calling from God."

Miriam had shifted even closer to her husband. Ephraim juggled his sleeping daughter so that he could fold his own fingers over the hand she'd laid on his arm as he went on quietly.

"Which is why for all the evils now besetting my nation, I for one do not pray for an end to the fighting and hunger and death, but that God would use these evils to purify us as a people. To purify us as a church. And so we have already seen. If the violence of these recent years has been a terrible thing, it has also been a cleansing of the church. Those who are truly Christian have been forced to stand up to be counted. To show the reality of their faith when all else is stripped from them and there is no longer a benefit, but great danger, to proclaiming the name of Yesu Kristo, Jesus Christ, as their Savior."

Ephraim looked at Robin, his expression one of determination and blazing conviction. "As a Congolese, it is my deepest prayer, whatever the cost to my people, my beloved family, my own life, that from the raging fires of war and evil, the church of our Lord Jesus Christ here in the Congo, my country itself, will be reborn in righteousness and justice. That as so many like the Stewarts from your country have been a light here in the Congo for many past generations, so the Congo with all its great potential will one day be known as a light of God's love to the nations roundabout, and not as Africa's 'heart of darkness,' as we are now sadly known around the world."

Tightening his grasp on his wife's fingers, Ephraim looked down into Miriam's face, upturned to his. "My sweet Miriam, wife of my heart and daughter of the Congo in spirit, is in full agreement. Which is why, though many told us it is foolish and dangerous, we have returned to this place. To hold high the light of Christ's love in the darkness. To set the example that there is an alternative to violence and hate for the future of the Congolese people."

Miriam's beautiful, oval face with its terrible scar. Ephraim's broad, dark features with the proud, high nose and full mouth. So striking in their differences. So alike in the intimacy and love that shone from their eyes as they looked at each other. Robin had a sudden image of that father-son pair she'd seen trudging down the street in Bunia.

Here was less acute destitution. But this cinder-block cube with its tin roof in the isolation of a rebel-infested war zone with only rain-forest villagers for neighbors was hardly the heritage in which Miriam might have expected to raise a family had she made it stateside for college as intended. Or Ephraim either as that scarce commodity in the Congo, a trained medical doctor.

Robin had often enough endured rustic living conditions on the ground during a field op. But for a lifetime? For her children?

I could never be willing to do what Miriam's done here.

So why was the strongest emotion surging into Robin's breast as she lowered her eyes from the intimacy of the couple's shared gaze hot, throat-choking envy?

CHAPTER EIGHTEEN

Robin was glad for the distraction of her hand radio crackling. This time the querulous demand belonged to Carl Jensen. "Duncan, where are you? Mulroney's online early. We're going live in five."

"Coming!" Robin jumped to her feet. As Ephraim and Miriam rose to accompany her to the door, Robin turned back. "You know, you shouldn't have to send a runner down to our camp when you need to contact us. Why don't I leave you my cell phone number and my Skype ID. That way, if there's anything you need, you can just drop me a call, and I'll pass it on."

Robin had already noted a pen and a scattering of papers beside the computer monitor. Grabbing the pen, she was writing out her information when she caught sight of a familiar printed photo among the papers. "I see Michael passed on our wanted photo of Jini, the insurgent leader. Have you had any response among your residents? Does anyone recognize the picture?"

The couple exchanged a glance. Then Ephraim reached a long arm to pick up the sheet of paper. He held the photo side by side with his own face. "Yes, Michael gave us your picture. It could be many men, including myself."

Now that Robin was looking at the picture so close to the Congolese doctor's face, she saw that his statement was only a slight exaggeration. The printed photo was not close enough in appearance to be a much younger Ephraim, but perhaps a brother or cousin.

"He has a look of this region. Not one tribe or the other, but both. Perhaps a mixed family like my own. But I know of none with the scar Michael mentioned."

Miriam spoke up. "It would help if we knew what year this photo was taken. If it's a university application ID, it could be a past Taraja student. But hundreds of students went through here, and it's been ten years. Without knowing what year, any number of students could have grown up to look like that. Certainly I don't remember any with such a scar."

Replacing the printout on the desk, Ephraim said gently, "If one of our residents identifies this man to us, we will inform you immediately."

Their blank expressions made it futile to press further, and Robin was already late. So she offered a swift good-bye and hurried down the path. But her thoughts were not happy. In the past hour she'd come to like and respect the Taraja couple. They exuded sincerity. But like Michael, they were definitely not being forthcoming with all they knew.

Or guessed.

Robin stepped into the communications trailer to find teammates already crowded around a video screen. The group was small since most Ares Solutions operatives were in the field. Besides Carl Jensen, there was only Pieter Krueger, Samuel Makuga, Ernie Miller, who was overseeing supply runs to the ground teams, and a Serbian who'd managed to sprain an ankle his first zip line down into the rainforest and so had been assigned base security duty.

On the video screen, their employer did not look happy. "What do you mean you've finished the grid search without finding a single sign of the insurgency? Jensen, are you telling me your lauded new surveillance package is a flop? Or are we talking sheer incompetence?"

Robin had originally pictured Carl Jensen flying around the jungle in the executive helicopter, spying out its inhabitants with his high-tech aerial gear. Instead the Shaggy clone never left his bank of computer screens, several of which currently displayed both real-vision and infrared images of the rainforest canopy. He shook his head now.

"This baby's worked flawlessly according to specs. The design company's going to be tickled pink at the field test results. It's counted every human sign in every village clearing right down to infants. And of course there's scattered hits within a reasonable radius of cleared areas. Usually one or two, no more than a half dozen. Village hunters and fishers, most likely. Our own units are showing up no problem. Every twitch. Every stroll to the latrine.

"So it's not the equipment. But there's definitely no human sign outside the charted villages big enough to be your insurgent band. Even if this Jini heard the chopper, guessed its purpose—you said he's an educated man—and scattered his force, we'd still pick up a pattern of movement with that many men." Carl cleared his throat before suggesting delicately, "Is it possible our mission parameters are the problem here? Maybe the targets had already moved beyond the perimeter coordinates before we started the search?"

"No way!" Pieter Krueger spoke simultaneously with Trevor Mulroney's face on the screen.

Mulroney continued on alone. "We know what this Jini wants. It isn't to flee the zone. He's been after the mine from the beginning.

Every attack he's made has been within a few kilometers of there. If he was going to simply abandon his mission and flee the zone, he'd have done it long before we showed up. Sure, if he's now figured out we're about to lower the boom, he could try to slip his force past our bush hunt perimeter. But we'd know it if he tried unless you've totally screwed up."

Even two thousand ground troops could hardly draw an impenetrable net around a chunk of rainforest whose radius began at the Taraja airstrip and ended at the mine, close to thirty kilometers away as a crow flew. But here, too, technology had come to the rescue in a form similar to the motion sensors guarding the Ares Solutions base camp perimeter, all part of the test package Carl Jensen had brought with him. The range of said sensors was among the design specs Carl Jensen refused to discuss. But each dropped field team was responsible for staking out a section of perimeter several kilometers long. As the bush hunt progressed over coming days, that perimeter would contract to a smaller and smaller circle around the mine, buttressed by aerial surveillance from the chopper. Any human sign approaching the sensors would show up on Carl's screens.

"Our perimeter line is up and running just fine," Carl Jensen countered obstinately. "Field units have already picked up a few hunters who've strayed close. I'm telling you this insurgency force is nowhere in the zone. It's not like we search one quadrant at a time so they can slide ahead of us from one grid coordinate to another. The way we run this is a spiral starting outward and circling the entire perimeter, then working our way inward toward the mine in concentric circles. Then we do it all over again in reverse. If a force was trying to slip out of the zone, we'd be crossing its trajectory with every rotation. If they're hiding under the canopy, we'd have found them by now. Believe me, there's no one out there but our own men and the native villagers."

"I believe you." The affirmation came from Ernie Miller. "You say this guy is a college boy? Got some outside education? So let's say he knows about surveillance gear. Knows what those choppers mean. There is one other place a sizable insurgency group could park itself."

"The villages!" Pieter Krueger spoke up with dawning comprehension.

Ernie nodded. "Jini and his men might have simply melted into a local community when he heard those Mi-17s coming in. Maybe even maintain a forward operating base there."

But Carl Jensen was again shaking his tousled mane. "You think I didn't factor that in? Those villages only run a hundred to two hundred max, men, women, children. An unbalance as big as a hundred extra adult males would pop up immediately."

"Unless the actual men of the village are no longer showing up in your head count," Ernie argued. "From what we've been told, it wouldn't be the first time Jini's force wiped out a village population."

"So what's your suggestion, Miller?" Trevor Mulroney demanded from the screen.

"We had a saying back in 'Nam. Wasn't original with us. Came from Ho Chi Minh himself or one of the other Commie warlords. 'Drain the sea, and the fish will die.' The villages are the sea."

"You mean, clear out the villages so the insurgency has no place to hide or find aid." Trevor Mulroney was already nodding. "We practiced a similar philosophy during Rhodesia's Bush War."

"We did something similar in Angola, remember?" Pieter Krueger spoke up. "Except that turned out one major screwup. Too many got away from the first assault to warn other villages. And the rebels."

"Because I wasn't in charge of that mission," Ernie responded calmly. "Like I told you back then, the only way to do this is to hit every target simultaneously. There's only a dozen villages within our current perimeter. So we're talking a dozen AS operatives and a dozen ground units. We've already got them in place, locked and loaded on our bush hunt perimeter. Every jungle resident makes sure they're back inside their own village perimeter by nightfall because they've no way to see after dark, not even stars or moon under that canopy, and lots of nasties that *can* see in the dark are on the prowl. So if we hit just before dawn, every legitimate civilian will be buttoned up in their beds. Once we've secured the civilian population, we count everyone left standing a combatant and go after them full force—napalm, Agent Orange, whatever present-day scorched-earth equivalent you choose."

"Except Wamba's militia are as leery at moving around in the dark as the villagers," Pieter Krueger objected. "We've got night vision goggles for our own operatives. But not enough for the ground troops, even if they knew how to use them."

"So we move the teams into place before dark," Ernie retorted. "They'll just have to hole up on-site for the night. That shouldn't be a problem. If there's one thing Wamba's troops are good at, it's sneaking around."

"I like it," Trevor Mulroney spoke up from the screen. "Krueger, I want those teams in place by dark. Jensen, I want a complete fresh aerial sweep of our zone by then. A repeat of Angola is not an option. Earth Resources lost an entire diamond concession to the rebels there."

Robin's companions clearly had more joint history than she'd realized. Robin herself was having to bite back dismay. When had the security operation she'd signed on for spiraled into a full war that could involve such terms as *napalm* and *scorched earth*? Would Robin have to be the one to ask an obvious question again?

But Carl was already speaking, sunburned features as troubled as when Robin had explained the facts of charitable handouts. "I'm not so happy about this. Even if Jini's force has taken over a village, it seems a little hard on other villages just going about daily life to attack them all. Especially since Wamba's goons hardly look the type to respect the difference. Shouldn't we be doing some ground reconnaissance? Figure out which village Jini's holing up in rather than attacking all of them?"

Carl's remarks drew a ferocious scowl from Makuga. Trevor

Mulroney frowned, but he answered civilly enough. "Obviously ensuring the safety of a civilian population is a priority. But our timetable doesn't permit an extensive intel op. Bottom line, as Ernie pointed out, Jini's forces have already burned out numerous villages in the immediate vicinity. So it's a reasonable conclusion any villages left undisturbed are at minimum guilty of collaboration with the insurgents. Such communities can expect to be searched, even interrogated, within the rules of engagement. *Rules of engagement* being the operational term here. Wamba's men will be under direct supervision of Ares Solutions operatives, and if there's one thing Wamba has drilled well into his followers, it's the ugly consequences of disobeying an order. Right, Makuga? More importantly, if this works, we could finish the mission in one blow. Which makes it worth any minimal risk or fallout."

When Carl made no further objection, the Earth Resources CEO spoke again. "One last issue. Makuga, I'm told your interrogation of the logging party produced no usable intel concerning Jini's most recent attack on the mine."

The militia commander hunched massive shoulders. "That is true. And we were not gentle, so I am satisfied none of them had advance knowledge of the attack or contact with the insurgents."

"Hmm, I could have sworn that's how they got the bomb in. If Jini's liaison wasn't in the logging party, we're going to have to rethink things. Well, carry on."

The image on the screen reached out a hand as though to sever the video connection. Robin reacted quickly, stepping into view of the camera. "Mr. Mulroney, there is one more thing. The Taraja clinic. They've been caring for the mine explosion victims and—well, they're running short of medical supplies."

Mulroney's hand dropped. "So they want reimbursement. That's reasonable enough. And expedient to keep our neighbors happy. Have them make out a list of what they want. We'll fly it in on the next cargo run. No need to be skimpy either. We may need their services ourselves at some point."

His equable response encouraged Robin to continue. "They're also asking for reimbursement for a medivac flight. They'll be evacuating the worst cases to Bunia tomorrow."

But at this the Earth Resources CEO stiffened. "A medivac flight. Who authorized that? Where's Makuga?"

Makuga's scowl was back. But it was Pieter Krueger who spoke up. "Ah, yes, I should have mentioned that, boss. It was the American surgeon Michael Stewart who arranged the medivac. I let him know it was not permissible without Wamba's authorization. He was . . . difficult. We can prevent their aircraft from landing. But Stewart has made it abundantly clear that if we don't permit the medivac, his organization will scream to the media."

"And Wamba will scream if prisoners do not follow his orders," Samuel Makuga rumbled.

Robin bristled. Would the militia commander bring up her own interference? But Mulroney was already reaching again for the screen. "I'll handle Wamba. We've got enough problems without ticking off an international organization as powerful and vocal as Doctors Without Borders. Krueger, Makuga, this is your mess. If you can't figure out a way to keep everyone happy without my spoon-feeding you, I'll replace you with someone who can."

Before either man could respond, the screen winked out.

CHAPTER NINETEEN

Incompetents! Maybe he should advance his flight back to the Ituri to handle the rest of this mission in person.

Except that Mulroney's appearance here at Earth Resources' London headquarters was vital if the remaining professional and personal plates he juggled were not to fall crashing to the floor. Nor did he want to rouse speculation as to why a Fortune 500 CEO should involve himself so intimately in a backwoods security op.

And in truth his subordinates were not incompetents. If not the best of the best, they were as good a team as he could have put together at such short notice. More significantly, enough of them were long-term comrades-in-arms to ensure mutual self-interest if not loyalty. Including Samuel Makuga, who'd been Wamba's liaison for some extremely profitable mutual dealings in coltan mines back when that Congolese warlord had still been a rebel commander. Mines sadly transferred to government control under the peace treaty.

No, despite the setback at the mine, Mulroney's plans were still progressing on a reasonable schedule. There was no rational reason for a mad dash back to the Ituri. If he could only banish the uneasy feeling that Murphy of the infamous Murphy's Law was still lurking in the shadows of the rainforest, just biding his time to strike again.

A feeling that didn't keep Mulroney from enjoying the adulation and five-star meal of an intimate banquet he'd arranged with certain Parliament bigwigs whose whisper in Her Majesty's ear could just about guarantee that knighthood. Trevor Mulroney had scarcely stepped off the elevator into his Chelsea penthouse before his phone rang.

He checked the ID first. Howard Marshall. Then the time. Almost midnight. Meaning 7 p.m. in Washington, DC. "Yes?"

"Mulroney. Was hoping I'd catch you still up. Just got out of a meeting that should interest you. Hypothetically, of course, but certain parties have expressed interest in what you have to offer. They don't know the source, only that I can guarantee delivery. But they are in full agreement that preventing China, India, or other bidders less friendly to my country from taking possession of this bonanza is now a matter of urgent national security. That being the case, I'm authorized to inform you discreetly that if you need the intervention of our assets in Kinshasa or Bunia, you've only to ask."

"Good. I may need that intervention. Tell your friends the deal is theirs."

He'd just signed away a treasure his own passport country would give its own collective eyeteeth to possess, but the fact disturbed Trevor Mulroney not at all. Despite that proffered knighthood, Mulroney felt no particular loyalty to the British Crown. On the contrary, he still owed a grudge for Parliament's decision to abandon Rhodesia's colonial leadership to its ungrateful majority population and despot Robert Mugabe. Howard Marshall's "friends" were far more profitable allies and business partners. And since an alliance with the Americans ensured a responsible Western government controlling said treasure instead of some despot, in the end the Crown would benefit too.

Trevor Mulroney was feeling almost cheerful as he rang off. A sensation banished by the jangle of a voice message downloading, its calling code the DRC's 243. Ituri province was two hours ahead of London's Greenwich Mean Time, which meant 2 a.m. Hardly an hour for social calls. Mulroney hit redial.

"Krueger? I assume you have good reason for disturbing my sleep." That he was already up, Mulroney forbore to mention. "What's the emergency?"

"Sorry about that, boss. I'd meant to leave a message. No real emergency. But I got a call from Rhodes over at the mine. Some of the off-duty guards were getting tipsy tonight. The new supplies arrived, and they've been celebrating. One of them happened to mention—well, maybe it's nothing, but you said you wanted to know immediately if anything turned up on that logging detail."

"Just get to the point!" Trevor Mulroney cut in impatiently.

"Well, it turns out there was one more member of that work party who was never questioned. I guess they didn't think of it."

"And why not?"

"Because he's one of the casualties who was airlifted out before the interrogations ever started. An older boy. Jacob by name. Maybe it doesn't make any difference. He's only a kid, and he'd hardly collaborate with blowing himself up, right?"

"On the contrary, it changes everything!"

The small girl sobbed softly into the darkness. The painful weight of her bound arm had stirred her to uneasy wakefulness. But it was another pressure that made her squirm with discomfort. Back home with her mother, she'd have scampered off to a corner of the kraal. Here there was no kraal, and when in desperation the girl had earlier relieved the pressure where she sat, a woman in a white coat had scolded her furiously before leading her through a door into an adjoining small room. There she'd demonstrated the purpose of two foot-shaped depressions on either side of a hole in the concrete floor.

But no one was responding now to the girl's whimpers. And the darkness was too complete for her to find her own way. In any case, she was afraid to move. She'd never slept anywhere but a mat flat on the ground. This metal frame on which she'd been placed was so high off the ground it gave her vertigo even to thrust her bare foot over its sharp drop-off.

If her mama or baba were here, there would be strong arms responding to her unspoken plea. A crooning voice soothing her fears. But first her father and now her mother had been snatched from her, and the small girl no longer dared ask where they'd gone. So she curled herself into a tight ball well away from the drop-off, whimpering with growing emphasis.

> > >

Out in the corridor, a guard had heard the child's whimpers but chose to ignore them. The second guard lay stretched out on a mat just outside the ward door, snoring. He himself was not striding back and forth from any sense of duty. A closed and latched door had shut away his charges for the night, and his assignment did not include mounting any guard on the clinic itself.

No, his wakefulness was of a more personal nature. A package of khat leaves and hand-rolled cannabis cigarettes had been an essential element of the guard's daily rations since he was press-ganged as a boy of just ten years into rebel commander Wamba's army of freedom fighters. The excitable euphoria produced by chewing khat leaves made the things he was forced to do in battle easier to endure. The cannabis offered solace and relaxation afterward.

Clinic personnel had made no objection to the two guards chewing their khat ration on duty, perhaps had not even been aware of it. But the *mzungu* doctor had come along just as the guard was lighting a cigarette, furiously snatching it from his hand. Samuel Makuga's stringent orders had precluded shooting the doctor. But the guard now lit his third cigarette as he paced down the hall. One more smoke before retiring for the night, this one out-of-doors.

Sliding the interior bolt from the clinic's rear door, the guard stepped outside. A full moon risen high overhead reflected palely from slow ripples of the river that edged the clearing's rear perimeter. The guard's own cigarette tip glowed fiery red against dark silhouettes of banana palms and fruit trees as he drew in a lungful of cannabis smoke, savoring the relaxed languor coursing through his limbs. A shadow flitting toward him, then another and another, roused no curiosity. When a sharp blade slashed the guard's carotid artery, the only emotion he had time for was astonishment.

"Rachel, why are you still awake? Be silent and go to sleep!"

The impatient demand from the dark was a voice the small girl had known all her short life. If she did not yet fully understand relationships beyond mama and baba, she knew Jacob was family, her *mjomba*—someone to whom she could confide her distress. Though her mumbled explanation elicited an annoyed sigh, this was followed by creaks and rustles of someone climbing out of the neighboring cot. Then arms lifted her down until her feet touched concrete. Fingers gripping her wrist guided her forward between cots until she bumped into a door. She knew now where she was. She pushed the door wide enough to slip through, her small feet unerringly locating depressions in the floor.

She was still tugging her clothing back into place when a crash of wood against concrete startled her. The corridor door slamming open against a wall, her ears deciphered. Then much closer she heard a sharply indrawn breath, followed by the warmth of a body crowding in beside her, the soft click of the lavatory door easing shut.

And just in time. A rush of footsteps entered the infirmary ward. Low male voices were accompanied by a beam of light that played across a gap at the bottom of the lavatory door. Its probing illumination cast into sharp relief her youthful relative's pain-drawn features above her. The fear she glimpsed on them silenced any thought of protest when his hand came down hard over her mouth.

Darkness returned as the beam moved away. The spastic trembling of her uncle's thin body against hers had now roused the small girl's own fear so that she remained as motionless under his grip as a duiker fawn spooked by hunters. From the other room, she could now hear thuds. Grunts. An anguished gasp of pain. A startled scream that subsided immediately to a bubbling moan.

A murmured babble rose to audible Swahili. "Is this all? Were there not more?"

"Shh, I hear voices coming. We must be gone."

A rush of retreating footsteps returned the night to stillness. But the hand over the small girl's mouth did not ease for several heartbeats. When it dropped away, a whisper against her ear commanded, "Do not move until I return for you."

The warmth of her uncle's body left her side. A creak signaled the opening of the lavatory door. Crouching down, the small girl waited obediently. But with restored quiet, her fear was subsiding. And among voices now approaching rapidly down the corridor was the scolding one of the woman in the white coat.

Emboldened, the small girl crept out into the infirmary ward. But she stopped almost immediately when her bare feet felt under them a viscous liquid that had not been there before. She slipped in the puddle, grabbing for balance at the nearest cot. But there, too, she encountered dampness. Jerking her hand back, she fell full-length on her belly.

The puddle beneath her was now soaking through her clothing.

Splashing across her face. And young though she was, she knew that metallic taste on her lips. The hot, iron scent in her nostrils.

She couldn't even whimper her terror. If her young relative was anywhere still in the room, she could make out no rustle or movement that might be his. The approaching voices out in the hall broke off abruptly. The only sounds were the scattered drip, dripping of liquid splashing against liquid.

Until the small girl remembered how to scream.

> > >

The flitting shadows that had entered the building were now melting away into banana patch and orchard. But a man pulling himself noiselessly into a mango tree inched forward until a low-lying branch offered him a direct line of sight through a screen window. Lanterns moving around inside illuminated a grisly scene.

Here was the collateral damage from that steam engine explosion. And now they'd been silenced so the dangerous truth might never come out. All but a small girl child, who screamed piercing anguish and confusion. How had she managed to escape?

"*Mon Dieu! Yesu Kristo!* What monster could do such evil? *Pour l'amour de Dieu.* Dear God, have mercy!" Exclamations in babbled French and Swahili—or were they prayers?—from a woman in a white coat rose above the murmur of several men crowded into the room.

Then he heard the name by which he'd become known. "Jini! . . . monster . . . evil."

I am no monster!

Or am I? In fighting to redress evil, have I now become the evil they accuse me of being? The evil I sought to defeat?

The man could summon little sorrow over the older burn victims. Even had they survived such terrible injuries, their future here in the Ituri would have been as great a burden to themselves as others. They were better off where they now found themselves.

But he could regret the young boy sprawled out like a broken doll on one cot. And the small girl crouched like a wild animal in the aisle between two cots. Would the things she'd seen and heard this night ever fade from her mind?

He told himself that collateral damage in war was inevitable. That none of this had been his instigation. That achieving his mission was worth the price of a few more casualties of war.

But he could no longer convince himself of such a lie. The blood spilled in that room—such streams of it, dark against the white sheets, rich scarlet where the lantern light touched—was now added to so much other blood staining his hands.

As to his mission, he was no longer sure it was still achievable. Not since he'd seen for himself the armed encampment spilling out onto the airstrip below this medical outpost. From the moment he'd spied the massive combat helicopters, spotted the smaller aircraft circling purposefully overhead, he'd had no doubt as to their target. If he still believed in miracles, he could consider it such that he and his men had been close enough to reach their sanctuary before those spying electronic eyes swept overhead.

But they could not remain in hiding forever.

Then he'd received the message that impelled him to this place. Only a fool traveled the jungle at night. Or a desperate man. What mattered was that the helicopters believed this, too, for they did not fly at night.

So he and his men had risked a river passage difficult even by day when one could spot loitering crocodiles and hippos, low-hanging snakes, snags that could flip a canoe.

And some protective presence seemed to have watched over their passage because the only snake dropping into their canoes had been a python—a struggle to subdue, but not poisonous. Under a rising moon, the crocodiles had remained slumbering on the riverbanks, while the lethal shadow of a hippo lunging at one canoe had retreated easily under the furious blows of several paddles.

And now they must risk the same passage again. Not only because night was fast ebbing, and they must be back within their sanctuary before dawn's first rays. But because the clinic personnel were no longer the only audible voices, and he could now hear as well the roar of an approaching vehicle.

Dropping to the ground, he threaded through banana palms toward the glimmer of water that was the river. Behind him, he could still hear the female clinic worker's shrill babble addressed to almighty God, to Jesus Christ. A pang of grief pierced the shield guarding his heart so that he stumbled needlessly over a tangle of vines.

If only he, too, could still pray!

There'd been a time when such prayer was a part of every day. The automatic response to all the good and ill of life. Jointly with his village under his father's headship and in his own individual thoughts. Even when he'd been exiled from his birthplace, during all the years of study and work, he'd never stopped praying. Never stopped believing in the Creator God to whom his father had taught him to direct such prayers.

When on that day he'd run away, as much in shameful fear as obedience to his father's last command, slipping and sliding over thrusting buttresses, snakelike roots, mud, and moss until he'd at last tugged from his feet those shiny city shoes of which he'd been so proud, even then he'd still screamed out his mental supplications.

But his prayers had only blown away unanswered like the smoke rising from the devastation he'd once called home.

And now he no longer dared to pray.

If his father, if his instructors, both *mzungu* and Congolese, who'd once taught him right here at Taraja, had not been deceived, if this earth did indeed have a Creator and Judge, then that Creator no longer chose to hear his prayers. Not after the terrible things he'd done. The rivers of blood staining his hands.

Which made it foolishness to dwell on past hopes and dreams. They only distracted from the path of action to which he was now irreversibly committed.

The man called Jini pushed away further introspection as he emerged through a patch of brush onto the riverbank. A gap in rain-forest foliage offered by the width of flowing water permitted light of moon and stars to outline human shapes. The elongated ovals of several canoes. Climbing into the nearest, he picked up a paddle. Without need of speech, his companions followed suit.

The other canoes had pushed away from the bank when he heard the low, urgent call. He stiffened, head turning to seek out the river-bank shadows from which that whisper had come. But he made no attempt to push off the canoe, his hand shooting out to stop his near-est companion, who had shoved his paddle into the current.

Because the name the whisperer had called out had been his own.

Not the name of the monster he'd been labeled.

But that to which the man now called Jini had been born.

CHAPTER TWENTY

A persistent jangle rolled Robin over on her cot. She focused blearily on the phosphorescent cell phone screen.

2 a.m.! Not good anywhere on the planet. Or had Kelli simply forgotten the time change from South Carolina to the DRC? Robin groaned. This had better be worth disturbing her sleep.

"Robin? You'd better get up here."

Michael's terse order snapped Robin to full wakefulness. She was already switching on a fluorescent lantern, reaching for boots as she demanded, "What is it? What's happened?"

"Just get up here. And bring whoever's in charge down there."

The phone went dead. But by the time Robin tugged on boots and snatched the M4 and knapsack kept always within arm's length on a footlocker, she could hear the revving of an engine. The camp jeep. If there'd been some alert, why had her own radio remained silent?

But when Robin emerged from her tent, the rest of base camp still drowsed silently. An earlier downpour had tapered off to the slightest drizzle, leaving the ground so slick underfoot Robin had to pick her way carefully through the tents. She spotted the jeep tearing out onto the airstrip just as she reached the camp perimeter. Reaching past the night sentry to release the mesh gate for herself, Robin sprinted across the jeep's path, waving wildly. As it screeched to a halt, she hurried around to the driver's door.

Pieter Krueger rolled down the window. A single passenger rode shotgun beside him. Samuel Makuga. "What are you doing up at this hour, Duncan?"

"What are *you* doing up?" Robin demanded. "I was actually heading to look for you when I heard the jeep. This is about Taraja, I assume. What's going on up there?"

The South African mercenary looked annoyed. "How did you hear about Taraja? Yes, there's been some commotion at the clinic. Makuga and I are heading there to check it out now. And since we'll hardly need a translator, you can return to your beauty sleep."

But Robin had already yanked open the rear door and was climbing in. "No way. Michael—Dr. Stewart—called and asked me to come. Ordered me, rather. And since Mr. Mulroney appointed me liaison to the Taraja people, I'm coming along."

"It's your lost sleep!" Pieter Krueger started the engine again. Samuel Makuga had not so much as turned his head to glance at Robin. How had the two men learned so quickly of the problem at Taraja? Of course Makuga had guards stationed there. But that could only mean—

The path leading from airstrip to clinic was designed for pedestrians. Pieter Krueger simply gunned the jeep's four-wheel-drive capacity through brush and over roots until they'd reached the open clearing. Jouncing headlight beams caught Michael Stewart and his brother-in-law, Ephraim, waiting for them on the clinic veranda.

"So what couldn't wait until morning up here?" Pieter demanded as the three new arrivals stepped onto the veranda.

"See for yourself." Picking up a kerosene lantern at his feet, Michael led the way into the clinic. Inside, Robin could smell immediately the familiar mineral-sharp odor that was spilled blood. Dread grew inside her chest as she followed the others down the corridor. The doors to the other two patient wards were closed, but she could hear agitated voices behind them.

Then the lantern's yellow glow touched a uniformed body sprawled on a mat. One of the AK-47s Wamba's militia carried lay near an outflung hand. A gaping slash across the throat made obvious the cause of death. Robin's two companions were already crowding past the dead guard into the ward. Robin froze in the doorway as Michael's raised lantern illuminated what lay beyond.

Michael came alongside her and spoke quietly. "You know, I grew up hunting game in this rainforest. Carried weapons as a combat medic all through Afghanistan. Qualified expert marksman with every gun I've picked up. Not once have I ever had cause to fire a weapon on another human being. Only twice have I really understood the impulse to kill one. When I got word of the attack on Taraja ten years ago. And tonight. If I had the people who did this in front of me right now, I'm not sure I could keep from taking out every one of them on the spot."

Robin understood exactly what he meant because the same fury was coursing through her own veins. The last time she'd witnessed such carnage had been in the aftermath of a Taliban attack in Afghanistan when she'd been called in to question surviving females. There, too, she'd stepped around pooled blood, averted her gaze from staring, dead eyes.

And there, too, had been a girl child huddled shivering and blank-faced among body parts that had once been parents, uncles, cousins.

Robin had not at first realized the ward held a survivor, its only visible occupant the Congolese female nurse Robin had met earlier. The woman was hunkered down beside an unoccupied cot in the farthest corner, a lantern on the floor beside her. Only when the nurse reached under the cot did it become evident her murmured Swahili was not directed at herself.

The cot frame erupted into frenzied motion. An agonized mewling underneath sounded more like an injured animal than any human being. When the nurse withdrew her arm, the eruption abruptly subsided. In the lantern beam, Robin could see fresh scratches on the woman's arm.

Hurrying over, Robin knelt down to peer under the cot. The youngest mine explosion victim was huddled back in the corner in a fetal position. Were it not for the black glitter of wide, unseeing eyes, that earlier explosion of movement, the rapid rise and fall of a small chest, Robin might have wondered if the child was still alive, so drenched in scarlet were her clothing, limbs, even hair.

"Rachel? Little one, don't be afraid." Robin made no attempt to reach under the bed as she formed the Swahili phrases carefully. "You're safe now. Won't you please come out?"

Perhaps it was the sound of her own name. Some lingering connection in the small girl's traumatized mind with this female *mzungu* who'd been present when she was ripped from her mother's arms to board the helicopter. A tenuous bond Robin had forged during her brief visit the day before.

Or maybe the child had simply exhausted her defiance.

But slowly, as Robin continued to coax, the little girl's expression under its mask of blood, tears, and smeared nasal mucus lost its blankness. Uncurling from her fetal position, she scooted forward, voicing at last an intelligible word. "Mama?"

The hopeful question in that single word threatened the dry-eyed control Robin had managed to maintain since walking into this building. Reaching under the bed, she gently tugged the little girl forward. As the child emerged, the Congolese nurse with a cluck-clucking of dismay snatched up a bedsheet from an unused cot, swiftly wrapping it mummy style over the little girl's filthy clothing.

The child offered no further resistance, burying her face against

Robin's shoulder when Robin scooped the bundle into her arms. This time her repeated query held less hope. "Mama? Baba?"

Fury competed with compassion for emotional supremacy as Robin carried the child into the hall. Pieter Krueger and Samuel Makuga had by now each produced a flashlight, their beams probing every cot in turn. One hand shielding the little girl's eyes against any further glimpse of that horrific scene, Robin spoke gently in Swahili to the woolly curls butting against her chin. "Your mama isn't here right now. But I will take you to her soon. I promise you."

Rounding on Michael, who still held a lantern in the doorway, she shifted into tight, furious English. "You see now why we're here? Why this mission is so important? You said people like Ares Solutions just cause more bodies for people like you. And I know you're going to try to blame us for this. To say it would never have happened if we hadn't come here. But this is precisely why we have to stop this Jini, no matter what it takes. I thought that mine explosion took pure evil. But this? To murder the survivors after all they had already been through? Who could even conceive of such a thing? The man is a monster. And I for one will do anything it takes to bring him down."

Though the child in her arms couldn't have understood Robin's English, the raw emotion in her tone was unmistakable in any language, and she began to struggle in Robin's arms. "Mama, mama, mama!"

With a swift stride, Michael was at their side, his own Swahili far more fluent than Robin's as he ran a gentle hand over the small wrapped body. "Be still, little one. You are safe. All is well. Tell me, does this hurt?"

At his quiet tone, the child relaxed her stiffness. Solemnly she shook her head. Dropping his hand, Michael switched to English. "She appears unharmed at least, just scared stiff, poor baby."

Michael's hooded gaze as he shifted it to Robin's face was grimly somber in the lantern light but without the accusation she'd expected. "Robin, you don't have to defend yourself. Or your team. You think I don't agree? Whoever killed those people in there is responsible for this, not your presence here. And however much I may wish otherwise or resent the need for a mission like yours, they do have to be stopped. For the sake of Taraja as well as every other community in the Ituri Rainforest."

Michael gave his head a quick shake. "But something doesn't make any sense. This Jini you're after may be a monster. But he's fighting an insurgency. And a fairly successful one until now. Why would he risk coming all the way here to the very doorstep of the enemy camp just to kill a handful of survivors from his assault on the mine? Especially with an all-out search going on for him. He'd have to be stupid or insane."

"Not so stupid. He got away with it, didn't he?" Pieter Krueger stepped over the dead guard and back into the corridor. "Not so insane either, it turns out."

"Yes, the ghost had reason enough." Samuel Makuga emerged from the ward, Ephraim and the nurse at his heels. "The same reason we came here tonight."

The huge militia commander swung around to loom menacingly above Ephraim. "Where is the boy? The older one. His body is not with the others! What did you do with him?"

Robin's respect for Michael's brother-in-law climbed a notch as the Congolese doctor stared at Makuga without flinching. "We removed nothing from that room. And I did not count the bodies, only checked to see if any still had life."

Reaching for the kerosene lantern the nurse was carrying, Ephraim stepped back into the doorway to shine its light across the ward. Then he lowered it. "You are right. There is a patient missing. The older boy named Jacob. Perhaps he escaped during the attack. Or was taken by the killers."

"Jacob?" Michael swung around to demand. "You're talking the leg wound I stitched up? I suppose he could have walked out of here on his own, but the amount of blood loss, the pain—it sure wouldn't have been easy."

"Either way, it settles Jini's reason for risking this attack," Pieter Krueger interrupted. "Makuga and I had just been informed when we heard all the commotion up here that we'd failed to interrogate one member of that logging party suspected of smuggling in the bomb. The reason being, he'd been airlifted here to Taraja. So I guess we now know who was Jini's contact in the mine."

"Jacob? The boy who almost died?" Robin said incredulously. A strong image rose to her mind of unconscious young features, of her own frantic pressure on that scarlet wad of cloth, the boy's frozen terror when she'd last seen him in the clinic. "I can't believe that of him. He's so young! And he was one of the victims himself. Why would he smuggle in a bomb just to blow himself up?"

Pieter Krueger waved a dismissive hand. "Don't kid yourself! I've run into thousands of insurgents younger than that boy. Take a look at Wamba's own militia. As to his injuries, maybe he miscalculated. Or didn't realize what Jini was asking him to do. Let's not be crediting the man with a concern for his own tools. Maybe the kid was even meant to die in that explosion before his role could be uncovered and tracked back to Jini."

"Of greater concern now is how the killers gained entrance." Samuel Makuga had not relaxed his aggressive stance above Ephraim. His tone grew harsher. "How is it that you and your staff maintain such poor security for a medical facility? This will be reported, and there will be an investigation. But first we must determine how this happened. There is a survivor. What has she reported? If she has not spoken, she must be made to talk."

As Makuga's fierce glare swiveled around to Robin's burden, Robin took an automatic step back. *Oh no, you don't!*

But Ephraim was already speaking up in his quiet, level tone. "We have tried to get the child to tell us what happened. Evidently she managed to hide so they did not know of her presence. But she could only say that it was dark and that she heard men's voices and screams. What else could she say that we do not already know? She is not of age to count killers or describe them. We know they killed with a knife or machete, so it would seem they possessed no guns. Or perhaps they simply wished to make no noise."

"And the boy Jacob? That he escaped, yet did not alert the killers of this child's presence is suspicious. She must be made to tell what she knows of him."

As the militia commander started in her direction, Robin retreated another step back. But Michael had already moved into the middle of the hall to block him.

"You are not going to interrogate this child. As her physician, I will testify she is too traumatized to be questioned further. As to any security lapse, you've got a lot of nerve casting blame on the Taraja staff. This may be an unarmed civilian facility, but a sizable inventory of pharmaceuticals and other medical supplies are kept stored here, for which reason doors and windows are secured at all times, the front door bolted from the inside by the night nurse after dark. I made the rounds tonight myself.

"Any door opened would have to be from the inside. And if you're trying to point a finger at this kid Jacob, he'd have to get past your own guards to let in the killers. Speaking of which, weren't there two of them when we locked up tonight? So maybe you're pointing a finger at the wrong enemy. Maybe your missing guard was the one who let in the killers. Or was the killer. Makes a lot more sense than this invisible Jini of yours. Guess we'd better check our drug inventory. But if you think you're going to make trouble for our staff here, you've got a fight on your hands. And that goes for you, too, Krueger."

The militia commander took a swift, furious step toward the American doctor. Robin saw the corresponding tautening of muscle under Michael's clothing, saw again that abrupt shift she'd witnessed before from unassuming civilian to dangerous warrior. She tensed.

"That's enough! Makuga, back down!" At Pieter Krueger's sharp order, Samuel Makuga retreated with a growl. "Interrogating a preschooler is hardly a useful exercise. As to your staff, Stewart, be assured we've no intentions of dragging the authorities into this. Right, Makuga?"

As the militia commander shrugged in grudging acquiescence, Michael relaxed fractionally.

"Besides, Stewart is right on one thing. Where is the other guard?" Pieter Krueger was already striding toward the rear door. The play of his flashlight beam revealed that its bolt was slid to an unlocked position. The South African mercenary switched off the flashlight before easing the door open a wide crack. He listened intently for a moment, then slipped out through the crack. A moment later, his sharp exclamation drew the others to the open door.

Pieter had turned his flashlight back on. Revealed in its beam was another sprawled figure. "All's clear as far as I can see. The killers must be long gone by now. But here's your missing guard, Makuga. More knife work. And here's how our killers got in."

As Pieter kicked at a small, thin cylinder still smoldering beside the body, Robin recognized the scent of marijuana. "Your boy must have stepped out for a smoke, Makuga. Either the killers simply seized the opportunity, or they've been watching long enough to learn his bad habits. Didn't I warn you to cut back on the controlled substances abuse until this mission is over?"

The militia commander was unapologetic. "Then it would not be this Jini whose rebellion we would face. At least it is now clear who is responsible for tonight's attack. The boy Jacob must have known enough to be dangerous to this Jini if he were to be interrogated. Perhaps even where he is hiding."

"So did they come here to kill the boy or rescue him?" Michael demanded. "And why kill the other survivors? They weren't in any condition to resist."

"They could have raised the alarm. If it weren't for the child, we would not have known of this until morning," Pieter Krueger said flatly. "Makuga makes a good point. If this boy was involved in tonight's attack, he at least knew the girl was there. Which leaves three basic options. Either the killers meant to take this Jacob out, but he managed somehow to make his own escape. Or the killers took him along, willingly or unwillingly, and he chose to protect the girl. Or he's dead somewhere, and we just haven't turned up the body. Either way, there's nothing much we can do until daylight. Meanwhile, let's get this body indoors before it starts drawing animals."

Both dead guards were carried into the ward with the other victims. Once the rear door was closed and bolted, Pieter Krueger brushed one hand against the other. "That's it then. Makuga, let's hope the rest of your men aren't stoned out of their gourds on khat and weed because I want every warm body left in camp ready to roll for a full manhunt at first light."

"Speaking of which, I'd better cancel that medivac flight," Michael put in heavily. "We certainly won't be needing it now."

Robin was still holding the little girl tight in her arms. "What about this one? We can't just leave her here. And I promised she'd see her mama again soon." The image of frantic cries and pleading arms being pushed back from the Mi-17 rose sharply to Robin's mind. "The poor woman must be worried sick about her by now."

Michael and Ephraim exchanged glances. It was the Congolese doctor who spoke up. "We had thought to release the child if a family member could be found to care for her. Her injury does not necessitate further hospital care, only supervision so that the stitches do not get infected."

"That should be easy enough for the mine healer." Robin looked toward Pieter Krueger. "I'm assuming it won't be any problem to arrange a ride-along on a chopper flight out to the mine?"

The South African shrugged. "You talked Mulroney into one mercy mission. I'm sure you can do it again. Meanwhile, we're done here until we've got some daylight. And if you think you're hauling *that* back to base with us, think again! The kid isn't our responsibility. So just put her down, and let's be out of here."

Glancing down, Robin could understand the South African's tone of disgust. The bedsheet enveloping her charge had not prevented dark-red blotches from seeping through, staining her own clothing. As though sensing revulsion in Pieter Krueger's glare, the little girl was beginning to whimper again against Robin's neck.

A fierce protectiveness surged up in Robin. In another world, another life, this could be a four-year-old redhead named Kristi Duncan, and it was simply not in Robin to walk away from her need. Instead of releasing the child, she tightened her arms. Pieter Krueger spun around, annoyance tightening his mouth. Samuel Makuga looked amused.

"I'll take her." The soft voice interrupting belonged to Michael's sister, Miriam. Stepping from the veranda into the clinic, she hurried down the hall, the night nurse tight on her heels. "Malaika came to call me. Told me there was a child up here in need of a bath, meal, and place to sleep."

As Miriam reached her, Robin could see Michael's sister was blinking drowsily, sleep marks creasing one cheek. But her smile was warm as she reached for the child in Robin's arms. "What is your name, little one?"

The girl raised her head immediately at Miriam's gentle, soothing Swahili. In the merest whisper, she admitted, "Rachel."

"Rachel. A beautiful name." Miriam turned her smile to Robin. "She can stay with our three until you make arrangements to reunite her with her family. One more won't make any difference to our circus."

It was the perfect solution, of course. And certainly Pieter Krueger was right that an Ares Solutions forward operating base was even less a place for a child than an empty clinic ward. So why did Robin's arms feel suddenly bereft as without protest little Rachel allowed Miriam to lift her into her own arms?

It was almost 3 a.m. by the time the jeep was back in camp, barely enough time to burrow into her army cot before dawn rousted her again. But Robin found herself reaching instead for her cell phone. When it rang through, her sister picked up. She sounded surprised.

"Robin, is that you? I wasn't expecting a call."

"Yes, I know it's getting late there. I was just hoping to say good night to Kristi." In the background, Robin could hear music, voices. Adult voices. "Is she still awake?"

There was a pause, the nearby murmur of a deeper, masculine voice. Then Kelli's voice returned. "Actually, I'm not home at the moment. I'm out having dinner. With Kristi's pediatrician, in fact. You remember Dr. Brian Peters. He wanted to discuss her care. Kristi's with a sitter. You could call the house, though I'm sure she's asleep by now."

Her sister's tone was calm, even cheerful, so whatever this pediatrician had to discuss couldn't be too alarming.

"No, I'll try another day. Just—enjoy your dinner." Punching an end to the phone call, Robin crawled back at last into the cot she'd vacated earlier.

But sleep did not return so easily.

CHAPTER
TWENTY-ONE

"Hey, over here!" From the river edge, Ernie Miller waved an agitated hand. "No, you there, back off! Don't step too close!"

Though pink still tinged the eastern horizon, the Taraja compound already swarmed with Wamba militia. Overhead, the executive chopper made wide, lazy loops, presumably putting to use its high-tech sensory equipment. As Robin translated Ernie's orders, she, too, was taking in muddy marks where canoes had been pulled up onto the riverbank. A maze of barefoot prints, not all the same size.

Ernie probed one footprint with a forefinger. "I count at least half a dozen individuals. Could just be local Taraja fishermen except these prints are fresh since last night's rain shower. And this."

Robin stifled a yawn as she bent to study a bloodied strip of gauze snagged by a thornbush. "That's the same bandaging our missing boy Jacob had wrapped around his leg."

"I'd say we found our perimeter breach. Have one of those goons call Krueger. He's going to want to see this."

But Pieter Krueger was already hurrying down through the banana palms, Michael and Ephraim with him. "Heard your call. What did you find?"

The South African studied footprints and gauze, then turned a hard, blue scrutiny to the brown curve of the river. "So the boy *is* still alive. Or was last night. And had help getting away. I'd say this confirms he was Jini's mole in that logging party. And we know now, too, how our ghost has been moving around without our chopper catching him. Though I'd have sworn no Congolese villager would be caught dead canoeing these rivers by night. Shows this Jini does understand surveillance equipment. Question is, where's he holing up by day? We've combed every inch of this jungle repeatedly."

Snatching a hand radio from his belt, Krueger snapped into it, "Jensen, I want an immediate surveillance run of the river between here and the mine. And forget sleeping until this is over. We'll be running night searches as well as day from now on."

Returning the radio to his belt, Krueger leaned down to pluck the bloodied gauze from its thornbush. "Of more interest is how Jini learned of the boy's presence here at Taraja to begin with. Someone had to have gotten that news to him."

Michael and Ephraim stiffened simultaneously. The Congolese doctor stepped forward. "I know every family who has returned to live here in Taraja. None would be involved in hurting others or helping a murderer."

Krueger's chiseled features hardened as he tossed the gauze strip into the river. "Yeah, well, you and I both know if this Jini didn't have support in the villages, his force would never have survived this long. For all we know, maybe last night's assassins and the boy are still hiding out right here in Taraja. Or maybe it was local sympathizers who carried out last night's raid, not the ghost himself. That makes more sense than crediting this killer with courage to brave the Ituri

Rainforest by night. Bottom line, at this very moment every village in this zone is being searched, every villager being questioned. You can hardly expect us to make an exception for Taraja. Especially after last night. And that includes the clinic and its personnel as well."

In all the upheaval, Robin had actually let this morning's scheduled raid slip her mind. In one brief instant, she saw comprehension followed by horror, fury, resignation, then blankness on Ephraim's dark features. *Don't look like that! It's not what you think!*

"Now see here, Krueger, are you accusing our staff of trafficking with murderers? That we'd bother saving your patients' lives only to kill them off? And what is this about the other villages? What gives you the right—?" Michael broke off as Ephraim laid a hand on his arm.

"My brother, it will be all right. Let them search. We have nothing to hide. We of Taraja are all followers of Jesus Christ, committed to peace. It is to our benefit these men satisfy themselves we had nothing to do with aiding or harboring the killers of innocents."

Michael made no further objections. But he watched like a hawk as militia fanned out through the compound, rousting villagers from their huts, dumping out grain sacks, rummaging through piles of drying cassava root. Only Robin's direct intervention rescued the Taraja communication equipment from being dismantled. Huddled under the thatched community shelter, Taraja residents shook their heads stoically when Jini's photo was thrust under their noses. None admitted to hearing or seeing anything the prior night.

Standing an hour later on the clinic veranda, Robin glanced around with dismay. Banana palms and cornstalks lay broken, vegetable plots flattened by careless boots. Cooking fires spouted noxious smoke where overturned pots had spilled their contents. An Mi-17 had hovered down to remove the massacre victims.

The last militiamen were finally retreating along the path toward the airstrip. Robin looked at Michael, standing beside her on the veranda, arms folded aggressively across his muscular chest, gaze focused on the receding uniforms.

"I am truly sorry, Michael. I'd promised you Taraja wouldn't be impacted by our being here. That Wamba's men would not set foot on clinic property. You can call me a liar. But I really thought at the time I was telling the truth."

Michael shifted his grim scrutiny from the retreating soldiers to Robin's upturned face. But he looked less angry than resigned. "It's okay, Robin, really. No matter how I add this one up, I can't make it your doing. I know you did your best to keep your promises. Some things you've just got to chalk up to life in the Congo. Something I've let myself forget in the last decade away from here." The stern compression of his mouth curved downward. "Which doesn't mean I won't twist Mulroney's arm to cough up reparations. Ephraim may be the forbearing type. Believe me, I'm not!"

Robin glanced through the clinic door where the Congolese doctor was crouched down with his nurses, sorting smashed bottles and vials for salvageable pills and other medications. "I really like your brother-in-law. He's quiet and kind but not a pushover. And clearly very competent at his profession. I can see why Miriam fell in love with him. And Ephraim with her."

Michael's glance followed Robin's. "Yes, it's Congolese like Ephraim who offer hope that this country really does have a future. He's a great guy. A man I'm proud to call my brother-in-law. But he's not alone either. Growing up here, Miriam and I have been privileged to witness a whole new generation of Congolese who are educated visionaries, entrepreneurs, determined to lead their country forward. Maybe not as many as there should be because of violence. But then it wasn't so long ago this place was still a brutally enslaved colony run by forced labor and the *chicotte*. Not so different, in fact, from Europe a few centuries back. I mean, just go to the Tower of London or other such places and see the instruments of torture and violence there. The boot. The rack. The guillotine. Peasants treated as property while aristocrats built their luxury palaces. Injustices that changed only when those who called themselves followers of Jesus Christ began putting into practice his teachings to the point where their societies were turned upside down. So who can say just where the Congo might be in another century if enough Ephraims come along to make a serious impact on Congolese society?"

Michael broke off to slope Robin a rueful grin. "And when I get on that soapbox, I don't know when to shut up. Sorry about the rant."

Something in Robin's own chest eased at Michael's less combative tone. Despite all the chaos surrounding them, standing here peaceably side by side felt . . . right! Countless times they'd stood just like this. Looking out over a desolate, war-shattered Afghan landscape. Exchanging easy, undemanding commentary on everything under the sun. Everything but their own personal losses and pain.

Though not on that last day. Then Michael's tawny eyes had blazed down at Robin. And she'd thought . . . It didn't matter what she'd thought because her pager had gone off, and nothing had ever been the same again.

I'd forgotten how much I enjoyed just being with Michael. How much I missed him when he was gone. I made myself forget.

Robin swung around abruptly, an action that left her only inches away from a muscular chest. She had to tilt her head back to search those lean, bronzed features, the pensive gaze fastened on her own face.

What was he thinking?

Was he sharing the same memory?

"Michael . . . about five years ago—"

An impatient beep cut her off. The camp jeep careened around the side of the clinic, Pieter Krueger behind the steering wheel, Samuel Makuga and Ernie Miller in the backseat. Something in the South African mercenary's expression as he pulled up to the veranda had Robin quickly stepping away from Michael, heat flooding her face.

But though Pieter Krueger's derisive glance took in Robin's flushed cheekbones, he addressed himself to the American doctor. "We're out of here."

Michael inclined his head fractionally. "So you found nothing, just like I told you."

The South African's shrug offered no apology. "Doesn't mean there's nothing to find. Only that it's not to be found within the perimeter of your community. Personally, I never expected our adversary to make things that easy for us. But I'm sure you understand we had a protocol to follow."

Only now did Krueger address himself to Robin. "If you're heading back to base, Duncan, the trolley leaves now. Mulroney's called another teleconference ASAP."

Michael disappeared into the clinic as Robin climbed into the front passenger seat. The interruption was just as well since Robin had no idea what she'd wanted to say.

In a few hours, the footpath down to the airstrip had become a well-defined vehicle track. The jeep jolted back into base camp to find all three helicopters settled to the ground. Crowded into the communications trailer were more of Robin's Ares Solutions teammates than she'd seen in camp since their bush hunt mission had started. Ernie's Green Beret buddy, Frank, was addressing Trevor Mulroney's face on a screen when the new arrivals entered.

"Insurgents are definitely not in the villages. At least not in any numbers. We hit at dawn as planned. All twelve villages, complete surprise. Searches turned up hunting bows and spears, but no real weapons or ammo. Nor the excess of fighting-age men we'd be seeing if they were harboring an insurgency. No one admitted to recognizing this Jini fellow. Nor did we find anyone with the scar you described. And believe me, we checked everyone, male and female, in case the perp was hiding behind a pagne."

"You didn't check everyone." The screen Carl Jensen was tapping seemed less an aerial shot of the Ituri Rainforest than an image one might expect through a pair of night vision goggles. In its center was a cluster of yellow-orange blotches. Additional blotches scattered out randomly.

"We've been rotating sweeps around each village since this morning's attack. That center cluster is the conjoined heat signature of rounded-up villagers and our own forces. But you can see here a dozen other signatures fanned out within a half-kilometer circumference of the village. This one's your takedown, Frank. Since you confirmed your unit was all inside the village clearing, those signatures are definitely not our men. And check this shot taken of the same village a couple hours later."

The second image showed a similar pattern of heat signatures but scattered more distantly from the center. "Every village shows the same pattern. These have to be locals escaping the attack. Not huge numbers. But rounding them all up under triple-canopy jungle is going to be as easy as chasing down individual ants from a smashed anthill."

"Then you'd better get started," Trevor Mulroney responded sarcastically from his screen. "I didn't call you together here for excuses but to hear results. Krueger, is this what Ares Solutions calls competence? You assured me this team could do the job."

"Boss, you know better than anyone here there's no such thing as a perfect surprise attack." Pieter Krueger moved into view of Mulroney's video cam. "There's always the early riser out taking a leak. Kids scrambling under a bush while we're rounding up the parents. Besides, we don't need to chase them down. There's only three directions they can head. Back to their homes, in which case they'll run into Wamba's militia we've quartered in each village for prisoner control. Or out of the zone, in which case they'll run into our perimeter line. Or if they head deeper into the zone, we'll round them up as we draw in our bush hunt net."

The South African stabbed Carl's satellite image with his forefinger. "If anything, these images confirm Jini and his men were never in the villages. Notice our escapees are all individuals, not a group signature anywhere. And let's not forget our ghost and his pals were out of bed last night. Did you scan that waterway like I asked, Jensen?"

"Of course I did." A new image Carl pulled up looked to be an aerial map. "As you can see here, the river flowing behind the Taraja compound does dump into the stream that flows past the mine. Which means a straight shot by canoe from where we last pegged this Jini to the back door of the clinic. It would take some doing to paddle it in a night. But with a full moon like we've got right now, if someone knew the river well, I suppose it's possible.

"Anyway, we just ran a full scan of the waterway. Not a canoe in sight. No surprise with all the local fishermen buttoned down in their villages. And the only settlement along that particular stretch is the mine itself. If your perps took this route, they must have beached themselves before daylight. But we ran reconnaissance to five kilometers back on either side of this river. No human signature anywhere."

Carl tapped a spot on the winding brown snake representing the waterway. "We did pick up something on our motion sensors right along here. A cluster of somethings. I thought we might have found our perps. But when we ran a visual sweep, it turned out smack in the middle of an empty river."

The image Carl pulled up on a neighboring screen showed brown water glinting bright enough under sunlight to reflect trees and vegetation along the bank but visibly empty of canoes or swimmers. "Unless this Jini's a fish as well as a ghost and can breathe underwater, I'm assuming we picked up a pack of hippos or crocs."

From Robin's side, Ernie stepped forward to study the screen more closely. As he did so, his buddy, Frank, spoke up. "The big question here isn't where a handful of perps in a canoe might hide themselves. But where is this full-blown insurgency we're supposed to be fighting? Is it possible Wamba came up with this insurgency just to explain away his own failure in controlling rebellious locals? That maybe our ghost doesn't really exist? After all, who's actually seen this Jini or his scar?"

"Those burned-out villages speak to a sizable insurgency," an Australian operative argued. "Besides, if not an insurgency, then what? I suppose there's nothing really in the sabotage of mine and convoys to date that couldn't have been carried out by a much smaller, determined band of anarchists. But then you'd be talking a compelling personal motive, or why the risk? I mean, it's not like they can walk off with a mountain of molybdenum to sell."

"Maybe it *is* personal," Frank retorted. "If last night's assault team traveled all the way to Taraja just to break out this Jacob kid, maybe it never was about the mine but about the workers. Has anyone checked on who the prisoners are? Could this be as simple as an op to break out some local equivalent of a drug lord or mafia boss Wamba's got locked up there?"

"Enough!" Trevor Mulroney interrupted forcefully from the screen. "This is a moot discussion. I can assure you with 100 percent certainty this Jini is real. He's out there. Catching him—not his followers, few or many—is your chief mission. Your only mission. As to his motives, that is irrelevant. If you want those hefty combat zone bonuses you've contracted, you'll find him for me—yesterday, if not sooner."

"And I think I may just have an idea where he's holed up." As Ernie's drawl broke into the discussion, every eye swiveled to where his calloused forefinger traced the image of a tranquil, empty stretch of jungle river. "Can anyone tell me what this shadow is?"

Even studying the image, Robin could make out only a ripple across the water, a hint of shadow she'd assumed came from the trees reflected in the water.

"A sandbar, maybe? Who knows? Who cares?" Carl Jensen answered defensively. "My equipment is calibrated to spot human beings under triple-canopy rainforest, not to map riverbeds."

"Not a sandbar. I grew up in a Louisiana bayou. I know a sandbar when I see one. That's a boat down there. Didn't you say that barge went down about here?"

Now it was Pieter Krueger who moved closer to study the screen. "Yes, it did. I suppose that could be the barge. But what does that have to do with anything?"

"A lot, actually," Ernie said. "What Jensen said earlier about breathing underwater gave me the idea. You mentioned detecting motion here but no human signature. So can this gear detect an accurate human signature underwater?"

Carl shook his head. "A composite human signature is differentiated from other mammals based on body temperature, weight, shape. All of which are distorted by water. Are you suggesting our crocs might actually be human? But we didn't just fly by. I had the chopper spend some time doing a visual search. You'd need scuba gear to stay down that long."

"Stay with me," Ernie said. "See that line? What's under there is on a slant. Maybe resting on an actual sandbar. You can't see because the water's so muddy. But that ripple says this end's barely under the surface. And a barge cargo hold's got to be airtight."

Robin got where he was going even as Trevor Mulroney spoke up from his screen. "You're suggesting an air bubble down there. Even if that's possible, it's a little far-fetched that it could still be there months after that barge went down."

"It's happened before. To yours truly, in fact. No barge, but a torpedoed gunboat I scouted out sneaking into a Vietcong command post. Boat was half rusted away, but I found air down there. When the mission went sour, I hid out forty-eight hours while Ho Chi Minh's goons scoured the jungle for me, sneaked out once they gave up. Here that wouldn't even be necessary." Ernie was now tapping the aerial map. "Notice this stretch of water is right around the first bend from the mine."

"That's right," Trevor Mulroney said slowly. "The ore barge had barely left the mine when it blew. A hundred tons of molybdenum ore still sitting on the bottom of that river."

"Which means the sunken barge would be completely hidden from mine security. At the same time, these trees right here—" Ernie pointed to tree trunks reflected in brown water—"are tall enough that if you climbed into their upper canopy, you'd have a perfect line of sight into the mine itself. Let's assume this Jini discovered an air pocket, maybe doing some salvage after sinking the barge. And that he's sophisticated enough to know about aerial surveillance. All he'd have to do is get his team underwater at the first sound of an approaching chopper. Meanwhile, does anyone notice that as the crow flies, it's a pretty easy trek from this river bend to the mine itself? I'm guessing we just may have located Jini's forward operating base."

"He could be right," Pieter Krueger admitted. "In fact, that's the same direction the logging party was cutting trees for charcoal. Why did I never notice this before?"

"Maybe I've appointed the wrong leader for this mission," Trevor Mulroney commented with a malicious grin. As Pieter Krueger stiffened angrily, Mulroney's grin widened. "So, Miller, you got any suggestions on how to smoke this guy out? For one, let's get a chopper back out there ASAP for a closer look."

But Ernie was shaking his head. "I'd hold off on the chopper. If this is Jini's FOB, we don't want to tip him off. My suggestion is a small, discreet insertion party after dark on foot. Our own guys, no Wamba militia to mess things up. Night vision goggles will cancel out a local advantage in this jungle. Oh, and one other thing. The mole. Say this Jacob was Jini's runner for getting that last bomb into the mine. What field commander's going to depend on a kid? And whoever tipped off last night's killers, it sure wasn't the kid because he was buttoned up tight. Only two groups knew about that medivac. Those at the mine. And here. Unless we're seriously pointing fingers at the Taraja medical personnel, the mine's a more likely leak."

"Or if you're right about the rest, maybe Jini just saw the choppers land and take off for himself," Pieter Krueger pointed out.

"Possibly. But how would he know where they were headed? No, our ghost has got to have another mole at the mine. Someone not on that logging party or the kid wouldn't have been needed. An adult. Maybe more than one. And they've got to have a means of getting messages out to this Jini." Ernie Miller paused before adding laconically, "So how about we offer them another urgent message to pass along."

Once the former Green Beret had explained, Trevor Mulroney nodded. "Let's do it. Ernie, you've earned yourself the ground mission. Krueger, as team leader you'll continue to move forward with the bush hunt. And take Samuel Makuga with you to do the saber rattling out at the mine. They're scared to death of him enough already to swallow anything. Be on notice I'll be flying back your way within forty-eight hours. I want this Jini in front of me when I get there."

Trevor Mulroney's screen went blank. Energized at the prospect of a worthwhile mission, operatives crowded around Ernie to volunteer. Robin found herself at the Vietnam vet's heels as they threaded out of the communications trailer. She seized the opportunity to ask a question nagging at her. "Ernie, does it seem to you our employer knows more about this Jini guy than he's passed on to us?"

Ernie swung around to cock an eyebrow. "I *always* assume Trevor Mulroney knows more than he's saying. Believe me, it's safer that way. I've worked with and for Mulroney since back when he started Ares Solutions. He always knows what he's doing. And he always gets what he wants."

Heading toward the supply depot, Ernie tossed over his shoulder, "So don't let the civilized shell fool you. I say that as a compliment. Mulroney also rewards generously those who get him what he wants."

Robin tagged on his heels, still curious. "And Pieter Krueger? You must have worked with him before too, then."

"Krueger?" Ernie didn't slow his stride. "Krueger's a company man. He'll do what he's paid for, no questions. And do it well, make no mistake. Why do you think he's still working for Mulroney? Mulroney doesn't suffer fools, believe me, whatever that little exchange back there. He figures pitting us at each other keeps us on our toes."

"Speaking of Krueger—" At the roar of rotors picking up speed, Robin glanced toward the airstrip. She gave an exclamation of dismay as she caught sight of Pieter Krueger and Samuel Makuga striding rapidly toward the executive helicopter. "Oh, great! They're leaving already. I was going to ask about arranging a ride-along to take Rachel back to her mother."

Ernie punched a code into the supply depot's lockbox. "That little girl we brought in? You need to get her home? No problem. The mine's our takeoff point for this op. I was just thinking an on-the-ground translator might prove handy if we take any prisoners. You want in, we can swing by the clinic to take on a passenger."

"That would be great!" Robin dug out her cell phone and punched Return on her most recent call. If Taraja's Internet phone service was up and running, she wouldn't have to make a trek up to the clinic.

It took several rings before Miriam answered the phone. Yes, she'd have Rachel ready and be watching for a helicopter. Robin spent the next hour helping Ernie sort out NVGs, ammo, radio batteries, and other mission gear from the supply depot before grabbing her own knapsack and slinging her M4 over her shoulder. She shouldn't need either for a brief run to the mine and back. But one unbending maxim both Colonel Duncan and the Marines had drilled into Robin was that you went into the field planning for the best but prepared for the worst.

As the Mi-17 hovered down where the trail from the airstrip opened up into the clinic lawn, Robin jumped out. But it wasn't Miriam she spotted waiting as promised on the veranda, Rachel in arms. Rather a much taller, distinctly masculine figure. Bent over to shield his burden from wind and dirt kicked up by the rotors, Michael ran forward. But instead of handing the child to Robin, he climbed through the Mi-17's open side door, swinging a large brown medical bag in with him.

"What are you doing?" Robin demanded above the noise.

"As her doctor, I'd like to hand her over myself. Make sure her caregiver understands what's needed to follow up with that injury," Michael shouted back.

His only reason? Or an excuse to nose around the mine situation?

Michael's next words gave the answer. "In any case, after last night, I'd like to see for myself what's happening out at that mine. Check out those other survivors you referenced. You mentioned all they had was some prisoner with paramedic training."

Robin looked at Ernie, seated in the copilot's chair next to the pilot. The Vietnam vet simply raised noncommittal eyebrows, but Marius, the Afrikaner pilot at the throttle, waved an impatient hand. Robin clambered inside after Michael.

Robin couldn't blame Rachel for breaking into a wail as the noise of rotors and engine rose to full throttle and the Mi-17 lumbered skyward. Michael offered no resistance when Robin eased his burden into her own arms. From the cockpit, Ernie called, "Hey, you two, up here!"

Supremely conscious of Michael's warmth at her back, Robin worked her way forward through a half-dozen teammates hunkered down with their combat packs. When they reached the cockpit, Ernie reached for Robin's charge. "Here, let me take the little one."

Evidently recognizing the burly warrior who'd cradled her on her last helicopter ride, Rachel broke off her wail. Within moments, she appeared asleep, face buried against the Vietnam vet's Kevlar vest. Which permitted Robin to shift her attention to the windshield. Her last flight in an Mi-17 had been spent crouching on the floor, holding a pressure bandage in place. Now she could see the entirety of Taraja spread out below. The straight ribbon of trimmed grass and dirt. Overgrown fields and broken buildings stretching well back on both sides of the airstrip. The relatively small cleared area around the clinic that was Taraja's new beginning.

Then the medical compound fell behind. Now the only break in endless green billows was a winding brown snake. The river down which last night's killers had disappeared in their canoes. The Mi-17 swooped low enough for Robin to spot the sudden slither of a crocodile from the riverbank into the water. Ahead on the horizon, a smudge of gray-brown rising above the rainforest canopy grew quickly into individual hillocks. At this distance, there was no evidence of mining activity, only serene, untouched beauty as far as the eye could reach.

Michael leaned in beside Robin to look out the windshield, his exhalation brushing her neck as he shouted against her ear, "Really something, isn't it? I won't say I didn't enjoy college stateside, medical school, seeing the world in the Navy. But this—well, this is coming home. What the—?"

Michael's warm breath had abruptly pulled away from Robin's ear. She felt the stiffening of his lean body before he exclaimed sharply, "What is that?"

Off to the helicopter's left, a second gray-brown smudge rose to bifurcate the paling cerulean of late-afternoon sky. Its lazy curl as the Mi-17 drew closer made clear this one was no rock formation but smoke. A lot of smoke.

Ernie had leaned forward to see what Michael was pointing out, but it was the Afrikaner pilot, Marius, who spoke. "That? Looks like one of the villages that put up resistance to this morning's raid. Bow and arrow against assault rifles is plain stupid, but you've got to admire their nerve. Wamba's boys weren't too impressed, as you can see. Good thing we were there to keep them from doing to the residents what they did to that village."

Robin felt Michael's withdrawal, the evaporation of that tenuous restored camaraderie she'd so eagerly latched onto these last hours, even before the American doctor straightened away from her. When he spoke, Michael's expression was blank, his tone carefully neutral. But Robin knew him too well to miss the subdued fury. "I was in that village just last month. Held a surgical clinic there." Michael clamped his jaw shut. Nor did he speak again during the remainder of the brief flight. But as the dynamited rock face came into view and the Mi-17 hovered down into churned red mud outside the mine enclosure, Robin could see one hand clenching and unclenching at his side.

Before the rotors stopped, her Ares Solutions teammates were on their feet and grabbing combat gear. Handing Rachel back to Robin, Ernie climbed out to direct his field team toward the gate. Robin juggled a now wide-awake Rachel to reach for her own knapsack and weapon. Stepping over, Michael resolved her dilemma by shouldering both along with his medical bag, then offered a hand to help Robin step down from the helicopter's high threshold.

He still had not spoken. Remembering her own initial consternation, Robin tried to see the place through Michael's eyes as they headed through the gate. No pick-and-shovel work was happening on the rock face. But that didn't signify a halt to the molybdenum ore processing. Most of the workers appeared to be occupied in an assembly line of hammering and chiseling at mounds of stockpiled raw ore. At each station, the rock handled was of smaller dimensions, until the final step closest to the slurry vats involved sledgehammers pulverizing gravel-sized pieces of rock to dust.

It was, in fact, a low-tech manual duplication of what the steam-powered rock crusher had accomplished before Jini's bomb blew it apart. Other workers were wearing a circular groove around the slurry pits as they pushed on the same long poles employed to move carts around the camp, their steady tread turning the huge paddles that stirred the mix of crushed rock, water, and chemicals. Female workers were scooping out sludge previously suctioned off by pump and pipes.

If an excruciatingly laborious method of processing molybdenite, Robin could see a sizable mound of filled ore sacks. She wasn't sure why she felt impelled to offer some defense to Michael's tightened mouth and critical survey. "If it's a mess now, you can thank Jini's destructive efforts. But once we can secure stability and open transportation, Earth Resources will be able to bring in some heavy-duty mining gear. Make this place a model for mining here in the Congo. Offer a chance for a real life to the locals."

"They have a real life." Michael clamped his teeth together as though the words had escaped him against his will.

"You know what I mean." Robin looked around for the young woman from whose arms Rachel had been dragged aboard the helicopter. Something she could not put a finger on was nagging at her. Something out of place. But other than the shift in work assignments, the only difference she could see in the mine clearing was that the debris from the explosion had been cleared away.

"Yes, I know what you mean." Michael's own scrutiny was focused on the workers. "And believe it or not, I've nothing against reaping the natural resources God provided this country. So long as it's done right and benefits the Congolese people, not just some expat mining conglomerate. I've seen government gold and coltan mines a whole lot worse than this. If Mulroney really means to do the right thing, more power to him. But this used to be such a pretty spot. I just hate to see that completely destroyed."

Robin glanced at Michael. "You know this place?"

"Not necessarily this place. But those hills are unique in the Ituri region. I remember visiting a village somewhere at the base of one of them when Miriam and I were kids. Climbing up to look out over the rainforest while my parents were holding a clinic. That was back before the fighting shut down all the roads."

A wail broke into Michael's commentary. "Mama! Mama!"

Immediately a scream responded from the nearest slurry pit. "Rachel! Rachel!"

The little girl in Robin's arms began to struggle as a young woman abandoned her skimming to rush toward them. "Give her to me! Give me my daughter!"

"Mama!" As the little girl heaved herself from Robin's arms, the young woman caught her close. Tears streaming from huge, dark eyes, she patted her daughter all over as if to reassure herself the child was truly whole and well.

The passionate relief in the woman's face tightened Robin's throat. *I did something good here. In this time, in this place, at least, I did the right thing.*

Then Robin spotted a white-haired man hurrying forward from the brush corral. "The boy Jacob—did you bring him, too? Is he well?"

Robin glanced at Michael. "That's him. The camp healer who said he knew your family. Do you recognize him?"

Robin saw Michael's tawny gaze narrow as he turned his head toward the old man. Saw the elderly healer stop abruptly in his tracks as he caught sight of Robin's companion. But Michael was given no opportunity to respond because now others were abandoning the stone-crushing assembly line and slurry pits to rush toward them. The elderly healer disappeared from view as workers swarmed around Robin and Michael.

"My son, where is he?"

"My daughter, is she well?"

"My woman, why has she not returned?"

Robin was stunned by the demands. This, she realized, was what had seemed out of place. The Mi-17 had evacuated the massacre victims from Taraja hours ago. A funeral, rather than a normal workday, should have greeted their arrival.

"What is going on here?" At the furious exclamation, workers fell back to reveal Pieter Krueger striding from the Quonset hut that served as mine headquarters. Samuel Makuga loomed huge at his side. Following behind were Ernie Miller and Clyde Rhodes, the South African mine administrator Robin had met on her last visit. The rest of the Ares Solutions team had vanished inside the Quonset hut.

"You all! Return to work immediately, or there will be no food rations tonight." Makuga's harsh Swahili scattered the crowd as the group reached Robin and Michael. Robin saw Rachel's mother dart with her daughter into the brush corral instead of heading back to the slurry pits. The healer followed.

Robin spun around and addressed Pieter Krueger in low, urgent English. "Why are these people asking about the other patients we airlifted? How is it they don't know about last night? I thought the bodies had been returned to their families."

"They don't know because they haven't been told yet. We didn't want anything to seem outside the usual before tonight's op. Which is why if I'd wanted you hauling the kid back at this juncture, I'd have said so! And dragging an unauthorized civilian into the middle of an op? Is that one of our weapons he's carrying? Are you out of your mind?"

Robin had actually forgotten Michael was still shouldering her knapsack and M4 until Pieter Krueger snatched the weapon from him. "This one you're not going to just brush off, Duncan. When I get done reporting to Mulroney, maybe this time he'll be smart enough to fire your sorry—"

"But . . . I was told—" Robin broke off her defense. In fact, Ernie hadn't actually given verbal permission for Michael's presence, and she was not about to pass along any blame.

But now the Vietnam vet was stepping forward. "Hey, ease up, Krueger. I'm the one who gave the kid and doc a green light. Mulroney assigned me this op, and I saw no harm. In fact, I figure some medical insurance for tonight isn't such a bad thing."

"That wasn't your call! Mulroney may have handed you this op. But I am still team commander here."

Body language bristled between the two operatives. Michael took a step forward. His interruption held no appeasement. "The question isn't what I'm doing here, Krueger, but what you are! I saw the village your men burned down. I thought you claimed Wamba's men were under strict control of Ares Solutions."

Pieter Krueger's glance toward Michael held contempt. "Yeah, well, it's called rules of engagement. Villages that didn't resist got rounded up nice and peaceful. Your peaceful villagers took out a dozen of Wamba's troops this morning. Surely you don't expect Wamba's men to just roll over when they're attacked!"

"And it never occurred to you attacking a sleeping village might provoke some defense from the locals? You punish that by burning their homes over their heads?"

Pieter Krueger turned furiously on Robin. "And this, Duncan, is why you don't drag civilians into an op. They can't grasp the simple principle that to have power and not use it is weakness. And weakness gets people killed."

The worst was that by every standard of Robin's own training, the Ares Solutions team leader had a point. Michael shouldn't be here. In truth, she'd been allowing herself to think of Michael as the comrade-in-arms she'd served with in Afghanistan, not the civilian outsider he actually was to this mission. It was not enough to say that the American doctor had barged in without Robin's invitation. That her teammates had raised no objection. Her concern for a young mother frantic about her child had overridden the professional judgment in which Robin took so much pride. Mingled shame and anger tightened her vocal cords so that she could only nod.

"To have power and not abuse it is courage, not weakness," Michael responded tightly. Then he glanced at Robin's miserable expression, and his taut posture eased slightly. "But, hey, you're right that I'm a civilian now and this isn't my op. I do apologize for intruding without authorization. Please believe it was none of Ms. Duncan's doing. I rather barged onto your helicopter without asking. But since I am here, I hope you'll allow me to make myself useful. I'd like to check out the other explosion victims. Maybe have a chat with your site medic on any other health issues among your workers."

Pieter Krueger's own body language did not ease at all. "Are you kidding? You think I'm going to allow you to compound one breach of protocol with another? You shouldn't be here to begin with. Now you know things you shouldn't. You've seen things you shouldn't. And not just last night's events. You've made your sympathies clear enough that I wouldn't trust you near our suspect pool! You'll spend the rest of this op inside that Quonset hut."

As the South African turned to Robin, the bite in his tone grew more pronounced. "Since you, Duncan, aren't part of tonight's action, I trust I can at least count on you to make sure your pal here remains out of sight and incommunicado until this all goes down."

It could have been worse in a thousand ways, if none came immediately to mind. Ernie Miller was already heading toward the Quonset hut. Robin turned to Michael. "This way, please."

But Pieter Krueger held up his hand. "Wait. Since you're here, Duncan, you might as well do your job first." The South African turned to Rhodes. "It's time."

The mine administrator headed toward a shiny new shed that had replaced the one destroyed in the explosion. In the brief passage of time since the Mi-17 had touched down, the sun had finished its plunge below the treetops, and in the swift onset of an equatorial night, the sky overhead was rapidly fading from twilight's pale green to dusk. Robin knew from the team briefing what was about to happen. As Rhodes ducked inside the shed, a generator that had replaced the shattered steam engine rumbled to life. Security spotlights blinked on from a total of seven watchtowers spaced along the perimeter fence. Above the Quonset hut's front entrance, an additional fluorescent tube flickered to pale white-blue light.

Once the lights were on, the door of the Quonset hut opened. Seven men in militia uniforms emerged. Each headed to a tower. As they climbed up, the guards atop the platforms handed the newcomers their weapons and climbed down.

The evening shift change.

The new generator's limited capacity did not provide sufficient lighting for the work zones. As though its rumble signaled the end of the workday, laborers who'd dispersed back to their work stations began gathering tools and heading for the brush enclosure. Pieter Krueger turned to Samuel Makuga. "Do it."

Stepping forward, the huge militia commander lifted a bullhorn. Pieter Krueger glanced at Robin. "Okay, I want to know exactly what he's telling these people."

Robin obediently set herself to translating the militia commander's shouted Swahili. "'The Congolese army has now successfully evacuated this region of civilians. Any individuals remaining outside the mine perimeter fence will be assumed to be insurgents. Beginning at sunrise, the Congolese air force will begin—' I don't know the Swahili, but I'm guessing he means a strafing campaign—'which will proceed until the rebel leader Jini and his men are killed or captured. To avoid—' again I don't know the Swahili, but I'm guessing he's referring to collateral gunfire from the choppers—'all camp residents must remain inside their living quarters until they receive orders to leave. Mining operations will be suspended until it is over.'"

The workers had frozen in place during Samuel Makuga's speech. A security beam spotlighted the elderly healer, standing in the opening to the brush corral. He melded into a stampede toward the corral as the militia commander lowered his bullhorn. Pieter Krueger offered Robin a grunt that might have been satisfaction, if not approval, before walking off with Makuga toward the generator shed.

Twilight had now completely faded to black. With the moon not yet risen, the rainforest night beyond pools of artificial light was as dark as it would get. To Robin's relief, Michael offered no resistance to following her toward the Quonset hut. They'd reached the white-blue glimmer cast by the fluorescent tube above the Quonset hut entrance when the door opened. The Ares Solutions team that had been on the Mi-17 stepped through into the light.

In synchronicity, the Mi-17 outside the perimeter fence rose from its muddy resting place to touch down again moments later in the now-vacated work area. The Mi-17 cut its engine, its rotors winding to a halt.

The commotion inevitably drew curious eyes. Human shapes scrambled to the top of the brush corral and crowded into its opening to watch the *mzungu* soldiers in their safari clothing and bulky body armor. But just as the Ares Solutions team headed for the helicopter, the generator's smooth rumble became a rough chug-chug. The lights flickered. Steadied themselves for a few more heartbeats. Then came a loud hiccup. An even louder clank from the shed. Simultaneously generator and lights went dead.

Consternated shouts from the shed echoed from watchtowers to brush corral. It took some moments before a pale glimmer of battery-powered lanterns blinked on from each watchtower platform. The only other available illumination was the Mi-17's running lights.

Bodies milled outside the Quonset hut. Then a flashlight came on, its narrow beam lighting a path for dark silhouettes threading their way toward the helicopter. The running lights created odd patterns as the group heaved ore sacks from the stockpile Robin had noted earlier into the helicopter. Once the pile was gone, the silhouettes climbed in on top of the ore sacks and the helicopter roared back to life. Standing in the Quonset hut's open doorway, Robin blinked away a grit of dirt stirred up by the rotors as the Mi-17 lifted from the ground.

Only Robin and Michael had been close enough to note that the dark silhouettes clambering aboard the helicopter were not the Ares Solutions operatives who'd originally stepped out into the light, but the group of day shift security guards who'd climbed down earlier from the watchtowers.

CHAPTER TWENTY-TWO

The helicopter roared into the sky. "And that's one of the things you probably shouldn't have seen," Robin tossed over her shoulder to Michael as he followed her into the Quonset hut.

Inside, this proved to be a single large, octagonal room. Around the walls, stacked crates and padlocked metal storage lockers alternated with bunk beds. At the rear, an office setup with both satphone and radio hookup jostled a propane stove and fridge. A narrow fiberglass unit stood open to reveal a camper-style chemical toilet and shower. A small television and DVD player perched precariously on a bunk were a reminder that the mining camp headquarters also served as Clyde Rhodes's personal living space.

A lantern on another bunk revealed the missing Ares Solutions team rummaging through duffel bags, stuffing ammo clips into utility belts, tugging night vision goggles into place. Ernie glanced up from snapping a water canteen onto his belt.

"Seven in, seven out—not including you, Duncan, and the doc

if anyone was counting. If Jini's got a watch posted, they'll assume we came to escort out that load of molybdenite. Doc, I'm told you've got experience in combat medicine. Afghanistan, right? Sorry about all that out there. Krueger's mission head. But I for one am tickled to have you both here for the duration."

Assenting nods and grunts from around the hut eased a hard knot in Robin's throat. Her teammates at least didn't appear to share Pieter Krueger's estimation of Michael's presence here. Or her own competence.

"Afghanistan and Iraq," Michael affirmed. "You were in Vietnam, I'm guessing?"

"Special ops till the politicians threw in the towel. Love to have a chat sometime. But the clock's ticking. Everyone ready?"

The six Ares Solutions operatives completing Ernie's team had now finished settling their gear into place. Shouldering his own pack, Ernie picked up the battery-powered lantern. "Okay, we're out of here. Any luck, you two will have a quieter night than ours. Duncan, you mind doing the honors?"

Ernie handed Robin the lantern. If she hadn't already known their plan, night vision goggles coming down from foreheads made clear what was wanted. Striding to the hut door, Ernie reached for the knob. "Now, Duncan."

Robin switched off the lantern, plunging the hut into absolute darkness. At least for herself and Michael. A gust of wind signaled the door opening. Bulky silhouettes were barely visible against the night as her teammates slipped noiselessly outside. A cessation of wind signaled the door easing shut again.

Only then did Robin switch the lantern back on. In its soft glimmer Robin saw that the pleasant facade Michael had presented Ernie and the Ares Solutions team had vanished, his strong-boned, bronzed features now grim and hard gaze accusing. They both spoke at once.

"You recognized that old man, didn't you?" Robin repeated.

"You're actually planning to firebomb the rainforest?" Michael demanded incredulously. "No wonder Krueger's worried about me blowing the whistle! That's what your employer calls rules of engagement? Are you kidding me? After what Wamba's goons did to that village and who knows where else, do you know how many refugees could be milling around out there? Not insurgents. Escaped villagers. Women. Children."

A truth Robin knew better than Michael because she'd already seen Carl's aerial images. Robin set the lantern down. "Of course we're not going to firebomb the rainforest. You really think we'd do that? Makuga just said that as a—well, a trick."

"A trick?" Michael's tone was as hard as his expression.

There was little point in withholding the information, not when Michael would be here to witness it. Not when he'd been there last night to see and hear all that had happened to this point. And Pieter Krueger had already ensured the American doctor would have no opportunity to leak the plan.

"We know someone's feeding intel to Jini. Someone besides that boy Jacob. Whoever told Jini that those casualties had been taken to Taraja is probably in this mine camp right now."

Immediate understanding slightly allayed Michael's hard expression. "I get it. So you're offering new intel, hoping the mole will be motivated to warn this Jini he could be firebombed in the morning. That generator didn't really break down, did it? You're using cover of dark to lure your perp into making a move. Hence the fake security guards and night vision goggles."

Robin didn't correct Michael's assumption that Ernie and his team were part of the sting operation. He'd worked out enough confidential intel on his own. The night's bigger mission was the business of no one outside of Ares Solutions.

"If we can catch the mole, we can figure out how he's contacting Jini, hopefully put a quick end to all this. I can't believe you'd actually think I could work for a group that would take part in firebombing a civilian pop—"

Robin broke off. She was assuming Samuel Makuga's threat had been only a bluff. But then she hadn't expected that burned-out village either. "At least—"

Michael pounced on Robin's hesitation. "You don't really know, do you? In fact, what *do* you really know about your employers? Ares Solutions? Trevor Mulroney? Especially Trevor Mulroney!"

"Why do you say it like that?" Robin cried. "As though we're hiding something? I mean, you've seen this place. It's a molybdenite mine. Hardly the Ritz, but you can't blame that on Trevor Mulroney! He has good plans for this place. For these people. Maybe soon if our trap works tonight."

Each of the octagonal hut's eight wall panels had a single window, a small, square affair with metal shutters standing open and a wrought-iron protective grille. Striding over to the nearest, Michael stared out into the night. His voice was so quiet Robin wasn't sure whether he was speaking to her or to himself. "Things aren't what they seem. 'Woe to those who call evil good and good evil.'"

Robin was at his side in an instant. Looking out, she could see that the window faced the brush corral, visible across the open clearing because of a faint glow that outlined piled-up branches. Cook fires inside, undoubtedly. "Then you *did* recognize that old man! Who is he? What is it you're not telling me?"

When he didn't answer, she said more urgently, "Michael, don't shut me out. I need to know."

Michael shook his head and answered slowly, "Are you asking me as the Marine I once trusted with my life in Afghanistan? Or the Ares Solutions hire who'll take anything I say straight to her mission chief?"

"Why does there have to be a difference?" Robin demanded.

"Believe me, there is!" Michael snapped his mouth shut as heavy footsteps sounded outside the Quonset hut. The door flung open. A flashlight beam entered the hut, followed by Clyde Rhodes, then Pieter Krueger and Samuel Makuga.

Pieter Krueger headed directly to a duffel bag tossed onto an upper bunk. When Robin saw what he was pulling out, she quickly dug into her own knapsack. Unearthing night vision goggles, she settled them into place as Pieter Krueger tossed a set to each of his companions. Which left only Michael sightless when Krueger clicked off the lantern and gestured for Rhodes to extinguish his flashlight. "Now we wait."

And so they waited. Surreptitious inspections of Robin's cell phone screen revealed the passage of multiple hours. Michael had retreated to a bunk where he appeared asleep, an arm wrapped around his brown medical bag. The other three men each stood at a window, all on one side of the room.

Adrenaline kept Robin from following Michael's example. Restlessly, she slid from the bunk where she'd retreated, slipping noiselessly forward to stand beside Clyde Rhodes. The mine administrator shifted to allow Robin a clear look out. It was easy to see why the three men had chosen these windows. All overlooked the brush corral where the mine workers were locked down for the night.

A full moon had risen high above the rainforest, brightening the ghostly green illumination of Robin's NVGs almost to daylight, emergency lanterns on nearby watchtowers an annoying blaze in Robin's peripheral vision. Inside the brush corral, cook fires must have burned out, the prisoners now sleeping, because the wall of dried brush and tree branches loomed black and silent except for the shuffling of two night sentries outside the corral entrance.

Another hour dragged by. Maybe the boy Jacob had indeed been Jini's only contact within the camp. Tired of straining her eyes against green gloom, Robin had pushed up her NVGs when she heard Pieter Krueger murmur a triumphant obscenity.

Tugging the NVGs quickly back into place, she saw it. A green shape rising phantomlike from the ground at the base of the brush corral.

It took no genius to deduce that a prisoner had managed to burrow out through the brush pile. The spot where the phantom rose was where the corral curved close to the river and out of sight from those two night sentries. Under ordinary circumstances this would make no difference since security spotlights on the watchtowers offered bright illumination.

The mine's chain-link perimeter fencing did not itself extend into the water. Instead, a stockade of trimmed saplings draped in concertina wire had been driven deep into the river mud, permitting a free flow of water for camp use while walling out crocodiles and any other dangerous aquatic fauna.

And walling in prisoners.

Now with only emergency lanterns glimmering atop watchtower platforms instead of bright spotlights, the human shadow rising to its feet was effectively invisible against piled brush. Or would have been without Robin's NVGs. As the phantom scuttled silently, hesitantly toward the riverbank, Robin could see something cradled in its hands.

Pieter Krueger let out his breath in audible satisfaction. "Now!"

Abandoning their lookouts, the three men headed for the door. As it clicked softly shut behind them, Michael swung his feet to the floor. So the doctor hadn't been asleep. Only when he reached unhesitatingly for the overhead bunk did Robin realize he'd stationed himself directly under where Pieter Krueger had left his duffel bag.

"Ah! I thought I saw another pair in here." Strapping on the NVGs, Michael strode over to join Robin at the window. Outside, the three men who'd just exited were nowhere in sight. The phantom evidently believed itself still invisible because it now strode confidently toward the river.

The shadow waded out into the water. Did it hope to climb over that snarl of wood pilings and barbed wire? But no, a meter or so short of the stockade, it paused waist deep. Whatever it carried rose in its hands.

As though the motion were a signal, a rumble broke the silence of the night. The generator. At the same instant, security spotlights sprang to life, their beam so blazing white in Robin's NVGs she snatched the goggles from her face. Out in the river, the phantom froze, impaled by a spotlight. Assault rifles in their hands, Pieter Krueger and Samuel Makuga sprinted into view.

The phantom must have seen men running toward him. But when he unfroze, it was to step toward the stockade, completing a tossing motion. Something vaguely spherical arced over the wooden pilings. As the phantom turned back toward the bank, empty hands rose into the air.

But his surrender came too late. At a staccato of automatic gunfire, the man in the water staggered. Recovering, he managed two steps toward shore, then collapsed on the bank, half in, half out of the water. At first Robin assumed Pieter Krueger or Samuel Makuga must have fired. Then as both men stopped dead, weapons still dangling loose in their hands, she took in the movement of a sentry atop a riverside watchtower, his assault rifle angled toward the water.

With a furious exclamation, Michael was already heading for the door. On the way, he snatched up his brown bag. Stripped a bedsheet from a mattress. Snatched a towel hanging over the end of a bunk.

Rushing after him, Robin grabbed at his arm. "You can't go out there! You heard Krueger's orders."

Michael spun around, his expression savage as he knocked Robin's hand away. "Maybe you can't. But I don't work for Krueger. I'm a doctor, and there's a man out there who needs me, no matter what he's done."

Robin made no further attempt to detain Michael, instead staying tight on his heels as he raced for the river. This was no more than twenty meters from the Quonset hut, so they reached the bank just as Samuel Makuga and Pieter Krueger tugged the fallen man out of the water and rolled him faceup.

Makuga was simultaneously shouting orders. "Get out there and find what he threw into the water! Secure the other prisoners!"

Pieter Krueger emitted a stream of obscenities that included at least three languages. "That idiot guard. He'd no business shooting before we had a chance to interrogate the prisoner." He broke off as Michael and Robin entered his line of sight. "What are you two doing here? Duncan, I thought I told you to keep our guest locked up. I want him out of here now!"

Michael had already dropped to his knees beside the fallen man. "What are you going to do? Shoot me, too? Because you'll have to shoot me to keep me from tending this patient. And if you really hope to interrogate the man, you won't want to stop me."

A logical enough assessment that when a triumphant shout rose along the riverbank, the South African strode away without further debate. A sentry had beaten his peers to the far side of the stockade by climbing the nearest watchtower and dropping down over the perimeter fence. Now he held up a round object to the chain links. A husked coconut, Robin recognized as the sentry heaved the object over the fence. Pieter Krueger caught it. "At least we've recovered the message."

But Robin had lost interest in the success or failure of tonight's mission. Her mind whirled with confusion and dismay as she dropped to her knees across from Michael as he leaned over the sprawled body. The gunfire had caught its victim across the midsection, his lower torso such a mass of torn flesh Robin was astonished to see he still breathed.

Leaving his face untouched and immediately recognizable. How was it possible the kindly old healer who'd fought so desperately to save the explosion victims could be the spy they hunted?

"Here, bear down on this for me." Michael had already put the towel to use as a pressure bandage and was now ripping the sheet into lengths. As Robin scrambled to follow his instructions, scarlet welling up around her hands evoked sharply a memory of this man's grizzled head and deeply grooved, worried features bent above a boy's limp form.

The same boy who'd vanished from last night's massacre.

Was that the connection here?

A mystery likely to remain unsolved, judging by the amount of blood trickling from a corner of the elderly healer's mouth. Though unbelievably, his lips were now moving. A grunt emerged. Not of pain, but of urgency.

"Don't try to speak," Michael said gently in Swahili.

The old man only made a fresh effort to move his lips. This time words emerged. Not Swahili, but the educated French Robin had heard from him before. "You are the doctor? Stew-art?"

Michael shot Robin a glance before he answered quietly, "Yes, I'm Dr. Charles Stewart's son, Michael."

"Michael." The old man's nearest hand moved in a gesture that might have been entreaty. He worked his mouth before another word came out. "Woe!"

A cough increased the scarlet trickle from his mouth to a stream, but still he battled for words. "'Woe to—'"

Raising the elderly healer's head so he wouldn't choke on his own blood, Michael finished for him, "'. . . to those who call evil good and good evil, who put darkness for light and light for darkness.'"

"Yes." The old man's voice was now only a thread of sound. "Your father knew. Things are not as they seem." Another paroxysm of coughing shook him before he spoke again, this time in such a low whisper Robin had to lean close to hear. "Son of Charles. Save . . . save my son."

"I will do what is possible." Michael's quiet reassurance sounded shaken. "Please, rest yourself."

The old man did not respond. But from him came a long exhalation of air that might have been relief, hope, satisfaction. Except that Robin knew too well that particular exhalation. Not until she felt warmth splashing on her hands did Robin realize tears were spilling down her cheeks. Why was she shedding tears for a traitor, a criminal?

Somewhere in the distance, a drone escalated until it drowned out the generator's rumble. Then flashing lights swept overhead, heading downriver. A helicopter. Not the Mi-17, but the smaller executive helicopter by the pattern of running lights. Its roar, the lights, that still, silent form on the muddy bank triggered something in Robin's chest so that she leaned forward to grab at Michael's T-shirt with one bloodied hand.

"Please, you have to do something! You can't let him die! Not this time! Promise me you won't let him die!"

Hope died in Robin as Michael's bleak gaze met hers, the thick-fringed, tawny eyes deep pools of pain and grief under the glint of restored perimeter lighting. Robin relaxed her grip on the cotton material. But before she could snatch back her hand, hard, warm fingers as sticky and damp as Robin's own closed over it, flattening her palm against a heartbeat.

With his other hand, Michael brushed across the elderly healer's still features, closing wide, staring eyes. The grim line of his mouth had softened to a tenderness and regret as profound as the sorrow that darkened his gaze. Michael's lips parted to release words. Apology? Comfort?

"Robin, I—"

The world exploded into a rain of heat and fire.

CHAPTER TWENTY-THREE

The man now called Jini had seen the helicopter's earlier arrival. Watched the *mzungu* warriors hefting ore bags aboard. His high perch was the same branch from which he'd witnessed the steam engine explosion. If not his original plan, one benefit of that event had been an end to the logging that had drastically reduced the rainforest camouflage separating his refuge from the mine.

He'd discovered his refuge while searching the sunken barge for weapons, food, and other useful items such as he'd recovered from disabled supply and ore convoys. The explosives he'd laid under cover of darkness had been positioned to sink the barge midchannel where its cargo could not easily be salvaged. But the river was not deep, and the barge crew had managed to snatch up any portable possessions before splashing ashore.

Two successful ambushes had ended attempts to raise a hundred tons of heavy ore sacks to the surface, Makuga's security force adamantly refusing to risk their necks to an arrow or bullet they couldn't see coming from the thick jungle foliage. Only after a week's abandonment had he risked diving on the wreck. Finding nothing in the submerged wheelhouse, he'd dived deeper to slide through the jagged hole in the stern. The list of the sunken barge had piled up ore sacks along one side of the hold, leaving an open channel to swim above them. But in his search, he'd penetrated too deeply, the river water so murky once away from sunlight filtering through the shattered hull, he'd found himself in utter darkness, unable to retrace his dive.

He'd been desperate for air. Certain the Creator's judgment had finally overtaken him. Then a last frantic lunge for freedom had brought his head out into a large air bubble trapped by the vessel's sharp upward list just under the undamaged bow. The trapped air reeked with petroleum seeping from some fuel tank to puddle on top of the water. But to his oxygen-starved lungs, its taste was the sweetest perfume. His bearings now recovered, it had been simple to retrace his course back to the opening.

Having found nothing of value, he'd thought little further of the submerged barge until the steam engine explosion brought combat helicopters packed with *mzungu* warriors. By then he'd begun to feel safe in his treetop eyrie. Vicious though they were, Wamba's demobilized fighters now masquerading as mine security thought like most rainforest outsiders—in two dimensions, not three. He and his companions simply lived and moved thirty meters or more above their heads, the tangle of creeper vines, mosses, and thicker lianas interweaving massive hardwoods into a single labyrinth allowing them to range widely without setting foot on solid ground except to launch ambushes against their adversaries.

Even the explosives, detonators, ropes, knives, and other items purloined from convoys were stashed only a few feet from where he now lay, inside a rotted-out hollow where branch met tree trunk, a hardwood plug wedged in tightly to shield against the thieving, clever fingers of monkey troops that shared their habitat. There were captured firearms, too. A handful of assault rifles. An Uzi machine pistol. Ammunition. But these were rarely unearthed since in the close quarters of jungle foliage, the silent stealth of the rainforest's own weapons—bow, arrows, spear, machete—far outweighed the greater reach of *mzungu* weapons.

Hidden behind him, too, was the single prized possession to which he clung. His only hope of finding a way out of this madness.

If such a way still remained.

Though combat helicopters were a new element to this fight, he'd grown familiar enough with the smaller aircraft. It had been the mine's sole reliable transport and supply line once he'd cut off land and river access. But its usual flight path from Bunia brought the smaller helicopter in over the opposite side of the mine clearing, at no time approaching his hideout or the sunken barge tucked out of sight from the mine by a curve of the river.

Aerial surveillance was among the many marvels he'd learned of during his university studies, and he'd quickly recognized the smaller helicopter's new flying pattern as a search grid.

Convincing his companions to hide underwater had been more difficult. That the patrolling aircraft carried a magic eye that could penetrate the thick foliage of triple-canopy rainforest seemed to them as implausible as the *jini* he was accused of being. But they'd learned by now to trust his leadership. The first time he'd heard the helicopter approaching their hideout, he'd ordered his band down to earth. Breaking off some bamboo stalks, he'd led the way under the river surface into the submerged hull, hoping if he could not pray that its air bubble had not bled away.

It hadn't, and he'd had just enough time to hand each companion a length of hollow bamboo before the roar of rotors swept low above the sunken barge. They'd remained submerged beneath the water, breathing through the stalks, until he felt certain the aircraft was not returning.

At least twice daily since that first heart-pounding retreat, a distant drone had sent the band scrambling for their underwater hideout. Enough that he'd ordered his companions to remain at root level, no longer such a risky move since the hiatus on logging had also put a halt to ground parties intruding into his territory. That there'd not been more alarms was less comforting than his unsophisticated companions assumed. It simply signaled his new enemy's search ranged widely enough that his small band dared not withdraw far from their refuge.

Excepting last night's terrible trek.

Many hours had passed after the explosion before he'd recovered a message detailing the airlift of young Jacob and other victims to Taraja. The message also included the orders prompting a dangerous canoe expedition up winding, treacherous waterways to reach the mission compound that in another lifetime had signified to him a place of knowledge and comfort and safety.

By then he'd ascertained that the *mzungus* showed no stomach for night maneuvers, and he hoped the newcomers were no exception. He had no other alternative. Preventing his youthful ally from spilling what he knew to interrogators was just a minor corollary to their purpose at Taraja. But by the time the boy stumbled over their band on the riverbank, it had become clear they could no longer hope for success in their primary mission. Jacob himself, when questioned, had little to contribute regarding the steam engine debacle. The wasting of his own careful preparations had simply been an unfortunate chance accident.

So they'd returned here to regroup. But now for the first time since all this began, he could offer his companions no proposal of what to do next. Twice already since their return, they'd had to retreat to their underwater refuge. This time the helicopter's slow, deliberate pass along the course of the river left no doubt his enemies had discovered his escape by canoe. At least they'd never find the canoes, buried under ore sacks at the bottom of the river.

But he was less sanguine about how long he and his companions could remain undetected. Did he not know just how great the resources his enemy could muster? What if some clever mind or instrument deduced where he and his companions had found refuge? Since the failure of last night's Taraja trek, a growing sense of doom was impressing upon him that he was running out of time.

Which was why he still lay on this branch while his comrades slumbered down on the ground. He'd grasped instantly the possibilities when the generator died and the *mzungu* warriors flew off into the night with their precious cargo. Surely his father would seize on the darkness so miraculously offered him to attempt a message.

He'd found the first message washed against a storm-toppled mahogany right where the river made its first sharp bend past the village. The underwater tangle of rotting branches offered a hazardous obstacle to canoes, but also a natural trap for debris. As any villager was well aware. He'd fished out the green coconut for eating when he spotted a whittled chunk of wood hammered into the husk to make an airtight plug. Breaking the coconut, he'd discovered its milk drained out, in its place rolled-up palm fronds etched with his father's neat lettering.

Go. Leave. Bring aid. Such the message's contents summed up to be. He had not obeyed. His father, who had not been out of the rainforest in decades, simply did not understand how today's world worked. The futility of his faith and optimism in human nature.

Instead he'd begun his own war.

With some success, but more failure.

And even should some semblance of victory be obtained, could his father ever forgive him?

Especially now that he'd failed his father's most recent directive. Nor without the logging parties could he get a message of his own through that chain-link barrier. Were any of his earlier preparations still in place? Or was all now lost?

Baba, tell me what to do! This time I will listen!

His straining eyes had to this point made out no shadow creeping from the brush kraal. But what could he expect to see in such darkness? A sensible course of action would be to join his companions. To get some sleep, then check the debris trap at first light.

Instead he lifted his gaze to the pale, round globe of the full moon floating high above the mine clearing. A light to guide his father's steps in the darkness. A light that offered comfort to all hunted things.

Beneath that silvery, forgiving radiance, the devastation greedy men had wrought to his birthplace was no longer apparent. A strong breeze rustled leaves and branches around him. Its soughing music, the open clearing, swaying treetops, a glimmer of moving water all offered a momentary illusion of the paradise an almighty Creator had once placed here for the enjoyment, not pillaging, of his greatest creation, man.

Yesu, nuru ya ulimwengu.

There was no reason why at this moment, under this quiet moon-lit sky with the sweet rustle of the rainforest's melody in his ears, a lyric learned in distant childhood should spring so strongly to mind.

Yesu, Light of the World. The shining central figure of childhood stories taught by his father, read from the Holy Book, reiterated by *mzungu* and Congolese teachers alike at the Taraja mission school. A light to those in darkness. To the hunted. The brokenhearted. The hurt and the weak.

But not to me. I am lost in the darkness. Lost with no way out.

No, he would not be distracted by self-pity. Nor could he continue to lean on a frail old man for counsel. A solution to their current impasse rested like all else on his shoulders alone. If neither justice nor redemption remained for himself, he would not relinquish hope of achieving either or both for his people.

The rush of wind so filled his ears, he didn't note the generator's rumble until the white glare of security spotlights stabbed at the night, destroying its illusion of peace and beauty. But he couldn't so miss the drone of an approaching aircraft. A helicopter flying by night?

He was already scrambling back from his lookout perch when he heard the gunshots. He dared not linger for a look. Nor did he call out a warning. His companions would also have heard that approaching drone. With practiced speed, his feet and hands sought out artificial gouges in tree bark that marked a path across treetops. Only when moonlight glimmered on water below him did he descend earthward, more swiftly than prudent because the helicopter was now almost upon him.

The riverbank stretched away silent and empty from his muddy feet. But a swirl of disturbed water out where the sunken barge lay beneath the surface indicated his companions had preceded him. He was sliding into the water when he spied shadows separating from the base of tree trunks onto the riverbank. He froze long enough to take in moonlight glinting on the knobby disfigurement of night vision goggles, body armor, automatic weapons.

"You there! Stop!" The atrocious attempt at Swahili confirmed these were no Congolese militia, but the *mzungu* warriors his own eyes had witnessed lifting off with their load of ore in the combat helicopter. Or so he'd believed. And if they'd spotted him, they must also have witnessed his confederates taking refuge in their underwater sanctuary.

He dived just as a bumblebee shape roared low overhead. Gunfire peppered the water as he swam downward. A hand found the hull of the sunken barge, then the jagged edges of the opening. Surfacing into the air bubble, he tugged free from his body harness a palm-sized fluorescent lantern—tough, waterproof, with an LED light that did not require batteries—also purloined from those convoys. In its light, he counted with relief eight faces around him, including the young features and awkward paddling of the boy Jacob. They'd all made it.

But they could not stay here. Not just because of a rattle of gunfire against the hull overhead, so close to the river surface. But one or more of those bullets must have penetrated the fuel tank because the sheen of petroleum on water had become a rapidly spreading rainbow shimmer, acrid fumes already making it hard to breathe.

"They know we are here," he told the others. "The gunfire comes from *mzungu* troops. They are between us and the mine. But if we dive deep and head for the opposite bank, perhaps it will be possible to escape into the forest. You know what to do then."

The pumping fuel was now a noxious pool a thumb's width in depth atop the water. They could wait no longer. Petroleum fumes burned his nostrils as he drew in as much air as his lungs would hold. "Now!"

Switching off the lantern, he dived through petroleum until his groping hands encountered ore bags, then forced his way through the passage with every bit of power still in him. He pushed out of the opening but remained underwater, swimming until another stroke would have him breathing in water before breaking the surface.

But he had not followed the instructions he'd given to his companions. This refuge was hopelessly compromised. They would not be able to return. But he at least could not simply flee. All hope that remained to him hinged on retrieving what he'd so cautiously hidden away in his treetop eyrie. His strenuous underwater sprint had carried him at least twenty meters downstream from the sunken barge. Not far from the opposite bank, he spotted another head breaking the water's surface. The first of his companions.

The *mzungus* had spotted it too. As his companion scrambled to the safety of brush and trees, their gunfire shifted direction. But even with their special eye gear, the far side of the river would be almost invisible from the *mzungu* position. With triumph he saw a second companion scramble to shore before turning his own powerful strokes toward the near bank.

But the *mzungus* had also recognized their need for more light. He was almost to shore when a flare shot high above the sunken barge. Its red blaze caught at the rainbow sheen now spreading out into the river. It illumined, too, several heads still bobbing in the water.

Shocked comprehension propelled the man dubbed Jini to faster speed. His feet touched river mud just as the flare splashed down into petroleum. The barge's fuel tanks must have been quite full, the air pocket transformed into a time bomb of built-up gases, because the resulting explosion was far beyond what he'd anticipated. Fire and thunder shot skyward. The barge itself lifted completely out of the water, splitting into pieces before crashing down with a force that sent a surge of water well up onto the bank. Flaming chunks of wood, metal, and rock cleared the treetops before raining down on river and forest.

Shouts of fury and pain from the *mzungu* position indicated that some falling debris had found a target. As they redoubled their gunfire, an anguished cry rose from the far riverbank. A limp body fell back into the water.

Jini had reached the near bank. But as he clambered out of the water, he realized with horror he was not alone. A thin, lithe figure with a dragging limp had scrambled to shore beside him.

The boy Jacob.

There was no time for reprimand. The roar of an aircraft was now sweeping back upriver. As a bumblebee shape soared into view, a searchlight on its belly caught both fugitives full in its beam. Above it, another *mzungu* in body armor leaned out an open door, assault rifle in his hands angled downward.

For one long, terrible heartbeat, the two fugitives remained pinned in that harsh, white beam. But the search beam had also revealed the high, protruding buttresses of a liana-infested African teak. Its upper regions offered access to the lower branches of a neighboring mahogany. Jini shoved his young companion ahead of him into the underbrush just as the gunman opened fire.

The boy had understood. A bare foot slapped at root buttresses while a hand grabbed a liana. As the boy disappeared upward into the dark camouflage of night and leaf cover, the man dubbed Jini followed. The first bullet creasing his ribs did not slow his upward rush. He was reaching for the safety of a mahogany branch when a second agonizing pain stabbed through his right shoulder. The liana in his grip slid from suddenly helpless fingers.

Then followed only the sensation of falling before blackness swallowed him up.

CHAPTER
TWENTY-FOUR

By the time Robin scrambled to her feet, the column of fire was sinking below treetop level, the last flaming debris drifting down like dying fireworks. Pieter Krueger snatched a radio from his belt. "Miller! What's going on there? What just blew? I need a situation report now!"

The radio crackled. "That was the barge you saw go up. Our mission's blown. Three dead targets. None of them Jini. Two injured on our end. Chopper's heading this way to evacuate them. Alert the doc to be on standby. No prisoners taken. Repeat, no prisoners."

Emitting a furious stream of Afrikaans and Swahili, Pieter Krueger and Samuel Makuga headed at a run toward the Quonset hut. Robin leaned in urgently toward Michael, still hunkered beside the dead healer. "You know I'll have to make a report on all this. So who was that man? What did it mean, all he was saying? Did I hear right that this prisoner might be our ghost's father? That would be one motive for helping a killer. And what's your connection here?"

Guards hurrying forward kept Michael from an immediate answer. As they took charge of the fallen prisoner, he walked instead to the water's edge, crouching down to scrub at hands and forearms. Replicating his action, Robin whispered forcefully, "If you won't talk to me, someone else is going to be pushing you for answers. And believe me, they won't be as patient or—well, as friendly to you as I've been."

Lowered eyelashes hooded Michael's dark glance. "You do what you have to, Robin. I've already told you I know nothing that could further your mission or your search for this Jini. That still stands. As for that man, like I've said before, a lot of people in this region know the Stewarts, especially my father. But . . ."

He shifted position to stare speculatively toward the brush corral, where frightened shouts and wailing indicated its occupants no longer slumbered. Robin had finished her scrubbing. Before she could rise to her feet, a wet hand shot out to grab her dripping forearm. Michael's lowered tone was urgent, compelling.

"Robin, I may not know anything, but there are things I'm beginning to wonder. Things I need to check out. Is it too much to ask you to hold off on that report? Give me twenty-four hours max. Trust me, a report now won't further your mission. Holding off—well, it just might make all the difference."

Robin stared at him without trying to shake off his grip. "Now you're asking me to trust you when you've made it clear you don't trust me."

"It isn't you I don't trust." Michael released her forearm. "So is that a yes or a no?"

Beyond the chain-link perimeter fence, flashing lights and a growing roar signaled the executive helicopter approaching. Robin's hand radio crackled. "Duncan, where are you? Get that doc over here now."

"We're on our way." Jumping to her feet, Robin met Michael's hooded gaze. "Twenty-four hours, then. Unless some compelling reason comes along to change my mind."

Neither operative they unloaded from the executive helicopter proved seriously wounded. One had been knocked out cold by falling debris, but his Kevlar helmet had saved him from worse injury. A chunk of metal shrapnel from the barge had sliced through the other's upper thigh but had missed any major arteries, Michael assured the man as he stitched him up.

At dawn came the funeral Robin had expected to encounter earlier. This included the three dead insurgents pulled from the river along with the elderly healer and the Taraja massacre victims whose delivery Pieter Krueger had ordered now that secrecy no longer offered any advantage. Accustomed though she'd become to its necessity, the haste with which such recently living, breathing human beings were thrust into the ground still seemed to Robin almost indecent.

Anguished wails and tears accompanied a brief service before slag was piled over the communal grave to form a crude burial mound. The prisoners were given little time to mourn, guards herding them back to their normal tasks before the rising sun cleared the treetops.

With his expatriate patients resting comfortably, Michael insisted on making a round of the camp's sick and injured. This time Pieter Krueger shrugged indifference. But a snap of Samuel Makuga's fingers scrambled a security guard to dog Michael's steps. Which might be why Michael's patient queries received little response beyond yes or no. Still, the remaining casualties of that earlier bombing appeared to be well-tended and healing.

Thanks to the man who'd shown himself this very day a spy and accomplice to the same injuries he'd tended.

Robin, who hadn't waited for Michael's invitation to tag along, glanced back at the security guard as they exited the brush corral. Reminding herself the militia uniform spoke no English, she looked at Michael. "If you won't say anything else, can you at least tell me the context of what that old man kept quoting? You said it was something your father preached about. Could it be some code he thought you'd understand? Something that would identify him or the son he mentioned?"

Michael slid the same glance back at the guard. "That's just it, I don't see how. It wasn't something my father said privately. He said it so often and so publicly, it was almost a joke in these parts. You've got to understand, my father was old enough to remember when the Belgians pulled out and Mobutu took power. And he was very much a product of his times. It wasn't that he didn't recognize injustices that concentrated wealth in the hands of white foreigners while reducing to servitude the local population. But he also remembered a stability long gone by the time Miriam and I came along. A time when one could travel from Taraja by road, train, and boat all the way to Kinshasa or Nairobi without so much as packing a gun. Like the Roman Empire, he used to say. The Romans weren't always just. But the stability, roads, and law they brought permitted early Christianity to spread the width and breadth of their empire.

"When the insurgencies started, Dad worried about his Taraja students and the local Christians listening to rebel promises of freedom and a more equitable society. He felt—with justification, as it turned out—that the insurgents were just thugs out for their own crack at the treasure chest. So he'd quote a verse to warn against sympathizing with the rebels. Isaiah chapter 5, verse 20: 'Woe to those who call evil good and good evil, who put darkness for light and light for darkness.'

"Of course the students and even the village leaders would argue back that the same verse could be applied to *mzungu* colonialists calling their system good instead of evil. And after independence, *mzungu* corporations who'd prop up their own pet dictators in exchange for lucrative mining concessions. My father would try to convince them Mobutu and his Western allies were at least better than the rebels. With less success as a new generation grew up. I remember going out to a village with my dad as a boy where their leader had some pretty strong words about making excuses for evil authority. He told my father that refusing to address injustices that pushed people into rebellion was as much calling evil good and good evil as the rebels themselves. That as a follower of Jesus Christ, he'd lived long enough to understand that teaching his people to live righteously was the only way true change would come to the Congo. But he could sympathize with the rebels' motivation and rage. That village was—" Michael's jaw suddenly snapped shut.

Glancing up, Robin spied a fleeting unreadable expression before his face went abruptly blank. "So you think he was making some oblique reference to Trevor Mulroney's local allies. That Wamba's so-called law enforcement being former insurgents somehow justifies the old man allying with Jini?"

But Michael was done reminiscing. Curtly, he cut Robin off with a sharp hand gesture. "If I had any specifics, you think I wouldn't spill them? That I don't want to stop a killer as much as you do? But let me say this. If you want to talk about calling evil good and good evil, you might want to look a little closer than Governor Wamba."

"Just what are you implying?" Robin stopped dead in Michael's path. "If that's another crack at Ares Solutions, all we're doing is the job we've contracted. And doing it well."

"That's what I'm afraid of."

She might have argued further. But a helicopter was angling in from the river, this one an Mi-17, and as Michael and Robin approached the Quonset hut, Pieter Krueger emerged, radio in hand, to call impatiently, "Duncan, that's our ride out, so wrap it up. And I need Stewart."

A disheveled, bloodied Ares Solutions team climbing down from the Mi-17 explained Krueger's demand. While assorted cuts and contusions had not been deemed serious enough to abandon their mission, there was a deep gash across Ernie Miller's cheekbone that had narrowly missed an eye. He reluctantly permitted Michael to clean the wound and put in stitches but brushed off his personal injury in fury at the mission's lack of success.

"We were right about the barge. Just as we'd counted on, the chopper spooked them into the river. We got a head count too before the op blew sky-high. Whatever force this Jini has stashed elsewhere, we counted only eight perps diving for cover when that chopper closed in. One of them looked small enough to be that boy Jacob. Whether that explosion was accidental or rigged, I couldn't begin to say. They couldn't have counted on getting clear in time, so I'm leaning to accidental. Either way, it created enough confusion that all but three insurgents escaped into the bush. We thought we'd treed a couple of them on this side of the river. Found a blood trail to indicate our door gunner in the chopper wounded at least one. But it turns out our perps climb like monkeys. Wounded or not, somehow they made it into the foliage where the chopper couldn't follow. Since we *don't* climb like monkeys, it was pointless to go after them until daylight.

"Once we did have light, we climbed the tree where the chopper team had seen two of them disappear. Managed to follow the blood trail across several hundred meters of canopy before losing it. Which means they could be kilometers away by now. And since Jensen tells me the rainforest is swarming with refugees from yesterday's raid, there's no way to pick out by aerial recon which are our fugitives!"

Ernie was even more furious over the elderly healer's death. "Who gave orders to fire? A mistake? How do you make a mistake like that, Makuga? If your guard didn't do this on purpose, he deserves to be strung up by the thumbs for sheer stupidity. Now we've not only lost our principal target, but we can't even question the mole. So where does that leave us?"

Samuel Makuga was scowling at the criticism, but Pieter Krueger responded calmly. "We still have our bush hunt. We froze the perimeter advance for yesterday's raids. If we'd nabbed Jini, we wouldn't need it. Since we didn't, we go back to our original plan. And we got the message, at least, so we know how news was getting to Jini. Clever using coconuts. As expected, this one warned of the threatened firebombing. But it also asked for an update on Taraja. Which indicates Jini *hasn't* been able to communicate inside the mine since the logging stopped."

"Which leaves the question, just who was our mole?" the Mi-17 pilot, Marius, spoke up. "Makuga, you handle prisoner labor. You must have some kind of database of prisoner IDs and criminal records. Who was this guy? What was his crime that sentenced him here?"

But the militia commander was unhelpful. "Who can tell? Prison workers are assigned by the authorities in Bunia. We do not ask who they are or what they have done, only if they can work. You will have to discuss such matters with Wamba himself."

"We do have some good news," Ernie interjected. "It took some climbing, but we followed signs from the river back to a nice little treetop hunting blind with a perfect line of sight to the mine. We found quite a cache of explosives, detonators, and other odds and ends. Even assault rifles such as your mine security carry, Makuga. Which means our ghost has been right under our noses since the beginning. And assuming he escaped empty-handed, we've at least crippled Jini's capacity to mount further attacks."

Robin saw Michael's intent gaze following the conversation as he packed up his brown medical bag. Was Krueger forgetting there was an outsider in their midst? Perhaps not because the South African immediately raised a hand to cut off discussion.

On their return flight, Marius again hovered onto the Taraja lawn to disgorge his extra passenger. Swinging down from the open side door, Michael shot Robin a pointed glance as he shouldered his medical bag. A reminder of her promise?

Though Robin had no time to make a report in any case as the C-130 cargo run was just taxiing toward the Ares Solutions camp when the Mi-17 touched down on the airstrip. Somewhere in its cavernous interior were medical supplies the Taraja clinic urgently needed. With the clinic no longer housing mine victims, Robin was anxious to deliver her requisition before someone—Pieter Krueger or Trevor Mulroney—decided such largesse was no longer called for.

Locating crates whose manifest matched her requisition list, she directed the militia uniforms unloading cargo to off-load them directly into the camp jeep. The militia had already uncovered their own private shipment because the entire group was chewing khat, pausing occasionally as they shifted pallets to spit out streams of green saliva.

It would be an easy matter to instigate a search for contraband if Robin's employer and Pieter Krueger both hadn't clearly opted for a hands-off approach to Wamba's underlings. And there was a point to be made that a stoned-to-the-gills militia might be less dangerous than a guard force with trigger fingers made twitchy by narcotics withdrawal.

So Robin simply directed several burlap sacks of cornmeal and rice to be added to the jeep load. *We won't miss them, and the Taraja staff have been feeding our patients along with caring for them.*

"That should be it. I'll have the Taraja people do the unloading, so you can return to your other duties." Robin slammed the jeep's rear hatch, then headed around the vehicle to the driver's side.

She might never have spotted the refugees were it not for the scream of terror and despair.

CHAPTER
TWENTY-FIVE

There were five of them, all children.

No, six. Robin modified her count, noting movement in a bundle tied around the back of the biggest child, a girl ten or twelve years old. They'd emerged from the shadows of towering hardwoods edging the end of the airstrip, and Robin might have assumed they were Taraja villagers were it not for their filthy, bedraggled appearance, lips cracked from dehydration, and the hollowed, bruised look in sunken eyes. Robin had seen that look of desolation too many times in the eyes of young war victims to mistake it.

Nor could she mistake the root of that terrified scream. The children had been running forward when they'd spotted the encampment, armed militia swarming around the C-130, the Mi-17 squatting just beyond. Already as Robin started toward them, the entire group was scrambling backward into the underbrush.

"Wait! Stop!" Robin called in Swahili. "Please don't go. We won't hurt you."

The smaller children had already disappeared under the foliage, but the girl with the bundle on her back stopped dead in her tracks. As she turned slowly around, Robin hurried forward. "Please, let me help you."

The girl remained poised like a deer about to take flight, but at Robin's soothing words, her shoulders eased slightly. "Is this Taraja, then? But the soldiers—"

"The soldiers won't hurt you. But no, this is not Taraja. See, up there is Taraja." Robin indicated the metal and thatched roofs protruding from vegetation across the airstrip. "But where did you all come from? How did you get here?"

"The soldiers burned our village." The girl's eyes were still wide with fear as she nodded past Robin. "Soldiers like those. My mother—when they came, she attacked the soldiers with a stick so I could run and hide with my brother. I saw the soldiers hit her! I saw blood. She had told me if there was danger, to flee to Taraja. That we would be safe there. We came once to the clinic by canoe, so I knew the way. Down the river toward the rising sun. Then to the right hand at the falls along another stream.

"When I heard shooting and saw the smoke of burning, I knew I must do as she said to save my brother. I found these others who had escaped too from the village. So I brought them with me. We ran from the soldiers all day. Then we hid in the forest all night. We heard noises of animals or hunting men that made the little ones cry. I told them they must be quiet or we would be killed. So they were quiet, and none came near us. This morning we came the rest of the path. I thought I had lost the way, but we are here."

Robin listened with horror and fury to the girl's simple narrative. It was one thing to see heat signatures scattering on a computer screen. Another to see and hear the living, breathing consequences of yesterday's raid. These children and their parents were the resisting villagers of whom Pieter Krueger had spoken so cavalierly?

Stooping down, the girl called softly. "You can come out. We are safe. The *mzungu* woman has sworn the soldiers will not touch us here."

There was a rustling in the brush. One by one, small bodies emerged. The smallest—another girl, by her twisted hair spikes, and no older than the massacre survivor, Rachel—whimpered, "Water? Please, water."

A responding whimper came from the biggest girl's bundle. Swinging it around from her back, the girl unloosed a knot to bring out a toddler perhaps two years old. Though limp and unresponsive, the child looked sturdy and well-fed, no light burden for a young girl's back.

"Please, my brother has not eaten or drunk anything since yesterday. These other little ones either. I have been so afraid some of them would die. If it is true those of Taraja will share food and water, I must take them there quickly."

The girl made no mention of her own needs, speaking matter-of-factly of what must have been a horrific ordeal, shepherding this band of children through a rainforest night and long jungle trail to safety. But Robin's heart twisted inside her to see tears coursing noiselessly down dirt-streaked cheeks. Anger and guilt battled inside Robin as well. All other horrors of this mission might be blamed on the insurgent leader Jini and his misdeeds. But these children's predicament could be laid at the feet of no one but the Ares Solutions team and their actions, however unavoidable and well-intentioned.

Robin was already hurrying over to the jeep to grab the knapsack she'd left sitting on the driver's seat. Her emergency food stash provided a protein bar for each child. Two bottles of water were emptied within moments. Once every crumb of food had followed, Robin nodded toward the jeep. "I am going up to Taraja right now. I will take you to those who will help you."

The children's furtive glances made Robin wonder how many motorized vehicles they'd ever seen. But they squeezed obediently into the front seat and on top of crates, the smallest on Robin's lap, their eyes wide with fear and wonder as the jeep jolted slowly across the airstrip and up the path.

By the time the jeep emerged from the tangle of brush and fruit trees to draw up at the clinic veranda, Robin had realized that her passengers were far from the first refugees to pour into Taraja. The veranda was packed with squatting bodies, some carrying bundles but most empty-handed. The large, open-sided thatched shelter that served Taraja as church and school also overflowed with humanity. More huddled in the open area between clinic and cinder-block mission house.

In all there had to be well upward of a hundred, the vast majority women and children, many small enough to be tied to backs. All had that exhausted, hollow-eyed look of fugitives from terror. A filthiness that came from mud and sweat and tears and in some cases blood.

To make matters worse, it had begun to rain. At first a soft patter. But as Robin stepped down from the jeep, it became a steady downpour that sent refugees squeezing even more frantically under cover of veranda and thatched shelter.

"Bibi Miriam. *Jambo*, Bibi Miriam. *Jambo.*"

Robin had already spotted Michael's sister among the huddled throng on the veranda. As Robin's passengers scrambled out, Miriam hurried over to the jeep. In a mass surge, the children threw themselves against the other woman's bright pagne. "Bibi Miriam, you are here!"

"Yes, I am here. You are safe." Wrapping her arms around as many small bodies as she could, Miriam looked up at Robin. "I know these children. We were out as a family at their village just last month. I did a youth camp with the kids while Michael and Ephraim held a medical clinic."

She spoke softly, coaxingly with the children in Swahili, then looked up again. "I'll take them to the mission house. I don't know where we'll squeeze them in. It's already full. But at least they'll be under a roof, and my two older boys can get them settled. They'll remember them from the village."

A village that no longer existed. Robin had been doing her best to keep the image of that village an ephemeral column of smoke rising anonymously from the jungle. Collateral damage, unfortunate but unavoidable. But Miriam's words, these children, made that village only too real a place. It had been a community, homes, families. Now it was gone.

But Miriam was looking past Robin into the jeep. "Oh, Robin, are those the supplies? Bless you! Ephraim, look what's here! And food, too. I don't suppose there's any hope there might be powdered milk in all that. As you can see, we're going to need it."

Ephraim had materialized from inside the clinic. As he called over volunteers to unload the jeep, Miriam shook her head with resignation. "When I was growing up, we learned to expect this kind of invasion any time there was insurgent unrest or attacks. With the hospital and airstrip, Taraja wasn't just the biggest community in the area, but the designated sanctuary. That stopped, of course, when Taraja was destroyed. Word's definitely out that we're back and open for business. We had an onslaught a few months ago, but nothing like this. But then those villages didn't have many survivors. At least we can now feed these ones, thanks to you."

"Yes, Taraja cannot thank you enough." The jeep now emptied, Ephraim walked over as crates and sacks disappeared inside the clinic. "Please convey our gratitude to your associates. Our brother, Michael, would wish to thank you as well, but he is in surgery. The removal of a bullet. Because of your generosity, there will be anesthetics for the operation."

The rain continued pouring, and as water trickled down her face, Robin fought to keep tears from intermingling. *You can thank us all right, but not for anesthetics! Would either of you be speaking to me so civilly if you knew just why these refugees have come here? Could it be Michael hasn't told you this isn't Jini's doing but ours? Maybe we needed to go into those villages. But did we need to burn them? To shoot people? Maybe one of these kids' parents is Michael's patient in there!*

Aloud she said stiffly, "It's a minimal compensation for all you've done. I'll see if I can round up more supplies for your new guests. I might even be able to do something about shelter."

By the time Robin reached her own base camp, the downpour had become a flood that threatened to turn the airstrip into a river. At least the C-130 had managed to take off. But the militia cargo detail were now out in the rain, sullenly stabbing shovels at the mud to create a runoff trench around the camp perimeter. Parking the jeep, Robin made a dash through water and mud up the steps to the communications trailer. There she found a dozen Ares Solutions operatives squeezed inside, but this time the video conference screen was blank. Pieter Krueger was speaking.

"That's it, then. The field teams will begin moving forward as soon as the rain stops. If all goes well, we'll start the final push at dawn. Any movement on ground level will be given opportunity to surrender. Now that we know our bad guys like to hide in trees, once a ground sweep is complete, we will assume any remaining human sign is a target. Marius, Willem, I want those Mi-17s ready if we need air strikes."

The South African broke off to direct a cool look at Robin as she joined the group. "You missed Mulroney's debrief. Not that you had much to add unless you know something about a short count in our cargo."

Robin recognized the paperwork on a clipboard he held up. "I just delivered the Taraja requisition. If you're talking about the missing grain bags, I'm going to need at least another twenty. Plus tents, blankets, and anything we can scare up for a couple hundred refugees. I'm thinking maybe three or four of the militia dormitory tents."

The field accommodations Ares Solutions had supplied their local allies were vintage campaign pavilions, each canvas structure capable of sleeping forty to fifty soldiers. With most of the Wamba contingent in the field preparing to spring that bush hunt trap, the tents stood largely empty at the moment. But even as Robin explained, Pieter Krueger was shaking his head. "Fugitives who've chosen to resist local law enforcement, then evade arrest, can hardly claim assistance or shelter from us."

"The majority are women and children," Robin argued. "And we're responsible for them being there. Responsible for any number of them losing their homes and villages. Unnecessarily too, as it turns out. Isn't this just the kind of PR nightmare Trevor Mulroney's been trying to avoid if we don't do something to help them?"

"And how exactly would that news get out?" Pieter Krueger sneered. "You think Trevor Mulroney's going to let the press anywhere near this op? But come to think of it, if you're talking refugees who've evaded our roundup, maybe it's not such a bad idea to gather them in one place. Give us a chance to interrogate them, make sure our escaped barge fugitives haven't slipped into the crowd."

Alarmed, Robin was already shaking her head. "You can't be serious! You saw how much you got out of the Taraja villagers when Wamba's men rampaged through there. These people aren't even local. You spook them, they're only going to disappear again into the jungle. There's infants among them, and some of the women are clearly pregnant. Do you want them on your conscience wandering around again without food and water in the jungle?"

"She's got a point," Ernie Miller spoke up. "You send Makuga and his boys up there, we just tip off anyone with intel to make a run. But Duncan here's another woman, no obvious threat. She speaks the language. She could move around that camp without raising red flags."

Pieter Krueger eyed Robin speculatively before giving an abrupt nod. "I can buy that. You get your tents and supplies. In return, I'm assigning you personally to check out every person in that camp. Run that photo past them. Make sure there's no male refugee with a scar meeting Jini's description. You got a problem with that, just say so, and I'll send Makuga instead."

"It's basically what I did as liaison in Afghanistan," Robin responded. "And I'll be happy to do the job if it'll keep Wamba's drugged-up thugs away."

"Then get a move on. Miller, if we're done here, you can borrow some of Wamba's boys to move those tents. I assume you have no objection to that," Krueger addressed Robin sarcastically.

"Actually, I do," Robin said. "If we can get the tents down and loaded into the jeep, I'll see if the Taraja staff can scramble volunteers to set them back up. That way the refugees won't have to come face-to-face with the same uniforms that burned their villages."

"Whatever!" Thrusting his clipboard under his arm, Pieter Krueger headed for the door. "Just don't forget Mulroney will be here tomorrow. You want that fat contract bonus, we need some serious progress by then. Preferably Jini in hand, dead or alive."

Want that bonus? Robin needed that bonus. Desperately. Robin suddenly realized she hadn't so much as thought of her sister and niece in a full day. How had she let herself get so caught up in the concerns of these Ituri residents that she'd lost sight of the most vital concern in her life?

The downpour outside had tapered off to a drizzle by the time she'd finished wrestling a fresh load of supplies into the jeep. With Pieter Krueger's lackluster go-ahead, she'd permitted herself generosity in pillaging the supply depot, adding jugs of vegetable oil, salt, sugar, and oatmeal to sacks of rice, corn, beans. She found no powdered milk but commandeered an entire flat of canned evaporated milk.

Her own task complete, she grabbed the chance to change her damp clothing while Ernie Miller tied the collapsed tents onto the roof of the jeep. Hanging the rain poncho she'd been wearing from a tent pole to dry, she unearthed her cell phone to hit Kelli's speed dial number. There was no answer, but Robin's voice mail proved to hold a new message.

"Robin, I'm heading to the hospital with Kristi, so no phone until we're home. She . . . she isn't doing as well as we'd hoped. But Brian's doing everything he can. And if you can hurry with—you know. I'm just a little worried time is running out!"

If there'd been the tears and melodrama she'd known so often from her sister rather than quiet, even resigned control, the message would have left Robin less worried. With deliberate effort, she shoved it from her mind. *I can't do anything about Kelli and Kristi right now from here. I can do my job. Do my part in putting an end to this. For Kristi and for these people.*

But as Robin hurried out to where Ernie was tugging tight the ropes that bound folded canvas material to the top of the jeep, she burst out, "Ernie, there's something I've wanted to ask you. What we've been doing these last few days. Attacking and burning those villages. The men killed last night. Those threats to firebomb the jungle. Is this the kind of thing you expected when you signed up for this contract? It just seems—well, I'll admit it's more than I counted on. We came here to help these people. But it seems so far all we've done is hurt them. And for what? Especially since it turns out none of the villages were harboring Jini and his men. I can't get out of my head those kids walking all night through the jungle. It's only our luck none of them died out there. At least that we know of. I guess what I'm asking is, would you have taken this job if you'd known what we'd be asked to do? And that threat to firebomb the rainforest—would you actually obey such an order if Pieter Krueger gave it?"

The Vietnam vet gave one last hard tug on the ropes as his grizzled eyebrows shot high. "What I expected? You bet it is! This is hardly my first op in Africa or the messiest. And you bet I'd carry out that fire-bombing if that's what's needed to take out our target. I'm surprised at you, Duncan. Why so squeamish? You're a Marine, right? Spent time in Afghanistan? How many night raids did your unit carry out? How many sweeps for Taliban in civilian villages?"

"But that was different." How was it Robin now found herself offering up the same arguments Michael had once made to her? "Our governments were at war. We were following the rules of engagement. Those villages were harboring Taliban. At least our intel gave us reason to believe so."

"You think the local Afghan villagers made that distinction?"

A twisted smile distorted the Vietnam vet's hard mouth. "I'm guessing you've never had to kill someone in combat. Of course not. You're a woman. For you combat training is an exercise in skill, not survival! Well, let me tell you something you didn't learn in boot camp. Or in Afghanistan, apparently. This is no love fest out here. It's war. We're not here to worry about the villagers' feelings. Or even their well-being. We're here to complete the mission. You're a good kid, Duncan. I like you. But don't get to thinking that just because Frank and I are fellow Americans we're some kind of knights in shining armor!

"You want to know why we quit the Green Berets to go freelance? Bottom line: after Vietnam, the tactics we utilized—tactics that could have won that war—were no longer politically correct back home. Frank and I went Agency for a while. CIA for you greenhorns. We put our particular skills on the line for our country plenty of times in Central America and other places. But eventually what we had to offer no longer fit the ethos of American foreign policy. So we ended up down here fighting for pay.

"Don't get me wrong. We're not butchers or monsters like some we've worked with. We've got our own rules of engagement we don't cross. But in the end, finishing a mission quickly can be the best way to save lives. Or have you forgotten how much civilian blood Jini's insurgency has left behind here already? Maybe it does seem harsh. And sure, the local villagers aren't happy right now. But if we can empty this zone of civilians, plaster it with firepower, catch this guy, then those same villagers will finally be free to rebuild in peace.

"And I'm sure Earth Resources will offer some kind of compensation for damages. It's not like they can't afford it. If you're so concerned, make that your mission when this is over. You seem to be good at talking favors out of Trevor Mulroney. In the meantime, collateral damage comes with the territory of making war. Having compassion on the enemy, even a civilian enemy, is a luxury you can afford only after the war is won. And if you can't deal with that, Krueger's right. You're a liability to this operation."

Robin felt as though she'd been slapped. Why had she assumed Ernie would see things her way? Because he was a countryman? And any countryman of hers wouldn't do things that Third World mercenaries like Samuel Makuga or even Pieter Krueger might do without blinking an eye?

With dignity, she responded, "I've never found showing compassion a liability to doing my job either as a Marine or an Ares Solutions operative. And rest assured you won't find me a liability on this mission. Now if you'll excuse me, I'll get this up to Taraja and start carrying out my orders."

Robin kept a smile on her face as she climbed behind the jeep's steering wheel. But inside she was rebelling. *They keep saying this is war! But it isn't! At least not as defined by any government or military I know. When the Marines went into Afghanistan, someone in authority sent us there. And watched to make sure we followed rules of engagement. Maybe Ernie's right that this is the best and even safest way to finish off Jini and his insurgency.*

But Michael's right too. Where is our accountability to make absolutely sure we're doing the right thing?

And for the right reasons?

CHAPTER TWENTY-SIX

It took the rest of the afternoon to get tents pitched, volunteers digging trenches to drain away rainwater before spreading the canvas floors. Robin ferried up two more loads of supplies in the jeep. On the final load, Ernie Miller accompanied her to drive back the jeep for camp use while Robin stayed on to make inquiries among the refugees. Miriam and the Taraja staff were everywhere, separating those needing medical care, setting up communal kitchens, mixing evaporated milk and boiled water for infants and toddlers without mothers to breast-feed. But Robin didn't catch sight of Michael or Ephraim until dusk, when the two doctors emerged from the clinic to walk around the encampment, stepping into each tent to speak to refugees who'd staked out sleeping spots on the canvas floors.

Robin had already completed one such round, satisfying herself no one among the refugees matched Jini's description or scar. But more refugees continued to filter in throughout the afternoon, so her original estimate had doubled. For which reason she'd begun a second round. She'd checked a male newcomer's left arm for scars and was showing him Jini's photo when Michael and Ephraim entered the tent with Miriam at their heels. The refugee held an infant in his arms, and a small boy clung to his side. He shook his head at the photo as he explained unhappily that his wife had been taken to the clinic. Did Robin know if the *docteur* was finished with her yet?

"Robin!" Michael crossed the tent with quick strides. "Miriam's told me you're responsible for supplying all this. So Mulroney did come through. Maybe I had the wrong idea about the man. I can't tell you how much we appreciate this."

"It was the least we owed you," Robin answered, then lowered her voice. "I—your sister seems to think this is Jini's doing. Why didn't you tell Miriam and Ephraim how these people ended up here?"

Michael made a dismissive gesture. "What would be the point? The damage is already done. The only purpose served by telling them who's really at fault here would be . . ."

As he trailed off, Robin finished quietly for him. "To make them think even worse of me than they already do. That wasn't necessary, but it was kind of you."

Michael's jaw tightened. "I wasn't thinking of you, but of Miriam. She's been through enough. She doesn't need any more disappointment. Above all from you."

But Michael's glance had now dropped to the photo in Robin's hand. Stunned realization banished any appreciation from his face as he snatched it from her grip. "So this is why you were checking that man's arm when we walked in? And why Mulroney's suddenly shown himself so generous! Not out of altruism, but to get a spy in here to poke around. Do you guys never let up? You really think your ghost is dumb enough to walk into this little trap?"

"No, I don't!" Robin hissed back. "But poking around, as you put it, was the only grounds on which Krueger would sign off for supplies and tents. And your choice was me or Makuga! I assumed you'd rather have me up here making discreet inquiries than a bunch of armed soldiers. And that you cared more about getting these people under cover and fed than your stupid little feud against Ares Solutions."

Michael didn't answer but strode away to speak to another refugee family. Hurrying up, Miriam slipped an arm around Robin's shoulder. "Don't mind my brother. Michael's normally pretty easygoing. But he's been in surgery all afternoon, and they just lost the final patient. Another gunshot wound. A young mother who's left two children. It's always hard to lose a patient, especially one who shouldn't have died. But she'd lost too much blood by the time Michael got to her. When he calms down, he'll be willing to recognize how much you've done for these people. I don't know what we'd have done without you today. Especially considering these people aren't your responsibility."

Yes, they are! We did this! Stop being so nice to me! Guilt and shame churned in Robin. Could it be the woman who'd died was the wife of that young refugee father, mother to that infant and small boy?

Then her turmoil hardened to anger. *No, we didn't do this. At least not alone! If there's a Creator of all this mess up there listening and watching, then he's allowed Jini to terrorize this jungle. Allowed today's events to happen. So where's the real responsibility? God, do you weep when you watch a mother dying on a jungle clinic operating table? A little girl having to shoulder her baby brother because her mother was taken away? A four-year-old living in and out of a hospital? Or do you just shrug and say, "Too bad, those humans got what they deserved"?*

"Come on, Robin." Miriam had a firm hold of Robin's elbow. "Everyone's fed and sheltered now. And you've been working hard all day. So how about we let the men finish their rounds and see what we can do about a cup of tea."

Like some irresistible whirlwind, Miriam swept Robin out of the tent. "And your niece—Kristi, right? How's she doing? My kids have added her to their bedtime prayers. They'll be asking for an update."

"Actually, I'm not sure. I got a voice message saying my sister has taken her to the hospital. But I couldn't reach them to get any details." Robin swallowed hard to keep her worry, frustration, anger, and exhaustion of the last hours from her even tone. But Miriam's searching look indicated she was not successful.

With the moon not yet risen and rain clouds still pregnant overhead, the only illumination as the two women headed toward the mission house was from the dying embers of a cook fire and a single lantern hanging from a rafter of the thatched community shelter. Near the front of the shelter, two men had begun a soft staccato on hollowed-out sections of wood. Robin recognized the drummers as Taraja residents who'd helped unload the jeep and set up tents.

The refugees had already finished a simple meal of rice and lentils, the cleanup easy since sections of banana frond had served as plates. But several women were pounding out cassava flour in a pair of waist-high wooden mortars to make *kwanga* bread for tomorrow's breakfast. In an open area between tents and mission house, children ran circles in some unidentifiable game. Among them Robin spotted Miriam's boys and small daughter along with the refugee children she'd directed to Taraja. Laughter rose from the scampering band, so it was hard to believe a few hours ago these playing children had been lost, terrified, hungry, and thirsty. A resilience of human nature to which Robin had also been witness in too many war zones.

A drifting of adults had emerged as well from tents and thatched huts to squat down under the thatched shelter. As the drummers shifted rhythm, voices rose in a chorus Robin had heard before from the Taraja residents. *"Yesu, nuru ya ulimwengu."*

"Jesus, Light of the World." An odd image in such a dark place.

The song switched to one familiar not just in Swahili, its simple words among the earliest songs learned by children in every corner of the planet. *"Yesu anipenda."*

"Jesus loves me, this I know."

In the midst of their game, the shrill soprano of children picked up the refrain. "Yes, Jesus loves me. . . ."

The song spread from thatched shelter to tents, so the drummers increased the volume of their syncopated staccato, its simple melody taking on bass, tenor, alto harmonies so rich and complex any additional musical instruments would be superfluous. *"Yesu anipenda."*

Robin should not have been astonished. The Congolese were a churchgoing people, Christianity deeply rooted in village life after generations of missionaries like the Stewarts. But after all these people had endured over recent days, over the space of their lives, the miserable history of their land, after all the contrary evidence offered up to them, how were those confident, optimistic lyrics possible?

The two women had now entered the mission house. Miriam reached to turn on a light whose power came from those solar panels on the roof. "Make yourself comfortable. I'll get the tea started."

As Miriam crossed the room, she sang along softly, not in the Swahili filtering through open windows, but the English of her own and Robin's childhood heritage. "Yes, Jesus loves me! Yes, Jesus loves me!"

Robin's reaction was as instinctive as it was harsh. "Don't! Stop! How can you sing that? How can *they* sing that? How . . . how can you let them believe such a terrible, cruel lie?"

Miriam ceased her singing, and though she did not lose her smile, there was astonishment in her stare. Then, more irritatingly, pity as she turned to nudge the teakettle onto glowing coals. "Oh, Robin, it isn't a lie. Far from it! It's their hope, our hope, that no matter what's happened today out there, no matter what will happen tomorrow, the almighty Creator of the universe loves us so much he came to earth to walk among us in the form of a man, Jesus Christ, to show us the way out of this world's darkness into his light."

"Hope!" Robin slid into a chair at the table. But she sat rigidly, hands clenched in her lap. This was not a discussion she wanted to have with a virtual stranger whose cheerful Pollyanna attitude despite the distortion of that badly healed scar was as incompatible with this setting as it was downright exasperating. But she'd held back for too long the words now spilling out in a stumbling, furious stream.

"What a joke! So do you believe in Santa Claus too? Oh, sure, I used to buy God's love. I sang 'Jesus loves me' as a kid in Swahili as well as English before my mother—" Robin choked off the rest of the memory. "I've always basically accepted the Bible. Even in Afghanistan with all I witnessed—well, going to chaplain services there, I . . . I started to buy it all again."

Robin stopped, blinking hard, until Miriam prompted gently, "Yes, Michael mentioned when he wrote that you and your brother attended services with him. So what happened to make you doubt God's love? You're so angry. I thought it was Michael you were angry at. But it's not Michael. It's God, isn't it?"

The absurdity of her words gave Robin voice again. "How can you ask what happened? I stopped believing in a God of love the same time I stopped believing in your brother. Okay, so I was wrong about Michael. But—God? What kind of God lets a twenty-one-year-old genius with so much to offer bleed out his life while he just watches it happen? What kind of God takes away your family and your dreams one after another until you can't bear to dream again? And you're afraid to love again because you know it's only a matter of time until God takes that away too! And you keep fighting because you can't just give up. But there's no point in that fight because there's no way you can win out against God."

Robin broke off again. She'd given away far more than she'd intended in that answer. Easing into a chair across the table, Miriam responded quietly, "You're thinking of Kristi. You're assuming because you lost your mother, your father, your brother, that you're going to lose her, too. That you have to fight for her life because God won't. And maybe you're right. Maybe you will lose Kristi, too. I can't pretend to know God's plan for your niece's life or yours. If you do lose another loved one, you're hardly unique in that."

Robin stared at the other woman. Soft though they were, Miriam's words carried an implacability at sharp odds with the unmistakable sympathy in amber eyes. "What you're really saying is you believed in God's love so long as your own life was going fine. And now that you've had to endure loss and suffering, now that your own dreams haven't all come true, that must mean God doesn't truly love."

Gently, kindly, but still implacably, Miriam went on. "So just who do you think you are to write off God because your own life hasn't turned out as you feel it should? Take a look around you! Take a look outside! You've hardly had a monopoly on human suffering. At worst, you've had food in your belly, a roof over your head, medical attention. Plenty of people in those tents have lost loved ones to sickness, war, famine, even before everything they've endured today. Or do you somehow think you should be exempt because you're a rich *mzungu* from a rich, comfortable country where parents don't have to watch their children starve to death and families don't have to watch loved ones cut down by war?"

The accusation stung—above all because it held some merit. Robin shook her head, again wanting to end this discussion but unexpectedly reluctant to leave her companion with such a poor and inaccurate opinion of her. *Why do you care what she thinks of you?*

"You have it all wrong. It's because I *don't* think I'm exempt, because I *know* I'm not unique, that I find all this . . . optimism of yours so untenable. Believe me, I never once asked, 'Why me?' when my mother died in that embassy bombing. After all, hundreds of Kenyans lost family members that day too. Nor when my father dropped us off like abandoned packages with a relative and we lost our dad, too. Nor even when Chris died, which seemed so much worse because we were so close. Nor when Kristi was born so sick. Like you said, what right would I ever have to complain? I've still had food to eat, a roof over my head, medical care for Kristi.

"If I'm angry, it's because I *have* seen so much worse suffering than my own. Haiti. Sierra Leone. Sudan. So many refugee camps. So many kids so malnourished they'll never be normal no matter how many nutrients we pour into their mouths. Women, little girls, and boys, too, who've been . . . wounded so badly they'll never be able to enjoy normal marriage and kids of their own. And those are the lucky ones we can reach. Or maybe it's the dead ones who are lucky."

The tears that had threatened all day pressed at the backs of Robin's eyelids, stung in her sinuses. But the very anger of which Miriam had accused her stiffened her shoulders, steadied her voice to dispassionate, analytical inquiry.

"You see, that's what I don't get. I'm not the heathen you seem to think. I believe what my mother taught me, what I learned in Sunday school. God created this world. God is all-powerful, all-knowing, all-present. God sent his Son to die on a cross for those lucky few who live somewhere in the world where they've been taught to believe in Jesus so they can be saved. Maybe 'Jesus loves me' is true for those few too. But what does that make the rest of humanity? Expendable crewmen?

"And that's where I have a problem. I would give my own life to stop the pain I've seen. To stop little girls and boys from being raped. Or just as bad, forced into armies where they're turned into killers like Wamba's militia. To keep families from being torn apart by war. Children dying of preventable diseases for lack of a dollar's worth of medicine. I don't have the power to do all that. But the Creator of this universe sure does!"

Robin's gesture encompassed the huddled refugees outside night-darkened screens and an entire world beyond. "So am I more compassionate than the God who created all these people, created all this beauty? There's the question, and I've never yet found anyone who can give me a credible answer. How can an all-powerful God who claims to love humanity look down on our planet and watch such unspeakable things happening, innocent people hurting and dying, bad guys winning over and over again, so *much* suffering, without it breaking his heart? And not just multiplied thousands, no, millions of times all over our world. But year after year, generation after generation, century after century without ever reaching down and putting a stop to it?

"Unless God *isn't* watching. The human experiment hasn't gone so well, and he's just walked away and left us to finish killing ourselves off from our own greed and stupidity and meanness. That I can understand. Bottom line, if God doesn't waste his compassion on a broken world, why should we? Me, I keep it simple. I love my niece. I love my sister. I'd give my life for them. Maybe . . . maybe someday, however unlikely that seems now, I'll even love a man and children of my own."

Robin had not heard the front door opening over the music outside, so only the lift of Miriam's eyes, her acknowledging nod, turned Robin's head. Michael's lean, muscled frame rested against the doorpost.

Michael's quizzical gaze met Robin's. How much had he heard?

Robin turned her head so she could no longer see Michael as she finished defiantly, "But if there's one thing I've learned these last few years, it's that you can't save the whole world. You can't love the whole world. Especially people you can do nothing to help anyway. Who only too likely would just hurt you if they had opportunity. All you can do is protect your own heart, your own life, your own survival. And sometimes, when you can, your own family."

In Robin's peripheral vision, boots crossed the concrete floor. A chair scraped back from the desk. As the solar-powered computer screen blinked to life, lean hands settled a Skype headset into place.

Robin added hastily, "Of course I didn't mean by any of that to criticize the admirable mission you and your husband are carrying out here at Taraja. I . . . I must sound horribly self-centered and negative."

Robin had prided herself on keeping her voice light and detached. This was a philosophical discussion, not the hemorrhaging of a long-contained heart wound. But something of those pent-up emotions had betrayed her in face or eyes, because unbelievably, the tears Robin refused to let spill now shimmered instead in Miriam's own gentle eyes.

"Oh, Robin, I wish I could show you just how wrong you are. Believe me, love is never wasted, no matter how much it hurts. As to loving people who are just going to hurt you, isn't that exactly what our Savior, Jesus Christ, did? 'Jesus loves me, this I know.' It's no fairy tale. It's an unshakable truth of this universe."

Miriam stretched a hand across the table. "As for you, have you been listening to yourself? If you were self-centered, you wouldn't care so much about the suffering of others. Be so angry at God on their behalf. And say what you like about protecting yourself—what you've done here today hardly seems like someone who doesn't believe in wasting love or compassion. All those medical supplies, tents, food. Those kids you found down in your own camp. You could have just walked away, shooed them off like the trespassers they were. I'll bet that didn't even occur to you, did it?"

"No, of course not," Robin began.

But Miriam cut her off with a dismissive wave. "There is no 'of course not'! Believe me, we've seen countless people walk away over the years. You didn't because you cared about those kids. Because that same compassion you speak of burned in your heart so that you couldn't turn your back on them. But can't you see that very compassion burning in you for hurting people is in itself evidence of how much God loves this world? Because like you said, do you really think you are more compassionate than the Creator of all these people? Who do you think puts that compassion for others in your heart?

"You asked why God doesn't just reach down into this world to put an end to suffering. But that's exactly what he did when he stepped into human time and space in the person of Jesus Christ. And that's what he's doing every time he sends someone like you here today to be the human hands and feet of his love to a hurting world. Wouldn't you agree, Michael?"

Miriam's query allowed Robin to overhear Michael's response on the Skype link. "You're sure about that? . . . No, I wish I could say it was a surprise. . . . Yes, I'll send you the info. . . . That's right. . . . Keep me posted. Over and out."

Michael's strong fingers now flew over the keyboard. But from his ironic glance across the room, he'd been following the two women's conversation. "I think Robin here would be the first to point out that those generous contributions you mentioned came from Trevor

Mulroney, not her own pocket. And believe me, Sister dear, a man like Mulroney does nothing for completely altruistic reasons."

Was Michael still thinking this was only about mounting a spy campaign in the refugee camp? Robin jumped to her feet. "Michael's right. I can't take credit for anything here today. That stuff all came from mission supplies, not from me. And now I've intruded on you long enough. If you need anything else, don't hesitate to let me know."

"Oh no, please don't go yet!" Miriam rose hastily to her own feet. "I haven't even served your tea. Or the scones I made. I am a terrible hostess! And Michael—he didn't mean it the way it sounded. Even if all that stuff came from your employers, do you think we don't know who went out on a limb to get it here for us? Michael, do you have something to add?"

The fierce look Miriam directed across the room was so un-characteristic of Michael's gentle younger sister—rather like a kitten glaring at a misbehaving Saint Bernard—that Robin had to swallow a smile. Michael didn't bother. His firm mouth quirking upward, he pulled off the Skype headset to stride over to the table.

"I didn't mean to downplay your role in this, Robin. Like my sister, I am not unaware that Trevor Mulroney would never have coughed up so generously without you pushing the matter. And I hope you'll reconsider rushing off. Miriam makes a mean pot of tea and scones. She'd be terribly disappointed if you didn't stay to try them."

Robin was already subsiding back into her chair. However uncomfortable Michael seemed to go out of his way to make her feel, she would not bring further distress to this sweet, kindly woman who was her hostess.

The teakettle was now singing its own quiet song. Miriam poured hot water into a teapot, then lifted a cloth to reveal a plate of freshly baked scones. She carried the plate along with a sugar bowl and jar of orange marmalade to the table and poured three cups of tea.

"I'm afraid there's no milk," she apologized, pushing sugar bowl, scones, and marmalade over to Robin. "We'd given out what little we had in stock before you brought up the new supplies."

"This is perfect." Robin spooned sugar into her tea, then accepted a scone, shaking her head at the marmalade. "But how in the world did you bake scones without an oven?"

"It's a campfire recipe my mother taught me. I bake them in a cast-iron skillet." Sliding back into her seat, Miriam smiled at Robin. "Please, eat up! And I hope you won't mind if I give an answer to what you asked earlier."

Miriam stirred sugar into her own tea as she continued. "It's just what you brought up is something I've done a lot of thinking about. You ask how a God of love can tolerate so much human suffering. To me, it's the other way around. The real question is how a God of justice can possibly tolerate human choices.

"You see, everything you've mentioned—all the war, starvation, suffering, broken and hurting families—they've all come about through human actions. Human choices. Not God's. Oh yes, there's natural disasters too. But for the most part it's human beings choosing to do selfish, unkind, cruel things to each other. Other human beings choosing not to take a stand to stop it. Preferring to look after their own comfort and their own interests and their own families and their own village and their own tribe and their own country and so on instead of working together."

Miriam set her spoon down on her saucer. "And that to me is one good reason why a God of love can't just wave a wand and void all human suffering. Not here in the Congo or anywhere else. Because if we never experience the ultimate consequences of our own actions, how are we ever to learn how ugly and evil those actions are? It's like some well-meaning parent who rushes to bail out their adolescent delinquent every time the kid indulges in petty theft, shoplifting, drunk driving, whatever, paying off the fines and restitution so their kid doesn't end up in jail. Then they wonder why the kid ends up instead a full-fledged criminal with no moral conscience as an adult.

"Call human suffering God's equivalent of tough love. Like those doting parents, maybe you and I *would* keep waving that wand and canceling out the ugly consequences of human choices. But God, who happens to see and know a whole lot more than we ever can, has in his infinite wisdom chosen to let the human race experience the ultimate consequences of our greed, violence, hate, war. Unfortunately, as you've pointed out, any number of those we would call innocent get swept up in those consequences."

Miriam's dark, silky eyebrows knit together above a slim-bridged nose as she laid out one measured phrase after another. "So the question is: Why doesn't God at least protect those who don't deserve to be hurt? Why should innocent people have to suffer for the sins of others? If the purpose for human suffering is to punish wrongdoing, well, that's certainly justified from the viewpoint of a holy God. But it's not so easy to see God's love in it.

"Unless God sees some greater purpose for the suffering he permits in our lives. A value to us that we just can't grasp while we're in the middle of it. You see, once you accept that God really, truly loves us, that he *is* love, that he wants nothing more than the absolute best for our lives, it's the only thing that makes sense."

Miriam looked anxiously at Robin. "Oh, dear, this must be way more than you wanted to hear."

"No, no, please, go on." Rather to Robin's own surprise, her quick reassurance was not simply politeness. The thought processes of this young woman were beginning to fascinate her. "I mean, I'm the one who asked."

"Well, if you're sure." When Miriam reached to pick up a volume sitting on a shelf, Robin was not surprised to see that it was a well-thumbed Bible. "I'll try not to get too preachy. But the Bible has a lot to say about God permitting suffering in our lives. The book of Job in the Old Testament is one such story that doesn't quite make sense to our human thinking. Satan makes an accusation that Job is only following God because God has given Job the perfect life. A wife and ten kids. Wealth. Respect of friends and neighbors. So God tells Satan he can strip everything from Job but his life. Which Satan does.

"I won't unload the whole thing on you, since I'm guessing you know the basic story. Job never renounces faith in God. But he sure throws a lot of questions at God. Yells and screams them, in fact. And though God eventually restores all Job had lost, he never does explain his reasons. Instead it's Job who ends up recognizing that God has every right to do whatever he chooses with Job's life. But there's one thing Job had to say even while yelling and screaming at God that has become engraved on my own mind. Especially since he wasn't saying it about Satan, but about God, whom Job very correctly pinpointed as the one ultimately responsible for his suffering. Chapter 23, verse 10 of the book that bears his name. 'When he—' that is, God—'has tested me, I will come forth as gold.'"

As she spoke, Miriam was flipping through pages marked with highlighted passages and scribbled notes. "The image is of a smith melting down gold in a blazing furnace to produce an unadulterated metal refined of all impurities. The same image is used over and over in Scripture in reference to God's purpose behind human suffering and tribulation. Not to be cruel. Or to punish. But to refine our character. To make us strong and mature in our faith. In fact, we're told we should actually rejoice in our tribulations because of their value to our lives. The entire first letter of the apostle Peter in the New Testament is one long treatise on that subject. But the verse I've come to cling to in the dark hours of my own night is in Paul's epistle to the Romans, chapter 5, verses 3 and 4: 'We also rejoice in our sufferings, because we know that suffering produces perseverance; perseverance, character; and character, hope.'"

Miriam's nose wrinkled as she looked up from the worn pages. "I'll admit I never paid much attention to all those bits of Scripture growing up. Maybe because my own life was so happy, so ideal in many ways. Surrounded by the beauty of Africa. A family that loved me. My Congolese brothers and sisters in Christ who also showed me nothing but love. I guess I was pretty innocent or maybe just plain selfish because I never really saw that even then the world was so much less sunny for so many around me."

Robin understood exactly where the other woman was coming from. Had she herself as a child in Kenya ever seen beyond the beauty of Africa to its suffering? Miriam's amber gaze grew shadowed.

"All of which meant that when the reality of a very dark, cruel world did come crashing in . . . well, like you, I couldn't understand how the heavenly Father whose love had always been the rock on which I counted could let such things happen to me. Much less expect me to actually rejoice in those trials. It took me a while, years in fact, to finally glimpse at least a little just what that Scripture means, about the fires of suffering and pain refining like gold. Producing character and perseverance. Yes, and hope. A hope that isn't only about everything going right."

Miriam focused her gaze on Robin as though withdrawing her thoughts from distant memory. "I guess what I'm trying to say is, you seem a really nice, caring person, Robin Duncan. You see all those people out there, the Congolese people as a whole, as victims who need rescuing and your pity. And you want to help them. To give them a better, easier life. Which is certainly laudable.

"But—please don't take this as criticism—but I've been in your country. My parents' country. People there have for the most part exactly the kind of life you're suggesting God owes every human being. A roof overhead. Electricity and running water. Plenty of food and clothes. Education. A car, maybe even two. Freedom from constant fear and war. And yet can you honestly say having so much has made all the people in your country smarter, better, harder-working, more caring human beings than the rest of the planet?"

Robin had no answer. How well she remembered that initial bewilderment coming from Nairobi to a South Carolina middle school. Her new peers focused on the latest MTV pop star, video game, designer label as though they had no consciousness of a vast, dark world where things like bombs blew up other children's mothers. Nor could Robin, the pampered daughter of privileged expatriates, claim any superiority, for all her pride in a wider worldview and the pain of recent tragedy.

She smiled wryly. "Hey, I'll be the first to admit it wasn't prosperity, education, or any of those benefits that taught me what little I can claim to know of character, discipline, honor. It was the meanest, nastiest drill sergeant a Marine boot camp ever possessed. And Afghanistan."

Robin's glance slid to Michael, quietly consuming his refreshment. His gaze met hers in a brief moment of shared memories before he sloped a half smile toward his sister.

"I'm with Robin. Coming stateside from a Congo rainforest, I figured I was tougher than my college peers. But it wasn't until the furnace blast of combat drops in Afghanistan that I really learned endurance and discipline. I guess it's human nature to want the next generation to have advantages we didn't have. I know what kind of dreams Mom and Dad had for the two of us. Problem is, prosperity can also spawn arrogance, entitlement, laziness. So when we get our way in making life easier for the next generation, we also discover they don't have the strength, resourcefulness, ingenuity that were the products of hardship in our own lives. In trying to make life easier for others, we can end up simply crippling them as human beings."

"That's just what I was trying to say!" Miriam responded eagerly. "Not that I'm suggesting deliberately making life hard for people. But—well, take the Congo, for instance. For all its problems, Michael can testify with me that we've seen this country, this life produce some of the most resilient, hardworking, sharing, compassionate people this planet holds. They have strength and endurance precisely because they've survived so much. They're unbelievably resourceful. Foreigners who would dismiss them as lazy have never seen a bicycle peddler pushing flour and salt hundreds of kilometers for no more than a few francs' profit to feed his family. The Congolese have a spirit of generosity that doesn't just care for their own but will take in every relative and neighbor left homeless by war when they don't even have food to feed themselves. And somehow, despite war, hunger, loss, they can keep on singing!"

Miriam's gesture was toward the nearest window, its open shutters offering a clear view of the drummers squatted below that dangling lantern, their sticks tapping across hollowed wood so quickly it was impossible to make out individual movements. The audience was clapping to the beat, and a few energetic souls had jumped up to pound out a rhythmic counterpoint with their feet.

"Though, believe me, much as I love this country, I'm not blind to the negatives. The Congo is such a rich, huge place that should work, should prosper, if its people would just lay aside their differences, forgive, work together. If its leaders would just pour resources into building this country instead of filling their own pockets. Even that spirit of generosity can work against them because it leads to nepotism, handing out resources or positions to family members and friends instead of the best qualified and most deserving. And I'm certainly not blind to those, far too many, who've chosen to kill, rob, oppress their own countrymen."

Miriam slanted Robin a rueful smile. "To sum up—and I do apologize for taking so long to get here—the biggest purpose I've come to glimpse behind why God permits so much darkness and suffering and injustice in this world is just what that life verse of mine says. Darkness, suffering, injustice are the very things that show the measure of a person's true character as peace and comfort never can. After all, without the darkness, how could we ever measure the light? Without the trials, without the option to choose unspeakable evil, we wouldn't truly be free to choose things like courage, honor, sacrifice, endurance.

"And that's just what I've been privileged to witness here in the Congo, in the midst of all the ugliness. The young man who, instead of picking up a machete to avenge his family, risks his life to save a village not even of his own tribe. The woman who, instead of grabbing as much aid as possible, shares her last cup of cassava flour with another hungry family. The pastor who refuses to escape the rebel militia in order to minister to wounded and dying in their last hours. So much beauty of human character and spirit. A beauty that would not be there without the ugliness because it's a beauty, as Job described, refined and purified to shining gold by the furnace of war and pain and suffering.

"Which brings me to the inescapable conclusion that somehow, somewhere beyond what my limited mind can grasp, God places a value on that beauty. On that shining pure gold born out of the furnace of human suffering and injustice. A value that outweighs all the ugliness, the injustice, the suffering that must break his heart far more than it does ours because it is his beautiful creation being ripped to shreds."

Beauty! Robin shifted uncomfortably in her seat. Had Miriam overlooked that the chief product to date of this Ituri Rainforest's darkness and human cruelty was hardly any beauty of character and spirit, but a killer named Jini? With Robin's tea now half-drunk, perhaps she could politely excuse herself. Her eyes slid to Michael, but his gaze was now fastened, somber, silent, on his sister's face.

Robin shook her head. "Look, I appreciate all you have to say. But, well, it's pretty easy to sit here drinking tea and holding a theoretical discourse on the theology and philosophy of human suffering. It just seems a little condescending to say to someone else, those people out there, for instance, 'Hey, look, I know you're suffering, but grin and bear it because it's for your own good and it'll make you a better person in the end.'"

"You're right; that would be pretty condescending," Miriam said quietly. "Which is why it is those who've been through suffering who are best equipped to help others. Nor does God simply abandon us to our suffering. The apostle Paul, who knew what it was to suffer for his faith, tells us in one of his letters—2 Corinthians chapter 1—that God comforts us in our suffering so we can pass on to others the same comfort he gives us. As to theoretical . . ."

Miriam's hand rose suddenly to the scar that pulled her right eye to a distorted upward slant. "This is hardly theoretical."

CHAPTER
TWENTY-SEVEN

Robin almost choked on her scone. How had she let herself forget for an instant that Miriam's parents hadn't been the only casualties that day? Robin placed the remainder of her scone beside her tea mug. "I wasn't trying . . . I didn't mean to imply—"

Miriam raised a hand to cut into Robin's apology. "No, I know you didn't. You don't know my story, and I don't tell it very often."

At a sudden guttural sound emerging from Michael's throat, Miriam looked at her brother. "No, Michael, I want to tell her. I need to tell her. You don't have to stay."

Michael made no further protest but rose in one swift movement to his feet, heading for the door with long, rapid strides. As its metal panel clanged shut behind him, Robin could see Michael through the window weaving rapidly through the dancers and running children. She turned her head to look instead at Miriam.

"Please, you don't need to do this. The last thing I intended was to bring up distressing memories. Or upset your brother."

Miriam shook her head. "I don't need to, but I'd like to if you wouldn't mind. You said Michael told you about his childhood but never mentioned how this place was destroyed. If you really want to understand what's happened here—Ephraim, me . . . and Michael—you really need to hear the whole story."

Michael's sister stood suddenly, abandoning her tea to walk over to the open window. After a startled moment, Robin rose to join her. Miriam's delicate profile was turned away to stare out the window, her voice so low Robin had to bend close to hear her above the drums and singing, the thud of dancing feet.

"I told you about the massacre ten years ago. How my parents and I missed the evacuation flight. What I didn't mention was that it was all my fault. I'd wanted just one last canoe ride and swim at a favorite waterfall before leaving the Congo. The rebels caught up to us at the falls. Funny, one of the things I remember best is how the foam at the base of the waterfall turned bright red like cherry fizz after my parents were thrown into the water. They didn't bother using their machetes on me, not until—"

Robin could see what was coming, and cold horror was already squeezing at her chest as the other woman went on quietly, even matter-of-factly. "I think they thought I was dead by the time they threw me into the waterfall. I remember the rapids carrying me downstream, slamming me against the rocks. What I don't remember is how I ended up on a riverbank. That's where Ephraim found me."

The single solar-powered light behind them, night streaming through the window cloaked the two women in shadow so that Robin caught only a softness of mouth as her companion turned her head toward where two tall, broad-shouldered figures had emerged from a tent. Michael and Ephraim.

"Ephraim missed the massacre only because he'd volunteered to come looking for my parents and me when we weren't there to meet the plane. He knew where I liked to go. He'd have died with all the rest of his family if he hadn't been looking for me. I certainly would have died if he hadn't found me. So I guess in some fashion we both saved each other's lives. Ephraim hid me for days in the jungle until the rebels pulled out of Taraja. By then some of the other survivors were filtering back in. The communication equipment was destroyed, of course, like everything else. But that same day a mission plane touched down to search for us. Michael was on it. He'd taken the first flight to Africa when he'd heard of the attack and that I was missing. He was . . ."

Miriam's amber gaze lingered on the dark silhouettes of husband and brother, who'd paused to face each other, animated gestures conveying earnest conversation, as she continued even more quietly, "It would be impossible to put into words how angry Michael was. About our parents, of course, but me especially. Like any big brother, he's always been a bit protective. If he could have dropped a nuclear bomb on the rebel camp, he would have.

"Ephraim went back with us to Bunia. Six months later I asked him to marry me because I knew he'd never have the nerve to do so however much we'd come to love each other. You've met my oldest son, Benjamin. Ephraim isn't his biological father, but he sure is his daddy. I don't know what a church back home would say about the pastor marrying a raped, pregnant teenager. Or even about a white daughter of missionaries marrying a Congolese village boy. But there was no judging here, just understanding."

Miriam turned from the window to face Robin directly. "You've already heard the rest of my story. But going back to what we were talking about earlier, I remember only too vividly that once we'd made it to Bunia, some well-meaning expat colleague of my parents visited me in the hospital and pulled out a Bible to quote those passages I referenced. 'God's refining you into pure gold,' she told me. As an eighteen-year-old lying in bed with a body that would never again be whole, just beginning to suspect I might soon be a mother out of wedlock, I gave her some polite answer. She was after all a dear friend of my parents and grieving herself over their deaths. But inside

I was crying out my rebellion. *I don't want to be made gold. I never asked to be made gold!*

"Which, I guess, is why God never asked my permission. And I am thankful now that he didn't. Yes, I went through pain. I would have never chosen it for myself. But I can testify today that God was there with me through all the pain, all the suffering. And that the value of all I've learned of God's love and presence in the midst of sorrow is so much greater than the pain that I would not go back and wish it away if I could. Or undo the creation of my precious firstborn son, no matter how it came about."

Robin could envy the steadfast faith shining from her eyes, the serenity on her pretty, scarred features that was not resignation but calm acceptance. Moving back to the table, Miriam began placing cold tea and abandoned refreshments onto a serving tray.

"I guess what I've been trying to say in all this is that I've come to understand at least a little bit that God just doesn't see suffering, death, even life the way we do. One year or one hundred, our lives here really are just a short breath by his perspective compared to eternity. What matters is what we do with the span of life he gives us, whether short or long. What kind of people we become. Because our real lives are still ahead. An entire eternity ahead. And therein lies the hope that verse I quoted promises. The hope those refugees singing out there know well. Somehow I don't think a thousand years from now, a hundred even, that we'll look back from all that Scripture says our heavenly Father is preparing for us in eternity and still be complaining that our short lifespan here on this planet was so hard and unfair. In the meantime, life isn't all pain even in the middle of a Congo war zone. I mean, just look around you."

Robin turned from the window to glance around. What was there to see in the dim flicker of a single lamp but a plain, square room with cinder-block walls and concrete floors, screen windows without glass, sparse furniture, and even sparser belongings?

Miriam paused in her cleanup to look directly at Robin. "I would never have believed that day by the waterfall that God's plan for my future could hold such joy and beauty. A comfortable home with three healthy children. A wonderful husband for whom I thank God every day. If there's one thing I would still wish to change if it were my choice, it would be to offer Ephraim a perfect body, an innocent, whole heart and mind and spirit, instead of . . ."

Miriam's hand again rose as though without will to touch the awful scar. "Well, this is only the most visible evidence that still remains of that day. But that Ephraim loves me, that he would lay down his life for me, has become to me the most precious illustration of just how much God loves me. Here I am, marred by human sin and weakness. And yet somehow God sees in me, in you, in all of us, a treasure worth stepping into time and space for as Jesus Christ, Immanuel, God with us. Living in a village little different from an Ituri Rainforest community. Putting up with all of humanity's ignorance and meanness and rejection. Ultimately laying down his life on a cross for our redemption."

The tray now loaded, Miriam picked it up. "This certainty, this hope, is why I don't fret myself because I live in an unjust world where too many evil people hold power. I can't fix it all. But I can hold high the single candle of hope and light my heavenly Father has given me against the darkness. I can have faith that in the end God's purpose for our world will not be thwarted. And if the darkness seems awfully big for my little candle, that's okay because there are a lot of other candles being held high out there. Including your own, Robin, dear, whether you see it or not. And together those candles make up a mighty bonfire against the night."

Once again Miriam's quiet speech was hitting too close to home for comfort. Outside the window, Robin could see Michael and Ephraim now striding rapidly toward the house. They were no longer alone but had gathered a swarm of children in their progress, including Ephraim and Miriam's children as well as the parentless group Robin had driven from the airstrip. Stepping forward, Robin scooped up the knapsack she'd let slide to the floor beside the table. Her mouth crooked as she shook her head.

"Hey, don't count me in that bonfire. If I had a candle, it blew out a long time ago. Look, I appreciate the tea. And the chat. But I really do need to get back before my boss gets to thinking Jini and his men carried me off."

The tray in Miriam's hand clattered back to the table. "Oh, dear, I knew I was preaching too much. You should have told me to shut up. It's just—you're so exactly how Michael once described you. A person of such beauty inside and out. A person who might have been . . . well, a close friend by now if things had turned out differently. And even if you're still angry with Michael, with me, I can't bear that you should be so angry with God. Not because it makes any difference to how God feels about you. He loves you whether you believe it or not. But because of what it is doing to you. It's tearing you up inside; do you think I can't see that?"

Miriam's step away from the table brought her close enough that Robin could see light glint on each individual eyelash, a renewed shimmer of distress in amber eyes. "Please don't leave here angry. In fact, you should ask yourself why you're so angry. At Michael. At God. Why is it you've been far angrier with Michael than with the Taliban who actually shot your brother? Don't you see? It's because you trusted Michael more. Cared about him. Even . . . even loved him if you were willing to admit it. So it hurt far more when you thought—wrongly—that Michael had abandoned you.

"Just as you are so much angrier at God than at the human beings who took your mother, who hurt those people out there, because you trusted God, you truly believed in that 'Jesus loves me' your mother taught you, however much you choose now to forget. And you feel God betrayed that love. But he didn't. Oh, Robin, if only I could open your eyes to see my heavenly Father as I do. To experience the depth of his love that I have known in the midst of unspeakable darkness. Michael has come to understand why I don't hate the men who did this to me."

Robin stopped cold in the process of swinging her knapsack over her shoulder to stare at Michael's sister. This young woman—so close to her own age but already a mother of three, a survivor of war, rape, assault, personal injury—was indeed the kind of person Robin would choose for a close friend. If circumstances were different. If Robin were not abandoning this rainforest as soon as possible. "Miriam, believe me, I'm not still angry with you. Or Michael. I just—"

Robin didn't finish because the door flew open, a flood of children pouring into the room, followed by Michael and Ephraim. "Mama! Bibi Miriam!"

Amid the babble of children's high-pitched voices, Ephraim took a quick, long stride toward his wife. "Beloved, there is something you should know. Something we have learned. The foreigners—"

He broke off as his glance registered Robin standing quietly beside his wife. Only then did she take in the piece of paper the Congolese doctor held in his hand. A computer printout.

The photo of Jini.

CHAPTER
TWENTY-EIGHT

What is it? What have you learned? Robin took a step forward, but Ephraim's expression—not anger, but a blank withdrawal of all earlier thawing and friendliness—stopped her cold. *So Ephraim at least knows now who's really to blame for all that out there.* If the Congolese doctor had not learned from Michael, perhaps stories told by fleeing refugees had enlightened him.

Robin had every right, even a responsibility, to walk over and demand what it was Ephraim had learned about that flyer in his hand. Certainly Pieter Krueger would expect her to carry out her commission here. But Robin could not force herself to such brashness. Behind Ephraim, Michael's raised eyebrow appeared to be asking why Robin still intruded on his home. Miriam was looking with perplexed expression from her two menfolk to Robin. Only the children acted naturally, running through cloth-draped doorways, climbing in and out of wicker chairs and sofa.

I promised you twenty-four hours, Michael, and I'll honor that promise. But you'd better keep yours to let me know of anything that would impact our mission. Shouldering her knapsack more firmly, Robin offered Miriam a wry smile as she gestured to the lively children. "Looks like you've got your hands full, so I'll get out of your hair. I really do appreciate . . . well, everything."

"We'll have to do it again soon." A faint shadow lifted in Miriam's eyes, but she made no effort this time to detain Robin. As Robin let the door close behind her, she could already see through a screen window Miriam and her two male family members gathering in a close huddle over the computer printout.

Threading through dancers and playing children, Robin tamped down a sharp pang of aloneness. Nearby, one pair of grinders was still at work, lifting and dropping a heavy pestle into a wooden mortar's hollowed-out bowl. Carved in one piece with its heavy shaft, the pestle's massive, rounded striking end was a tree burl, one of those bizarre but oddly beautiful knots Robin had so often seen growing from the trunk of some hardwood. Itself, Robin was suddenly reminded, the product of some wound the tree had suffered in its past, the burl forming over time from the scar tissue of its healing.

From experience, Robin knew she'd barely be able to lift a pestle that size. But taut arm muscles flexed effortlessly as the two women took turns smashing the pestle down on heaped-up cassava root. And somehow they still had breath to join their ululating soprano to the singing, the rise and fall of the pestle keeping flawless rhythm with the syncopation of drums. At a second mortar, other women were using gourds to scoop cassava flour into a sack. As a toddler raced by, one woman dropped her gourd to sweep up the child in a mutual extravagance of kisses and giggles.

Miriam was right, Robin conceded achingly as she left behind light and dance and community to head down the unlit path toward the airstrip. Even in the middle of a refugee camp, there was joy.

A child's laugh. A mother's love. The companionship of people bonded together by adversity.

Impulsively, Robin pulled out her cell phone and punched her speed dial. Still no answer, but this time the voice mail response was different.

"I'm at the hospital with Kristi. Leave a message after the beep. I'll try to answer when I can. And please . . . please pray for Kristi!"

The break in her sister's voice, the request for prayer, said more than any update. Even as she composed a short, reassuring message, Robin sent up a plea. It was hardly the first such prayer she'd hurled heavenward in the last five years. Angry, demanding prayers. *God, please don't let Kristi die! You can't let Kristi die! I don't think I could go on if I lose her, too! Are you even listening? Where are you? Do you hear me?*

Bitter anger turned against herself. How had Robin let herself get so distracted these last days from her real mission here? Not succoring refugees nor even catching a killer, but carrying out that lucrative contract as team translator quickly and efficiently enough to save one little girl's life.

If only I could get through to Kelli! Find out just how big a loan it will take to secure Kristi's treatment, even if I have to work off the debt for the rest of my life! Poor Kelli—she must be so frantic!

Though the voice so like her own had sounded more composed than Robin would have expected, holding weariness, concern, but none of the hysterics to which Robin was accustomed. Maybe she was overestimating the urgency of Kristi's situation. Maybe routine medical tests were all that had placed Kristi in the hospital.

And yet there'd been Kelli's plea for prayer.

Leafy boughs of fruit trees closing in above the path had now blocked out the last glimmer of lantern and cook fire from the Taraja clearing. But Robin didn't reach again into her knapsack for a flashlight. The equatorial night was warm, a breeze rustling through foliage redolent with the fruity sweetness of mango, guava, citrus. Now that she was some distance from the singing and drums, Robin could hear other sounds of a rainforest night as well. The chitter of a monkey troop. The flapping of fruit bats settling down for the night. The shrill whine of some insect.

A louder rustle sent Robin's stomach flying up into her throat. She froze midstep, ears straining against the darkness. Did that quick, hard breathing belong to an intruder, or was it her own? Maybe this trek alone on foot at night had not been such a good idea.

Unfreezing, she completed her stride. But before she'd taken another step, she caught the snap of a dry branch or twig close at hand. Robin whirled around, Glock pistol instinctively sliding from the small of her back into her hand.

"Whoa! Put that thing away." From up the trail, a thin light beam played over the gun in Robin's hand, rose to touch her face. As the beam dropped away, its bearer closed the gap between them in a few swift strides. "Sorry, I didn't mean to startle you."

Cast into dark shadow above the penlight were broad shoulders, a trim male frame. Robin slipped the Glock back into its holster. "Why are you following me, Michael? What do you want?"

"You left so quickly. I had things to say to you. Without company." Michael twisted the flashlight, and the narrow beam winked out. "Excuse me if I turn this off. Batteries are hard to come by out here."

"I was managing fine without it before you showed."

What could Michael have to say to Robin he didn't want Miriam or Ephraim to hear? Was he angry that she'd lingered in his home? Permitted Miriam to resurrect painful memories? *I tried to stop her!*

"I left because you made it clear I'd overstayed my welcome. It's not like I planned to crash your evening. But your sister is rather persuasive. And persistent. Kind of like her brother! Not that I didn't appreciate her hospitality," Robin tacked on hastily. "I'd hate for Miriam to think I didn't enjoy myself, and I hope you'll let her know that. I'll admit I don't quite get her. How she can be so loving and full of hope with what happened to her. How she can forgive the men who . . . hurt her. How she and Ephraim can bear to come back to this place where it all happened. But whether it's all she's been through, like Miriam says, or just the kind of person she always was, I can admit your sister is truly an incredible person."

"*Unlike* her brother, you're saying?"

Robin could hear a laugh in Michael's query. He'd moved closer since switching off the flashlight. So close Robin could now feel a heat that came from his body and not the warm, humid night. Hear the gentle, unhurried sigh of air entering and leaving a broad, muscled chest. His scent filled her nostrils. A scent that combined the musk of male perspiration and a whiff of hospital antiseptic with the faintest tang of orange and cinnamon and other spices from the marmalade he'd eaten with Miriam's scones.

As cologne, it would hardly make a fortune. So it wasn't really fair that its proximity should leave Robin's own heart beating more rapidly against her breast. Her own slighter frame stiff with the effort not to step forward into his arms. She stepped back instead to introduce a space of night between herself and that fragrance.

"You know that's not what I meant. I'm sorry if you didn't want Miriam to tell me her story. But I'll admit I don't understand—all those hours we used to talk in Afghanistan—why you felt you couldn't even mention you had a sister! Or a brother-in-law, either. Did you think I would judge Miriam, Ephraim, their marriage?"

"Believe me, that wasn't it at all." From his quiet voice floating out of the night, Michael had made no effort to eliminate the space she'd inserted between them. "It's just—to start talking about my family would mean telling the whole story. And it was Miriam's story to tell. I guess at the time I thought . . . I hoped maybe someday you'd have opportunity to hear it from her. Though not like this! In any case, back then I still hadn't come to terms with it all to be able to talk about it, even with such good friends as you and Chris."

Good friends. Was Michael still including Robin in that category, or had that been a slip of the tongue? As Michael broke off, Robin spoke up quickly. "Okay, I get that. And I can't blame you. If it were my sister or parents, I don't think I could ever forgive what those men did. What I don't get now that I know the whole story is how you ever used to get up there in Chaplain Rogers's place and speak so convincingly about trusting God's love and goodness. And here I was thinking *I* had a lot to forgive God for!"

Robin heard a sigh from the darkness before Michael answered quietly. "Actually, it may sound sanctimonious, but forgiving the rebels wasn't as hard as you might think. It's like—well, when a jaguar attacks a herd. Or a crocodile carries off a small child. You hate what happened, but there's no point in hating the predator. It's life in the jungle, animals acting according to their own nature and need. The rebels—they're worse than any jungle predator precisely because they're thinking human beings to whom God has given a will and a conscience. And of course I hate what they did, everything they represent. But still, neither Miriam nor I have ever seen what they did as anything personal against our family, if that seems odd to say, just being in the wrong time and place when the storm hit. I can even understand some of the built-up rage and despair and sense of injustice that sent them on that rampage.

"No, I can forgive the men who assaulted my sister and killed my parents, if only because Miriam has forgiven them. As to forgiving God, I'm not sure that was ever really an issue for me. Not when I'd seen so many others suffer all my life. As you brought up earlier, it never crossed my mind that God owed it to me to exempt my own family. Truth is, it wasn't the rebels or God I had a long, hard time forgiving. It was myself. I should have been here to protect Miriam, my parents, Taraja. Maybe they'd all still be alive and safe if I hadn't gallivanted off thousands of kilometers away to follow my own dreams. Or so I kept telling myself."

Maybe it was because she knew him so well that Robin heard the depth of pain beneath the low, even words. A pain that twisted in Robin's own heart, brought sudden dampness to her eyes, hot words to her lips.

"Oh, Michael, how can you blame yourself? If you'd been here, you'd likely be dead too; you've got to know that! After all, you'd have been on that field trip with your parents and sister. And the rebel army had hundreds of armed men. Besides, you weren't gallivanting on some . . . some frivolous vacation! You were studying to become a doctor, to help people. Miriam would be the first to say you couldn't have done anything to change that day. That God was the one who permitted it all to happen. And you came home as soon as you could!"

Robin cut herself off. Could that possibly have been a chuckle floating her direction? Hurt and fury erased any sympathy roused in her. Balling her fists, she struck out, blows landing against a hard chest. "Are you—? You're laughing at me, aren't you?"

"Ouch!" The smile she'd suspected was in Michael's amused exclamation. "You've got quite a punch there. Hey, I'm sorry—don't hit me again."

Catching Robin's fists, he held them still and impotent against his T-shirt. "I wasn't laughing at you, really. It's just . . . you sound as fierce as a mama tree leopard defending her cub. You don't have to convince me it wasn't my fault. I know that. It may have taken time, but I've come to terms with it all. Just as I've come to terms with my best friend dying in my arms. You disappearing. Losing three months of my life in that coma. A year in rehab with them telling me I'd never walk again.

"Not that I can claim to be some super-saint. Or that many times the grief and loss and painful memories haven't felt more than I could handle. But Miriam's right about that, too. God's light shines brightest in the darkest, loneliest night. And what I've learned about God's love—his mercy and compassion—these last few years, I wouldn't trade if I could go back and undo everything that happened here. Everything that happened in Afghanistan."

Grief.
Loss.
Painful memories.
Loneliness.

Robin's heart was pounding so hard her chest hurt. Was it only the loss of his parents, of his best friend who'd also been Robin's brother, the pain of his sister, his own injuries of which Michael spoke? Or did his quiet words hint at what Robin had once thought, hoped, dreamed, passionately trusted to be reality?

For years Robin had sought to suppress the vivid memory that now succeeded in thrusting itself to the surface of her mind. A painful memory only because at the time it had been anything but.

It was, in fact, the last memory of unadulterated, unbounded joy Robin could recall.

She'd been standing just like this, face-to-face with Michael, hands resting open on his broad, hard torso. But it hadn't been some jungle trail. The trek up to Afghanistan's high Band-e Amir lake region had been permitted because the Taliban had been quiet recently, the presence of off-duty Marine units a test for opening up to tourists the beautiful Himalayan valley with mineral-rich waters responsible for the famed aquamarine tint of its lakes and ponds.

By then friendship had grown to a far deeper understanding. Robin had known it couldn't last forever. She was committed to at least one more tour of duty. Michael would soon be transferred out for his medical studies. But that afternoon it was enough to be together. As the sun dropped below the ridge, the mountain pool's crystal-clear aquamarine had deepened to a translucent sapphire that below the surface darkened almost to violet.

"Just the color of your eyes," Michael had told Robin with a rare, warm smile.

Robin had teasingly batted her eyelashes in response. She could still remember his abrupt sucking in of breath. The sudden erasure of distance between them so that she'd had to tilt her head back to see his tawny eyes, now aglow with strong emotion. His camouflaged arms around her were so tight she could hardly breathe, his heartbeat pounding against hers even through their fatigues.

"Robin, I wasn't going to tell you until we got back to base.

But you should know my transfer papers came through for medical school. No date yet. But it could be any day. I know you've another year here at least. But—you must know how I feel about you. I can't leave without asking. Without hoping—"

That was when Robin's radio crackled. She'd wanted desperately to ignore it. Michael was the good soldier who'd stepped away, nodded toward the radio, and waited courteously for Robin to respond. The caller was her brother's platoon leader. Could Robin take the place of their sick female translator? A last-minute raid on a suspected Taliban compound. Her brother had assured him she'd be willing to help.

A moment later another Marine had bellowed from the campsite they'd just finished pitching beside the lake. Weekend leave was canceled, choppers flying in to retrieve all available units for the raid. Robin never got to hear what it was Michael had wanted to ask. What he hoped.

Instead all hands scrambled to repack the camping gear. Michael and another medic remained behind to drive the Hummers back while the Marine contingent climbed aboard two Black Hawks hovering down. The next and last time Robin had seen Michael before setting foot in the Democratic Republic of the Congo was when he'd lifted her brother aboard that medivac helicopter shortly after dawn the next morning.

What did that Band-e Amir lake memory hold for Michael, if anything at all? Disgust? Relief that he'd never voiced those words on his lips? Though his musings just now indicated at least some regret.

I loved him so much. I was so sure he loved me. That it was only a matter of time and patience before things worked out for us to be together. I'd even have given up the Marines for Michael. Then I lost both Michael and the Marines. And ruined everything by blaming Michael for Chris's death, waiting for him to come after me like some stereotypical romance novel instead of going after him.

No, it wasn't quite true she'd ruined everything. What had Miriam said to Robin on their first encounter? *You couldn't destroy Michael if you tried. . . . He's become a stronger, better person for it.*

And Miriam was only too evidently right. Both Michael and his sister had emerged from their own night of suffering as stronger, better human beings with such faith and conviction in God's love and purpose for this universe as Robin could only envy.

And Robin?

Am I so different from those rebels, from Governor Wamba or Jini, using the darkness as an excuse to turn from the light, wallowing in my own self-pity and self-absorption? Maybe Michael is a better person for these last five years. But I sure am not! So maybe God was just doing Michael a favor in permitting all the confusion and taking me out of Michael's life.

One step forward would have bridged the gap of five years, placed Robin back into those strong arms. Instead Robin took a long step back to say coolly, "Well, I'm glad life has worked out for you after all. And for your sister. Is that all you followed me down here to talk about? Or was there something else?"

A silence from the darkness dragged on so that Robin could hear the singers and dancers up at the Taraja compound shift to a new song. When Michael did speak, his voice was just as detached. "Actually, I didn't come down here to talk to you about any of that. Sorry to have wasted so much of your time. But you did ask me to let you know if I found out something pertinent to your mission."

Robin's interest revived. "Then you did find something out! I wondered when I heard you on Skype. And saw Ephraim with that printout."

"Yes, I did find something. More than I expected, in fact. I'll be honest, if I hadn't given my word, I'm not sure I'd tell you. I'd rather *not* tell you. I'm not sure it couldn't be dangerous. For you. For Taraja. Especially if you run straight to your superiors with it. But since you've made clear you'll have a posse on Taraja's doorstep tomorrow if

I *don't* speak—well, I asked you earlier to trust me. I guess I'm going to have to trust you now to do the right thing with this info."

Robin stiffened. "What is it you're saying? Just spit it out!"

"I'm getting to it. When we arrived back here this afternoon, I contacted a journalist friend in Bunia. A stringer for the BBC. He did some digging for me. That Skype call was him getting back to me. Here's the first thing. The Bunia prison system has no record of who that old man actually was. But more than that, there's no record of *any* prison inmates being transferred within this past year from Bunia to a mining labor camp, here in the Ituri or anywhere else."

"So you're saying Samuel Makuga was lying when he told us the mine workforce came from the Bunia prison system?" Robin demanded. "What are you insinuating? That Trevor Mulroney can afford an Ares Solutions op, but he's too strapped for cash to pay the pittance locals make here to work his mine, so he kidnaps innocent civilians instead? Maybe your journalist friend just didn't look in the right file."

"I'm not suggesting anything." Michael's tone hardened to match Robin's curtness. "I am only reporting what I was able to find out. And since my journalist friend has a Congolese wife whose cousin is superintendent of prisons in Bunia, believe me, his intel is accurate. But that's not all. The bigger issue here is that I've got a good idea now just who your healer really was. And his son—your insurgent."

Shock squeezed the air from Robin's lungs. "You told me you hadn't recognized that old man, the healer! Then you *lied* to me?"

"I didn't lie. I wasn't sure when I saw him. Or the others. After all, it's been ten years since I lived here. Far longer since I was out in those villages. Those rock outcroppings spread for miles. It never occurred to me that strip mine could be the same area where I'd climbed them as a kid. The Congolese like to joke that all white men look alike. Well, I thought I was just seeing similarities when a couple mine workers looked so much like students who'd attended the Taraja school. Or when one of the older women looked the spitting image of

Mama Wambura, who used to feed Miriam and me cassava porridge after we climbed those outcroppings. Or even that your healer bore some resemblance to the village leader who argued with my father about his pet verse. But once my journalist pal let me know those workers out at the mine had not come from Bunia, I had Ephraim show that picture of Jini around to some recent arrivals from the village closest to where the mine now is."

As Robin herself had done not an hour earlier. And every refugee there had denied recognizing that photo. Sarcastically she demanded, "So your refugees up there lied to me too?"

"Not at all. No one admitted to recognizing your rebel leader. It was Ephraim who told me that he and Miriam both had seen a resemblance to a young student who'd just begun studying here at Taraja when the massacre happened. A boy named Joseph. So named because he was the petted late-born son of a large family who knew their Bible stories well. Funny thing is, I'd noted such a resemblance too. Not to this boy, but to a much earlier Taraja student. Simeon was quite a bit older than myself but similar in age to that picture last time I saw him before he left Taraja and returned to his village. So it turns out this Joseph was Simeon's youngest brother, which accounts for the resemblance. Of course neither had any such scar as you described, and I'd been told the entire family and village was wiped out in the massacres. Which is why I didn't bother mentioning it to you. Besides, Ephraim and Miriam both say this Joseph was one of the brightest students Taraja ever had. A bookworm, not a brawler. Not the type who'd ever hurt anyone, much less ever become a rebel leader. So like me, Ephraim assumed he was only seeing things when he noticed a resemblance.

"Until this evening, when I was filling in those village leaders on the same details I gave the BBC stringer. An elderly man with paramedic training who spoke fluent, educated French. That's when Ephraim informed me Joseph's father was just such a man. A government civic administrator assigned to the Ituri during the early

Mobutu era, who'd stayed on to marry and raise a family here. But here's the kicker. According to Ephraim, Joseph's village was a day's travel from here down the old road on the bank of a river at the base of those rock outcroppings. Quite likely the same village where my father used to let Miriam and me go climbing until the civil war got too bad for travel."

Robin's head was swimming with her effort to piece together Michael's revelations. "What is it you're suggesting? I mean, so what if the old man is this Joseph's father! Or if his sons studied at Taraja. Doesn't that make it even more likely he's our insurgent leader? Especially if the family survived the massacre and are maybe less forgiving than you or Miriam. After all, our intel on Jini cites specifically that he is highly intelligent and has a certain level of education. So maybe that old man ended up under arrest because he *was* this Jini's father and was also involved in the insurgency. Maybe the prisoners didn't come from some Bunia jail but were rounded up in recent fighting."

Robin broke off with stunned disbelief as the implications of Michael's words, of her own question, sank in. "Wait a minute! If you're suggesting the molybdenite mine actually was the site of Joseph's village, that those prisoners looked familiar because they're the villagers you used to visit there—exactly what *are* you suggesting? About Trevor Mulroney and Earth Resources? About Ares Solutions? About me?"

"Like I said, I'm just passing on intel," Michael answered evenly. "But when you run to your boss and tell him who your ghost really is, you might want to ask what happened to the local community that used to be where he has his mine. Best scenario, maybe he's got no idea and would be glad to know his local muscle like Wamba and Samuel Makuga haven't been completely forthright with him. Worst-case scenario—"

Robin must have imagined that voice in the darkness had ever held a smile for her because now it carried only bleakness. "I won't go there. But maybe while you're asking other questions, you need to be asking yourself exactly what kind of people you've chosen to fight with and for."

It was so unfair—it echoed so closely Robin's own earlier self-doubt—that she felt as though she'd been punched in the stomach. Through clenched teeth, she gritted, "I know who I'm fighting against, which is what counts. I'm fighting against a killer who butchers villagers and murders innocent people in their hospital beds. Have you forgotten that?"

And I know who I'm fighting for! A little girl who deserves to live as much as any of these refugees.

Michael didn't get a chance to retort because this time the crack of dry wood snapping was too loud and abrupt for either of them to miss. Long experience and training told Robin exactly what it meant in the split second it took her to react. That earlier rustle and snapping of a branch had not been Michael as she'd assumed, but someone else. Someone hiding close by while Michael and Robin argued. Someone whose muscles had grown weary of immobility but, in trying to ease stiffness, had stepped unwittingly on a fallen limb.

Robin's Glock was out and up even as Michael stepped forward, the thin ray of his flashlight scanning underbrush beneath the fruit trees.

"Show yourself!" he called out in Swahili.

Another rustle. A shaking of ferns and bushes. Then a dark shadow rose against a mango trunk. Michael's flashlight flickered up a gangly, adolescent frame to brush across a young face too gaunt for the huge, black eyes, high-bridged nose, elongated jaw.

The boy Jacob.

CHAPTER TWENTY-NINE

"Who are you?" Michael demanded. "What do you want? Why are you hiding? Is there anyone else with you?"

His flashlight probed the underbrush as their captive obeyed a wave of Robin's gun to step forward onto the path. Only once the beam of light returned to play again over their captive did Robin take in what Michael had immediately recognized.

This was not in fact the boy Jacob, but a youth several years older and as many inches taller. Perhaps as old as seventeen or eighteen, despite an emaciation that made age difficult to judge. It was the very similar gaunt, dark features, the same bruised, haunted expression in the eyes, the pain lines grooving a full mouth, the tattered shorts that were the newcomer's only article of clothing, even a bloody, dirt-encrusted bandage wrapping one thigh that had created the illusion of their missing patient.

"I am alone. I was looking for Taraja. For the *docteur* Stewart." The youth's black eyes blinked rapidly under the flashlight's glare.

"I saw you come, heard you speak. But I could not understand your words. And when I saw the woman had a gun, I hid."

Just another refugee then. How many were still out there in that black rainforest night? Robin slid the Glock back into its holster. Michael simultaneously lowered the flashlight so it no longer dazzled the youth's eyes. "I am Dr. Stewart. And the woman will not hurt you. She is leaving now to her own place."

He nodded up the trail. "Taraja is this way. If you'll come with me, we will tend to your needs."

Robin didn't linger for some polite farewell but headed down the trail. Already behind her, she could hear a flood of low, urgent Swahili. She wasn't sure if she was annoyed or relieved at Michael's cool assumption of authority. Especially since Robin hadn't missed that when he'd stepped forward, he'd done so in such a way that placed his broad frame between Robin and whatever was hiding in that brush.

Robin quickened her steps. She could no longer hear Michael or the youthful refugee. But the staccato of drums, hand clapping, and singing followed Robin all the way out onto the airstrip. Here in the open, the long slash of close-trimmed grass and leveled earth permitted a vista of night sky unknown under the rainforest canopy. The moon had not yet risen above the treetops. But earlier rain clouds had retreated enough to offer a scattering of star patterns against black velvet overhead. Across the airstrip, the harder, brighter glitter of the military encampment's security lights offered a reference point for Robin's steps.

Robin did not head immediately toward those lights. This close to her own base, she no longer felt the lingering apprehension that had dogged her down the blackness of the trail. Wandering a few dozen meters to the very end of the airstrip, Robin stretched out in the pool of shadow cast there by the massive hardwoods that marked the boundary of virgin rainforest. She slipped the uncomfortable lump of her Glock from her back holster and laid it close at hand, then impulsively slid her night vision goggles from the knapsack.

Once she'd settled the NVGs into place, the stars visible overhead immediately multiplied by a factor of ten: bright clusters, swirls, patterns no naked eye could ever envisage a rain-drenched night sky holding. A reminder that this universe held far more than Robin's own limited vision could grasp? That perhaps, as Miriam insisted, an almighty Creator really was working his own immutable purposes, even if Robin could not see them?

Straight ahead, the brighter luminosity of the NVGs had transmuted the airstrip into a long, silver-green ribbon, marred only by the hulking insect shapes of the Mi-17s squatting near the Ares Solutions base. Even as Robin tucked her knapsack under her head, the two helicopter engines roared suddenly to life, their rotors picking up speed until their furious beat and the noise of the engines had completely drowned out the singing and drums. Slowly the two Mi-17s lifted from the ground to bank over the rainforest canopy in the direction of the mine.

As music and starlight recaptured the night, Robin let tension slip away. Tilting her head against the knapsack so that star clusters and constellations filled the vista of her NVGs, she deliberately shut all else from her senses. The military encampment. The lethal weaponry of the Mi-17s. The horrible events of the last twenty-four hours. Her worry that she still had not heard from Kelli.

Which left only the serene, perfect beauty of that night sky and the music still wafting down from the Taraja compound. Even as one song followed another in glorious harmonies, a single word stood out.

"*Yesu ni wangu wauzima wa milelee.*" "Jesus my Savior is mine forever."

"*Yesu anipenda.*" "Jesus loves me."

"*Yesu, nuru ya ulimwengu.*" "Jesus, Light of the World."

Yesu.

Jesus.

The musicians' simple expression of faith and hope lifted up against the unrelenting darkness of the jungle night did something in Robin's chest, brought those annoying tears springing again to her eyes. Those refugees up the trail in the Taraja compound were survivors of far more horror and death than she'd ever encountered. Yet they had clearly found something she had not.

Was Miriam right? Could it really be as simple as that last chorus? The darkness was no less profound around these refugees, their universe filled with no less pain. But a Light moved through the darkness with them. A Light filled with so much love and warmth and comfort that Robin found herself shaking with her longing to possess it.

The drumbeat had slowed, the lively melodies giving way suddenly to a song that was also slow and minor of melody and hauntingly, piercingly sweet. *"Baba Mungu yetu uliye mbinguni . . ."*

The song was a prayer. Robin translated the phrases to English in her mind. "Our Father God in heaven . . . teach me your ways. . . . Give me an obedient heart. A heart of humility and full of love so that I may be able to do your will. . . . Give me a heart full of justice that I might find rest and peace."

It might have been a prayer for all the Congo. For an entire planet where peace and justice and love appeared to be in such short supply. As the final sweet refrains died away, silence fell at last over the night; even the animals and birds nesting overhead finally settled into slumber so that the sighing of wind through leaves and branches and the rumble of the generator at the Ares Solutions base alone remained to make music. Robin found herself shaking with sobs, tears pouring down her cheeks, so she pushed the NVGs up onto her forehead to grope for a tissue packet tucked into a pocket of her knapsack.

Baba Mungu yetu uliye mbinguni, she cried out silently, repeating the words that had been so familiar in her childhood. *Father God in heaven. Jesus, Savior, Light of the World, who once walked this earth and took upon yourself the weight of human evil and sin. If you're listening to me right now, won't you please let me know you hear? It's not that I don't believe you're up there somewhere beyond those stars. Nor even that you've got some ultimate purpose of your own in this world's darkness and suffering. I have no right to judge your actions or inactions. You are so great and powerful. I am so very small.*

But that's just it! What good does it do to pray when you've already made up your mind and will in the end do whatever you choose? How can I even ask you to hear my prayers for one little girl when you let go unheard—or at least unanswered—the cries of so many heartbroken mothers, starving babies, little girls being raped, fathers seeing their children hacked to pieces, even if it is for some vital divine reason only you know? How can anything I say or do move the Creator of this universe from what you've already decided for my life, for the lives of my sister and my niece?

And yet those refugees at Taraja sing of their heavenly Father as someone they can know and love and trust. Someone they are convinced loves them back. Who cares about their pain. Me, I guess I've always seen a heavenly Father as I have my own father. Someone whose love you have to earn and who's just waiting to pounce if you don't measure up. Maybe I misjudged my father. Maybe he really did love me in his own way, even though he never let me know any of those nice things he told Kelli about me. Maybe like a drill sergeant does with raw recruits, he figured if he ever praised us, we'd stop striving for excellence.

But I don't care anymore what Colonel Christopher Robert Duncan thought of me if I could only know, as those refugees and Miriam and Michael and Ephraim seem to know, that I've been wrong about my heavenly Father. That human suffering and God's love really aren't mutually exclusive. Yesu anipenda—Jesus loves me. *I want to know in the very core of my being that it's no fairy tale but the ultimate truth of this universe. I want to know, not just hope, that your light is stronger than the darkness. And that in the end, your purpose on this planet will truly bring forth something so beautiful and shining and pure, it will be worth all this blazing furnace of killing and pain and death!*

Robin could not have said how long she sat there, arms wrapped around her knees, staring out into the darkness that had replaced the star-studded splendor of the NVGs. At least until tears had dried to salty streaks that puckered and pulled at her skin. If an answer came from somewhere beyond that night sky, she didn't hear it. But at long last she heard something else. A rustle in the brush near where the trail led to the Taraja compound. If an animal, it had to be a big one. After her earlier fright, Robin did not take any chances this time but immediately tugged her night vision goggles back into place.

As always, it took a moment to adjust to the odd green light. To find through lenses the exact spot where she'd seen underbrush sway. Yes, there it was again. A ripple among ferns, banana palms, a patch of bamboo, following the edge of trimmed vegetation toward her own position. Robin dropped her angle of vision slightly. Two moving shadows emerged against the backdrop of vegetation, distinctly human and male in shape. The leap of Robin's heart identified the taller, broader shadow.

Michael.

And what was he carrying in his right hand? Robin's NVGs dropped farther. A bag. From its shape, the same medical bag he'd lifted aboard the Mi-17 yesterday. Then this was definitely no stroll in the night. The other shape, thin, lithe, leading the way with sure, quick strides despite almost total darkness, matched the youth they'd encountered earlier on the trail. Where could the two men be going in this dark jungle night? The youth had said he was alone. But that did not preclude other refugees left behind in the rainforest in need of help.

Yes, that was a logical explanation for the two men's presence and that medical bag.

Though Michael's steps were less certain against the green glow of her NVGs—twice she saw him catch his balance as a boot met root or vine—already in the few moments she'd been spying, the pair was closing in on the same high, black wall of untrimmed rainforest at the end of the airstrip where Robin had sought solitude. They skirted close enough to where Robin sat huddled against a mahogany buttress that she could hear their breathing, a muffled thud of boots that must be Michael since his companion was barefoot.

Why she didn't call out a greeting, why she rose noiselessly instead to follow, Robin could not quite have defined. Perhaps it was the stealth with which the two men had made their way along the tangle of under-brush when a far easier course would have simply struck out across the airstrip. Perhaps it was that Michael had not turned on his flashlight though here existed no rutted trail for boots to feel out in the darkness.

Or perhaps it was that Michael had changed his clothes since Robin had last seen him. She could remember jeans and a light T-shirt in the thin beam of his pencil flashlight. Gray or pale blue.

So why would he now be wearing camouflage fatigues?

CHAPTER THIRTY

Not just camouflage fatigues either. Night fatigues. Without Robin's NVGs, the dappled olive, brown, and black pattern would have made Michael as invisible against the backdrop of rainforest and night as his companion's mud-streaked black limbs.

Leftovers from Afghanistan?

Or hunters' gear?

Either added up to a deliberate evasion of the militia standing guard around the Ares Solutions base camp on the far side of the airstrip. Hurt and a burgeoning anger replaced idle curiosity as Robin slid around massive hardwood trunks, stepped over protruding roots. Despite the grudging information he'd divulged on the trail, Michael had made clear he didn't completely trust Robin.

Or at least not her associates.

Was Michael still pursuing his own investigation? But what could this youth offer to draw Michael alone into a black rainforest night?

And with his medical bag? If there were refugees who could not make it to sanctuary on foot, why not an entire party? Stretchers? Even a request to the Ares Solutions camp for one of those Mi-17s as a medivac?

A sudden thought leaped in her heart. The boy Jacob. Was there a reason this newcomer looked so much like him? An older sibling or relative with whom the fugitive had found refuge? That bloody strip of gauze they'd found. If his wound had worsened, if Michael's careful stitches had been torn open again, those who'd orchestrated the boy's escape might seek clandestine aid. After all, to return openly to the Taraja clinic would surrender the boy straight back into Samuel Makuga's hands.

But that would make Michael's youthful companion an insurgent! And Michael an accomplice.

No, just the committed surgeon he was. Hurt and anger eased in Robin's chest. It would be like Michael to see the boy as his patient rather than a fugitive who should be reported immediately to the Ares Solutions team. To take matters into his own hands rather than risk being delayed or stopped. Robin could admit that if he *had* alerted her, she'd have felt obligated to alert in turn her field commander, Pieter Krueger.

Still, if Robin had pieced this mystery together correctly, Michael could be walking himself into serious trouble. She could not have left her chase to seek backup now, had she chosen. The necessity for stealth was making her slow, and the two men were barely visible up ahead in the green light of her NVGs. Without that advantage she'd have already lost their trail.

Literally a trail, as Robin could now see. The very trail, she suddenly realized, from which those refugee children had emerged—could it truly have been only the previous morning? With worn, packed earth under their feet, the two men were moving even faster. Robin broke into a trot, heard the slap of her own boots against hard ground, and dropped again to a fast walk.

That she could have snatched a radio from her belt and alerted her colleagues, even scrambled one of the Mi-17s to fly overhead, Robin brushed from her thoughts. She had only suspicions, however plausible, and Robin did not even like to think of Krueger's or Makuga's reactions if they saw Michael in his current guise. Somehow she doubted either would consider humanitarian impulses an excuse not to arrest him—and his young companion—on the spot. Besides, if she was right about who needed Michael's medical services, Robin would not want to risk spooking a patient back into hiding, perhaps to his death. Whatever he'd done, whoever he'd gotten himself involved with, Jacob was still only a child.

So Robin settled herself to a distance that maintained her two targets at the very edge of her NVGs' field of vision. It was years since she'd had to put her own field skills of stealth and speed into practice, but the shift came automatically—breathing through her mouth for greater quiet, sliding her boots along the trail to feel out obstacles before stepping on them. So long as Michael did not turn on his flashlight, she was safe from discovery.

She'd hardly voiced the thought when light blazed into her field of vision so that she had to push her NVGs to her forehead. Perhaps feeling he was beyond spying eyes from the Ares Solutions base, Michael had in fact turned on his flashlight. Robin stepped instinctively from the trail to crouch behind a high mahogany root. And not as silently as she'd hoped because the beam swung instantly around to scan the trail.

The thin ray played over the gnarled maze of buttresses and creeping roots, then withdrew. Robin waited for three long breaths before rising again to her feet. By the time she'd stepped back onto the trail, the flashlight beam and the men were no longer visible. Sliding her NVGs into place, Robin hurried down the trail. Less than fifty meters later, she discovered how the men had so completely disappeared.

The trail dead-ended at a road. Just a one-lane dirt track such as jeep tires had worn from the airstrip up to the Taraja compound, but wide enough to permit passage of a sizable cargo truck. Washed-out ruts and a knee-high tangle of weeds, vines, and ferns carpeting the central median made clear the road had not seen recent use. Well off to Robin's left, a dot of light in her night vision goggles was the flashlight beam. From its rapid bobbing up and down, the two men had now broken into a run.

Robin could guess where she stood. This was the original colonial-era road linking the Ituri Rainforest with the outside world. If Robin correctly remembered Jensen's satellite maps, the road's trajectory skirted through Taraja's burned-out fields and houses not far beyond the Ares Solutions base camp to join up eventually with the dilapidated highway system linking Bunia with the Congo River, then went on through nearly two thousand kilometers of rainforest to Kinshasa, the capital. Trevor Mulroney had forked over a considerable sum not even a year ago to clear this road so that his convoys could ferry supplies and workers from Bunia and return with processed ore.

Only to have it closed down again under the assaults of Jini's rebel force.

All of which meant that the direction in which the flashlight had disappeared led toward the molybdenite mine, a full night's march on foot; Robin could only hope that wasn't the two men's destination. With no advantage remaining in stealth, Robin, too, broke into a trot. But the unevenness of the washed-out ruts required caution. She couldn't afford to find herself stranded alone in the night with a sprained ankle. Even worse, while minimal rain made it through the rainforest canopy to the jungle floor at least fifty meters below, there'd been enough to leave these ruts sticky and slippery with mud, so Robin had to wade instead through the central median's knee-high vegetation. She was further slowed by the necessity of checking both sides of the road for trails, since she could not assume the two men's trajectory would not leave the main road.

But though she could hope Michael and his companion faced similar limitations, not a glimmer of light had reappeared in Robin's night vision goggles by the time she dropped to an exhausted walk. Were the two men even still ahead of her? Or were they long gone down some side trail so that Robin could end up trekking all the way to the mine without coming across them? Either way, this was getting ridiculous. And two-legged predators were hardly the only danger in an equatorial rainforest. Pieter Krueger would rightly ream her out for abandoning every mission protocol in her impulsive pursuit.

A looming obstacle blocking the road ahead solidified Robin's indecision. A massive hardwood toppled across the track, she confirmed as she approached, its girth as tall as a two-story building. Like some beached octopus, the huge limbs of its vast crown sprawled several truck lengths in all directions. Storm fall or one of Jini's exploits?

Even if Robin weren't dog tired, she would have zero interest in clambering over rotting limbs or scaling that colossal trunk. Not alone at night when a breaking branch could mean far worse than a sprained ankle. Surely Michael and his companion had turned off well before this. She'd take her return trip more slowly. Check more carefully for side trails. Either way, she'd already gone much farther than was prudent.

God in heaven, you know exactly where Michael is, even if I don't. He has such faith in you. So much love for this place. So much passion to help its people. Whatever you choose to do with my life, won't you please, please at least protect his?

Robin had turned back from the fallen tree when that very action captured a glimmer at the edge of her peripheral vision that was not the green glow of NVGs. She froze, moving only her head to probe the darkness.

Nothing. Had she imagined that single flash of white light? Swinging around, Robin slipped into a tangled labyrinth of limbs and leaves until she was brought up short against a chest-high bough. But it had been sufficient. At this angle, though still obscured by vegetation and fallen limbs, there was no mistaking a light somewhere beyond the fallen tree's crown. No, make that two lights.

Cautiously reversing course, Robin emerged again onto the road. A search revealed no side trail, but she did discover broken and trampled vegetation leading around the felled hardwood in the direction of those lights. Robin eased herself through the vegetation, sorely tempted to dig out her own flashlight since the NVGs' green glimmer made a single snapped twig or crushed frond difficult to mark. Losing the trail, she had to retrace her steps until she found a snapped-off elephant ear.

But it was only a dozen paces later when Robin stepped around a tree trunk to see a light now fixed unwaveringly up ahead through her night vision goggles. Another few paces, and Robin could hear a murmur of voices. When the light grew too bright for her NVGs, Robin again pushed the goggles up onto her forehead. Her rambling trajectory would seem to have brought her all the way around to the far side of the fallen tree's crown because she could now make out the road with the looming bulk of the tree trunk across it.

Much closer, the fork of two fallen limbs formed a triangular shelter. Robin had been right that there were two lights, not one. The youth she'd already surmised to be Michael's companion was angling the penlight downward to where Michael knelt on the ground, medical bag open beside him, bloodied hands busy with gauze bandaging and a bottle of hydrogen peroxide.

The patient was stretched out full-length on his side. Like Michael's guide, he wore nothing but a pair of tattered shorts, his body streaked with mud except where Michael had cleaned it away from a section of rib cage and upper back. Vines tied odd tufts of leaves and feathers to biceps and thighs as though some bizarre attempt at jewelry. Just beyond the patient's outflung hand sat the second light. No flashlight this, but a palm-size fluorescent lantern such as Robin's own Ares Solutions field kit might contain. Hardly a piece of equipment one would expect a rainforest villager to be carrying.

But then, this was no ordinary villager.

Nor was it the boy Jacob.

If Robin recognized instantly the broad features, full mouth, and prominent nose, it was because they'd had little reason to change since that university ID photo. Why had Robin assumed the picture to be an old one, the rebel leader a much older man? This one could not even now be far out of his teens. Surely no older than Robin's own brother when he'd been killed in Afghanistan.

But if she'd doubted, there was no missing what the play of light from that fluorescent lantern revealed. A poorly healed burn running up the underside of that outflung arm from wrist almost to armpit, the scar tissue fissured and pale against surrounding chocolate-brown flesh.

Robin's first impulse was triumph and relief. Against all odds, unbelievably, she'd completed the mission for which her team had been contracted. A radio call, an Mi-17 filled with Ares Solutions operatives, and this would all be over.

I can go home! Kristi can have her operation!

But as she slipped closer, relief was giving way to stomach-roiling agitation. Robin had understood an impulse to help the boy Jacob, whose life Michael had already once held in his hands, enough to forgive a clandestine mission to save that life again. But offering succor to the very enemy Robin had committed herself to capturing? A mass murderer of women and children, destroyer of his own countrymen's homes? And while the man's injury looked ugly enough, it was clearly in no way life-threatening.

Worse, Robin could not even convince herself Michael had been brought here under duress or false pretenses. While a man-tall bow and deadly looking sheaf of arrows lay on the ground just beyond the patient, both Congolese appeared currently unarmed. Nor did Michael seem under any coercion as he finished swabbing clean his patient's right shoulder and shifted to a long, curved needle and surgical thread.

On the contrary, he and his patient were engaged in a low, swift Swahili conversation, interrupted only by a single groan from the patient as Michael pulled the first stitch tight. Nor did that conversation seem in any way hostile. Michael's speech was patient, his expression calm, compassionate. His doctor face, Robin thought of it. The patient's swifter tone was filled with distress and urgency, but it held no overtones of anger or threat. The youthful guide shining a flashlight on Michael's rapidly moving fingers was nodding earnest agreement, occasionally adding a phrase of his own.

Robin slipped noiselessly, cautiously from one shadow to another. The American doctor was just tying off the final suture, clipping it with a small pair of scissors, by the time she'd approached close enough to make out what Michael was saying in his fluent Swahili.

Unbelievable words.

Impossible words.

The words of a traitor.

"Joseph, I promise I will not let this go. Not all *mzungus* are faithless. Your father did right to send you to me. I only wish I had known before. I am not sure what I can do to help. But whatever it is, you can count on me."

Robin listened no longer. Sliding her Glock from its holster, she allowed the fury to build up in her if only because tears of disappointment and betrayal were not an option for a Marine.

For a Duncan.

No longer making any pretense of stealth, she strode out into the open. Deliberately, she trod on a branch underfoot. At its snap, three heads jerked her direction, three pairs of eyes mirroring the same startled astonishment.

Robin's narrowed glare was only for Michael. But when she spoke through clenched teeth, it was in her own halting Swahili, each cold word deliberately chosen. "So this is the *jini* for whom we've searched. Thank you, *Docteur* Stewart, for delivering him to us."

CHAPTER
THIRTY-ONE

As she'd hoped, Robin's statement threw into confusion this cozy little rendezvous of conspiracy and treachery.

With a cry of horror and denial, Jini—no, Joseph—jerked himself to a sitting position, bare heels scrabbling at the dirt as he scrambled back from Michael. Dropping the flashlight, Michael's guide dived for bow and arrows. But Robin was already striding forward, Glock angled downward to center on the youth's chest. "Drop those, or I will blow a hole in you."

Black eyes glared, but bow and arrows fell to the grass.

"Joseph, stop. You will tear open your wound again. You must not believe her. It isn't true. I did not bring her here!" Michael looked up at Robin, hands still filled with scissors and suture needle. "Robin, please put the gun down. This isn't what it looks like! Joseph isn't who you think!"

"Things are not as they seem." Dying words of the old healer.

Robin shook them off to demand hotly, "Are you saying this isn't the insurgent leader they call Jini? That isn't the scar we were told to watch out for?"

She'd addressed Michael in English, her Swahili already stretched to its limit. But while the youth on the ground showed no comprehension, Joseph's snatching up of his scarred arm against a bare chest indicated a more extensive education. Michael answered patiently, "Yes, this is the man you call Jini. As we'd surmised, his real name is Joseph, youngest son of Jean-Luc, the healer you met at the mine. I've just had to tell him of his father's death."

That explained the man's distress, killer or not. "But just about everything else we—you—thought was the truth is not. 'Woe to those who call evil good and good evil.' Jean-Luc was right. You've got to listen to what Joseph has to say."

"Listen! Has he bewitched you?" Robin cried out. Down on the grass, Michael's youthful guide was twitching ominously. Would he risk launching himself at her? Joseph's scooting retreat now placed him outside the angle of her weapon. Robin took two long steps backward to cover all three men with her gun.

"Just tell me one thing," she seethed through clenched teeth. "Tell me he didn't set that bomb at the mine. Tell me he isn't responsible for the dead bodies I saw with my own eyes. For women and children burned and bloodied beyond restoration. Tell me he didn't butcher innocent victims in their beds. Then you can try telling me things aren't as they seem. Because from where I'm standing, things look exactly as they seem! You aiding and abetting a fugitive and murderer. Me holding you prisoner and getting ready to call in backup."

Shifting her Glock to a one-hand hold, Robin reached for her radio. But just then the man named Jini spoke, his voice so unexpectedly young and unhappy Robin dropped her hand from her radio. "No, I did set that bomb. But I did not mean to hurt anyone."

His English was careful but far more fluent than Robin's Swahili. "I will never forgive myself for their deaths. And the others killed at

Taraja. But I did not kill them, I swear. How could I? They were my family. My aunt, my cousins, my uncle. It is for them I am fighting. But I failed them, too, as I have failed in all else."

"You haven't failed yet, Joseph," Michael interjected urgently. "And this isn't your fault, if it was your doing. Mistakes happen. In fact, Robin, I'm beginning to think very little of what we've been told, of what you've been told, is true. Tell her, Joseph."

Genuine pain in the rebel leader's tone carried conviction. But then this man had already proved himself a master strategist as well as killer. Robin's exhaustion, confusion, the plea in Michael's steady gaze were making decisions difficult. But one thing she could cling to in making a choice.

Her duty.

Robin reached again for her radio. "If there are mitigating circumstances, I, as well as the rest of my team, will be happy to hear them—back at base. I'm calling in a chopper and ground team. The jeep should make that road in no time. Whatever Jini—Joseph—has to say can wait that long. One way or another, it's time to put an end to this."

"Why, so you can collect your bonus and run back to your sister and niece? Is the money more important than justice?" Michael half rose from the ground as Robin keyed her radio. "Robin, you can't do this! If you're the person I think you are, you *won't* do this. You'd be signing Joseph's death sentence. Maybe even mine and yours."

Michael's accusation stung most because such a consideration had actually crossed Robin's mind. "Don't be ridiculous! I'm doing this because it's the right thing to do. And you seem to have forgotten what side you should be on! If it's Governor Wamba you're concerned about, believe me, we're not stupid. We're not just going to hand over a prisoner to the locals without checking out the situation, even if it means flying him to Kinshasa or out of the country. He'll get a fair shake. On that you have my word. Or is that no longer worth anything to you?"

But now it was Michael who gritted his teeth. "As I've said before, it's not your word I doubt. It's your associates'. And I'm not talking about Governor Wamba. 'Woe to those who call evil good and good evil.' Remember I told you how Joseph's father argued about that with my dad. Only it wasn't local warlords he was referencing."

As sudden suspicion tightened Robin's face, Michael nodded. "That's right! It was the hypocrisy of *mzungu* colonialists and profiteers like Earth Resources. The real bad guy here isn't Jini—Joseph. Or his father. Or even Governor Wamba. It's Trevor Mulroney, your boss! Now do you see why we can't let you call in the troops?"

But his demand came too late. Robin had already lifted her radio to her mouth. "Duncan to HQ. Duncan to HQ. I've got a situation. Requesting—"

She'd no opportunity to finish. As a bare foot kicked the gun from Robin's hand, a hand simultaneously slapped the radio to the ground. Robin was still registering the two mud-camouflaged men in loincloths who'd dropped from overhead tree branches when Michael snatched up the radio. His falsetto was a disturbingly accurate facsimile of Robin's voice. "Never mind. Found what we needed. Everything under control. Heading back soon."

Dropping the radio into his medical bag, Michael looked at Robin. "Did you really think your dangerous rebel leader wouldn't have the forethought to post guards?"

Both Joseph and Michael's youthful guide were now on their feet, the latter once again snatching up bow and arrows, Joseph scooping up the Glock. As one newcomer shoved Robin to her knees, another bound her wrists in front of her with a vine. Robin glared at Michael. "I will never forgive you for this!"

Sadness crossed Michael's face. "That's your prerogative. For now, you're going to listen. Joseph?"

But now it was the rebel leader who shook his head sullenly. "What is the purpose? She is the enemy. An ally of my enemy Mulroney, who seeks to destroy me. We must leave here at once. We have already lost too much time."

"She isn't an enemy but a friend I trust. A friend who will help you once she knows the truth." Michael shot Robin a warning glance as she opened her mouth to refute the claim. "And if it has been this long, a few more minutes will not change the situation. Not for Jacob, at least. Please, Joseph, just tell her what you told me."

"Quickly, then." The rebel leader lowered himself gingerly back to the ground. Grabbing for his medical bag, Michael began plastering a bandage over his earlier stitches as Joseph spoke. "You must understand I never wanted to become a fighter, only a geologist like others who uncovered the treasures of my country. When I went to Taraja to study, it was all I dreamed of. But then came the attacks. Because there was room, and I was the youngest, I was given a place on the plane that came."

The place that might have been Miriam's and her parents'. Robin listened at first grudgingly since she could hardly stop her ears with bound hands. But by the time Joseph described that last flight out of Taraja, finding himself a boy of eleven in a Bunia refugee camp, his story had gripped her so she no longer wanted him to stop.

"I heard in the camp of the massacres. That my own village had been destroyed. Certainly no survivors from there arrived in the camp. I found work translating for the many foreigners who came to Bunia, and later they brought me to Kinshasa. When they saw my desire to study, they arranged a scholarship to attend university in London. They arranged employment, too, in a laboratory. That is where this happened."

The rebel leader lifted his left arm to reveal the scar. "It was a year ago now. My own carelessness. But though I had realized my dream to become a geologist, though I believed my family dead, my heart still yearned to return to the Ituri. Then I found the means."

As Joseph told of his discovery that the gray, chalky "graphite" of his childhood pebble collection actually contained high-grade molybdenum, Robin's mind was working furiously. If he'd been eleven when the insurgency swept through Taraja, then this hardened rebel leader was no more than twenty-one now. And the scar. If it had happened only last year in a European laboratory, how had Trevor Mulroney come to know of it? Unless some survivor of Jini's attacks had reported it.

"So it was just over six months ago that I returned to the Ituri to discover with joy that my father, my older brothers and sisters, cousins, all my village had not in truth been destroyed. And then to discover with grief that I had been betrayed. That in returning home, my dream, my discovery had not brought a new beginning for my people, but only death."

"My father ordered me to flee, so I did. Then I wished I'd disobeyed when the soldiers burned the village, killed those who resisted, took captive the rest. Including my father. I remained free only because a party of hunters was just arriving back to the village and the soldiers did not discover them. They helped me get away."

The two newcomers had taken up silent, hard-eyed sentry positions on either side of the rebel leader. Joseph gestured toward them, then toward the youth who'd snatched up the bow and arrows. "My older brother Simeon. My cousin Caleb. My nephew Nathaniel."

Yes, Robin could see now a strong family resemblance. Michael interjected, nodding toward the oldest man. "I mentioned that Simeon studied at Taraja when I was a kid. He confirms Joseph's story."

"There were eight of us who escaped. But some no longer live." Grief thickened the rebel leader's voice. "We tried to free the rest. But the soldiers were too many. Then soon more arrived. Fences and watchtowers rose. So we found other ways to impede the invaders. Uhh—!"

At the groan, Michael dropped his hands away from Joseph's ribs. "Okay, I've done all I can do without a real medical facility. The bullet's out and the stitches should hold if they don't get too much strain. But you've got at least two bruised ribs. The good news is if you made it this far, I don't think they're broken. Unfortunately, I have no morphine on me. But I can give you some ibuprofen for the pain."

Shaking capsules from a pill container, Michael handed them to Joseph, who washed them down with one of Robin's purloined water bottles.

The interruption gave Robin opportunity for her own interjection. "Yes, we've witnessed how you chose to impede! Organizing a rebel army. Attacks on the mine and convoys. Stealing ore. That's bad enough. But looting and burning neighboring villages? The bomb and attack on the clinic? In any case, why would these soldiers care about keeping your village prisoners? Especially women and children. After all, if it's workers they need, surely bringing in healthy male prison labor as has been claimed would make more sense. You understand how hard it is to buy your story. And even if someone did hijack your molybdenum find, that doesn't make you less guilty of all the rest. Being an insurgent. Leader of a rebel army."

"Lies! All lies!" Joseph threw the water bottle to the ground, fury engorging his broad, dark features enough to bolster every story Robin had heard of this man. The rebel leader leaned so close Robin could feel his spittle on her face.

"There never was an army—can you not see that? Only the eight of us. Five now with those who have died. Six if you count the boy Jacob who is now with us. I make no apology for waging war against the soldiers at the mine, against the convoys. Not when they held our families captive. But the villages—it was not us who destroyed them. It was the soldiers. To make it seem we were the guilty ones. To give excuse for their war against us! As to the bomb—"

Joseph squeezed his eyes shut as though to shut out painful images. Fury ebbed from his features so they were once again young and lost. "That was a mistake. The explosives were not intended for the steam generator, but to blow holes along the fence during the night. We had planned an attack. A diversion so the prisoners could escape through the river wall to where we had canoes waiting and then into the rainforest. Those who died were friends, family. I will carry their deaths to my grave.

"As to why they hold my people hostage, that is simple. For the same reason they killed the injured you took in the helicopter to Taraja. The same reason they still seek me. Because of what they know. Because of what I know. They dared not let those you saved speak freely to outsiders, so they killed them in the night. All but the boy Jacob, also my nephew."

With the strong resemblance, it was no surprise when Joseph nodded to Michael's guide. "They are sons of my oldest brother, among the first killed when the soldiers attacked. When Jacob escaped to us, he told us what had been done to the others. If they have not killed the rest of my family, my village, it is only to use them as bait, as hostages to trap me. Because I alone know the full truth of what treasure resides in the rocks of my birthplace. I alone know just who is our true enemy. And the weakness by which he might still be defeated."

Joseph's dramatic pause seemed to invite response, so Robin conceded him one, keeping her tone conciliatory, and not just because of the fierceness of his glare, the bonds on her wrists, or the weapons his henchmen carried. Despite that spittle still dampening her face, she could actually feel sorry for the man. His story was, after all, similar enough to countless other such tales of corruption, oppression, and injustice across the Congo, across Africa, to be plausible.

But was the rebel leader really naive enough after months of fruitless conflict to think he could still win a fight against the powers that be in Kinshasa and Bunia? Or even against a hired team like Ares Solutions? At best, the kind of a truce that had placed a warlord like Wamba in the governor's palace might permit the rebel leader to lay down arms and walk away. But if Joseph believed he could stuff the genie of discovered mineral wealth back in its bottle so his people could return to quiet village life, he'd discover soon enough that was an impossible outcome.

"Actually, the molybdenum discovery's no real secret anymore.

It's been pretty well publicized. And since you've studied and worked overseas, I hope you can understand that even if your authorities unfairly seized your discovery, that has nothing to do with the mining consortium who've brokered a deal to develop the find. Earth Resources, in this case. Did it ever occur to you that your people haven't been released, that you're still being hunted, because you won't stop attacking the mine? That if you'd lay down your arms and make peace, they would too? In fact, I'd be happy to volunteer as a go-between. I'm sure my boss, Trevor Mulroney, would be willing to pay reasonable reparations, help your village start over elsewhere, if he can just get the mine open again."

Robin hesitated before adding more delicately, "As to what happened at the clinic, you say you learned about it from Jacob. But we found your footprints. Canoe marks. Signs of where you met up with Jacob. If you didn't go there . . . well, to rescue Jacob and keep the others from talking, what were you doing there in the middle of the night?"

She'd gone too far. The rebel leader jumped to his feet so violently Michael put out an admonishing hand toward the bandage he'd just taped into place. But it was not Robin's insinuation that he might indeed be a murderer that Joseph chose to address. "Do you think I am stupid? That I do not understand my enemy or know who he is?"

A whistle of sharply indrawn breath, a hand pressed against his ribs were Joseph's only concessions to pain as he paced back and forth. "It is true I did not at first know the commander of the soldiers who came that day in the helicopters. Not until much later did I know him to be Wamba, one of the very warlords responsible for the massacre of Taraja, now sitting in power in Bunia. Nor did I know the aide who carried out his orders to destroy my village until he returned to direct the defenses of the mine."

Samuel Makuga. This time it was Robin who drew in a sharp breath.

Joseph sank down again in front of Robin. "But I did recognize one of the *mzungus* who came with the soldiers because he was my employer as well as yours. Trevor Mulroney, for whose company I worked in London, Earth Resources. The man I believed to be my benefactor. A friend, even, who could bring at last peace and prosperity to my birthplace. This—" Joseph eased his arm away from his ribs to display its scar. "Trevor Mulroney was in the laboratory the day I so carelessly permitted the crucible to spill valuable metal. Instead of punishing me, he had me taken to the hospital. Paid my salary while I healed. Then took me back as employee. So of course it was to him I ran with what I'd discovered in those small pebbles I'd clung to like some amulet of good fortune since childhood. But they proved instead to be the worst of fortune as he proved to be no friend, but one more greedy, deceitful *mzungu* whose only interest in my land, my people, was to steal its treasure."

Robin shot Michael with a glare. "*This* is what you were insinuating? I might have swallowed Wamba's involvement. Makuga's, too, since there's little I'd put past either of them. But Trevor Mulroney? CEO of one of the world's biggest and most reputable mineral consortiums? The guy's up for a knighthood, for goodness' sake! More than that, he's not stupid. Why should he swoop in and attack some local village when all he's got to do—what in fact he *did* do—is fork over considerable funds to purchase that molybdenum concession for Earth Resources legally?"

Robin cast a flicker of contempt from Michael to Joseph. "Considering all the damage your friend here has cost Earth Resources, it says a lot about Trevor Mulroney that instead of just cutting his losses and investing elsewhere, he's committed himself to restoring peace to the Ituri people. My guess is your pal here was so busy running away that day, he didn't recognize one *mzungu* from another as well as he thinks. Or else he's flat-out lying. But without any possible motive, there's no way you're going to convince me that a Fortune 500 CEO as well vetted as Trevor Mulroney is some kind of awful villain just because he's been successful in business. And therefore by proxy, Ares Solutions is too."

"You've raised a valid question." Michael's stark admission took Robin by surprise. He was taking her side now? "Joseph hadn't got to that point when you popped in. But since I *do* believe him, I'm sure he's got a motive in mind. Joseph?"

As he threw Joseph a questioning glance, Robin turned her own gaze with some trepidation back to the rebel leader. If her earlier queries had roused antagonism, to what rage had her defiance pushed him? But to Robin's surprise, Joseph's dark features had drained from fury to calm, his full mouth curving into a confident smile.

"You say you need only a motive to believe me? Of all you have asked tonight, that is the easiest. It is not the molybdenum for which Trevor Mulroney has seized my birthplace, but a far greater treasure. Rhenium."

CHAPTER
THIRTY-TWO

"Rhenium?" Joseph's statement had left Robin only more confused. "Isn't that some kind of rare heavy metal?"

"Yes, one of the rarest. Its high melting point and strength as well as malleability permits its mixture with other metals to form some of the strongest alloys ever created. But because it is so rare—no more than forty or fifty tons produced worldwide each year—much of its use is reserved for military applications. Above all for producing jet engines that will stand up to the heat of supersonic fighter planes. Most rhenium is produced as a trace by-product of gases released from processing copper. But the quantities are so low an entire copper mine might produce fifty kilos of rhenium in a month, a year. Which is why one kilo of rhenium is worth a hundred and fifty kilos or more of processed molybdenum. When I left London, molybdenum was selling at thirty of your dollars a kilo. Rhenium at more than five thousand."

The rebel leader's explanation had settled into a lecturing tone more characteristic of a classroom than a jungle clearing. A reminder that this young man had not always been a mud-daubed, half-naked insurgent fighter.

"But rhenium has also been found naturally in some molybdenite deposits. Usually only .1 or .2 percent, though some samples have tested as high as almost 2 percent. But only in the smallest amounts. Until I tested my rock collection. Though I had collected the samples from all over the rock outcroppings that rose behind our village, each gave the same result: at least 3 percent rhenium. You see what a treasure I'd found? In one month's production, such a molybdenite mine could generate more rhenium than the entire planet generates in a year."

The excitement of that memory lit up Joseph's eyes in the dim glow of the tiny fluorescent lantern. Then his features clouded over, his voice growing soft and resigned. "I should have thought what it would mean for rhenium to be no longer a rare metal, but as common as tin. I should have listened to the rumors inside my laboratory that all was not well with Earth Resources. But like you I believed Trevor Mulroney to be a man of honor. And there still would have been profits enough for any man if he were not greedy."

Robin was doing the math in her head. A hundred metric tons of ore on that barge. Another hundred in the convoy Jini had blown off that dirt track beyond the fallen hardwood. At 3 percent, that would be six thousand kilos of rhenium. At five thousand dollars a kilo, right there would be thirty million dollars. Not even counting the molybdenum profit itself. No wonder Trevor Mulroney had been so furious at the loss. Or considered a few million euros a worthwhile investment to restore production.

If it was all true.

As Joseph stared broodingly down at hands that had once held beakers and chemicals instead of a bow and arrows, it was Michael who summed it up aloud. "What you're saying is that once word got out of such a huge find, rhenium prices would tumble. Not to mention Kinshasa would hardly let Mulroney scoop that kind of profit at the price tag of a molybdenum concession. As things are now, Mulroney can stockpile the rhenium. Release it at will onto the world market. He could make billions. That enough of a motive for you, Robin?"

Now Robin wished desperately her hands were free so that she could shut out what she was hearing. If only she could go back a few hours to when she still had absolute conviction of what was evil and what was good. And that she, Christina Robin Duncan, was fighting squarely on the side of good. Back to when her mission was a simple one.

Catch a killer.

Finish her contract.

Earn a bonus.

Save a small girl's life.

Looking at Michael, Robin demanded harshly, "You realize there's not a shred of proof to back up any of this? That you're asking me to take the word of an insurgent killer with every reason to lie against one of the most respected businessmen in the world?"

"But I have proof."

The quiet conviction of Joseph's words banished any last hope that Robin might still be permitted to slide away into yesterday's certainty and ignorance. Reaching behind him, Joseph drew from the underbrush a briefcase, inexpensive, battered, caked in mud. As he snapped open its latches, his nephew stepped forward eagerly, juggling bow and arrows to shine Michael's flashlight directly across its contents.

The briefcase held glass vials and packets of chemicals. A file stuffed with papers. A laptop. A cell phone. How had Joseph kept all this intact during months as a fugitive in the rainforest?

Joseph lifted out a plastic envelope that glinted a metallic silver-white. "My employer wished me to tell him where the rhenium was to be found. But there are no street signs in the Ituri such as in London. How could I pinpoint one bend on one river? Nor did I know how many other rock outcroppings there might be. I had to come myself to mark the place where I was born. And since the war that drove me from my home was said to be over, I was not afraid, but eager to return.

"Trevor Mulroney purchased my ticket to Bunia, provided funds for a motorcycle, a cell phone. I brought testing equipment, a canister of fuel tied to the motorcycle. The road from Bunia to Taraja was long abandoned. But old tracks were sufficient for a motorcycle to follow. Once I saw the overgrown airstrip, the burned houses, the abandoned fields, I knew I had reached Taraja. From there I knew well the exact course to my birthplace. So I arrived home to find instead of ruins my father, my family, my village. I called on the cell phone to tell Trevor Mulroney I had arrived. Then I made tests on more ore. Again, I found high concentrations of rhenium."

Joseph lifted aside the laptop, opened the paper file to reveal unintelligible figures and graphs, held up a flash drive. "These papers contain all my research from the laboratory. The computer holds the new reports. This flash drive contains both. Once I finished my tests, I took my father up onto the rock outcropping to tell him my good news. But instead of excitement, he was angry and afraid. Then we saw the two helicopters. They were not like the one that flies often to the mine but like those I have seen overhead these last days."

Russian Mi-17 combat choppers, then. Perhaps even the same ones. Joseph went on. "I did not think at first it was Trevor Mulroney as I had not yet given directions to find the place nor results of my new testing."

"Cell phone triangulation," Michael murmured. "He didn't need directions if he had the right contacts."

"Perhaps. When I recognized Mulroney, I thought he'd come to celebrate with me. Instead soldiers came out of the helicopter firing their weapons. And not only Wamba's men. *Mzungu* mercenaries. Do you see now why Trevor Mulroney cannot permit my people to speak of that day? Of who they saw? Why he will not rest until he finds me? Though I do not believe he has told Wamba or Makuga why he hunts me so relentlessly. Because they too are greedy and would want such treasure for themselves. As to the other things of which you accuse me—here!"

Joseph pulled out the cell phone. "I could not stop Wamba's force from doing terrible things in the villages. He had hundreds of men commanded by Samuel Makuga. We were only eight. But we followed his men to one village where I took video and photos until my cell phone battery died. They will prove whose hand was truly behind the atrocities of which I have been accused.

"I have no such proof at Taraja except the word of my nephew, who saw the killers. Yes, I was there that night. But not to kill. Nor to seek release of Jacob and the others. Why should I? I was grateful when I learned they had been taken to Taraja. Since I could not then see the future, I thanked the almighty Creator I would not have their blood as well on my hands. No, it was to see Dr. Stewart that I came to Taraja."

Robin had thought she was past being surprised. "Michael? How did you even know he was there?"

"You told my father. From the beginning, he had sent messages written on palm leaves and hidden in coconut shells. Dr. Stewart has told me you found one such last night. I would let him know I found a message by leaving markings known to our hunters in places where they cut wood."

Robin pounced on Joseph's admission. "Not just markings, from what I understand. Did you have to get a child like Jacob involved?"

Mud-daubed shoulders rose and fell. "He was proud to do his part. Was not his father among those killed by the soldiers? Though my father did not approve of our plan. He feared more people might get hurt. And as was his habit, he was right."

Joseph's tone again held pain. "From the beginning my father wanted me to go to the authorities. He believed with such proof as I carried, I could impel justice for our people. But my father is a peaceful man who has not been outside the Ituri in long years. To what authorities could I go? Trevor Mulroney is a man of great influence even in his ruler's own palace. In Bunia, Wamba *is* the authority.

"So I chose instead to fight with the help of those who escaped with me, using the very skills I learned working for Trevor Mulroney to disrupt his operations. I thought if I could free the hostages so I need no longer fear what Mulroney might do to them, then I could take my proof to others who would gladly seize his prize, if only for themselves. But though I have been able to stop Mulroney from profiting by his treachery, I have not yet succeeded in liberating his prisoners. A stalemate, but one I fear in the end I must lose, for Trevor Mulroney has time and resources that I do not.

"After the terrible events with the steam engine, I was losing hope. I wondered even if I should surrender myself to plead Mulroney's mercy on the others. Then you came to the mine. Yes, I saw you. There are few women with hair the color of a rising sun. I saw you speaking to my father, helping to care for the boy Jacob. The next day I received a message that a Stewart had returned to Taraja. Not the grandfather or father who had befriended our people, but a son who was also now a doctor. My brother Simeon remembered this son from visits to our village, from his own studies at Taraja."

Joseph's gesture indicated one of his two flanking sentries. "My father's message said that if this new Dr. Stewart cared for the Ituri people enough to return here, then like his father and grandfather he must be a man of justice who could discern evil from good, darkness from light. And being also a *mzungu*, who better to advocate our plight among those with power to intervene on our behalf. Perhaps even among the United Nations force in Bunia.

"And so because I too remembered Stewarts who were my teachers at Taraja, who were kind to me, true followers of the almighty Creator, I came. At night because we had seen the helicopters and knew such aircraft carried spying eyes. Though I believed we had walked into a trap when we saw the soldiers' encampment below Taraja. Even more so when we witnessed a unit of Wamba's militia entering the clinic where we had hoped to find Dr. Stewart."

"Wait!" Robin interrupted. "You're saying Wamba's militia killed those people? But that would mean . . ." She felt newly sick as it hit home just what it meant. She'd wondered how Samuel Makuga had known so quickly of the incident at the clinic. Especially once it became apparent his two guards had been surprised before they could have gotten off an SOS. It wasn't hard to imagine Makuga's drugged-up recruits as killers. But that they would slit their own soldiers' throats to add credence that Jini was the killer was beyond evil. Besides, Robin had witnessed Makuga's stunned fury. The frenzied search he'd instigated.

But no, both fury and search could have been over Jacob's escape, not to find the killers. And it had been Makuga who was so insistent the patients not be permitted to speak to their caretakers. It all made horrible, obvious sense now.

And what about Pieter Krueger, who'd accompanied Makuga that night? Could he or any other on the Ares Solutions team have known any of this?

CHAPTER
THIRTY-THREE

The rebel leader dropped his head bull-like against his chest. "If only I'd surrendered that first day instead of running away, perhaps I alone would be dead today. Perhaps that would have been the best outcome, even if it meant triumph for Trevor Mulroney. Instead, my aunt, my cousin, my youngest nephew . . ."

Anguish twisted Joseph's features. "So much blood on my hands! My father was right. Meeting violence with violence has resolved nothing. Even if he had lived, I could never have hoped for his forgiveness. As the almighty Creator would himself turn his face from me. So all that remains is to bring justice for those who have died. For those who still live. Then it will not matter what becomes of me."

Joseph raised his scarred arm and pressed it across his face. But not before Robin glimpsed tears in his huge, bloodshot eyes. With that glimpse an image shifted irrevocably in her mind. She no longer saw the man crouched on his haunches before her as a ruthless killer she'd been assigned to hunt down, his very half-naked, mud-daubed appearance emblematic of cold-blooded, vicious savagery. Instead she saw a youth barely into adulthood as lost and grief-stricken and despairing as the Robin who'd cried out her own heartache to an almighty Creator not so long past on the airstrip.

Yes, and a very angry youth too. But how might Robin have reacted were Kristi and Kelli behind high chain-link fences? Would she have made wiser choices? Have shown as much courage?

Michael interjected roughly, "Joseph, you cannot take all the blame for what's happened. Perhaps surrendering would have saved lives. Or perhaps you would have thrown your own life away along with theirs. Hasn't the death of helpless wounded made clear how far your enemy will go? As to forgiveness, you must believe me: if your father were here, he would forgive you. He did forgive you. Robin here can testify he died thinking of you, his last request that we aid you."

The bowed head lifted slightly. Black eyes flickered toward Robin. She nodded. "Michael's right. Your father asked us to help you. To save you."

"As to the almighty Creator, believe me that there is nothing you can do, nowhere you can go beyond his ability and willingness to forgive."

Michael's quiet conviction further lifted Joseph's head. "You truly believe it is possible?"

"I know it is. I would stake my life on it. I *have* staked my life on it."

Robin squeezed eyelids tight when she saw the blaze of hope dawning in black eyes. *And this—the man you've just shown yourself to be, Dr. Michael Stewart—is why, wherever I go from here, whatever happens this day, I will love you until the day I die!*

Michael was now rising to his feet. "In any case, the blood of those who died, even in that unintended explosion, is on the hands of Mulroney and Wamba and Makuga, not yours. Nor is it your decision or theirs when it is another person's time to step into eternity. Their Creator holds each person's life and death in his hands. But to make a stand against evil is always the right decision, whatever the consequences.

To surrender will only embolden evil. The only way to truly end this bloodshed is to stop Mulroney and his cohorts once and for all."

Michael slung a repacked medical bag to his shoulder. "So can you move now, Joseph? Has that painkiller kicked in?"

Slamming shut the briefcase, Joseph probed gingerly at his bandages. Michael had not engineered this hiatus just to tell Joseph's story, Robin realized suddenly, but to give him time to tend the rebel leader's wounds. "It will do. We have lost too many hours already."

As the young man rose, a companion hefted Joseph's briefcase while another scooped up the lantern. Robin scrambled to her own feet. "Wait! Where are you going? What are you planning to do? Michael, you can't possibly be thinking you can somehow take on Mulroney yourself!"

Though Michael swung immediately toward Robin, it was Joseph who spoke up. "We must hurry because it was not my own needs for which we sought Dr. Stewart this night. This wound—" the rebel leader touched his bandage—"would have sent me falling to my death had not the boy Jacob pulled me to safety. He carried me to hiding among the treetops. Applied leaves and mud to stop the bleeding. Tended me until I recovered thought. But in the effort, his own injuries were torn open again. He has lost much blood. And another companion who remains to care for Jacob was also shot by your fighters. He will live but cannot travel far until the bullet is removed."

So these were the very men who'd been hiding in the sunken barge. Ernie Miller's report bolstered Joseph's story. But it also jogged a sudden unpleasant reminder in Robin's thoughts. "Michael, you can't go out there now! You don't know—"

Michael didn't know because it was an Ares Solutions operational secret. For one long moment, duty and training warred against urgency in Robin before she burst out, "Wamba's men and the Ares Solutions team will be closing in around the mine at dawn. Anyone left inside their perimeter—well, let's just say Makuga's threat yesterday was not entirely a bluff!"

"So what are you suggesting? That I leave a boy to bleed out inside a kill zone to protect my own skin? If you're really so concerned, maybe you should do something to call off your pals." Michael's tone hardened as he adjusted the medical bag's strap over his shoulder. "Question is, what are *you* planning to do, Robin Duncan? You're the one with a decision here. You know the truth now. If your loyalty still lies with your mission and your contract after everything you've heard, you've forfeited any right to know where we're going or what we're planning!"

"So what then?" Robin held up her bound hands. "You're just going to leave me here like this?"

Michael's mouth tilted downward at a panicked note in her voice. "No, but if you don't mind—or even if you do—I think I'll borrow these. I'm not quite as good in the dark as this bunch."

Plucking the night vision goggles from her head, he looked at Joseph. "I'd like to make sure Ms. Duncan here is returned to a place of safety. Can you spare someone to lead her back to Taraja?"

"Of course. Nathaniel will return her safely. But I had hoped she too would be willing to help us." As Joseph signaled to the youth who'd guided Michael, he held out a palm to Robin. In it lay the cell phone and flash drive.

"Ms. Duncan, my father's message declared you were a friend to Michael Stewart. I had hoped once you learned the truth, you would be a friend to us. Since Dr. Stewart must come with us, I had thought you instead could ensure this information reaches the right ears and eyes outside the Ituri. It is time the truth was released."

Caught off guard, Robin stared at Joseph's palm as though it contained deadly venom. Seeing her consternation, Michael spoke up harshly. "No one's asking you to breach your conscience here, Robin. Just take those to Miriam or Ephraim and ask them to get that intel to my BBC pal in Bunia. For any friendship we've ever had, will you do that much? I'd do it myself once I tend to Jacob, but . . ."

But you're not sure you'll have the opportunity! The realization was a stab to Robin's heart even as she snatched the two items from the rebel leader's palm. "I never said I wouldn't. What kind of person do you think I am?" Robin addressed Joseph. "I don't know what I can do about tomorrow's assault. But I'll take a look at this. If it's what you say, I will make sure it reaches Michael's BBC friend, if I have to take it there myself."

With a nod, Joseph took the bow and arrows from Nathaniel's grip and slipped forward into the night. As his two companions followed, the fluorescent lantern blinked out, leaving only the small flashlight Nathaniel still carried to leaven the pitch-black of an underground cavern—or a jungle floor at night.

Michael lingered. "Thank you, Robin. I knew I could count on you. Here's the name and Skype address of my BBC pal, in case Miriam can't find it at hand."

Scribbling swiftly with a pen and notepaper taken from his medical bag, Michael lifted flash drive and cell phone from Robin's bound hands, tucking the items and note into her knapsack before handing the bag to Nathaniel. As the guide shouldered it, Michael went on quietly. "Look, you've made clear you're a big girl and make your own decisions. So I'm not trying to tell you what to do so long as you keep your word to get that intel into the right hands. But if you do believe Joseph, I hope it's crossed your mind that letting Mulroney know you're now in on the truth might not be the wise thing."

"I'm aware of that," Robin answered steadily.

Michael's mouth quirked. "Yeah, I know. Just those protective instincts kicking in. Speaking of which, would you mind keeping one eye out for Miriam and Ephraim until I get back?"

Robin nodded. "You know I will. Nothing is going to come back on your family because of this. On that I'll stake my own life."

Michael stepped closer to Robin. So close another inch forward would have been an embrace. Looking deep into Robin's upraised eyes, he answered quietly, "Yes, I know you will. As I know just what kind of person you are, maybe better than you know yourself. Watch your back, Robin Duncan. Until we meet again."

Nathaniel had stepped away, the penlight probing the brush. In the dark, a hand passed over Robin's hair, her face. Was that the lightest brush of warm, firm lips across her cheek? Then Michael tugged night vision goggles into place, swung around.

An instant later, even his footsteps had disappeared as though they'd never been.

> > >

Trevor Mulroney did not consider himself a greedy man.

Desperate, yes.

"Are you all idiots down there, incapable of running an op without me standing over you?" he snapped into his satphone. "Whose call was it to blow up that barge, anyway? If this was your doing, Krueger—"

"It was no one. An unforeseeable accident. Or maybe Jini wired it to blow when we got too close. We're still not sure what set it off."

"Yeah, well, it's your job to foresee things," Mulroney cut into his mission overseer's defensive protests. "Consider yourself relieved of operational command as soon as I get there."

The barge's loss was the final straw that had Trevor Mulroney canceling nightclub reservations with a Swedish model to charter the Gulfstream jet in which he'd just flown from London to Nairobi. A charter paid for by one more juggling of corporate credit cards. The first hundred tons of molybdenum ore had been irretrievably scattered across rainforest canopy when Jini's insurgency blew up the road. But Mulroney had counted on raising the sunken barge cargo the moment Jini's capture brought peace. If not enough rhenium to pay off this entire operation, it would be ample to stave off creditors until the mine was producing again. The measly twenty tons that would be returning with Trevor Mulroney in this same jet's cargo hold would not keep Earth Resources afloat till the end of the week.

Mulroney's strong hands clenched and unclenched. Tightening them around someone's throat right now would be a relief. But the only throat he wanted to crush under these fingers had once again managed to slip right through them. If Mulroney above anyone didn't know otherwise, he'd start buying his subordinates' inept excuses that his enemy was a *jini*, a ghost.

Down on the tarmac outside the nearest cabin porthole, Trevor Mulroney could see a young Kenyan airport worker manning a hose that was refueling his charter flight. White teeth flashed under security lights as the youth wrestled with the thick hose as though he counted himself privileged to extend a long day's shift well into the night to service some wealthy foreigner's private aircraft. Mulroney abruptly yanked down the window shade.

How well he remembered such an enthusiastic smile on the young man whose stubborn existence his clenched hands itched to choke out. He'd been visiting the London lab that processed samples from Earth Resources exploration projects, searching for that next mineral jackpot. He'd brushed past a station where a Congolese intern on scholarship at the Royal School of Mines was working when his briefcase snagged an electrical cord, spilling molten metal down the intern's left arm. The Congolese intern had fortunately blamed only himself for his injuries. His groveling apologies, a jumping to servile attention every time Mulroney stepped into the lab, was at first gratifying, then annoying enough to contemplate how one might revoke that scholarship.

But then the Congolese had come to Mulroney with a garbled story of strange rock outcroppings, a childhood pebble collection, rare metals—a story that had checked Mulroney's initial impulse to throw the youth out. Was not Africa full of such stories of hidden treasure?

A discreet independent sample test confirmed Earth Resources had hit the jackpot.

There'd actually been a moment when Trevor Mulroney had considered the intern's rambling proposal of joint ventures, new beginnings, a showcase of modern mining in the Ituri Rainforest. After all, Mulroney was not ruled by greed. The planet's first reliable source of rhenium offered profit enough for any empire, even with such scraps as its discoverer might demand.

But desperation proved a stronger motivation than avarice. The collapse of his Equatorial Guinea oil deal, the seizing of his coltan concessions in southeastern DRC, the embargo on his Central African Republic diamond fields was no single flood, but an entire tsunami washing at the sand on which Mulroney had so carefully erected his empire. And though Trevor Mulroney had long ago chosen disbelief in any Supreme Being who might expect some accountability in return, Joseph's knock at the door still seemed as fortuitous as any fairy godfather or genie of the lamp.

The United States already consumed nearly half the world's supply of rhenium, but growing economies like China and India now also had ever-larger appetites for the rare metal. Demand that kept rhenium prices sky-high.

If authorities in Kinshasa and Bunia found out the true value of the find, by the time they each grabbed their piece of this pie, said pie would be reduced to crumbs. And other bidders for the rare metal would never stand idly by, allowing Earth Resources to develop the Ituri concession in peace. The reason Howard Marshall and his influential allies had jumped at Mulroney's appeal.

So much easier to keep the pie intact and to himself. All Trevor Mulroney needed was a year. One year of developing the mine, openly selling off the molybdenum, stockpiling the rhenium and releasing it at discreet intervals into the market. One year would put Earth Resources on such a firm financial foundation it would no longer matter if—as was inevitable with enough time—the truth finally became known.

It should have been so easy. After all, how much of an obstacle was a single eager, young employee naive and loyal enough to offer Trevor Mulroney the world on a silver platter?

One might almost think something or someone out there ruling this universe was taking gleeful and malicious pleasure in deliberately setting up, then thwarting his every endeavor.

Maybe there really was a God.

CHAPTER
THIRTY-FOUR

The entire long, dark, toe-stubbing, silent trek back to the airstrip, Robin alternatively offered up mental curses to Michael, Joseph, her guide, Trevor Mulroney, the universe in general. Above all the first two since, deliberately or by oversight, neither had thought to remove the vine shackles binding Robin's wrists. Did they think she'd still make an attempt to run away? Try to follow?

Well, maybe, Robin could admit.

When she'd held her wrists out to her guide, he'd simply stared at her before setting off at a pace that made keeping up with his bobbing flashlight one continuous tightrope act. After a stumble left her sprawling full-length in the mud, he'd at least fractionally slowed his strides. Once they'd reached the road again, the flashlight's thin ray permitted Robin to pick her way along the overgrown median between ruts. At some point, a roar of engines passed overhead that had to be the two Mi-17s Robin had spied earlier taking off.

Robin could have sworn they'd traversed the distance of her outgoing trek several times over when her guide finally led the way off the road up a side trail. Only then did he tug a knife from his tattered shorts. Before Robin could muster apprehension, he'd slit her vine bindings. Handing over her knapsack along with Michael's borrowed penlight, he broke into a trot back down the trail.

"Thank you," Robin called softly after him in Swahili. "I hope your brother Jacob will be okay."

But night had already swallowed the youth up. *How do they do that without NVGs? They could make a fortune marketing it to special ops!*

Rubbing sore wrists, Robin headed in the opposite direction toward a pale glimmer of light. As she'd anticipated, a few more paces brought her out at the end of the airstrip. Robin didn't bother turning on a flashlight. Now that she was safely back, she'd no desire to rouse curiosity among Makuga's guard force or anyone else with eyes on the night.

Nor did she need such illumination. While she'd been tucked under the rainforest canopy, the moon had risen, its full, silver-yellow orb shedding a luminescence across the airstrip bright enough to read a newspaper headline, if not the finer print. But Robin did not immediately abandon the concealing shadows of the huge hardwood under whose branches she'd emerged. Instead she crouched in dark shadow to grope inside her knapsack. Two unfamiliar shapes were Joseph's flash drive and cell phone. Robin pulled out her own phone and checked the screen. No new text or voice messages, but—

Robin blinked. She'd endured a lifetime out there in the rainforest. Or at least a night. But her phone's screen read 9:09 p.m. Less than two hours since she'd rushed out of Miriam's house and down to the airstrip.

Rising again to her feet, Robin shouldered her knapsack. Michael's suggestion—make that order—had been for Robin to ferry Joseph's data up to Taraja, then walk away. Following that option was not even on the table. For two reasons. One, no matter how convincing the rebel leader's story, Robin had every intention of examining Joseph's evidence for herself.

More urgently, if getting this intel to Michael's BBC friend should involve risk—and Robin wasn't naive enough to gamble that it wouldn't—she wanted to keep that risk as far as possible from Miriam, Ephraim, their children, the refugees sheltering at the Taraja compound. Even simply uploading data files to the Internet would leave an electronic trail back to the computer system involved. In this case, Taraja's solar-powered satellite dish communications setup. As it was, a Skype trail already linked that BBC journalist with Taraja.

If Joseph's proof held what he'd vowed, if this story did break wide open, there would be fallout. And while Robin would soon be gone from this country, Miriam and her family had to live here. Live here with a corrupt warlord like Wamba as the hand of law. A warlord whose current position as governor was ample evidence that proving Joseph's accusations would not necessarily guarantee justice.

Using the Ares Solutions wireless system was a small enough risk since no one was likely to suspect Robin's involvement or search for such a connection. If anyone eventually did, hopefully by that time Robin would be long gone from this place.

Decision made, Robin headed toward the Ares Solutions camp. Following Michael and Nathaniel's earlier example, she threaded in and out of shadows edging the airstrip rather than across the bright band of moonlight. A prudent precaution since airstrip and encampment proved to be boiling with activity as Robin slipped closer. Militia uniforms were stringing out into a line along both sides of the airstrip. Closer at hand, the two South African pilots and several other Ares Solutions operatives swarmed over the two Mi-17s, checking missile mountings on one, the underbelly guns on the other, bolting on huge floor guns to angle downward from open side doors.

It seemed, as Robin had feared, tomorrow's dawn aerial assault was no idle threat. Had that earlier takeoff she'd witnessed been some sort of trial run?

But Robin didn't approach to ask because the glare of security spotlights now revealed as well the extent of mud, twigs, and sticky sap staining her own clothing, limbs, and face. A situation to be remedied before she drew that unwanted attention she'd been trying to avoid. The Serbian whose sprained ankle had relegated him to permanent sentry duty appeared to find nothing unusual in her belated arrival or filthy appearance. But Robin felt a need to offer explanation. "Things got pretty muddy setting up tents at the refugee camp."

The Serbian pulled back the mesh perimeter gate to let her through. "Yes, I saw the helicopters bring the new refugees."

A comment that made no sense, but Robin didn't linger for a clarification because Ernie Miller was heading their direction from the helicopters, and dodging his sharp eyes was easier than inventing a more plausible explanation. Ducking into her tent, Robin let her knapsack slide from her shoulder. She shook its contents onto her army cot, then removed her iPad from its protective sleeve and powered it up. In the dim glow of the iPad screen, Robin stripped off muddy clothing, sponged down quickly with hand wipes, and pulled on clean khakis.

Activating her Skype function next, Robin spread out Michael's scribbled note and typed in the username he'd written out. Contact information for an Alan Birenge popped up immediately. The profile photo showed a male with the café au lait complexion and narrow features of mixed African-European heritage, an intelligent gaze peering through wire-rimmed glasses. Bio info listed Kenya as birthplace, British citizenship, journalist as occupation. With Birenge's Skype username was also listed a phone number, by its calling code an international cell phone service like Robin's.

Robin jotted down the number, then reached for Joseph's flash drive and cell phone. But here she ran into a snag. To fulfill Michael's request and Joseph's, Robin had to load the material onto her iPad's hard drive before she could e-mail photos or files. But Robin's iPad did not include a USB port, and while she always packed a cable for her own digital camera, it didn't match Joseph's devices.

Robin's hesitation was brief. She might not possess equipment to coax the flash drive's contents or the cell phone's photo album onto her iPad, but she knew someone who undoubtedly had every cord and adapter in existence. Grabbing iPad, flash drive, and cell phone, Robin headed over to the communications trailer. Out on the airstrip, both helicopters were lifting into the air again. But this time they settled almost instantly back down onto a patch of grass and weeds at the edge of the airstrip. Robin had just reached the trailer steps when she saw the sputtering neon green of a flare being lit. Then another farther up the airstrip. They winked out as immediately as they'd been lit.

The helicopter rotors cut off again just as Robin stepped through the trailer door. As she'd expected, Carl Jensen was inside, huddled over his precious computer screens. Even better, she'd found him alone. "Hey, I saw them moving the helicopters out there. And setting up flares down the runway. What's going on?"

Carl didn't even raise his eyes from the screens, but he removed a set of MP3 earbuds to respond. "Prep for Mulroney's arrival. Flight should be here in a couple hours."

Robin set her iPad down abruptly on the nearest workstation. "But—I thought Mulroney was flying in from London tomorrow. And it's already after dark. Surely there's no commercial flights in or out of Bunia at this hour!"

"That's what the GPS and flares are for. Guess Mulroney decided he wanted in on tomorrow's kill. He's chartered a private jet." Carl tapped the screen in front of him. Against a high aerial shot of ghostly green rainforest canopy, Robin could make out a ragged circumference of the orange-yellow blotches she knew to be human heat signatures.

"You see this? Our bush hunt perimeter has now contracted to an eight-kilometer radius around the mine. Troops rounded up a few dozen more refugees, none of them our fugitive yet. Choppers dumped the strays at Taraja with the others. But we've still got scattered signals beyond our own guys. Dawn tomorrow we'll finish tightening our noose, then go after every remaining intruder individually. Worst-case scenario, if they don't surrender, Miller's team out there's getting ready to bomb the dickens out of them."

A reminder of the urgency of Robin's mission. Michael, Joseph, and the boy Jacob would be among those heat signatures still out there when dawn came. And if Trevor Mulroney was on his way here tonight, Robin had further motivation to get this behind her before considering how to face the Earth Resources CEO. Carl Jensen glanced up as Robin pulled out Joseph's cell phone to lay it beside the iPad. "Tech problem, eh? Network or hardware?"

His tone evinced neither interest nor annoyance. Mercenaries were not a particularly techno-savvy bunch, and bailing them out of their frequent electronics troubles was among Carl's many duties. Robin handed him the cell phone and flash drive. "Not a tech problem, just need a cord or something to download this phone's camera memory and any files on this drive to my iPad."

"Shouldn't be a problem." After rummaging through a box, Carl unearthed a selection of cords. He plugged a cable into Joseph's phone and connected to his own computer setup. The flash drive he inserted into a USB port. The device's memory folder showed up immediately on the monitor. Carl dragged its single document onto his own screen. "Let's take a look at what you've got here."

The pink-faced, stoop-shouldered Shaggy clone looked so eager, so benign, so *nice* that Robin was tempted to spill her entire errand to him and elicit his help. Except this wasn't Robin's secret to share. She put out a hand as Carl reached to joggle the mouse. "No, I don't want anything opened, just shifted straight to my iPad."

Carl asked no questions, simply choosing a separate cord to connect computer and iPad. A few clicks of the mouse dragged the first folder into the iPad's memory. His fingers flew next over the cell phone keypad. Within moments a moving image filled the screen.

Carl's disinterest abruptly vanished. "Hey, that one of our ops?

Wow! That's some action! Mind if I get a copy for the mission reports? That's not a shot I have from any of our cameras."

"Just some footage someone took. But I'd have to get their permission before passing it along."

Robin tamped down her impatience as Carl shifted video and photo albums from the cell phone to her iPad. The instant he'd finished, she snatched up the cell phone, unplugging both cords. As the file folders vanished obediently from the computer screen, she tugged the flash drive from the USB port. The single file Carl had dragged over onto the computer screen remained behind. Reaching for the mouse, Robin clicked to delete it. But something in her fumbling opened it instead, filling the screen with a meaningless jumble of letters, numbers, and graphs that included the terms *molybdenum, ore yields, rhenium trace*. Carl had leaned in for a closer view by the time Robin managed to close and delete the file, berating herself for her carelessness. With any luck, the contents of Joseph's flash drive would be as incomprehensible to him as to Robin.

As she'd hoped, Carl straightened up almost immediately with a slight grimace. "Molybdenum yields, eh? *Not* my cup of tea. Though I wouldn't have put you as the geology type either. Or are you one of those mercenaries who've caught the African treasure bug?"

"Neither," Robin answered with a calm she wasn't feeling. "But I like to know the basics on any new assignment. And this one includes a molybdenite mine, so I've been doing a little research."

"Yeah, well, wherever you got that particular research, it's clearly an error. Or at least a misplaced decimal. Rhenium trace levels at 3 percent? *Point* 3, maybe." Carl clearly misunderstood Robin's startled jerk. "Yeah, boring, I know. Just as well you haven't caught the bug. Odds of finding Africa's next big bonanza are somewhat less than winning the lottery. At least without a few million to invest in mineral exploration."

Robin had taken advantage of his digression to scoop up both flash drive and iPad. "Really? I've got to say my research for this mission is pretty well all I know on the subject. How do you know so much? I thought you said geology wasn't your cup of tea."

To Robin's relief, Carl had turned his interest back to his computer screens. "It isn't. But I come from a long family line of mining interests. Studied it in college until I figured out IT research was more my gig. You need anything else? 'Cause I've still got to get GPS coordinates for these heat signatures out to the ground units before I can turn in."

"No, that's it. Thanks!" Robin did not completely release her breath until she was back inside her tent. At least it had been Carl Jensen and not Pieter Krueger or even Trevor Mulroney who'd been witness to that little fiasco. As single-minded as the tech guru had shown himself to be, he'd likely forgotten Robin and her errand already. And at least she had the pictures.

Robin called up first the video Carl had inadvertently drawn to the screen. It was only a few minutes long, but by the end Robin's hands were clenched, her emotions a raging tempest between fury and heartbreak. The backdrop was a rainforest village indistinguishable from hundreds of others. But the fetishes and amulets, the bone-and-teeth necklaces draped over Congolese army uniforms had become too familiar to Robin to be anything but Wamba's militia, as Joseph had claimed. Robin wanted to cry out a warning as torches were tossed onto thatched roofs, occupants mowed down by gunfire as they scrambled out narrow doorways, women and even young girls grabbed and thrown to the ground.

When the video ended, Robin opened the photos, several dozen of them. The brutality they revealed was as sickening as it was unnecessary if the only purpose was to make Jini out to be a war criminal. How had Joseph managed to remain silent and immobile long enough to document these atrocities? No wonder the rebel leader battled such overwhelming guilt. And yet to step out into that militia rabble would surely have accomplished nothing beyond throwing his own life away.

One more video clip was even shorter than the other. But by the time its images ran their course, Robin found herself stabbing at the volume controls to mute the machine, then stepping to the tent flap to ensure no one was close enough to have overheard. Only then did she play it through again. Joseph was right. His proof was as compelling as it was explosive. And far too dangerous for Robin to risk having it found in her possession.

For in the interval between filming the first and second video, daybreak had arrived at that horrific scene. And if most of the militia shown in video and pictures were too hazy of feature for positive identification, one man had caught the light of dawn full on his face as he strode directly toward where Joseph must have been hiding with that cell phone.

He was clearly the commander, his harsh voice issuing orders in Swahili that his companions scrambled to carry out. Robin recognized the face and huge, powerful frame as she'd recognized the voice before she'd silenced it. The security chief for Trevor Mulroney's mining operation and field commander of the Ares Solutions team's local allies.

Samuel Makuga.

CHAPTER
THIRTY-FIVE

Maybe Trevor Mulroney didn't know just how far Makuga planned to go out there!

Robin opened her iPad's Skype function and tapped Alan Birenge's username. *I've got to get this sent off, then erase it from my hard drive!*

Robin had been furious when Joseph and Michael scoffed at her cavalier suggestion that the rebel leader surrender himself and let the proper legal authorities sort things out. But now Robin herself was supremely conscious of being a virtual captive on a rainforest base with no way out except aircraft controlled by the very man Joseph accused, while those proper legal authorities consisted of two thousand militia under the very commander she'd just witnessed on her iPad screen ordering unspeakable atrocities.

What would Makuga do if he found out I have this? What he did to silence those mine victims at the clinic?

Because whatever excuses or disclaimers Mulroney might still offer for his own actions, she'd no longer any doubt after watching those videos that the Taraja massacre had been by Makuga's orders, whether he'd been personally present or not. Robin let the Skype call ring again and again until it became clear no one would answer. Perhaps Alan Birenge was simply away from his computer at this hour. Grabbing her cell phone instead, Robin punched in the contact number listed in the journalist's Skype profile.

"Who is this? Where did you get this number?"

Robin was so glad to hear a crisp British accent, she ignored its angry suspicion. "Is this Alan Birenge? I . . . Can you talk?"

"Speak up! I can't hear you."

Robin didn't dare speak too loudly. Not with possible listening ears outside her tent. Already she was stuffing iPad, flash drive, cell phone back into her knapsack. Slinging it over her shoulder, she hissed into the phone. "I'm going somewhere I can speak louder. I'm a friend of Dr. Michael Stewart. He asked me to contact you."

"Michael!" Suspicion abruptly left the other voice. "That's all you needed to say! Where is the doctor? I'd like to speak to him too. Is this about the intel he asked me to check yesterday? You wouldn't believe the hornet's nest that's stirred up on my end!"

While the journalist spoke, Robin had ducked outside and was hurrying through tents and around the storage hut toward the rear of the encampment. She stopped at the perimeter wire. Breaching the electronic fence would trigger all kinds of sensors in the communications trailer. But the only person now in sight was a militia guard patrolling outside the perimeter fence. By the glowing red ember that rose and fell, he was also smoking. And not cigarettes but cannabis, from the sickly sweet smoke a breeze wafted her way. He did not even turn his gaze from the rainforest in Robin's direction. Nor would he likely speak any English.

Which left Robin feeling safe enough to raise her voice slightly. "I'm sorry, but Michael's kind of unavailable at the moment. We've got a bit of a hornet's nest here, too. Which is why he asked me to contact you. I've got some photos, video footage, and other files he said you'd know what to do with. I can upload them right now if you have an e-mail address to receive them."

The British accent sharpened to sudden interest. "Are you talking Wamba or Trevor Mulroney? I wanted to let Michael know my dead end yesterday on that prison labor business turned out to be a hotter potato than if I'd found something. Within hours of slipping me that non-intel, my informant had Wamba's police knocking down his door. Thanks to a tip-off, he'd already skipped town. But I grabbed the next flight out to Uganda, along with my wife and kids. Whatever trouble Michael Stewart has found out there at Taraja, I'd rather not be in Bunia when Wamba figures out who my wife's cousin passed that non-intel to. We're just exiting the Kampala airport now, in fact."

"Oh no!" As her exclamation drew a lethargic glance from the strolling guard, Robin lowered her voice. "I don't think Michael would want me to put your family in danger by sending you this information. What I've got to send is pretty explosive. Is there someone else I could contact? Your embassy, maybe?"

"I doubt you could find intel more explosive than I've seen in a decade of covering this region's nasty little wars." The journalist's response was bone dry. "But if you've got dirt on Trevor Mulroney, I want it. I've been digging into that man for years. Natural curiosity since like me he arrived in the UK from Africa with hardly a shirt to his back. But something about his rags-to-riches story always smelled a little off. A mercenary turned billionaire may be legit, but when you're dealing with this part of the world, the odds of funny business are off the charts. Especially if he's hooking up with a lowlife like Wamba. All to say, I'll handle worrying about my family's safety. As to me, this is what I do. Trevor Mulroney may think he's hot stuff. But in the UK, nothing beats power of the press! You give me the goods, and it'll be Mulroney breaking on this story, not me. So what do you have?"

Robin hurriedly summed up Joseph's narrative. "The pictures and video prove it wasn't rebels but Wamba's own troops who massacred those villages. And Joseph says the technical data will show the true value of the discovery. But it's Michael I'm worried about. He's out there in the jungle right now. If Trevor Mulroney finds out what he's doing, what he knows, what I'm sending you—well, running some whistle-blowing news story isn't going to help much here on the ground."

"Don't let Mulroney find out, then," the journalist responded uncompromisingly. "And if you've got what you say, believe me, it won't be just a story I'll be stirring up on my end. Not when Michael Stewart's involved. I don't know if he's mentioned my wife's from Bunia. Our youngest daughter was born there just three months ago with a hole in her heart. While the local docs told us to plan a funeral, Michael Stewart performed open-heart surgery few docs would care to attempt outside the Mayo Clinic. Our little one's doing fine now, thanks to him. So if Michael Stewart asks me to check a story or walk on coals, he can count on it."

Another Michael Stewart conquest.

Robin could hear a roar of jet engines in the background, an excited chatter of children, the wail of an infant. The British drawl was now hurried. "Look, I've got to go. Give me an hour to reach the hotel, another to arrange Internet hookup. If you want to send those files so they're waiting for me, my e-mail address is just my first and last name at BBC.com. Meanwhile, something else you might do for me. If you've got a camera, maybe you can take some discreet photos of your own encampment. The militia. Those combat choppers. Any evidence of aggressive intent. If you can catch Mulroney on-site, even better."

The journalist broke contact. Hurrying back to her tent, Robin pulled her iPad out again. She grouped the cell phone photos into a zip file, the document folder from Joseph's flash drive into another, then attached both to an e-mail, hitting Send with a feeling of inordinate relief. But the video clips were another matter. Each clip was tenfold the megabytes of both zip files combined. After her Internet connection jammed twice, Robin abandoned her efforts and slipped outside with a digital camera. Even on the highest night setting, her discreet snapshots proved dark. But the impression of a military encampment, especially those two combat helicopters and armed guards, was clear enough.

Returning to her tent, Robin uploaded the photos, then sent off a third zip file. Another attempt to send the video clips failed. The BBC journalist would just have to settle for photos. Robin itched to scrub her hard drive clean of the telltale files, bury that flash drive and cell phone in some hole in the ground. But caution dictated she confirm first that the files had arrived intact.

Robin stretched out on her cot, but she was too keyed up for sleep. Had Michael and Joseph reached Jacob yet? Was the boy still alive, or had Robin's interruption delayed them too long? *No, don't go there! He'll be fine. He has to be!*

Robin's thoughts jumped instead to her own earlier harsh words. *I told Michael I'd never forgive him! I hope he knows I didn't mean it! At least once I understood his reasons. That he can forgive me for once again not trusting him!*

But that was an even less pleasant subject to occupy her thoughts. Giving up attempts to doze, Robin reached for her phone. But her sister's speed dial number elicited only the same message. *If they're still at the hospital, it can't be good. Maybe the crisis came faster than Kristi's pediatrician expected. Which means I've failed them in not finding funds in time. And now I'm not even there to be with Kristi. And with Kelli. Kelli's always fallen apart when the smallest thing goes wrong. If anything happens to Kristi, she will completely lose it.*

Or was Robin not giving her sister enough credit? Impulsively Robin reached for her iPad. What was it Miriam had quoted from the biblical story of Job about suffering and trials refining a person like gold?

Robin's packing had not included a Bible in years. She wasn't even sure what had happened to the small leather-bound volume engraved with her name that had been a birthday gift from her mother that last year in Nairobi. Maybe still among effects shipped home from Afghanistan that Robin had never bothered to open. But that was what online search engines were for. It took only a few keywords to find the quote in Job 23:10: "When he has tested me, I will come forth as gold."

The site cross-referenced similar Scriptures. Because she needed a distraction, Robin followed their links.

Psalm 66:10: "For you, O God, tested us; you refined us like silver."

Zechariah 13:9: "I will refine them like silver and test them like gold. They will call on my name and I will answer them; I will say, 'They are my people,' and they will say, 'The LORD is our God.'"

James 1:2-3: "Consider it pure joy, my brothers, whenever you face trials of many kinds, because you know that the testing of your faith develops perseverance."

1 Peter 1:6-7: "In this you greatly rejoice, though now for a little while you may have had to suffer grief in all kinds of trials. These have come so that your faith—of greater worth than gold, which perishes even though refined by fire—may be proved genuine and may result in praise, glory and honor when Jesus Christ is revealed."

The final reference came from the same epistle of the apostle Peter that Michael's sister had called a treatise on suffering. Robin read it through again more slowly. *Okay, so I get Miriam's point about why God would let human beings suffer the ultimate consequences of their own constantly awful choices. If nothing else, we just plain deserve it! And I can get the concept of testing and refining to make or break us the way a drill sergeant does at boot camp. I can even understand God doing it for our own ultimate good. Like when I'd take Kristi in for her vaccinations when she was a baby because Kelli couldn't bear to hear her cry. And it nearly broke my heart too. But I knew it had to be done to prevent far worse pain and sickness down the line.*

But rejoicing in trials and grief and pain? That's the piece I just can't grasp. I hated the drill sergeant who tormented me at boot camp. As I've hated my father and Kelli's no-good husband. Even Kelli, too, at times. And Michael. And yes, God, too, for not giving me the fairy tale. For hurting me whether it was for my own good or not!

And yet when I'd take Kristi in for those vaccinations, she never hated me. No, she trusted me, even though she knew I was the one submitting her to such pain. She trusted my love for her so much that she somehow knew I'd never subject her to a sharp needle if it wasn't for a purpose, for her own good. And though she still cried because it hurt, she would put her little arms around my neck, let me comfort her, and just keep on loving and trusting me in return.

Something in her line of thinking caught Robin. Then suddenly her fingers were flying over the screen.

Yes, there was the link she'd brushed through, a passage Miriam had referenced from 2 Corinthians chapter 1:

"Praise be to the God and Father of our Lord Jesus Christ, the Father of compassion and the God of all comfort, who comforts us in all our troubles, so that we can comfort those in any trouble with the comfort we ourselves have received from God."

Four times the passage repeated that single word *comfort*. *Miriam said that in the darkest night of what those men did to her, she felt God*

in the darkness with her. Comforting her. Loving her. Bringing meaning
and hope to her suffering even when he didn't just whisk it all away.

Robin's fingers were flying again. She lingered over a passage in
Lamentations 3, finding its heart cry to be so familiar.

> "I remember my affliction and my wandering, the bitterness
> and the gall. I well remember them, and my soul is downcast
> within me. Yet this I call to mind and therefore I have hope:
> Because of the LORD's great love we are not consumed, for
> his compassions never fail. They are new every morning;
> great is your faithfulness."

According to a footnote, the author of Lamentations was the
prophet Jeremiah, writing during the final days of his nation's destruction as Israel was carried off into exile by King Nebuchadnezzar to
Babylon. Jeremiah had been a servant of God. Yet he, too, had known
bitterness, suffering, wandering, depression.

But he'd also known hope. The same hope Miriam had expressed.
A hope that though the darkness was only too real, God's love, compassion, and faithfulness were equally real.

A word search for *hope* brought up the other reference Miriam
had quoted from the book of Romans, chapter 5.

> "We also rejoice in our sufferings, because we know that
> suffering produces perseverance; perseverance, character; and
> character, hope. And hope does not disappoint us, because
> God has poured out his love into our hearts."

Robin read on, transfixed.

"How can you sing?" she'd demanded of Miriam only a few
hours ago. "How can they sing? How can you let them believe such
a terrible, cruel lie?"

"It isn't a lie. Far from it! It's their hope, our hope," Miriam had insisted.

And here, leaping from her iPad screen as though in neon lights, was the explanation for such an improbable statement. The hope that permitted Congolese fugitives to sing with such joy and sincerity in the middle of a refugee camp. That allowed the teenage daughter of foreign missionaries to rejoice despite rape and scars and a child born out of horror and cruelty. That permitted Jeremiah to watch the destruction and exile of his nation with faith instead of despair.

"You see, at just the right time, when we were still powerless, Christ died for the ungodly. Very rarely will anyone die for a righteous man, though for a good man someone might possibly dare to die. But God demonstrates his own love for us in this: While we were still sinners, Christ died for us."

Christ.
Jesus.
Yesu.
The common thread of all those Swahili worship songs.
Yesu, Light of the World.
Yesu, my Savior.
Yesu anipenda. Jesus loves me.
This then was the secret to Miriam's joy. Not what she knew. But whom she knew.

Jesus Christ, living evidence of God's enduring, boundless love for his creation. Light in the darkness of human suffering and evil. God himself, Immanuel, as Miriam had so vividly described, stepping into the confines of his own creation, human time and space, to offer up his own life for an ungrateful, sinful humanity in the ultimate outpouring of divine love and redemption.

Robin was so engrossed in thought that when an aircraft roared in low above the tent, she jerked upright, knocking her iPad from the army cot. It didn't seem possible enough time had passed for Trevor Mulroney's chartered flight to have arrived. But when Robin scrambled to pick up the iPad, the clock on the screen read 11:07 p.m. Late enough that Alan Birenge should be calling back any moment as well.

A reminder of the journalist's final request. Snatching up camera and cell phone, Robin slipped out of her tent. A graceful white bird was banking against the moonlit night to line up with the airstrip. Along both sides, militia had now lit their flares to mark a corridor. Touching down, the Gulfstream taxied to a stop just beyond the encampment perimeter.

Robin lingered in the shadows between tents to snap photos as steps unfolded from the fuselage and Trevor Mulroney descended from the plane. But others were already hurrying forward, including Pieter Krueger and Samuel Makuga. Just seeing Makuga after what she'd witnessed on those videos roiled Robin's stomach. But she maneuvered near enough for several close-ups of Trevor Mulroney greeting the Ares Solutions mission chief and Congolese field commander. She'd just angled around for a single snapshot of the registration number on the Gulfstream's tail when her phone rang, its generic ringtone loud enough in the darkness to jerk every head in her direction.

Including Trevor Mulroney's.

Robin fumbled to slide her digital camera discreetly into one pants pocket while sliding her cell phone out of another. Had her employer seen the camera? *It doesn't matter! He's got zero reason to suspect you of anything! Unless you draw attention by acting like you've got a guilty conscience!*

And certainly Trevor Mulroney and his companions were already turning away as Robin strolled casually back toward her tent, cell phone to her ear. She ducked inside before breathing into the phone, "This is Robin Duncan."

"Alan Birenge here. You said there was video. I need it."

Robin settled herself on the cot where the iPad's screen still glowed against the dark. "The files were too big for e-mailing."

"Then upload them to YouTube and send me the link. Can you do that?"

"I've never done it. But I've put video clips on Facebook." One of the ways she'd let Kristi share her travels. Robin checked to make sure the wireless connection had not been affected by her iPad's tumble to the ground. No, it was still connected. "I assume YouTube is similar?"

"Actually, if you're accustomed to using Facebook, you can upload the clips there and send me a friend request. If I'm to make a case against Mulroney, I need that clip showing Wamba's second in command to prove those weren't just random insurgents. And something, anything connecting this Makuga with Trevor Mulroney."

"Actually, Trevor Mulroney just arrived. I got a couple shots of him speaking with Samuel Makuga." Robin was already reconnecting her camera to her iPad. "I'll send them right away."

"Good. Because I was wrong about ever being handed a story more explosive than this one. Those lab reports alone have staggering political implications. International markets will have a field day on this. As to a Fortune 500 CEO with aspirations of British knighthood being tied to war atrocities and a plot to steal billions in mineral wealth from a friendly government—that's TNT! If I can get that final intel, this will be on every cable news channel and head-of-state desk in the industrialized world by morning. Which reminds me, I'd suggest getting yourself well away from there before this all hits the fan. What you've sent me confirms my own experience of how far Mulroney and Wamba both will go when anything gets in their way. I'll do what I can to scramble a relief force over there. Meanwhile, just lay low." He paused briefly. "Got a call coming in. You upload that last intel right away. I'll call back to let you know I've got it."

As the line went dead, Robin lowered her phone, unease growing in her stomach. In carrying out Joseph's request, she'd anticipated initiating some sort of official investigation, not a global news blitz. Though Trevor Mulroney currently had no reason to suspect what Robin was up to, once Joseph's evidence hit news channels, Carl Jensen at least would guess immediately who was responsible. And it was wishful thinking that he wouldn't mention seeing a certain female team member with the very same video clip or rhenium yield graph.

> > >

Carl Jensen was not proud of what he'd done, but neither was he particularly ashamed. A besetting curiosity had propelled him to his current position in life and was a chief reason he'd been chosen for this assignment. The video clip he'd glimpsed on Ms. Duncan's iPad had roused avarice if only because he'd seen nothing similar in his footage of yesterday's dawn raid, from which the clip appeared to have originated.

Some operative's personal memento, undoubtedly, of this mission's most extreme action sequence to date. And not Ms. Duncan since she hadn't participated in the village raid. Carl could track down the operative's identity, ask for a copy. But how much simpler to surreptitiously copy the files to his own hard drive while transferring them to Ms. Duncan's iPad.

Carl resisted a glance at the new intel until he'd finished his current task, tapping a foot to the hip-hop rhythm blasting through his earbuds. So long as the remaining knots of human heat signatures did not move again before morning, his coordinates would have a team of Ares Solutions operatives and their local allies in place to hit each at dawn. If, like last night's barge fugitives, they retreated into the canopy, Carl would track them like an electronic hound after rodents and call in the Mi-17s. This was more fun than video games, if a million times more expensive.

That his targets were flesh and blood didn't enter Carl's calculations. This was how he preferred his involvement with humanity. At a safe distance. Behind the clean shield of a computer screen. Not like that horrible mob attack at the Bunia airport, which his pity for a human child had sucked him into. A blunder that reinforced why mathematical calculations based on ample and accurate data were a far more reliable basis for life's decisions than emotion.

When he finally turned his attention to the new video, it took only a few frames to recognize this footage had not come from the recent Ares Solutions dawn raid, however similar its rainforest village backdrop. Nor were the tactics such as any private military company would authorize.

Carl froze the final video clip on a close-up of Samuel Makuga. On a neighboring screen, he started a Google search. There were advantages to possessing a photographic memory. But the opening lines of that report Ms. Duncan claimed to have pulled from an Internet search produced no results. Nothing even similar.

Carl stared at the screen contemplatively before removing his earbuds to replace them with a Bluetooth headset. "Uncle Howard? Carl here. Yep, everything's on schedule. Yes, package is still working fine. You've received the intel reports? No, actually, that's not why I'm calling. Is there something out here you haven't filled me in on? Something dealing with—say, the subject of rhenium?"

If silence was the Bluetooth's only response, the same could not be said from behind Carl. A clang of the trailer door slamming shut was not as loud as the furious roar that followed.

"What did you just say?"

CHAPTER THIRTY-SIX

Robin prepared a fresh e-mail to Alan Birenge with the latest photos, then opened her Facebook account. She sent off the friend request before selecting Joseph's two video clips to upload into a new video album. But she did not immediately click on the upload icon or send the waiting e-mail.

I don't have to do this now. If I hold off sending these last photos and that video clip Carl Jensen saw until I've put myself out of Trevor Mulroney's reach, there won't be enough to connect me. Or for that matter, for Alan Birenge to convince his superiors to run the story before I'm safely away. The C-130's making another cargo run tomorrow. I could put in my resignation, fly out to Bunia, then send it from there. Or even from the air once I've booked a flight across the border.

Surely Michael, Joseph, and the BBC journalist, too, would understand if they knew the risk. After all, beyond any threat to herself, Robin had to think of Kristi and Kelli, for whom Robin was the sole means of support.

The worst was that she'd no doubt the others would agree her safety was a top priority. But that was also a coward's way out. Nor could Robin be confident that time remained for such dawdling.

Michael asked how I could expect him to think of his own skin if it meant abandoning Jacob out there in the rainforest. What if delaying this story places Michael and Jacob and Joseph and the others in greater danger? I have no idea what strings Alan Birenge thinks he can pull. But if he's to have any hope of scrambling some kind of relief force before tomorrow's assault, he needs this intel tonight. So how can I even factor in some hypothetical risk to my own safety?

Despite the heat of the jungle night, Robin found she was shivering slightly as her hand remained poised above the iPad screen. Not even in a combat zone in Afghanistan could she remember feeling this alone and unsure.

No, admit it—you're just plain scared! In Afghanistan, Robin had never been alone. Always she'd been able to count on her fellow Marines to have her back. And behind them, if necessary, was the entire might of her nation's formidable armed forces.

Here Robin was entirely on her own, her enemy the very leadership in whom she'd placed her trust.

But was she truly so alone?

Robin abruptly brushed the screen, but to neither the Facebook upload link nor her e-mail. Instead she restored the Scripture passage that had been on the screen when her iPad had toppled from the cot.

"We know that suffering produces perseverance; perseverance, character; and character, hope. And hope does not disappoint us, because God has poured out his love into our hearts. . . . When we were still powerless, Christ died for the ungodly. . . . While we were still sinners, Christ died for us."

Robin dropped her hand, squeezing her eyes shut in an attitude of prayer. *God, if you're listening—no, I know you're listening! It's just that I feel so powerless right now. If anything in my life has produced an ounce of perseverance or character, I'm not seeing it. I've been so angry with you for so long! I've yelled at you and begged you to do what I want. But what I haven't done is trust that you know what you're doing in my life. That whatever it is you are doing is because you love me so much.*

Right now I'm so afraid. Afraid of making the wrong choice. Afraid of what will happen to Kristi and Kelli if something happens to me. Afraid of what will happen to Michael, to Joseph and Jacob and Miriam and Ephraim and the others if I don't act.

And I'm so tired of being afraid. Even more tired of feeling I always have to be brave and independent and self-reliant because I'm the only one I can count on. I'm not sure I'm quite ready for what Miriam and all those verses had to say about rejoicing in suffering. But what I do choose at this moment is to place my trust in you. To trust the truth of "Yesu anipenda"—"Jesus loves me." To trust also your love for Kristi and Kelli and . . . well, anyone else I love. You hold them in your hands. And whatever happens this day, I choose to entrust their future into your care. Give me the courage to do now what I know you've called me to do, whatever the consequences turn out to be for me or anyone else.

Robin's surrender evoked no thunderous reply from heaven, no brilliant white light. She hadn't expected it. But neither was she prepared for the profound calm settling over her so that she was no longer afraid. A breeze had inserted itself through the dangling flap of the tent. Even as it brushed cooling fingers over Robin's heated face, some long-frozen core deep within Robin's heart unlocked, flooding her with such a gentle realization of love and warmth and comfort that she might have been wrapped in the embrace of her mother's arms.

God's arms.

I am not alone. Yesu anipenda, *this I know.*

Opening her eyes to the waiting iPad screen, Robin hesitated no longer. A swipe on the screen brought up her e-mail, where she composed a quick note to Birenge and hit Send. Then to her Facebook page. She tapped again to upload the first video clip.

But a moment later she stared with dismay at the notification on the screen: *Access denied.*

> > >

"And just who are you speaking to?" Trevor Mulroney fumed even as shuffles and knocks outside the trailer swung him back around. He'd instinctively slammed the door in the face of Pieter Krueger and his other companions when he'd heard Carl Jensen's incredible question. As the doorknob rattled, he reached to lock the dead bolt, calling, "Wait for me at the aircraft. Jensen and I have some communications issues to sort out."

The doorknob stopped rattling. Across the trailer, his reconnaissance tech's mouth hung open, a guilty expression confirming that Mulroney's ears had not deceived him. With two long strides across the trailer, Trevor Mulroney snatched the Bluetooth headset from Jensen's head. By then he'd spotted the Google search on one screen, a frozen image of Samuel Makuga on another. Stabbing at a keyboard, he released the image so that the video clip began to play. "What is this? Where could you possibly have got your hands on it?"

"Hey, y'all, what's going on over there?"

Mulroney had no difficulty recognizing the tinny drawl coming from the Bluetooth. "Howard Marshall? Put him on speaker now!"

As Jensen fumbled to obey, Mulroney demanded, his fury rising, "You want to tell me, Marshall, what you're doing discussing a certain subject with my tech here? No, let me guess. He's your man. He's been your eyes and ears since the beginning."

"Hey, you asked for a sneak preview of our latest reconnaissance package," the Texas drawl reminded. "I had to send someone with it. Better my own nephew than an outsider."

"Your nephew!" Mulroney glared at the tech. "So let me guess— he's in the family business too."

A snort through the speaker acknowledged that Mulroney's gibe wasn't referencing Marshall Corp, but the less publicized, if well-documented role that powerful clan had played for the last three generations in their nation's intelligence networks.

"Not officially. More of a temporary consultant. I sent Carl to handle your reconnaissance package, nothing more or less. Count the occasional intel report as a perk for the considerable investment Marshall Corp has riding on this too. Of more interest is why my nephew has raised that certain subject."

"Just what I'm trying to find out," Mulroney responded grimly. "Jensen, you got an explanation? Where did that Makuga clip turn up? That's not an Ares Solutions op. And why this particular Google search?"

Curiosity had replaced guilt in the pale-blue eyes rising speculatively from keyboard and computer screens. "To be honest, I hadn't realized till now there was anything to explain. The video clip was something our team translator brought in with a bunch of other photos. Asked me to download them from a cell phone. The Google search—well, I happened to see on Ms. Duncan's iPad a document showing molybdenum and rhenium yields, graphs, that kind of thing. She said it was just some Internet research. Weird thing was the grade of rhenium, ranging around 3 percent. I assumed it was a typo. Except when I tried to verify that document on the Internet, I couldn't find anything that matched."

Jensen shrugged. "Like I said, it didn't seem like much. But Uncle Howard was adamant to give him a buzz if anything popped out of place. So I did."

Trevor Mulroney had gone completely still. But his mind was racing. It couldn't be! Yet what other explanation was there? "Where is Duncan now? No, wait, I saw her outside taking a phone call. Jensen, you got some way here of tracking phone, e-mail, Internet activity? Duncan's specifically. Say, for the last twenty-four hours."

"I can't access her personal cell phone without some serious hacking. But I can pull up anything done through the Ares Solutions server." Carl Jensen's fingers were already typing furiously. "Here we go. She accessed Skype a couple hours back. Would have been right after she had me transfer those images. No actual calls made. Then she got into her e-mail, where she sent a couple messages. Then she spent the next hour or so surfing the Internet."

The reconnaissance tech looked up suddenly. "She's back online right now! Trying to send another e-mail."

"Then kill it!" The sharp order came simultaneously from Trevor Mulroney and the Bluetooth speaker.

Carl Jensen's fingers danced. "I've terminated her access to the server. That last e-mail didn't make it out, and she won't be able to get online without reactivating her account."

"Good, let's pull her in, then." Trevor Mulroney had taken a stride toward the door when he swung back. "No, wait, let me see first what she mailed off earlier. And what she's been researching."

The first zip file held JPEGs of a rainforest village. Trevor Mulroney's jaw tightened as he shifted through image after image. It tightened further when another file proved to hold shots of the Ares Solutions encampment itself. But it was a third zip file that left him stunned. How could documents he'd seen last on his desk in London six months ago possibly have found their way into the hands of Lt. Chris R. Duncan in the middle of the Ituri Rainforest? Only one explanation was possible, incredible as it might be.

"What is it?" Marshall's voice demanded from the speaker. "Do we have a problem here?"

"Oh, we've got a problem, all right!" Mulroney responded. "It's bad enough I'm seeing some extremely compromising photos of Wamba's security ops on our behalf. But that initial report I told you about—well, I'm looking at it."

"And just where did that turn up?"

"Only possibility is the original source. Which is the good news. It means we're getting very close to accomplishing our mission here."

"Not close enough!" the Texas drawl snapped. "Are we going to need damage control? Do I need to call—family contacts?"

"No!" Trevor Mulroney responded sharply. "Nothing has changed. This is my project, my mission. We have everything under control.

Damage completely contained. Matter of fact, I'm expecting our snooping translator to hand us our target by morning."

"Good. Because understand—nothing personal, of course—that if you can't bring these little 'problems' under control, I will have to reconsider my own investment in this venture."

As the speaker went silent, the pale-blue eyes glanced up again. "Okay, so I know Uncle Howard too well to ask what's going on here. I gather our pretty female translator has been naughty. But I'm not spotting anything in Ms. Duncan's browsing history to explain why she'd be suddenly throwing in with the opposition. It's nothing but a bunch of Bible references. You think the woman's flipped some kind of religious lid? Developed some sort of guilty conscience about our mission here? Women can be funny about combat missions, collateral damage, all that stuff."

"Yeah, something like that," Trevor Mulroney answered grimly. If Jensen hadn't put together the implications of the recipient's BBC e-mail address, he wasn't about to enlighten him. Striding from the trailer, Mulroney snatched up a hand radio to page Pieter Krueger. "Get Duncan in here now! And put together a posse. We've got some bush meat to round up."

> > >

No sooner had the Earth Resources CEO stormed out of the communications trailer than Carl Jensen quickly busied himself. Not surprisingly, the Bluetooth jangled again before he'd finished. Howard Marshall was on the line.

"I'm sure you know why I called back."

"Yep, sending it right now." Carl Jensen hit a key, forwarding the e-mails with their attached files that had so interested Trevor Mulroney. To them had been added the video clips.

"I'll have my people take a look. Some of them should still be in the office on that side of the Atlantic."

"That side of the Atlantic?" The curiosity that was Carl's besetting characteristic unfurled its antenna. "So what side are you on, Uncle Howard?"

"Kinshasa."

"Kinshasa! What are you doing there?"

"Don't ask."

"What are you going to do with—?"

"Never mind. Just shut up and listen to what I need you to do."

An inquiring mind knew when it had hit an impenetrable wall. Carl snapped his jaw shut and waited for his uncle's orders.

CHAPTER
THIRTY-SEVEN

Robin's first assumption was that the Ares Solutions wireless server had malfunctioned. But when a check proved the iPad was still connected to the Ares wireless service, Robin pulled up her status. It read, *IP address not valid.*

Robin's heart chilled. It could hardly be coincidence that with Trevor Mulroney's arrival, her company Internet account had been mysteriously terminated. *Mulroney knows.*

Even as unpleasant scenarios churned through her head, Robin had jumped from her cot. Stuffing the iPad, the two cell phones, and the flash drive into her knapsack, she tucked in water bottles and protein bars to replace what she'd given the refugee children. *But where can I go? There's no way I can outrun Carl's surveillance gear.*

Panic had now propelled Robin from the tent. Since she'd last ventured outside, the earlier rain clouds had drifted back in to blot out the star patterns, and while moonlight still filtered through a break in the clouds, a soft drizzle was again falling. Which perhaps explained why the Serbian sentry had retreated to the open hatch of the Gulfstream a dozen paces away. Beyond him, interior lighting revealed other Ares Solutions teammates milling around inside the plane's cabin. All was quiet, so clearly no alarm had yet been raised. Robin ducked back into her tent long enough to snatch the rain poncho hanging there, tugging its plastic shield over both clothing and knapsack. The Serbian watched without comment as Robin emerged moments later through the mesh perimeter gate.

Maybe it really was just a glitch in the system. Or maybe Mulroney's still trying to figure things out. Which might buy me some time for a head start. The worst is, I never got off the data that really counts. Without the footage and new pictures, there's nothing to implicate Trevor Mulroney. Or prove where those rhenium samples came from. Even if Alan Birenge pursues an investigation, Mulroney will have time to cover his tracks, come up with a plausible story. Joseph's right! Trevor Mulroney always wins. He's just too powerful.

Robin reached for that earlier calm, the sensation of being wrapped in loving arms. *Heavenly Father, Yesu, my Savior, I thought I'd found courage. But I'm so afraid again. I've failed Michael and Joseph. And I don't know what to do!*

Oh yes, you do!

Was that quiet reassurance from Robin's own mind? Or an answer from heaven itself? Either way, panic ebbed from Robin. *Yes, I do know what to do! There is a way, especially if the alarm hasn't been raised yet. If I can get up to Taraja, I can send that intel through their server. Now that I have the files, I can just connect my own iPad to their wireless, so there will be no trace of Joseph's files left on their computer. Once I get that evidence to Alan Birenge, it won't matter so much if Mulroney catches me. One way or another, there will be justice for Joseph and his people.*

With deliberation, Robin kept herself in full view of the Serbian guard as she threaded between tents occupied by Wamba militia toward the burned-out shells of the original Taraja township beyond. *If he reports seeing me, they'll think I've headed toward the old road to Bunia.*

But as soon as she reached a toppled wall, Robin slid behind it into deep shadow and began working her way through uncleared brush. It took longer than she'd hoped to reach the end of the airstrip, wind through hardwoods to the other side, then angle through ferns, banana palms, bamboo until she hit the trail to Taraja. But once under cover of fruit trees overhanging the track, Robin turned on Michael's penlight and broke into a run.

A single light glimmered from a clinic window when Robin emerged into the clearing. But the cinder-block mission house appeared as wrapped in sleep as the refugee tents. Robin didn't knock or call, fearing to rouse the whole camp. Instead she slipped around to an open bedroom window, shining the tiny flashlight through metal bars in hopes of rousing some sleeping resident.

But that proved unnecessary. Even as the narrow ray panned across a sprawl of small bodies, she heard Miriam's sweet alto humming a Swahili lullaby. The woman was seated on the edge of a cot, rocking a bundle in her arms. Her head jerked up, the lullaby breaking off, as Robin's flashlight beam brushed over her.

"Miriam, it's me, Robin Duncan."

At Robin's urgent whisper, Miriam hurried over to the window. The child in her arms was not her own, but the toddler whose older sister had carried him to Taraja. "Robin, what are you doing out there?"

"Please, can you let me in?" At Robin's urgent plea, Miriam immediately laid her small burden on a cot to hurry across the room. By the time Robin reached the front door, she could hear the other woman sliding back a metal latch. Robin slipped inside as soon as the door opened enough to let her through. Her flashlight caught Miriam reaching for the solar light switch. "No, no light, please! No one can know I'm here! Are you alone? Is Ephraim not here?"

"Ephraim's spending the night at the clinic. There are a lot of patients under observation, and Michael . . . he's not here right now."

"Yes, I know. That's why I'm here. Do you mind if I use your Internet? It's . . . I'm in a bit of trouble. And a hurry."

Miriam took a swift step forward. "Trouble? Is it Michael? Joseph?"

"So you know where Michael went." Robin breathed out relief. It would save precious time not to have to explain.

"Michael just told me someone had come requesting medical care for that boy who escaped. And . . . well, not to believe what your people are saying about Joseph and his men. But if you know about Michael—" Miriam's pretty, scarred features showed consternation in the flashlight beam—"does that mean they've been caught? Is Michael okay?"

"No, they weren't caught. Michael's fine. Joseph's fine. For now. I'll tell you all about it, but first I need your Internet because I don't know how much time I have. I've got to send some information to Michael's BBC friend right away. Information Michael and Joseph asked me to send."

Robin could have hugged Michael's sister for asking no questions but sitting down immediately at the desk and powering up the communications system. The glow from the computer monitor allowed Robin to turn off the flashlight. By the time Miriam brought the Internet online, Robin had unearthed herself from the rain poncho, retrieved the iPad from her knapsack, and was bringing up her interrupted video upload and e-mail.

Connecting to the router, Robin sent the e-mail with the attached photos. As she began uploading the two video clips, she gave the other woman a synopsis of the last few hours. Again, Miriam accepted Robin's narration with neither questions nor disbelief, only shaking her head when Robin finished.

"So Joseph really is this Jini you've been trying to catch. It's still hard to picture. You didn't know Joseph as I remember him. Sweet. Funny. The best student to come through Taraja in years. But also— well, not lazy because Joseph loved to study. But definitely a little spoiled, youngest of his family, darling future hope of the village and all that. Intellectually arrogant too. Rather like his biblical namesake, in fact, before that Joseph got carried off as a slave into Egypt.

"His father and the rest of the family were all counting on Joseph to step up as the next village leader, medic, schoolteacher once he'd finished his education. But Joseph's only ambition was to get out of the jungle. Have a job that involved a briefcase and cell phone, not a hoe and machete. He was only eleven or twelve when the rebels hit Taraja and we were all separated. I honestly would never have thought he had it in him to survive in the jungle like this. Or give leadership to a rebel force that's managed to fight Wamba's militia to a standstill. If nothing else, hardship has turned a spoiled little boy into a strong man."

Robin recalled an image of bitter fury on dark features, a spittle of rage splattering her own face. "Well, he's got the briefcase. But I don't think you'd recognize your sweet, funny boy in the angry, vengeful man I saw tonight. Justified or not, Joseph has proved himself willing to resort to violence to accomplish his objectives and revenge himself on those who've wronged him."

Miriam let out a sigh. "Yes, you have it right that suffering doesn't necessarily produce better people, even when it does make them stronger. Wamba started out just like Joseph, with a very similar story of personal tragedy, his family butchered by the other side in all the civil fighting. No one would deny Wamba's emerged a strong and competent leader, one reason the locals are willing to accept him so long as he can maintain some semblance of stability.

"But it's not only strength of character forged by adversity, but rather what you choose to do with that strength of character that determines whether a person ends up as dross or pure, shining gold. I'll keep praying that the sweet, smart, ambitious little boy I once thought I knew so well will become the strong man of God he was created to be, not just the capable killer everyone else seems to have written him off as being."

Taraja's solar-powered communications system was much slower than the Ares Solutions satellite link, but the first video had finally loaded. Beginning the second upload, Robin offered Miriam a wry half smile. "I can echo that prayer. And while I still don't condone

Joseph's methods, after hearing his story, I can certainly understand his motives."

Miriam studied Robin's face in the blue-green glow of her computer monitor. "You know, Robin, there's something different about you. You look—well, serene, peaceful!"

The curve of Robin's mouth grew to a full smile. It would take a blind man to see anything serene or peaceful in Robin's current disheveled condition, the mud and twigs hand wipes had missed, the dampness of both drizzle and perspiration. But Robin knew what the other woman meant. "I don't know about peaceful, but maybe at peace. I've come to understand how right you were."

A scarred eyebrow rose. "About?"

"Everything. There really is light in the middle of the darkness. And love. God's love."

"Oh, Robin! You don't know how happy I am to hear that." Miriam's swift hug came perilously close to knocking Robin's iPad from her hand. On its screen Robin saw that the second video had finished.

"Yeah, well, speaking of darkness, I'd better get going while I've got plenty of it." Robin began shutting down her iPad even as she returned the hug. "Hopefully my Internet difficulty really was just some fluke and Mulroney thinks I'm asleep in bed right now. In which case it'll be morning before they realize I'm gone. I've got food and water for two days. If that doesn't bring me to Bunia, it'll at least bring me to where there should be enough vehicle traffic to hitch a ride."

Robin looked at Miriam as she slid the iPad into her knapsack. "I don't suppose I can talk you into asking your pilot friend to drop in tomorrow. Take him up on that visit he suggested to Bunia. Whatever this Alan Birenge can do, it could take time. I'd feel a lot better knowing your family was safely out of the zone."

But Miriam was already shaking her head. "You know we can't leave the patients or refugees."

Robin rose to her feet. "I had a feeling you'd say that. I would hope a humanitarian medical compound is one line Mulroney won't dare cross. But if they come asking about me, the last thing I want is you getting yourself in trouble on my behalf. Just tell the truth—that I was here and asked to hook up to your Internet. It won't make any difference by then. Oh, and if you see Michael before I do, let him know I did what he asked."

Miriam was standing now too. "You know I will. I hate letting you go out there into that night. But you're right; this is the first place they'll come looking. Now you said you've got food and water. Is there anything else I can get you for the road? Wait, here, take this."

As Michael's sister snatched a worn volume from the desk, Robin recognized the Bible Miriam had read from earlier. "When I've been alone and afraid in the dark, this gave me comfort. No, please take it," she urged as Robin began to protest. "We have others. When it's all over, you can bring it back. I . . ."

Again she hugged Robin, this time more tightly. "Robin, maybe I shouldn't tell you this. Michael would kill me! But the e-mails he used to send. The way he described you. I thought then we might be sisters someday. And now whatever happens, we really are sisters. Sisters in God's family. I'll be praying for every step of your road."

Robin found herself shaken by Miriam's confession. *You can't know how much I hoped the same, even when I didn't know you existed!* Sliding the Bible in after her iPad, she hugged the other woman back. "Sisters. I like that."

Separating herself, Robin pulled out her cell phone. "And now let me alert Alan Birenge the intel's on its way. Then I'm gone."

But she'd just punched Return on her last call when she heard the slightest of scraping noises at the front door. Robin froze. Dropping her voice to a whisper, she demanded, "Did you lock the door again?"

"No, I was going to do it after you left." Miriam took a single step toward the door. But it was too late. An explosion against the roof tiles overhead was to Robin's experienced ears unmistakably a tossed grenade. The computer monitor and every power light on the Taraja communications system abruptly blinked out, plunging the room into absolute darkness. A screeching of broken metal was followed by a heavy object sliding across the roof. Even in moonlight, Robin could identify the metallic concave shape of the satellite dish falling past the kitchen window to smash into the ground.

Simultaneous with the crash of its landing, a second explosion of light and sound and surging bodies burst through the front door.

CHAPTER
THIRTY-EIGHT

"Got her, boss!"

A powerful flashlight probed Robin's face, blinding her. As the beam dropped away, the surge of bodies fanning out around the small room separated into four of Robin's own Ares Solutions teammates. All were in battle gear, automatic rifles raised to cover the two women. Outside Robin could hear screams, furious shouts, pounding feet, then a *rat-tat-tat* of gunfire. From the children's bedroom, startled cries and wails rose. The curtain of flowered material moved aside to show the frightened face of Miriam's oldest son, nine-year-old Benjamin.

Taking a quick step toward him, Miriam said in low, soothing French, "Everything will be fine, Son. Do not be afraid. Just keep the children inside."

"Lady, you stay right there!" Unbelievably, the harsh order came from Ernie Miller. His companions were not teammates Robin knew more than by sight, two South African commandos and an older white Rhodesian who'd fought with Trevor Mulroney during Zimbabwe's war of independence.

Miriam's beautiful, scarred features were pale in crisscrossing flashlight beams, but she raised her head bravely to face the intruders. "What do you want here? We are a humanitarian mission under UN sanction. You have no right to do this."

Ernie looked grim, his glance uncomfortable as it slid from Miriam to Robin. "Ma'am, I apologize for the intrusion. All we're after here is one of our own. We get her, we leave. No one moves, no one gets hurt."

"Don't apologize." Trevor Mulroney ducked through the doorway. A stooped frame and flushed, round features ambling in behind him ended any doubt as to the reason for this invasion. Robin read avid curiosity in Carl's glance as he headed past her to the communications station. So much for any hope the reconnaissance tech was someone to whom Robin might appeal. *Like those villagers on his surveillance screen, this is just a game to Carl!*

Carl played briefly with keyboard and mouse before announcing, "There's no way to tell if there's been recent use here, boss. Might have been smart to wait before knocking out the power and smashing that sat dish."

His Ares Solutions teammates glowered at the criticism. But Mulroney was advancing on Robin. As he snatched the knapsack from her shoulder, the cell phone in her hand squawked a tinny demand. "Hey, what's going on there? Ms. Duncan, are you okay?"

So her call to Alan Birenge had rung through. Robin dared not shift a muscle, but she raised her voice to answer, "No, we're not. Please check your—"

How much the journalist had heard, Robin couldn't know because Trevor Mulroney had already grabbed the phone. Throwing it to the concrete floor, he ground it to fragments under a boot heel. Then he ripped open the knapsack, dumping its contents. "This iPad's still warm. She's been busy here all right."

Robin bit back a cry of dismay as her iPad, too, became shards of plastic and metal. With a triumphant grunt, Mulroney retrieved Joseph's flash drive and phone from the heap. "Now where is he?"

Robin's heart was racing, but her eyebrows rose innocently. "Where is who?"

The openhanded blow across her mouth was as unanticipated as painful. "Don't play with me, Duncan. Where's Jini? The only way you could be in possession of that intel you showed Jensen is straight from Jini himself."

"Uh, boss?" At Trevor Mulroney's slap, Ernie had stepped forward, looking even more uncomfortable. "Just what's going on here?"

Mulroney threw the Vietnam vet an annoyed glance. "What's going on is that we've got a mole in the camp. Our translator has been fraternizing with the enemy. Worse, she's been passing on intel for him to a journalist. The BBC, no less."

If he'd accused Robin of communicating with a serial killer, there'd have been fewer stunned and accusing expressions. Mercenaries had not traditionally fared well at the hands of the international press, above all white mercenaries involved in Africa's many wars. And almost every man in this room blamed just such insurgents as Jini for ending colonial dominion in their homelands. As they blamed the international media for taking the side of African rebels. Consorting with native opposition, spilling an op to a journalist ranked with the highest acts of treason.

"You've all experienced the drill," the Earth Resources CEO went on contemptuously. "An insurgent leader cries foul to some sympathizing journalist, and all of a sudden he's David fighting Goliath, while the media makes us out to be the bad guys."

Robin could see on her teammates' faces she'd lost any sympathy that blow might have roused. But she was given no chance to defend herself. Outside, there'd been no further gunfire but plenty of screaming and shouting. In contrast, absolute silence reigned behind the curtain where Benjamin had retreated. That such small children knew so well to freeze into silence was more troubling than tears and screams. And now a newcomer was ducking through the door. Pieter Krueger.

"Boss, the target's not on-site. And there's someone else we can't find anywhere. The American doctor, Stewart."

"Stewart! I might have known!" Brutal fingers bit into Robin's upper arm as Trevor Mulroney leaned forward to loom above her slighter frame. "Your boyfriend from Afghanistan, right? Let me guess, he's the one who passed that intel to you. I should have trusted my gut feeling that you were trouble, Lt. Chris R. Duncan! Now where is your traitor boyfriend? Where is Jini? And your journalist pal—what does he think he's up to?"

Robin wanted to cry out at the pain of his grip. Instead she pressed her free hand against a cut lip to answer coolly, "Dr. Michael Stewart is a humanitarian volunteer who seeks nothing but peace for this country. What possible motive could he have to take sides with any insurgent leader who's done the kinds of things you accuse Jini of?"

An abrupt chilling of Mulroney's ice-blue glare would have been a dead giveaway had Robin still needed confirmation. *It's all true, then! And he doesn't want the others to know why Michael would take Jini's side. Which means they're not completely part of all this! If I can make them see the truth . . .*

But the Earth Resources CEO only said bitingly, "Why should some bleeding heart humanitarian take the side of a native rebel above his own kind? Good question if it didn't happen every day. Bigger question is how a Marine lieutenant, a veteran Ares Solutions operative, takes the side of a bleeding heart humanitarian. Guess it's not such a big question, is it? Love does strange things."

Her colleagues had bought it, Robin could see. Pieter Krueger's handsome features especially were tight with fury. "Stewart grew up here. If Jini's from the zone, they could even be old pals." He glared at Robin. "As for Duncan, I've had concerns from the beginning that her relations with the locals, especially with Dr. Stewart, went beyond the bounds of professionalism."

Liar! Robin spoke up steadily. "That isn't true. I hadn't seen or heard from Dr. Stewart in five years when I came here. I've always done my job to the best of my ability. As to why Michael Stewart would aid and abet your Jini—ahh!"

This time Robin could not contain a gasp of pain as Mulroney's grip tightened further. With attention shifted from her, Miriam had knelt to scoop the remaining contents of Robin's knapsack back inside. But at Robin's indrawn breath, Miriam jumped to her feet, dropping the knapsack to move to Robin's side.

"Please let her go. My brother isn't here, and we don't know where he is. Nor do we know anything about where this Jini you're looking for might be. A man did come and ask Michael to tend to some wounded out in the rainforest. And yes, Michael went with them. He's a doctor. He doesn't take sides in whom he helps! Please, Robin hasn't done anything wrong. Just let her go!"

"Let them go!" The echo came from Ephraim, who burst through the door. Samuel Makuga was close on his heels. As the Congolese doctor's black eyes narrowed on Robin's cut, swollen mouth, his usually calm, reserved voice quivered with anger.

"You would hit a woman, one of your own people? Whatever it is you want, you have seen it is not here. These are not the days of our ancestors when you could come into my home and my clinic only because you are a *mzungu*. You will leave at once before we report you to the United Nations."

As much to Robin's surprise as to her relief, Trevor Mulroney released his grip and retreated a full two paces as Ephraim swung around in front of the two women. But that only made room for Samuel Makuga to stride forward, spitting out in Swahili, "You dare to give orders here? You think because you have become a *docteur* that you may speak? You are a worm, a dog!"

Because Makuga had not shifted his automatic rifle, Robin didn't take note of his handgun until the Congolese field commander fired. Ephraim stumbled, blood spurting from his right thigh. As he slumped to the concrete floor, Miriam rushed forward with a cry of horror. Snatching up a drying dish towel, she pressed it against the wound. As it turned scarlet, Trevor Mulroney looked at Makuga to inquire mildly, "Was that really necessary?"

Massive shoulders shrugged indifferently. "The woman is your people; he is mine. Now they have reason to cooperate in telling us where to find the American doctor."

"I can't believe you did that!" Now it was Robin who stepped forward to spread her arms wide in front of the couple on the floor. "Miriam's telling the truth. Neither of us have any idea where Michael is. Or Jini, either. But I'm the one Jini gave those things to. Not these people. Not Michael. Whatever you want to know, I'll tell you. Only please leave them alone."

Robin looked straight at Mulroney. "About the other matter, I'm willing to make a deal. In private!"

He bought it. Robin knew the instant his brilliant-blue eyes narrowed. *If I can just get them away from Miriam and Ephraim. Delay long enough to give Alan Birenge more time to do his thing.*

Trevor Mulroney gave an abrupt nod toward Pieter Krueger. "We got what we wanted. Let's go. It's not like these people can go anywhere or contact anyone. Not anymore." A sneering glance swept over the inert communications system. "Leave a watch posted. If Stewart comes sneaking back in, I want him. Meanwhile, have your posse ready to jump as soon as we've got usable intel. Duncan, you come with me."

Robin hated leaving Miriam kneeling beside her husband's prone body. But clearing out this invasion so Miriam could send for the clinic's nursing staff was the best help Robin could offer. As she leaned down to scoop up her now-refilled knapsack, she whispered, "It will be all right! For Michael, for all of us. Don't lose hope."

Miriam's hands against her husband's thigh were bloody, her face pale and strained. But her amber eyes blazed unyielding determination as she glanced at Robin. "Never! Nor you. Now go, go!" she added as Trevor Mulroney stepped close.

Outside, militia uniforms roamed in the drizzle and moonlight, but refugees and residents alike had been permitted to return to their interrupted slumbers. The Ares Solutions unit piled into the jeep in which they'd evidently made their sneak assault. But Mulroney steered Robin into the executive helicopter now hovering into the clearing. When it touched down moments later on the airstrip, he grabbed her arm again, half-dragging, half-pushing her out of the helicopter and up the steps into his charter jet. The jet's pilot was resting on a sofa inside, but he exited the cabin at his employer's jerk of the head. Releasing Robin, Mulroney pulled up the steps to seal the fuselage. Only then did he shove Robin down into a leather seat.

"Okay, one more time. Where are Jini and your boyfriend? What have you been told? And exactly how much have you passed on to Stewart's BBC pal in Bunia? Oh yes, we know all about Alan Birenge. Seems his wife's cousin runs Wamba's prison system, and your doctor boyfriend had him doing some snooping on our labor force."

Robin could almost have smiled. So Mulroney didn't know yet that Alan Birenge had escaped Wamba's clutches. Though she'd have sworn she hadn't let relief touch her expression, Mulroney's gaze narrowed instantly on her face. "You know differently, don't you? I just knew you were too confident for the cornered rat you're supposed to be."

His mouth twisted in a sneer as he seated himself across the narrow cabin from Robin. "Nor am I surprised to find you willing to deal, badly as you've been needing money. Something about a young namesake with expensive medical needs, do I have it right? Lives in a nice little white house on a corner lot in South Carolina? Port Royal, to be precise. So what kind of a check do I need to cut for you to walk away and forget about anything but helping your sister get that cute redhead back on her feet in time to ride a certain pink bicycle she's expecting for her fifth birthday?"

His offer was a far more effective threat than it was a bribe. Icy fingers wrapped themselves around Robin's heart, squeezed at her stomach. *That bike—I just ordered it online. It hasn't even been delivered yet.*

Trevor Mulroney scrutinized Robin's expression with satisfaction. "Oh yes, it's quite something what you can dig up when you've got an asset as talented as our young Jensen. Now, can we make a deal?"

Wiping a damp arm across the sheen of moisture her face had acquired while she was dragged to and from the helicopter, Robin forced herself to relax against the leather seat. There was nothing further to be gained by shading the truth, and Robin had already made up her mind as to her next move.

The only move she could see that had any hope of ending this without further bloodshed.

"Look, I really don't know where Michael and Jini—Joseph, rather—are. Yes, I was with Michael tonight when this Joseph sent a man to request help for some wounded from last night's raid. And yes, he told us everything. How he used to work for you. The rhenium. What you did to his village. The massacres Samuel Makuga carried out to point fingers at Joseph. And he did ask me to help get that flash drive and photo evidence into the right hands."

Robin raised her chin to meet Mulroney's glare squarely. "Sir, I've been a good soldier and a good employee to Ares Solutions. I've never blabbed to the press before. But believe me, this time I was glad to make an exception. Anyway, once I was given the intel, I came straight back here, and Michael left with Joseph to try to help those wounded. They could be anywhere by now, so there's no point in hassling the Taraja people any further since they know even less than I do.

"As for me, if you think shutting me up will make this all go away, it won't! For your information, Alan Birenge made it safely out of Bunia hours ago. And I got that intel off to him before you took out the Taraja satellite dish. Including some nice close-ups of you and Makuga together to go with that video of Makuga ordering the massacre of innocent civilians. In any case, it's one thing to make a Congolese employee or an Ituri Rainforest village disappear. Or even someone like me. You wouldn't find it so easy to explain away a Doctors Without Borders surgeon or a BBC journalist."

Mulroney's face had become a mask of fury, but he said coolly, "So what was the deal you mentioned? Are you offering to sell out your confederates? Or is this a shakedown you and Stewart have cooked up together with Birenge? I don't really care. All I want is a figure to ensure the destruction of any remaining files and a binding confidentiality agreement. A hundred thousand American dollars? Five hundred? I can go that high if not in one lump sum. How about a hundred thousand now and a million in installments once the mine is moving ore again?"

Did he really think Robin was stupid or just plain greedy enough to fall for his offer? That she didn't know there was no way he could afford to let her walk away with this knowledge inside her head? Aloud, Robin asked, "How do I know you'll really pay me?"

Trevor Mulroney raised his eyebrows. "How do I know you'll really keep quiet?"

"You don't! And I won't," Robin admitted. "At least not for money. But I've got a much better deal in mind. A win-win for everyone. Bottom line, it's too late to take back those files. One way or another, you're not going to be able to keep the rhenium a secret any longer. But you can still walk away from this. We all can!"

"Walk away from this," Mulroney repeated skeptically. "A win-win. What exactly are you proposing?"

"Open the gates of the mine and let those people go free. Then make your own preemptive announcement that you've discovered the molybdenum concession contains an even more valuable mineral wealth. Make yourself a hero by offering the first reliable source of rhenium to the world. And by bringing peace to the Ituri, because I can guarantee Joseph won't keep fighting once you've let his people go. Once the rhenium's public news and the people are free, what would Alan Birenge really have left to come back on you? I can promise you I'd have no reason to say anything further."

As thoughtfulness replaced skepticism in Mulroney's expression, Robin eagerly pressed her plea. "Don't you see? All Joseph wants, all he's ever been trying to do in attacking the mine, is to free his family and the other villagers. He's not after the rhenium, at least not anymore. If you'll just call off this mission, maybe even pay some compensation so his people can rebuild elsewhere, he's made clear he'll be willing to let things go. Especially if you let him and his men walk away too. Ensure Wamba leaves them alone in the future. After all, they never were the army everyone's thought. And now there's only a handful of them left. But you've got to call off any air strike tomorrow in the perimeter zone because they've got wounded out there. And Michael, too!"

Robin did not recognize her blunder until a cruel smile banished introspection from aristocratic features. "So Jini has only a handful of confederates left. That we didn't know. Which makes things so much easier."

The Earth Resources CEO rose to his feet. "This has been most instructional. But if you think I've come this far to walk away, you are an extremely naive and foolish young woman. And you have no concept what I can get away with. What I *have* gotten away with! You imagine you've succeeded because your journalist pal managed to flee Bunia. Which might be true if I didn't know exactly where he is. Once Wamba discovered he'd gone missing, tracking Birenge and his family on a UN flight to Kampala was hardly a challenge. Checking the handful of hotels where a BBC journalist might book was even easier. And since there's not a major city on this continent where I don't have useful contacts, a certain police commander should be kicking in Birenge's hotel room door right about now. Your friend will not be given opportunity to pass on what you gave him."

Heading toward the plane's exit hatch, Trevor Mulroney reached for the handle. "As for giving Jini what he wants, that's a proposal I do like. Instead of wasting time firebombing stragglers, we let our prey come to us. A Congo Trojan horse. Excellent operational planning, Duncan. Too bad you aren't playing on my team."

Had she ever hated anyone as much as this man? Desperately, Robin tried to amend her blunder. "It won't work. Joseph will never fall for that! Especially after last night. You think he wouldn't recognize a trap after the way his father was killed?"

Trevor Mulroney bared his teeth as his smile turned savage. "On the contrary, thanks to you, he will fall for it. He clearly has faith in you to carry out your word. So when he sees the guards and mining personnel airlifted from the mine, the gates standing wide open, what will he assume but that you've accomplished your mission and we've fled in advance of the oncoming cavalry?"

Mulroney was already lifting a hand radio to his mouth. "Krueger? Get your posse to the comm trailer. We've got a new plan. And have Makuga send over a team to take custody of the prisoner."

Robin's heart dropped into her toes as the exit hatch unfolded into steps. Trevor Mulroney was as right as he was despicable. Her brilliant proposal had not effected salvation for Michael, Joseph, or his people as she'd hoped.

Instead she'd just handed their archenemy a blueprint for the perfect trap!

CHAPTER
THIRTY-NINE

Hope.

Joseph had not felt such an emotion for so long he could not at first allow himself to recognize the irrepressible bubbling of lightness pushing at his grief and anger. *My father forgave me! He spoke of me as his son when I had lost all right to claim that name, disobeying him, defying him, causing so much pain and death. He loved me enough to seek my salvation.*

And if this was true, what of that other incredible declaration the *mzungu* doctor named Michael Stewart had asserted? *Is there indeed hope that Baba Mungu, our Father in heaven who is the almighty Creator, will also forgive me? That he has not cast me completely aside?* If only he could ensure no further bloodshed.

Joseph recalled the dangers he'd already imposed on his small, loyal band—most recently, the journey to seek medical help. He had chosen the fallen hardwood as rendezvous point for the same reason he'd originally toppled it at that location. A sharp bend in the river that wandered from mine to Taraja brought its banks close enough to the road for easy access with explosives and arms. The foreign soldiers who'd blown up the barge had not found the canoes they'd submerged. Once the *mzungus* had departed by helicopter, his band's own survivors had waited only until near nightfall to slip down to the river and haul a pair of canoes to the bank.

By then they'd scouted out hundreds of uniformed militiamen filtering forward through the rainforest to form a long, ragged circumference several kilometers from the mine. Among them were other foreign warriors such as had blown up the barge. Joseph had instantly grasped the tactic. Was he not a native of this rainforest, his small band hunters?

A bush hunt with himself and his companions as prey!

But a bush hunt was effective only on earthbound quarry. And if the militia had drawn their perimeter so close to the mine, that only meant Joseph and his men need not fear the hunt once beyond that line. The greatest danger for their own passage was where the river pierced the militia perimeter. But they'd timed their approach just as twilight darkened to full night. Once a glow of campfires was visible, they'd turned their two canoes upside down, binding them with vines to a pair of snags they'd pulled along for the purpose. Of greater fear had been the aquatic fauna through which they kicked their way beneath the canoes. But flailing limbs had attracted neither crocodile nor hippo, and if guards had noted two snags drifting with the current, they'd raised no alarm.

Still, even once they'd been able to paddle freely, they'd been slowed by debris, sandbars, the fear of an unseen lunge or dropping snake, especially since the moon had not yet risen to pierce through the overarching foliage.

Not so on the return trip, which proved much faster than hoped, thanks largely to Michael Stewart. Joseph had heard of night vision goggles, but he'd never had opportunity to observe them up close.

Taking up a steersman's paddle with expertise, the *mzungu* doctor had called back warnings that permitted them to quicken their paddling until the canoes were flying through the water.

Though Joseph had not dared risk returning through enemy lines as they'd come. Even a careless guard would notice a snag moving against the current. So they'd taken to the treetops, greatly helped now by the soft, silver illumination of the moon. With his strange goggles to aid him, the *mzungu* doctor had slipped through the rainforest canopy with little less ease and speed than his own band. Perhaps Michael Stewart's claim to be a child of the Ituri was not to be scorned.

They'd now reached the hiding place where Joseph had left his nephew and their wounded companion who'd stayed behind to tend him. The foreigners had shown some tracking skills in uncovering the band's primary sanctuary. But only a fool provided for a single bolt-hole. This one was another high perch in a hardwood's leafy crown, but close enough to the rock outcroppings that the outermost branches brushed stone. If its distance from the river made this retreat less convenient, it was also less likely to be discovered. A hollow even held a few backup supplies, including their only remaining stash of explosives, detonators, and weapons captured from the supply convoys.

The rainforest canopy's dense foliage offered protection from a deepening drizzle, but thickening rain clouds had now swallowed up the last glimmer of moonlight, the resulting darkness such that Joseph had risked turning on his palm-size lantern. They'd arrived to find the boy Jacob still breathing, but unconscious, so that his companion had found it necessary to lash him with vines to a branch to prevent him from rolling out of his treetop eyrie. Shielding the light with fronds so that it could not be glimpsed at any distance, Joseph adjusted its beam over the *mzungu* doctor's shoulder. "Will he live?"

The doctor's hands were busy with the same sharp instrument with which he'd stitched Joseph's own wounds. "He lives. He breathes. I have repaired the torn stitches. But he has lost much blood, and he was already weakened by his earlier blood loss. He needs to get to a surgical ward to have this repaired properly. And he badly needs a blood transfusion."

The *mzungu* doctor was speaking Swahili for the benefit of Joseph's companions, words not in a village vocabulary like *surgical* and *transfusion* added in a hodgepodge of English and French. Crouched beside his unconscious charge, Jacob's attendant cradled against his own chest the bullet-shattered forearm that had kept him from traveling with the rest of the band. Shifting position cautiously to reach his second patient, the *mzungu* doctor waved for Joseph to redirect the lantern beam.

"To complicate matters, we've got to be out of these trees before dawn when Mulroney and Wamba's forces make their assault. What about the rock outcropping over there? That's close enough to the mine workings they won't want to be firing on it. Are there any caves or crevices where we could hole up? At least to give time for my journalist buddy to make his move."

Joseph shook his head as the *mzungu* doctor began swabbing dried blood and flesh. "Dr. Stewart—"

"Dr. Stewart is my father and grandfather." The lantern beam caught a flash of teeth. "Michael is the name my friends call me. I hope you believe now that I am your friend."

"My friend, yes. I do not know of any caves or crevices close enough to provide shelter. But perhaps with the blasting abandoned, we might find a place among the broken rock to lie hidden. Only we dare not show a light for such a search."

"We can use the NVGs. Just let me finish here." Pronouncing the broken forearm a simple fracture, the *mzungu* doctor—no, Michael, his friend—rebound the arm with gauze and two thin branches as splints. Then he adjusted into place the night vision goggles. The rest of the band settled in to wait as Michael followed Joseph unhesitatingly out of the tree fork.

To ensure a safe distance from the ore blasting, the band's secondary sanctuary was far enough back along the rock outcropping that it did not permit a view of the mine encampment. Its advantage was that creeping along the huge branches offered an easy leap to the outcropping's nearest flank. The full moon was again peeping through a gap in the rain clouds, and even without NVGs, Joseph's hardened bare soles had traced this path often enough to take the lead. They had covered half the distance, keeping well below the ridge where their silhouettes might be visible against setting moon and starlight, when the noise of multiple approaching aircraft dropped both men to their bellies.

Joseph did not move again until the roar of rotors and engines abruptly died. This time it was his companion who took the lead, slipping forward as silently as any Ituri native until the two men reached a spot where they could stretch out to look down over the mine.

Joseph didn't need goggles to see what had brought the helicopters. Indeed, with the blaze of perimeter lights below, his companion had pushed them onto his forehead. Abandoning their watchtowers, the guards were marching through the front gate to where the helicopters had settled down on the barren, muddy field outside. Joseph watched, stunned, as they clambered into the helicopters.

Light skin and hair identified the mine administrator as he climbed in after the guards. The helicopters were lifting skyward when the generator's rumble died, plunging the encampment into darkness. Joseph waited for emergency lanterns to spring to life. But this time the encampment remained dark and still. As the helicopters winked out of view over the rainforest canopy, the heavy metal panels of the mine's main gates yawned abandoned and wide open.

Joseph reached out to grab his companion's forearm. "Look! We will not need to find a hiding place. They have fled the mine. They are letting my people go! Your friend must have succeeded."

But Michael's low response did not hold Joseph's own excitement. "Or it's a trick to draw you out. I saw them do something very similar last night. If it isn't a trick and your people aren't still being held prisoners, we should be seeing them down there."

Hope had been dashed often enough in recent months for Joseph to see wisdom in the warning. The two men watched, unmoving, to the count of a hundred heartbeats, then another hundred. Joseph's companion had pulled his night vision goggles down again over his eyes and was scrutinizing the encampment vigilantly. But by the time drifting clouds again swallowed up the last probing ray of moonlight, there was still no movement from the encampment.

"I fear you are right, and it is a trick," Joseph admitted sadly. "We must find our hiding place and return quickly for the others."

But even as Joseph began sliding backward, his companion let out a soft exclamation. Joseph stopped his retreat. A single shadow had glided forward through the opening of the brush kraal. It moved hesitantly toward the yawning gate, stopping at frequent intervals to turn a head from one side to the other. Reaching the entrance, the shadow stepped outside, then back in. Only then did he raise a shout. A moment later other shadows emerged from the kraal. But these ones were now lighting torches.

"Would you recognize these guys? Here, take a look." Pulling the night vision goggles off his head, Michael held them out so Joseph could peer through them. "Are they anyone you know or security guards pulling another trick?"

It took a moment for Joseph to adjust to the strange green light. The drizzle gave the images displayed a hazy shimmer, but a blaze of white light was identifiable as a torch, while the face below it was unmistakably familiar. "Yes, there is my uncle Kito. And beside him my cousin Moses. They too must have waited to see if it was a trick. We must go get the others."

With no urgency to remain hidden, it took only minutes for the two men to reach the hollowed tree fork. Joseph voiced caution. "The *docteur* is right that we must still be careful. Perhaps it is best to wait until daylight to be sure the soldiers will not return. If our enemy has truly fled from the proof we sent out, others will soon be coming here. Once we see help actually arrive, we will know for sure it is safe."

But his words were lost on his companions.

"If it is a trick, then the more reason we must hurry," his cousin Caleb argued. "We have not seen our families, our wives and children, in months. We must seize this opportunity."

Kavuo, the second cousin with the fractured arm, was even more adamant. "Jacob has told me it was my little Rachel who survived the killers at Taraja. She is now returned to her mother. I must see them."

Even the *mzungu* doctor abandoned his support. "The mine has first aid equipment. I could rig up a transfusion. Joseph's right that for him it might be best to remain in hiding until we're sure what's happening down there. But for Jacob here, I for one have to risk this."

In the end they all went, hoisting Jacob between them in a rough cradle of vines. They also took explosives, ammunition, and the two automatic rifles remaining to them. With the moon now set, footing was precarious along the ridge and down the cliff face. The *mzungu* doctor picked a route through blasted rubble with his night vision goggles. A watchtower joined the chain-link perimeter fence to the face of the cliff. But here, too, a secondary gate stood open, permitting access without circling around to the main entrance.

A dozen torches blazed in the open area between brush kraal and main entrance. As someone climbed one of the watchtowers, a fluorescent lantern blinked on. By now the newcomers had been seen. As torches and shadows raced in their direction, Joseph turned on his own lantern and held it high. "It is I, Joseph. We are here!"

His own band could not run without jostling their burden. The two groups collided just beyond the shattered hulk of the steam engine. The encampment prisoners appeared as astonished at their sudden freedom as the new arrivals. Exclamations turned to joy and wonder as family members found each other. Despite his splint, Joseph's second cousin had managed to hoist his small daughter into his arms, his young wife patting them both with inarticulate cries of joy.

Then Joseph, too, was enfolded in a sea of arms. Brothers. Cousins. Uncles. Aunts. No words of censure, but only welcome. Hope blazed into joy as he returned their embrace. *It is true! I am forgiven!*

The doctor had already laid Jacob gently on the ground. Family members crowded close with murmurs of "Stewart" and *"docteur."*

"Look! What is happening?" The startled shout put an abrupt end to the celebration. All heads turned to follow a young boy's outstretched arm toward the main gate. Even in darkness, the gate's tall double panels could be seen swinging slowly, silently, without any touch of human hands toward each other.

"No!" Joseph broke into a desperate run. But he was too late. The two panels came together with a loud clang. A dozen other men had joined Joseph, but no amount of pounding, tugging, pushing budged the gate.

And now in a play right out of Joseph's own war manual, he caught sight through the chain-link fence of human shapes dropping down on vines or ropes from tree branches on the far side of the clearing. A solid line of them was moving into the open all along the edge of the rainforest. Once again without human touch, the generator rumbled to life. The perimeter security lamps came on, transfixing the prisoners with their bright light.

All the renewed hope that had persisted in bubbling up in Joseph these last hours evaporated as, in that light, he caught anguish and despair overtaking joy on faces all around him.

The trap had been sprung.

His enemy had won after all.

CHAPTER FORTY

Robin had long ago replaced a wristwatch with her now-splintered cell phone. So she had no idea how much time had passed. Several hours, surely. Nor in those hours had she glimpsed any Ares Solutions colleague. Her employer was not going to let Robin explain her actions to her teammates.

Instead Mulroney had dragged Robin to the door of the plane where Samuel Makuga was just arriving outside with several other uniforms. "This woman knows nothing further of value to finding our enemy. Her services have been terminated. You will take charge of her removal from these premises. I do not wish to be troubled by her again."

An exultant gleam springing to black eyes was more frightening than anything else Robin had undergone that night. How cleverly Mulroney had phrased his orders so that no one could accuse him of wrongdoing. Yet Robin had no doubt she'd just heard the order given for her execution. Nor after what she'd seen in that massacre footage could Robin hope Makuga's concept of "termination" was clean or merciful.

Desperately she strove for a calm tone. "Look, what is your hurry on this? Fire me if you want. I'll . . . I'll even give up claim to past wages. But you may still need me. To . . . to talk to Joseph. Or Michael. Maybe even get them to surrender before anyone else gets hurt. I'm sure you want that as much as I do."

Robin would let a personnel carrier roll over her before asking Joseph or Michael to surrender to this man. And surely Trevor Mulroney was too astute to swallow that Robin had misinterpreted his directive as a simple job dismissal. But he'd stopped shoving Robin forward. "I'm not looking for surrender. But you've got a point that you may still have value as a hostage. As you say, what's the hurry?"

Mulroney had locked Robin inside a sleeping compartment at the rear of the plane. Its door was hardly the reinforced bulkhead of a cockpit, and Robin had no doubt she could have kicked the lock open. But she had smelled on Makuga's accompanying detail the sickly sweet fumes that were not tobacco, seen their dilated pupils. Suggestions at least two separate guards called out when she rattled the doorknob made Robin thankful for a lock between them. A porthole showed more militiamen mounting a perimeter guard around the plane. Beyond them she could see Mulroney and Makuga striding toward the communications trailer.

So Robin retreated instead to the couch that unfolded into a bed. As prisons went, this one could be far less comfortable. She took advantage of a connecting bathroom. Mulroney hadn't bothered to confiscate her knapsack, so she fueled herself with a protein bar and bottled water. Eat, drink, sleep—the first priorities of any deployed soldier to be ready when a call came for battle.

But if she'd managed the first two, sleep did not come so easily. Had Trevor Mulroney truly succeeded in reaching across international borders to grab Alan Birenge and his family? And Ephraim. Had Miriam been able to stop the bleeding? Would Mulroney leave the family alone now that he'd gotten his own way? Or would he consider what they might tell friends outside Taraja an unacceptable risk?

Then there was Kristi. With Robin's phone in splinters, there'd be no way now for Kelli to get in touch if she tried to call back. *Father God, I promised to leave Kristi in your hands. But it's so hard not knowing! Please be with Kristi and Kelli both in that hospital. And please send your angels to protect Alan Birenge and his family! And Miriam and Ephraim and their beautiful children. Joseph, Michael, and the others, too. Trevor Mulroney thinks he's so powerful. That he can get away with anything. Like Joseph's father said, he calls evil good and darkness light. But you are more powerful. You are our light in the darkness. So please, whatever your plans for my own life on this black, horrible night, don't let Mulroney win. Don't let evil triumph over good, darkness over the light!*

Out on the airstrip, Robin could now see action. Militia soldiers and Ares Solutions operatives alike were crowding into the Mi-17s. Then a roar of rotors and engines shook the Gulfstream as the two huge combat helicopters lumbered toward the night sky. Robin watched them bank over the rainforest in the direction of the mine.

Despite the late hour and exhausted muscles screaming for oblivion, adrenaline was not going to permit Robin to doze. Digging through her knapsack for some distraction, she pulled out the Bible Miriam had given her before Trevor Mulroney's posse burst through her front door. Without her iPad search engine, Robin could find few of the references she'd researched earlier. But eventually she stumbled onto the epistle of 1 Peter Miriam had mentioned as offering comfort in her own darkness.

Yes, there in chapter 1, verse 6 was the reference her earlier Google search had turned up. "In this you greatly rejoice, though now for a little while you may have had to suffer grief in all kinds of trials."

Robin skimmed through the brief chapters, found herself lingering over certain passages, going back to reread again and again. Miriam had called the epistle a treatise on suffering. And certainly, according to background notes, this letter had been written to early Christians undergoing fierce persecution, even martyrdom at the hands of a Roman emperor whose lust for power and violence seemed little different from a modern-day Wamba, Makuga, or Mulroney.

Yet as Robin pored over the pages, what caught her notice was that its author referenced hope as much as suffering. Starting with the apostle's very greeting: "Praise be to the God and Father of our Lord Jesus Christ! In his great mercy he has given us new birth into a living hope through the resurrection of Jesus Christ from the dead, and into an inheritance that can never perish, spoil or fade—kept in heaven for you."

Not just hope. A living hope. Because that hope was made possible through a living Savior, Jesus Christ. And not just a living Savior, a living and powerful God. A little further in that same chapter, the apostle urged, "Set your hope fully on the grace to be given you when Jesus Christ is revealed. . . . Through him you believe in God, who raised him from the dead . . . so your faith and hope are in God."

Robin stopped to read over and over chapter 2, verse 9. "You are a chosen people . . . belonging to God . . . who called you out of darkness into his wonderful light." There it was—the light in the midst of this horribly dark night!

Chapter 3 included a reference to Sarah, wife of Abraham, the founding father of the nation of Israel. Peter described her as putting her hope in God, not in the husband who, according to the footnotes on the page, had dumped her twice into a king's harem to save his own skin.

"You are her daughters if you do what is right and do not give way to fear," Robin read in verse 6. She lowered the worn volume abruptly.

Do what is right. Robin could hope with all her heart she'd done so in this night's choices and actions. But to not give way to fear? Robin's throat was tight with it, her stomach churning, her hands shaking so that she had to be careful not to tear pages as she turned them.

Robin smoothed the pages flat as she bowed her head above them. *Heavenly Father, I definitely don't deserve to be called Sarah's daughter because I am so scared! But I pray you will give me the courage you gave Sarah to do the right thing no matter how afraid I am.*

Again there was no audible voice from heaven, but some of that earlier calm Robin had found settled over her, giving her strength of mind to keep reading and rereading. Because Miriam was right that 1 Peter addressed suffering.

Peter's mind-boggling command in chapter 1 to rejoice in trials was succeeded by his call in the next chapters to be willing to suffer for doing the right thing.

"But if you suffer for doing good and you endure it, this is commendable before God. To this you were called, because Christ suffered for you, leaving you an example, that you should follow in his steps. . . . If you should suffer for what is right, you are blessed. . . . It is better, if it is God's will, to suffer for doing good than for doing evil. . . . Since Christ suffered . . . arm yourselves also with the same attitude."

Later in chapter 4 came again that mind-boggling command to rejoice: "Dear friends, do not be surprised at the painful trial you are suffering, as though something strange were happening to you. But rejoice that you participate in the sufferings of Christ. . . . If you suffer as a Christian, do not be ashamed, but praise God that you bear that name."

Hope.

Suffering.

That the author could so easily juxtapose two such concepts was a paradox that still had Robin shaking her head. Until she stumbled upon the promise that made sense of it all. Over and over she read the words until they remained engraved upon her memory.

"And the God of all grace, who called you to his eternal glory in Christ, after you have suffered a little while, will himself restore you and make you strong, firm and steadfast. To him be the power for ever and ever. Amen."

Suffering and hope.

Hope and suffering.

Not diametrically opposed as Robin had thought all her life, but a beautiful paradox. The paradox that suffering did not after all destroy hope, but that enduring, living hope could be birthed out of the most terrible of suffering. A paradox made possible because suffering was transitory, ephemeral, the shortest of little whiles. While hope—that living hope in a living Savior—hope was forever.

Robin found that she was brushing dampness from her cheeks as she closed the worn volume and laid it carefully back in her knapsack. She who had prided herself on self-discipline and emotional control had shed more tears since beginning this mission than in the last five years. But she no longer felt shame or weakness at her own vulnerability as she lifted her prayer heavenward.

Miriam was so right! This world isn't all there is. It's barely a trial run for what you have waiting for us, heavenly Father. That eternal inheritance Peter talked about that will never perish, spoil, or fade. Even better, a family. Spiritual brothers and sisters like Miriam said, millions of them. But blood family too. All these years I've resented that you took my mother and Chris. But they'll be waiting with Grandma and Grandpa O'Boyle and so many others. And we'll have all eternity to make up for a few missed decades here.

Meanwhile, for whatever time we have left on this dark planet, Yesu—Jesus—walks with us, our Light in the darkness. And if that darkness still seems so full of Wambas and Makugas and Mulroneys with their cruelty and their thirst for money and power, it is also filled with so many Miriams and Ephraims and Michaels who have emerged from the furnace of suffering as pure gold. Who are holding high the light of your love in the darkness. I want to be more like them. Maybe I never could be. But right now I ask only that you help me face this coming dawn, face Trevor Mulroney with love instead of hate. Courage instead of fear. Forgiveness instead of anger and bitterness.

At some point Robin heard the helicopters roaring in overhead.

At an even later point she heard them lift off again. Robin would not have thought sleep was possible, but when the rain that had been threatening all evening deepened from a drizzle to a downpour furious enough to shake her prison, she barely stirred. The night had grown quiet again when the locked cabin door slammed open.

Jerking upright, Robin blinked away drowsiness and alarm as Trevor Mulroney strode through the door. His large frame crowded the small compartment. Robin did not trust the amiability of his smile.

"On your feet, Duncan. I've found a use for you after all."

CHAPTER
FORTY-ONE

The attacking force was now racing forward. Among them he spotted battle armor, helmets, the knobby shape of night vision goggles that were worn not by militia, but by their *mzungu* commanders.

Then, as suddenly as the heavy metal gate panels had clanged shut, they shuddered in obedience to a new command. Only this time it would not be to shut in captives, but to let in that flood of attackers.

Rage surged where hope had been. His enemies may have sprung their trap. But they'd overlooked one thing. They were not just dealing with Joseph, the eager university student with a lab coat and a dream. They were dealing with Jini, the ghost who'd held superior forces at bay with little more than his brain and a handful of willing hands and feet.

Rage became immediate action. "Simeon, Jobari, hold them off!"

The automatic weapons too noisy for guerrilla warfare came off his companions' shoulders, magazine clips slamming into place.

Remaining under cover at either side of the gate, the two men thrust gun barrels through the chain links and opened fire.

As Joseph had hoped, the advancing line froze. No one in the attack force was volunteering to be among those who would not return to base this day. Not when their enemy was already securely corralled and could not go anywhere. But it would not take long for someone to realize how little ammunition the defenders possessed.

Whatever mechanism was permitting remote control of the gates had suspended movement with the first gunfire. Then abruptly the panels clanged shut again. Which allowed Joseph time for the task he'd set himself. Already he had the plastic explosive out of its wrapping and was inserting a detonator with speed gained by months of practice. By then he'd located a small metal box on a gatepost.

Slapping the plastic explosive against the box, Joseph lit the fuse. "Everyone back! Back!"

His two companions firing automatic rifles hastily yanked their weapons free of the chain links just as a loud bang left the remote control mechanism dangling free. But at the same moment, Simeon, to Joseph's left, dropped his weapon, crying out in pain. Almost instantaneously, a second gunshot pinged against the gatepost precisely where Joseph's hand had been a moment earlier. No machine gun fire, this, but a sniper shot.

Despair again battled Joseph's rage. Even if they could hold off the assault, those *mzungu* warriors out there with their night vision goggles had only to pick off the defenders one by one from a safe distance. And now a long roll of thunder overhead was being drowned out by an escalating roar approaching from the direction of Taraja.

"Joseph, their helicopters are coming!" Despite his splinted forearm, Joseph's wounded cousin, Kavuo, had returned his small daughter to his wife and had raced forward to catch Simeon when he stumbled back. "They will be able to shoot us from the air. We must get the people under cover."

As Kavuo looked instinctively toward the brush kraal, Joseph shook his head. "No, that will not be defensible. Take them over there. See, where the *mzungu* doctor is taking Jacob. It is not big. But it will have to do."

The Quonset hut that served as headquarters to the foreign mine administrator was designed for the security and comfort needs of such an isolated outpost, its metallic bubble no flimsy aluminum but steel reinforced and insulated against tropical heat or bullet. "The doctor will tend to Simeon. And you, look there too for anything that will help us fight. You know what to do."

Yes, his men knew what to do. If only they had time. The running lights of the helicopters were now visible above the jungle canopy. No further shots had come from beyond the perimeter fence, perhaps because the milling crowd inside the gate made it difficult to separate combatant from noncombatant. But the assault force was again advancing across the muddy field, if more warily this time. Easing his assault rifle back through the chain links, Jobari opened fire, but he retreated immediately as a hail of high-powered bullets rattled chain-link fence and gate panels.

Please, if I had just a little time! An hour, a half hour! A deafening roll of thunder rebuked Joseph's mental cry as the foolish, useless plea it was. A simultaneous crack of lightning lit up roiling banks of cumulonimbus clouds. Against them, the insect shapes of two helicopters could now be seen skimming the treetops that separated the mine clearing from the river.

But just when Joseph surrendered himself to despair, as though an almighty Creator truly had heard his plea and leaned down to intervene, the heavens chose that moment to open up, releasing with a whoosh the storm that had been threatening all evening.

This was not the soft, steady rainfall of earlier that afternoon but blinding sheets of water whipped around by the wind so that visibility was instantly reduced to an arm's length. Certainly the foreign mercenaries' night vision goggles would be rendered useless by the storm's fury. Already the two approaching helicopters had wisely chosen to make a precipitate landing on the far side of the muddy field, outside the perimeter fence. Angry shouts and cursing could be heard as the attacking force retreated to the shelter of tree trunk and rainforest canopy.

For Joseph, it was all the visibility—and time—he needed. As camp residents scrambled in turn for the shelter of the Quonset hut, Joseph was already racing toward an aluminum awning where he'd earlier noted the mine's new generator. As he ran, he shouted orders into the wind and rain.

"Caleb, Nathaniel, search the storage shed for fuel, chemicals. Uncle Kito, Moses, find me carts, logs, brush from the kraal. Anything that can be used to create a barrier wall outside the hut."

Ducking under the downspout now pouring water off the aluminum awning, Joseph quickly located the device that had rigged the generator for remote control. Another explosive charge shut down the powerful security spotlights, leaving the mine encampment again in darkness except for scattered fluorescent lanterns.

One of these permitted Joseph to take inventory of the drums and barrels his companions were already rolling from the storage shed. Ammonia. Sulfuric acid. Casks of aluminum sulfide crystals. A wise enemy would have removed such dangerous materials. But perhaps there had not been time or room on the helicopters.

Or perhaps they simply were not aware how much Joseph could accomplish with such a bonanza. Kavuo rushed up, brandishing a bottle of French brandy. "Will this help? I found two cases inside the *mzungu* overseer's quarters. And a crate of lamp oil."

"It is perfect. Though we will need more glass containers if you can find them."

Men were now trundling handcarts with the first load of brush and logs. Braving the soaking deluge, women and older children pitched in to pile it chest high, leaving a space between barrier and Quonset hut. If they could get enough firing blinds into place, they would not be reduced to cowering inside but could mount a 360-degree defense around the base of the hut. Under shelter of the generator's aluminum awning, two of Joseph's own band were already funneling a mix of generator fuel and brandy into glass bottles.

Entering the Quonset hut, Joseph found a better fortress than he'd hoped. Supply crates and bunks lined the walls, and several village men had taken the initiative to remove mattresses, propping them between bunks and walls as additional fortification against gunfire. Women were unpacking crates. Joseph's defense force snatched up jugs of cooking oil. But canned meat, bottled water, boxes of MRE packets were passed among hungry prisoners. Dumping out jelly, Joseph confiscated its glass jar. "Bring me empty water bottles as well. We can use plastic if we do not have enough glass."

He'd hoped for more weapons and ammunition, even explosives used for dynamiting ore. But these at least the evacuating mine security had thought to take with them. By now Michael had unearthed the first aid supplies, and a neat white bandage wrapped Simeon's left shoulder. Jacob lay on a bottom mattress, an IV bag suspended above him from the upper bunk, its tubing already threaded into one of his veins. To Joseph's relief, his nephew was recovering consciousness. But moans of pain and restless tossing made this more a drawback than a gain.

At his side, Michael was applying a tourniquet to his own arm. He raised his voice to explain above the din of rain on the metal roofing. "I'm a universal donor—type O. Find me a couple volunteers to hold him still."

As Joseph motioned a pair of women over from the food supply, Michael shifted from Swahili to English, ensuring private conversation. "Joseph, you must understand I've been a soldier. I know what you can do with all this material. But even if we might be able to hold them off temporarily, once this rain calms down and they can move freely again, sheer mathematics guarantees we'll eventually be overrun."

We, he'd said, not *you*. An emotion that was not rage surged in

Joseph. "I know these things. But we must defend ourselves. We cannot surrender now. You know Trevor Mulroney will never let us go free."

"We can defend ourselves. But we won't win. I know those men out there. Not Wamba and Makuga's troops, but the *mzungu* mercenaries. They know what they're doing and they're armed for full-out war. You've made it this far by attack-and-run guerrilla tactics. But there's no way we can fend off a full frontal assault."

"I know that, too. Why do you think I am preparing for a siege? But I do not wish the others to know how hopeless it is. There is no reason to frighten them further before it is time."

"Time is all we need. Nor is this hopeless. We can't fight these guys off. But we can delay them long enough to give my friend Alan Birenge more chance to act. Because I refuse to believe Robin Duncan has not done what she has promised. And I know Birenge. If he thinks I'm in trouble, he won't care who he's got to roust out of bed to send the cavalry riding our direction. We just need to buy him all the time we can. And for that I've got an idea."

"I'm listening."

When the *mzungu* doctor finished explaining, Joseph shook his head in disbelief. "Michael, you would do this? To work, it would have to be real. The risk—"

A gesture of tourniquet-wrapped arm cut him off. "Joseph, even when I was a soldier, I was a healer, not a killer. Those men out there—they are not all evil. Many too have families, dreams of peace. Though I cannot stop you, I will not take up arms to fight and kill them. But this—yes, this I will do gladly. For this boy. For you and for your father, who was friend to my father and grandfather. For your families, the people of the Ituri whom I also love. Maybe it won't work. I'll take that risk. But if my read on those *mzungus* Trevor Mulroney has working for him isn't totally off the wall, it might buy us the time we need."

The rage was gone now. Was it hope that stirred again within?

Not just hope, but something more powerful. Michael had

spoken of love. Such love as had filled Joseph's own heart when he'd begun this journey. A love that had turned with betrayal to equally fervent hate. A hate that had consumed him until its weight had grown heavier than he could bear.

And now here was one of the *mzungus* against whom his heart had raged. And the love of which this man spoke was not just a word but shone in light-colored eyes so different from his own, breathed in the sincerity of every word.

On impulse Joseph leaned in, taking care not to disturb IV tubes and tourniquet, to give the *mzungu* doctor an embrace such as he would have given a countryman, a family member. He shook his head again in disbelief, but a shedding of despair had brought the glimmer of a smile to his own black eyes.

"Michael, my friend, my brother, your idea is crazy such as only a lunatic would propose. Perhaps crazy enough to succeed!"

CHAPTER FORTY-TWO

Robin had slept longer than her estimation because the night sky above the mine's perimeter lighting had paled fractionally to the darkest of grays. Dawn would arrive within the hour. Stepping down gingerly into a quagmire of mud and puddled water, she felt shards of glass crunch beneath her boots.

The executive helicopter had settled down in an open area between the main gate and the Mi-17s. Their armored insect shapes blocked all view of the Quonset hut. But to Robin's left, the brush corral that had housed prisoners was no longer a complete enclosure. Huge sections of dried branches and foliage had been pulled away, offering a clear view of thatched huts and a communal shelter.

But no residents.

Behind Robin, the gate's huge metal panels lay twisted off their hinges on the ground. Robin bent to pick up a blackened glass shard.

Its soot came away greasy, leaving her fingers smelling like engine exhaust.

A Molotov cocktail—the poor man's bomb.

AK-47 rounds littered the ground. And was that an actual arrow sticking into the ground near the gate? Smoke thickened the air, fumes of burning fuel, gunpowder, and chemicals stinging Robin's eyes. She coughed as Trevor Mulroney's grip on her elbow steered her directly toward a puddle of blackened and melted plastic that smelled strongly of rotten eggs.

"Don't touch the plastic." Pieter Krueger strode out from between the two Mi-17s. Beyond him were a handful of Ares Solutions operatives, the only combat troops she could see inside the chain-link fence. Ernie Miller. Krueger's fellow South Africans and an older Rhodesian. The same posse, in fact, that had burst through Miriam's door to capture Robin.

But outside the fence, the perimeter lighting cast into sharp relief hundreds of bodies hunkered down in the muddy field separating mine workings from rainforest.

Letting out a string of curses, Mulroney released his grip on Robin to inspect a streak of melted plastic that had transferred itself to one of his boot soles.

"Sorry about that, boss. The plastic bottles are some kind of gas bomb and as toxic as they get." Only as Krueger kicked dirt over the blackened, melted puddle did Robin recognize it as having once been a two-liter water bottle. "That's one we hadn't expected. Your Jini's a clever little stinker."

"So where is he?" Robin took advantage of her sudden freedom to step forward. "Where's Michael? And the prisoners. The villagers. What have you done with them?"

"Michael?" Krueger raised flaxen eyebrows. "You mean Dr. Stewart? Haven't seen hide or hair of him. But if he's still with Jini's bunch, he'd be inside the Quonset hut with the others. Whether as hostage or accomplice, there's no telling. If he's in there, we could sure use him right now. No body bags so far. But we've got a couple dozen wounded, one of them ours. Maybe that could be a first negotiating point, boss?"

Trevor Mulroney recovered his grip on Robin's elbow as the Ares Solutions mission chief turned to lead the way between the two Mi-17s. "More pertinent, Krueger, is why you've dragged me out here to negotiate. What's the holdup? We're talking a handful of virtually unarmed opponents and a bunch of civilians. You should have been able to overrun them in five minutes."

"A handful, yes. Unarmed, no. As to the holdup, blame your local allies." Pieter Krueger gestured contemptuously toward the militia hunkered down beyond the chain-link fence. "Turns out Wamba's boys are happy to go to war so long as it's an enemy that can't shoot back! A couple of Jini's men had automatic weapons. Once they started firing, our allies refused to continue the ground assault. Then we had that downpour, grounding the choppers. And NVGs aren't much good under a waterfall. Unfortunately, while we were holed up trying to keep from drowning, Jini and his boys were keeping busy. Really busy, as you can see over here!"

As Mulroney steered Robin with him into the open, she spotted instantly the missing debris from the brush corral. It was heaped up at intervals around the curve of the Quonset hut. Stacked drums and casks formed precarious towers between the piles. A solid wall fashioned from two twenty-gallon drums sitting atop two larger fifty-gallon barrels shielded the metallic bubble's single door. French lettering identified diesel fuel for the generator. Kerosene. Ammonia.

Other casks bore chemical names unfamiliar to Robin. But she was only too familiar with the tangle of dynamite sticks, plastic explosives, and fuses duct-taped to the exterior of barrels, drums, casks. And the detonator cord connecting them.

The Quonset hut had been wired into one huge bomb!

The hut's window shutters were closed to slits. The door stood open, but only a hand span was visible above booby-trapped barrels and drums. If the hut's interior really contained a hundred-plus men, women, and children, they were being remarkably quiet.

"As soon as the storm died down, we sent up choppers, of course. But our opponents can shoot. And not just with automatic weapons. They knocked Etienne off his gun post with an arrow." Krueger nodded toward an Mi-17. Robin recognized the man in body armor squatting beside a massive door gun as a French Algerian operative. One hand pressed a bloodied cloth against his collarbone where the broken-off shaft of an arrow pierced the gap between Kevlar vest and helmet.

"With Wamba's men declining to budge, we thought it wise to pull back and let Jini waste his ammo. We knew they couldn't have much since we'd left none behind. We kept poking at them, drawing their fire with the choppers. Once it was clear they were out of gas, Wamba's men got up enough nerve to rush the gate. But that's when we discovered Jini's second tier of defense. The gate blew as soon as Wamba's men got to hammering on it. And not only explosives. They'd rigged those plastic water bottles so that when the gate blew, they released some kind of gas. After getting a whiff of that in the face, Wamba's men refused to move forward at all, even when Makuga threatened to shoot them himself. It's just confirmed their superstition that Jini's some kind of sorcerer who can poison even the air against them."

"It's no magic." Ernie Miller's gaze avoided Robin as he strode over. "It's actually a trick I learned in 'Nam. The mine uses aluminum sulfide crystals for ore processing. Add water, and the stuff turns into hydrogen sulfide gas. It's also highly flammable, as Wamba's boys found out when they crashed the gate and set off those explosives."

"In any case, it took some time before we'd cleared the area well enough to land the choppers. All the while being pummeled from behind that barricade by Molotov cocktails and more of those gas bombs. I'd guess they've run out because they eventually retreated inside. That's when we were able to get to the generator to bring the perimeter lights back on line. As to why we haven't gone in after them, I think that's pretty obvious. The Quonset hut is standard field command specs. Even those guns—" Krueger nodded toward the two Mi-17 door guns swiveled to place the metallic bubble directly within their crosshairs—"couldn't blast through those walls. But the bullets just might be enough to set off those fuel drums. Which would be one way to end this fight, except they've got a full house of hostages. Women, children, wounded, even one expat if the doc's in there. Since they've indicated they're ready to negotiate, I figured you'd want to make the call on this one, boss. We've set up an FOB over there."

Their forward operating base was actually the new aluminum storage shed that had replaced the one blown up in the steam engine explosion. It stood empty because its fuel barrels, drums, and casks were now barricading the Quonset hut. Someone had overturned a cart outside its open doors to form a makeshift table heaped with ammo clips, grenades, smoke bombs. The older Rhodesian operative manned a heavy field gun set up on the table. Two others cradled M4 assault rifles. A pair of rocket grenade launchers leaned against a wall.

Leading the way over, Ernie Miller spoke up. "All I can say is this Jini's got to be more than just some local yokel with a bit of college education. There's serious knowledge of chemicals here."

So her colleagues still had no idea who Jini really was. Which gave Robin hope they were not fully part of this. As much hope as that mention of negotiations. Robin's spirit lightened fractionally.

But Mulroney brushed aside Ernie's suggestion. "This stuff doesn't take a college education. Like you learned in 'Nam, these are just the kind of guerrilla tactics insurgent leaders teach their followers. You can find most of it online these days. And what do you think you're doing here? This isn't some police standoff."

Releasing Robin's arm to stride forward, Mulroney snatched up one of the RPG launchers. "It's battle! You know the rules of engagement."

The RPG launcher stood half as tall as the Earth Resources CEO, so he balanced it across the cart to insert a grenade as he shouted, "Jini, if you're in there, you've got to the count of three to get out here before we open fire."

There was no immediate response. Unless Michael and Joseph were inside, there'd be no others in any case who could understand Mulroney's English. Not a factor the Earth Resources CEO would have overlooked.

"One!"

Mulroney's move had left Robin free to step beside Ernie Miller. Dropping her voice to a low, urgent whisper, she demanded, "Ernie, surely you guys aren't going to let him fire on a building filled with hostages!"

For the first time since her arrival, the Vietnam vet met Robin's gaze. His low response was brusque. "You don't get it, Duncan! Take a look around you. You see who Krueger picked for this op? We're all old Africa hands, including myself for the last thirty years. We've all fought for Mulroney since clear back when he founded Ares Solutions. And we've all fought a lot dirtier battles than this. You think that's by accident?"

"Two!"

Across the clearing, Robin saw a shutter crack open. A glint of dark eyes peered out.

Ernie cast a somber glance toward his employer. "But it's more than that. When Trevor Mulroney first came here all those months back, the bunch of us you see right here were his security detail. We'd been told the site was overrun by guerrillas, so we raised no objections when Wamba's men came out swinging. Once we realized no one was fighting back, we stepped in to call a halt, but . . . well, sometimes collateral damage is the price for an op like this. And Wamba's his own man, the authority in this region. But why do you think we've been riding Makuga and his cohorts so hard this time round to avoid unnecessary casualties? Bottom line, Krueger, me, the others here— we've hitched our wagons to Mulroney's star. We've no choice but to see this through. And if your journalist pal starts pointing fingers, we're following legal rules of engagement. Our target in there wants to avoid bloodshed, all he's got to do is step out and surrender. You'll find neither friends nor support here, Duncan!"

"Legal rules, maybe. But hardly moral," Robin whispered back urgently. "And you don't know what else is involved. Mulroney's lied to you about everything. Including what he's really digging out of this mine. Why do you think he's so anxious to shut up Joseph and the others instead of negotiating? There's women and children in there. And Michael, too—I'm sure of it! Whatever you've done before for Mulroney, whatever the rules of engagement, I can't believe you're the type of man to stand by and see unarmed civilians blown up."

"Three!"

At Mulroney's bellow, Robin abandoned her pleading to rush forward, just in time to see Mulroney raise the RPG launcher to his shoulder. "Michael! Joseph! He's going to shoot!"

Whether coincidence or in response to her shout, Robin spotted immediate movement from the doorway of the Quonset hut. She let out her breath slowly as Trevor Mulroney lowered the RPG launcher. Not that the weapon was any longer necessary. Every Ares Solutions operative in the shed had stepped forward, leveling assault rifles on the hut entrance. In that moment, Robin could have easily slipped away, made a run for it. The option didn't even cross her mind.

"I want you out in the open, Jini, you and your men," Trevor Mulroney called out. "Step completely away from the building, hands where we can see them."

A shadow cast by the security light above the doorway moved first out across the ground. Elongated, distorted by the superimposition of the barricade's own shadow, it was definitely human and definitely male. Trevor Mulroney's grunt of satisfaction was echoed by the loud click and release of assault rifles being cocked to fire. But it was not

Jini or any other Congolese who stepped into the narrow opening between stacked barrels and brush firing blind.

It was Michael.

A cry of dismay escaped Robin as the light fell full on him. Michael's hands were spread wide above his head in surrender, his expression calm. The long, muscled frame displayed no injury except a bandage of white gauze wrapping the left elbow. But bound to his torso with an overkill of duct tape was the same tangle of dynamite sticks, plastic explosives, and detonator cord that was taped to the fuel drums.

Nor was Michael alone. A second dark shadow could be made out behind him, shielded from clear view or gunshot by Michael's taller frame as well as the piled-up barrels and drums. But the tautness of the detonator cord twisted around Michael's neck indicated his controller held it in a tight grip.

Michael had flinched at the sound of Robin's voice, shock widening the briefest flicker of eyes in her direction. Had Robin read dismay there as well? Recoil? *I'm not here with them! Can't you see? I'm a prisoner too. I'm trying to help!*

But Michael did not glance her way again as he moved farther into the light. "As you can see, I'm not in any position to obey orders. Jini's got this thing rigged to blow if his demands are not heard."

As several weapons abruptly shifted aim, he raised his voice. "Before you think of trying to take Jini out, if you shoot him or me, this place still blows. I served in Afghanistan. I know a dead man's switch when I see one. But Jini's also made clear he's ready to negotiate a cease-fire, including a full release of the hostages, as well as an eventual surrender on his own terms. I've got patients inside among the hostages. I'd like to get them to a hospital in one piece. So can we please just lower our weapons and dialogue rationally? There's no reason for anyone else to get hurt here today."

Michael's plea was not intended for her employer, Robin recognized, but for her Ares Solutions teammates. Trevor Mulroney had good reason not to swallow Michael's shift from accomplice to hostage, but the kidnapping of an expatriate doctor by insurgents would seem imminently plausible to Mulroney's Ares Solutions subordinates.

Michael gave a head gesture over his shoulder. "Jini's demands are simple enough. He doesn't trust the forces of Governor Wamba who have been fighting against him. But he will surrender to the United Nations peacekeeping force in Bunia. He wants a UN negotiation party airlifted immediately to the mine along with a medical team from Doctors Without Borders. Once the United Nations officials accept his surrender, he will release the hostages for direct transport to a UN refugee camp in Bunia."

It was as logical a demand as it was brilliant. Mulroney would have a hard time explaining to the Ares Solutions team any reason not to accept UN intervention. And once in UN hands, even should Jini eventually be turned over to local law enforcement, he'd have opportunity to tell his story.

Still, Trevor Mulroney had already turned down Robin's own very similar and sensible proposal. Would it make a difference with the Ares Solutions team looking on? Or was he so sure of his control over these men?

Michael had finished speaking, his silence becoming a dragged-out pause when Trevor Mulroney made no response. Michael's expression remained composed as the seconds ticked by, his long, lean body relaxed under its deadly burden. But for just an instant, a spread-out hand curled convulsively into a fist before stretching deliberately flat again.

Robin's own body was a tightened coil so tense her jaw ached with it, her eyes glued to Michael's face as though memorizing it. The narrow, bronzed features looking unnaturally pale and drained under the security light's bright white gleam. The firm mouth that could be so stern and yet so tender. The jawline clenched with determination. The steady tawny gaze that flickered again her way before returning to Trevor Mulroney.

Could Michael read Robin's own fear, worry, anguish for his safety?

Her sorrow for having failed him?

Her love?

The Ares Solutions team had not lowered their weapons, but Robin could see among them a definite relaxing of battle readiness. Pieter Krueger spoke. "What do you think, boss? Is Jini bluffing? Would he really blow up himself and his own men?"

"Oh, he's bluffing all right!" The grim satisfaction in those words cut through Robin's brooding reverie, drew her startled glance upward. Only to find her erstwhile employer's brilliant-blue gaze intent on her own features.

Beyond him, Krueger's eyebrows shot up. "What makes you think that?"

"Because *she* thinks they're bluffing!" Yanking Robin close, Mulroney twisted her chin to tilt her face toward a security spotlight. "You see that! She's shaking in her boots right now. But not about what our perp might do to her doctor pal. About what *I* might do to the both of them!"

Mulroney's grip suddenly became a steel bar across Robin's neck. Powerful fingers biting into her cheeks dropped instead to Mulroney's belt. Only to rise again holding a 9mm pistol. A Beretta instead of a Glock as an American would carry, Robin's stunned brain found time to note as its muzzle ground into her right cheekbone.

Dragging Robin forward into the security spotlight's white beam, Mulroney called out, "You should know I don't negotiate with terrorists, Stewart. Nor do I stand for traitors on my payroll. You want to play chicken? Here's the deal. You send out the coward hiding behind you, or I blow the head off your girlfriend."

This time Mulroney's action did draw disbelieving stares from the Ares Solutions team. Ernie Miller took a quick step forward to say quietly but urgently, "You're bluffing now, boss, right?"

If her Ares Solutions teammates thought Mulroney in turn to

be bluffing, Robin knew otherwise. The painful grinding of metal against her molars, an anticipatory quiver in the hand holding the Beretta, a quick, sharp breathing above her ear all told Robin her captor was aching to pull the trigger. Mulroney's chin brushed her hair as he turned his head toward Pieter Krueger.

"You got a shot, you take it! The hostage is not a factor, understand?"

"Got it, boss!" Krueger's weapon rose unhesitatingly, shifted fractionally. They were not even going to give Jini a chance to surrender. And if Michael was in the way, too bad!

No, that's exactly what Mulroney wants! If Michael's shot in the process of killing Jini, Mulroney can write it up as a hostage standoff gone bad. He'll have witnesses, too. And if it sets off an explosion, even better. Then he can say Jini chose to commit suicide, taking the hostages with him. Conveniently leaving no witnesses against him. Except me!

Robin's despairing train of thought did not delay her instinctive reaction. A kick of her boot backward missed her intended target, the groin, but caught Mulroney's inner thigh viciously enough to draw a grunt of pain, a relaxing of that grinding metal against her face. A deadweight sag forward, a twist to the left broke the hold on her neck.

Then Robin was free and racing forward, toward the Quonset hut. "Don't shoot! Don't shoot!"

Would her former teammates actually shoot her in the back? Or would Robin's intrusion into the line of fire be, as she hoped, enough to give them pause? Robin's shoulder blades itched, bracing for a bullet. But none had come by the time she reached the barricade and spun around. "Please, you're not going to shoot me, are you? Pieter? Ernie? Just give me ten minutes to try to talk them into a no-conditions surrender."

Trevor Mulroney had recovered his balance, the Beretta coming up in his hand. But Robin's plea, her use of their names, was having its intended effect. Her teammates were looking at Robin now, not through her to the targets behind. On their faces she could read discomfiture, uncertainty.

"Please, just ten minutes," Robin repeated.

Without waiting for Mulroney's orders, they were lowering their weapons, Pieter Krueger last of all. Robin drew a deep breath as she saw Trevor Mulroney slip the Beretta in unspoken acquiescence back into his holster.

In the next instant, a hard hand was again grabbing Robin's arm. But this time to drag her behind the barricade and into the Quonset hut.

CHAPTER
FORTY-THREE

The Quonset hut was a seething mass of bodies crowding every available inch of floor and bunks. Among them Robin spotted little Rachel curled up on her mother's lap. A man beside them carried one arm bound in a sling. At the windows, sentries mounted a lookout with assault rifle or bow in hand. But a glance confirmed the rifles had no clips, the bows no arrows.

One bunk held the boy Robin had last seen in the Taraja clinic. To Robin's relief, Jacob was sitting up, eyes alert, leg freshly bandaged. But she'd already taken in the IV bag hanging from an upper bunk, a bandage matching Michael's above Jacob's right elbow. A field transfusion. No wonder Michael had looked so pale!

Dark faces, black eyes had all swiveled to stare at the intruder. Though Robin read in them fear and worry, she spotted neither tears nor hysterics. Just a patient, somber resignation, even on children's faces, that twisted her heart. But it was toward a single set of lighter features, the long, lean frame that stood tall and whole and only inches away, not limp and bleeding on the ground, that Robin stepped instinctively forward.

"Careful!" Releasing the grip with which he'd yanked Robin inside, Michael raised an arm to block her advance. "Let me get this off before it blows!"

Joseph had already moved to Michael's side, machete in hand. Robin suppressed the wobble that threatened her voice as she saw the caution with which the rebel leader sawed wires, duct tape. "I was sure that was all a bluff."

Joseph looked up from the wires. "The dead man's switch was a bluff. But this had to be real. Trevor Mulroney is an expert on such things. He would know if it was not genuine."

"And the explosives outside?"

Joseph carefully lifted the mass away. "The explosives are real. But the barrels now hold mostly dirt and debris. We used their contents to fight. It was our hope to hold off our enemy long enough to give Michael's friend time to send help. Do you bring news from him?"

"A bigger question—what are you doing here?" The moment Michael stepped clear of the explosive vest, it was he who closed the gap, yanking Robin against him in a hard embrace. Now it was Michael's deep voice that shook as he spoke into her hair. "In all this mess, I was thanking God you at least were out of reach and safe. I just about lost it when I saw you out there with Mulroney, that gun to your head. I should never have dragged you into this."

Robin wrapped her own arms around Michael's torso, where the duct tape had been. Let her head rest against his T-shirt. Under her right ear, she could hear the fast, hard thump of his heartbeat, feel a quick rise and fall of muscle. Her nostrils were filled with the wonderful, *live* perfume of perspiration and smoke and gunpowder and that particular masculine musk that was Michael's own scent.

Robin did not want to move. How long she had waited for this. Longed for it with a ceaseless, yearning ache that carried not the slightest hope of realization. Dreamed of it with such vivid clarity as to awaken her in the night with tears on her face.

This was spring after endless, dreary winter.

A stream of cool, rushing water in the most barren and thirsty of wastelands.

It was coming home.

But however much Robin would have liked to stay just where she was for the rest of her life or a year or an hour, there was no time for personal indulgence. Reluctantly she lifted her head.

"I had to come! They were going to shoot you both. I heard Trevor Mulroney give the order to take Jini out without even giving him a chance to surrender. And to take you out, Michael, if that was necessary to get a clean shot."

Letting out a sigh, Michael straightened, his arms falling away from Robin. "I was afraid of that. So I'm right that your presence out there means Mulroney's found out just what I'm doing here with Joseph. And therefore that I'm not really Joseph's hostage. Does he know also about the pictures and files? Were you able to get those to Miriam? And what about Alan Birenge? Any hope he's galloping to the rescue?

"I sent off the images and files myself to your journalist friend." Feeling suddenly bereft as Michael released her, Robin folded her own arms across her chest. "Believe me, I made no reports to Mulroney or anyone else about Joseph. Once I'd seen those pictures, that video, I just couldn't! But I knew the Taraja computer would be the first place our tech people checked once that material went public. So I decided to send it from my own. But that backfired because our tech guy somehow managed to dig the stuff from my own personal accounts. And he passed it on to Mulroney."

What had happened next at Taraja, to Ephraim, Robin didn't elaborate. It would only be more worry for Michael now if he knew. And by the time it was necessary to tell him, one way or another this would be all over.

"By then Birenge had the intel. And he said he'd help. But Mulroney says he's tracked down where Alan is and has contacts there going after him. That he'll never be given opportunity to air Joseph's evidence. And even if Alan Birenge and his family got away, Mulroney's pretty much told me he's not going to back down. Those M4s aimed at you out there won't cut through these walls. But Mulroney's got an RPG launcher locked and loaded. And he's not bluffing about using it! The explosives you've got rigged out there— even if those drums are mostly empty of flammable material—will they go off if an RPG launches through the front door?"

Tawny and black eyes exchanged a grim glance before Joseph nodded. "Yes, such an attack would detonate the explosives, destroying this place. But we had no choice. Without the threat, Trevor Mulroney's force would have rushed us an hour ago when they discovered we no longer possessed ammunition for defense."

"Then—I don't know what to say. To suggest." A Marine always had an answer. Always found a way to turn defeat into victory. Never gave up, never surrendered. That was the creed on which Robin had based her life.

It was also a lie. Sometimes when you'd done all you could, done the right thing, taken a stand on the side of justice—sometimes life still threw a curveball. The bad guy outfought the hero. The Joker caught Batman. Lex Luthor defeated Superman. Instead of Tripoli's white sands or the halls of Montezuma, those brave, young Marines found themselves stranded ashore at the Bay of Pigs.

And maybe Captain James T. Kirk could wriggle his way out of a fictional no-win scenario by rigging the Kobayashi Maru test, but Robin had nothing to offer. Only an apology that must be made before it was too late. "There's something else I have to tell you. It's no happenstance Mulroney found you here, planned this trap. It's all my fault."

Robin could not bear to watch conviviality fade from the two men's eyes, so she permitted her own gaze to roam across the sea of dark faces who thankfully could not understand her English, and so if they comprehended their peril, at least they did not know how close it was.

"If my slipup hadn't alerted Mulroney about Joseph and his evidence, there'd be plenty of time for Alan Birenge to go for help. And Mulroney would still be unaware that Michael knows the truth about Joseph and the rhenium. Even this trap you walked into—it's my fault too because Mulroney got the idea from me. Not intentionally. I was trying to talk him into letting Joseph and his people just walk away from the mine and the rhenium.

"Instead he got the idea to open the gates and make Joseph think I'd been successful with Birenge so he was pulling out. In trying to help, I've placed you all in terrible jeopardy. And what he's planning out there now—I wish I had better news. I told them I'd try to talk you into surrendering. But the truth is, Trevor Mulroney doesn't want you to surrender. He wants you to resist so he has an excuse to kill you. To kill everyone who knows the truth. He still thinks he can get away with it all. And I—"

Robin could no longer keep the tremor from her voice. "Bottom line, without a miracle, I'm not sure he isn't right."

Across the crowded hut, all eyes remained on the three-way conversation just inside the doorway. In them Robin could glimpse now expectancy jostling worry and resignation as though the listeners assumed that conversation, Robin's own intrusion, promised succor. Earlier she'd been glad they could not understand the English. But now as Robin turned back to Joseph, she did so in Swahili, her glance addressing the entire hut. The boy Jacob, watching from the bed. Joseph's older brother Simeon, holding a bow at one of the windows. Little Rachel wrapped tightly in her mother's arms. All the men, women, and children squeezed into this inadequate refuge who'd turned out not to be, as she'd believed, targets and victims of a vicious rebel and killer named Jini, but Joseph's family and neighbors.

"Can you forgive me? All of you. But especially you, Joseph. For all the trouble I've brought upon you. For being part of the team that came here to capture or kill you. For the evil perpetrated against you by a man of my own race in which I too have played a part."

> > >

Forgive?

Joseph could only stare at the *mzungu* woman. Robin Duncan was requesting his forgiveness? After what he had done? After his own terrible conviction that he himself was beyond forgiveness, redemption?

But the sincerity of her plea, the sorrow and remorse in eyes the odd blue and green hues of an ocean wave, were no illusion.

For Joseph, it was the last straw.

Not of hope.

But of hate.

For too long since he'd returned to the Ituri, every pallid *mzungu* face had held for him the sneering, arrogant features of his betrayer and enemy, Trevor Mulroney, so he could admit it to be one reason he'd resisted his father's advice to seek help from such as Michael Stewart. He'd come to understand the cruelty and violence of his countrymen who'd risen up to wreak their revenge on such invaders. Burned to have it within his own power to execute such revenge.

But in so doing, he'd allowed himself to forget others of pale skin who had not been cruel and greedy and deceitful. The Stewarts and others of their race who had been not only his boyhood instructors, but his friends at Taraja. The volunteers in the displaced persons camps who'd labored long and hard for refugees not of their own people. The foreign journalists who'd employed him, perhaps for their own purposes and a good story, but who'd troubled themselves to reach into their own pockets to provide a Congolese orphan, as he'd believed himself to be, an education and a future.

For all of this. For all the anger and bitterness he could now let go forever, worthless thistledown to be swept away by a monsoon wind.

For the healing brought to his heart and soul when these two *mzungus* chose to stand with him this day. Who had been strangers but were now friends. For all of this and more, Joseph could speak in a voice that was not his own but held a joy and release he'd left shattered at his father's feet on top of a rock outcropping.

"If the almighty Creator can forgive even me, if my people here can forgive my many mistakes, then who am I to speak of forgiving you? But such as I can give, I grant freely. If you will but forgive me too for the hate that has been in my heart against those like you."

The *mzungu* woman blinked her ocean-hued eyes. "Yes, of course I do."

"Good. And now you have shown to me what it is I must do." A peace he'd not known it was possible to feel in the midst of such darkness rested upon him. This exhilaration was not the gladness he'd known in promising Paradise to his father; it was far greater. He had prayed for deliverance. And though he had not at first recognized it, the almighty Creator had indeed brought deliverance. Not the deliverance he'd desired, imagined, demanded from his Creator, resulting in an enemy bloody and destroyed on the ground.

Deliverance from hate.

Deliverance from the crushing, choking rage which had so blinded him that he had not been able to see light in the darkness.

Deliverance from despair. Whatever happened this day, if like his father he did not survive to see the dawn, the truth had gone out. And were not the times and end of the wicked also in the almighty Creator's hands? Trevor Mulroney would not remain victorious forever.

Joseph looked around at the crowded room. His people. His family.

He groped for the heavy, slick feel of metal in the harness he wore. Sliding the weapon free, he handed it to the *mzungu* woman. "Let us end this now. I will do what you were sent to ask. Inform your commander that I am coming out unarmed and alone to surrender."

CHAPTER FORTY-FOUR

Robin took the gray, metallic object he was holding out. Her Glock. Automatically she ejected the clip, confirmed it was empty, snapped it back in even as she protested, "Joseph, you can't just walk out there! Didn't you hear what I said?"

Robin switched to swift English as she slid the Glock into the holster on her own belt. "Trevor Mulroney has given orders that you are not to be allowed to surrender. You step out there unarmed and alone, and they will shoot you! You'll be throwing your life away."

Joseph answered in the same language. "And if I do not, they will destroy all of us. Is that not also what you said? I did not surrender before only because my enemy would have no further reason to keep my people alive. But now my surrender is their only hope. Perhaps if he has me, Trevor Mulroney will spare these others, at least the women and children. If not, it will at least offer additional delay for the journalist to send aid. What other choice remains?"

What other choice? Robin looked pleadingly at Michael. His expression had gone bleak, but not with the condemnation for which Robin had braced herself. "Joseph's right, Robin. You can't be blaming yourself for this any more than Joseph should for being in the wrong place and time to offer Mulroney the rhenium. You did what you could. What is, is. But if Mulroney won't let us surrender to the UN, and we can't count on Birenge riding to the rescue, I can't see another option either. Would you choose differently if these were your people?"

No, she wouldn't, Robin recognized helplessly. Michael straightened his long body. "In any case, Joseph won't be going out alone."

Robin stiffened as his intent sank in. But Michael's hand was now at Robin's back, urging her forward. "But first, those ten minutes of yours must be about up. We'd better get you out there while you still can."

As Michael exchanged a swift look with Joseph, his tone hardened. "Give Mulroney a message from all of us. We don't negotiate with terrorists either!"

But Robin held her ground against Michael's propelling hand. "If you think I'm leaving, think again! Were you listening? If Mulroney's not going to let you walk away, he's sure not going to let me."

Michael's jaw clenched. "Out there you've at least got a chance. Teammates you can appeal to. Are you forgetting why you came to the Ituri to start with? Your sister and niece are counting on you to come home."

This time Robin did move, but not toward the door. Inches from Michael's solid frame, she tilted her head back to say softly, "Kristi and Kelli are in God's hands. Your own sister and you, too, taught me that. As for you, Michael Stewart, I left you once before when I should have tracked you down to the ends of the earth. Should have trusted the man I knew when I never heard from you. I'm not leaving you again. Where you go, I go. Not unless you're going to bodily remove me. And let me tell you, I kick, claw, and bite!"

The seriousness of their situation hardly warranted the half grin thawing Michael's stony expression. "I'd sooner tangle with a mother leopard. Which I guess leaves only one option."

Michael's grin vanished as he stepped nearer, a hand rising to gently cup one side of Robin's face. Though he did not close the remaining gap, a blaze of fire in his eyes, the tender curve of his mouth so near her tilted chin was as intimate as any kiss. "Shall we give Joseph some company? Together?"

Robin's voice shook as she answered. "To the end of the world."

"To the end of the world," Joseph repeated. He had paused in the doorway, intently watching the exchange. Now he spoke again in Swahili, his glance including the entire crowded room. "Michael, you remember the message you brought me from my father. What your own father used to say. 'Woe to those—' whether they are *mzungu* or African—'who call evil good and good evil, who put darkness for light and light for darkness' in pursuit of their own power and wealth. But there was something else my father also said often. Words from the Holy Scriptures your own grandfather first brought to our village. 'The light shines in the darkness, and the darkness has not overcome it.'"

"Yes, of course." Michael had eased back from Robin, his cupped hand dropping away. "From the Gospel of John."

"I was so sure the darkness had overcome the light," Joseph went on. "But now I know it was only my own eyes that were blind to its presence. These men—Trevor Mulroney, Samuel Makuga, General Wamba, and the others—they can destroy our bodies as they have already destroyed this beautiful paradise our Creator gave to my village. But they cannot destroy the light because the light is more powerful than the darkness. And we have another paradise awaiting us. Did not your father and mine teach that as well? We will meet again."

We will meet again. Looking at Michael, Robin saw the same peace that had settled over her own mind. She stretched out her hand. As strong fingers tightened around hers, she turned toward the open door to call out, "Mr. Mulroney, we're coming out—Joseph and Michael and I. There are wounded and children in here, so please don't shoot."

Hand in hand, Michael and Robin moved after Joseph toward the door. Only as a rustle behind them spread across the Quonset hut did Robin take in that their other companions had risen to their feet, falling into step. Sentries were abandoning their window look-outs, setting down empty guns and bows. Whirling around, Robin announced urgently in Swahili, "No, no, you need to stay here."

Jacob's older brother Nathaniel spoke first, tossing his own bow onto a bunk. "If Joseph goes, I go with him."

Behind him, Jacob struggled upright from the bunk bed, yank-ing the IV from his arm with a grimace of pain and determination. "And I go too."

Robin looked from Joseph to Michael, shifting into English to plead, "Tell them they can't go out! That it's not safe or necessary. That if they'll just stay here, we'll try to negotiate some kind of safe passage for them."

Joseph made no answer, but Michael shook his head, shifting also into soft English. "Robin, these people are not children that I, any more than my father or grandfather before me, should make decisions for them. This is as much their choice as it is yours, mine."

A middle-aged man had stepped forward beside Nathaniel. If he could not understand their English, he'd read Robin's expression well enough. "The almighty Creator brought my youngest brother home when we believed him dead. It is on our behalf he has fought evil men, both *mzungu* and Congolese, who have come here to kill us. If their honor is so small they will kill an unarmed man who surrenders in peace, they will not hesitate to destroy all of us. So let them look on our faces when they do so. We are done hiding. And we will not let our brother die alone."

Nods swept the room. A battery of steady, dark eyes held deter-mination, courage, peace. Robin's eyes were blinded suddenly with tears. She'd prayed for a miracle. Had she just witnessed one after all? She closed her eyes to squeeze the tears away.

Father God, you are in charge here. I don't have the wisdom to understand what you are doing. Sometimes you deliver miraculously. Other times you allow human courage and sacrifice to be its own miracle of light in the darkness. Whatever your choice for this day, I leave Kristi and Kelli to your care.

Opening her eyes, she smiled at Michael, around the room. "Then let's go."

Joseph attempted to step out first. But other villagers were already crowding forward to form a phalanx around him as well as around Michael and Robin so that it was a tangle of bodies that pushed and squeezed together through the narrow entrance. Robin heard Trevor Mulroney's sharp order as the first villagers began pouring out between brush barricade and stacked barrels. "Shoot! Shoot! What are you waiting for?"

But no gunshots came. Then Robin, too, was in the open, Michael's arm hard around her shoulders, Joseph at her other side. Limping badly, Jacob managed to insert his slight frame in front of Joseph. The rest of the villagers fanned out to form a solid mass in front of the Quonset hut. Parents lifted infants in their arms, pulled back small children who tried to run forward. Robin jostled forward to ensure her paler features and red hair could not be missed. Joseph's older brother had it right. If her teammates were truly willing to shoot her, unarmed and unresisting, let them look Robin in the face as they did so.

But still no gunshots rang out. In the brief time Robin had been inside the Quonset hut, the equator's swift shift from night to day had lightened the stretch of sky overhead from dark gray to pale green. Across the muddy field beyond the chain-link fence, a few stars still lingered on the western horizon. But behind the Quonset hut, the faintest streaks of orange and red were already tinting the eastern horizon above the rainforest canopy.

Security spotlights were no longer needed to highlight the automatic weapons the Ares Solutions operatives held trained on the Quonset hut. The loaded RPG launcher still lay across the overturned cart. At some point during Robin's absence, Samuel Makuga had joined the others in the storage shed, his subordinates out on the muddy field no longer squatting shadows, but an army of camouflage and assault rifles.

The surrounding rainforest was still, its daytime twitter of birds, caw of parrots, chitter of monkeys not yet stirring to greet the approaching dawn. But somewhere in the far distance, Robin caught a drone that was not of nature but an engine. A reminder that their Ares Solutions operation was not alone in flying aircraft over this jungle.

Then from behind Robin rose a new sound. Deep, rumbling, hauntingly beautiful. *"Yesu, nuru ya ulimwengu."*

A treble took up the harmony, then alto and tenor and the high, shrill melody of children. Robin heard Michael's deep baritone join in before the words from her childhood rose unhesitatingly to her own lips. "Jesus, Light of the World."

Behind the overturned cart, fury was naked on Trevor Mulroney's face. "What are you idiots waiting for? Do your job! Take them out!"

It was Ernie Miller who first lowered his assault rifle. "Can't do it, boss. Not when the perp has surrendered. Not when there's any risk of collateral damage to the hostages. It's just too easy for that whole thing to blow."

Robin broke off her song to draw in a sharp breath. The sudden tension in Michael's body, the tightening of his arm around her shoulders, said that he, too, had heard and seen what she was witnessing.

Then with a shake of his head, the French Algerian lowered his weapon, followed by the two South African commandos.

Mulroney whirled around. "Hostages! Don't you get it? There are no hostages here. They're Joseph's relatives, his accomplices, the whole bunch of them. They're as dangerous to this mission as he is. Krueger, you've got the shot. Take it now!"

Robin did not breathe as the barrel of Krueger's assault rifle shifted slightly to center on Joseph and the boy Jacob, standing tall in front of the rebel leader as though his thin frame could offer an adequate shield. But it was Ernie Miller who stepped forward into the South African's line of sight. "Not this time, Krueger. Not unless you plan to take me out too. Because that's the only way you'll keep this one quiet. Think what you're doing, man! Mulroney may pay our contract, but he doesn't own our souls."

The grizzled American mercenary swung toward Trevor Mulroney. "You just called the perp Joseph. That's what Ms. Duncan called him earlier. Then you knew who this Jini was all the time. Duncan's right that there's a whole lot more to this story—and this mission—than you've told us."

Robin could not see Pieter Krueger's expression behind Ernie's brawny bulk. But after a hesitation that seemed like an eternity, the Ares Solutions mission commander laid his rifle down on the overturned cart. "I don't really care who Jini is, and I don't want to know his life history. But Miller's got a point, boss. We've got the target now. Whatever you want to do with him we'll carry out. But there's no advantage here to risking unarmed women and children."

Robin let out her breath slowly. Was it over then? At least for the villagers?

The multitude did not need to understand the conversation. They had seen the weapons being lowered. Their song rose louder. So did the drone of an aircraft engine.

But it was not over so easily. Letting out a torrent of curses, Trevor Mulroney snatched the RPG launcher up to his shoulder and leveled it. Not at Joseph or the choir of villagers, but smack center on the stacked barrels and drums with their attached explosives, just outside the Quonset hut entrance.

How had it ever come to this?

Trevor Mulroney's convulsion of grip on the RPG launcher contained as much perplexity and mounting panic as rage. He was not a bad man. At least not in his own estimation. If he'd killed often enough in Africa's bloody wars, he'd taken no particular pleasure in it. He'd remained true to his own code of honor. Never go after women and children, unless unavoidable as collateral damage. Never kill one's own—a white man or woman—unless absolutely necessary or an enemy. Some might consider him ruthless as a businessman, but until recently he'd never crossed the line of international law.

Mulroney's first step over the line had not seemed a major one at the time or even avoidable, his need so desperate, his salvation so fortuitously dropped into his lap. One man's life had seemed acceptable collateral damage.

After all, this was a war. Not just for his own personal survival. For the survival of an entire way of life. Of free market capitalism, stability, prosperity. For Africa and the Congolese people themselves. If the Ituri had already been ripped apart by warring factions and greed for conflict minerals, only let word get out that an unlimited supply of a scarce military component had been discovered here. How quickly this zone could become a killing field between battling world powers, as Howard Marshall had cautioned. Not just China and India, but Russia with its renewed global ambitions. Perhaps even Iran and other Islamic states.

Was not keeping this treasure in friendly, democratic hands, ensuring stability and peace for the Ituri residents as well as the mining venture, of greater urgency than the life of a single insignificant Congolese native?

And so Trevor Mulroney had barely hesitated when he'd stepped at last over that invisible line.

Unfortunately, it had been necessary to leave the youth free until he'd pinpointed the exact location of his discovery. Then Joseph's tale of a destroyed and abandoned birthplace proved to be false. Still, a single village was not beyond acceptable collateral damage. After all, how many villages might be wiped out should war come to this region? And when the young man's stubborn tenacity had made the operation more difficult than expected, that too was part of war.

But now it was all spiraling out of control. Every time Mulroney trussed up one knot, another began unraveling. To kill a bunch of rainforest natives was one matter. Such things weren't so difficult to hide. To blame even on local allies like Wamba and Makuga.

Explaining away two American citizens would be more difficult. Doctors Without Borders would hardly leave unquestioned the loss of one of their own. And now a journalist as well? BBC, no less.

Perhaps he should have accepted Duncan's proposal. Perhaps it was not too late. As the troublesome female translator had suggested, Mulroney could walk away. Even still retain some return on his investment, however vastly reduced.

Except reduced profits would not cover Mulroney's debts. Perhaps not even permit him to hold on to the concession.

Nor was it too late to win this war. For every unraveling thread, there was an answer. Today's assault would handle most of it. His Kampala contacts would have the journalist by now. If further fallout arose at Taraja, Makuga would deal with it as he had the other night. If suspicions arose concerning expatriate casualties, a story could be planted. Collusion with an insurgent leader in return for mineral rights was a common enough tale to work. Mulroney's loyal Africa hands like Krueger and Miller would fall into line once no other option was left them.

And Howard Marshall had pledged to deal with any wider fallout. The American understood the inevitability and necessity of collateral damage. His vast connections would ensure this all went away.

It would all work out.

Some might say Trevor Mulroney was no longer entirely sane as he settled the rocket-propelled grenade launcher to his shoulder and closed his fingers around the firing mechanism. That his desperate grasp for power, wealth, renown, the months spent watching all to which he'd committed his life and future washing inexorably away like sand in an outgoing tide, had left him no longer capable of sound judgment or moral compass.

Mulroney knew better.

He was completely sane.

Entirely sober.

Fully aware of what he was doing.

And wholly satisfied with his decision as he closed his fingers on the trigger, releasing the lethal combination of projectile and explosive that would at last secure him victory.

CHAPTER
FORTY-FIVE

A clap of thunder put an end to the singing.

Robin's move to leap in front of Rachel and other small children was as instinctive as it was futile. A shower of dirt and debris rained down across the mining encampment. Eardrums screaming in pain, it took Robin the space of several heartbeats to recognize she was not only still alive, but unhurt.

Turning her head, Robin discovered she was not the only one to have moved. As futile as her own gesture, Joseph had flung himself in front of the explosive-rigged barricade toward which the RPG had been directed. Michael was still racing toward the storage shed, where Ernie Miller had knocked the weapon off target and now struggled to wrench it out of Trevor Mulroney's grip. Hurdling the overturned cart, Michael joined the Vietnam vet in wresting away the weapon. Robin turned her head again cautiously to take in the dust and smoke rising in a thick cloud above fire-scorched branches and thatch, where the RPG round had struck the dismantled brush corral.

And in all this time, the noise did not abate but grew. As the painful ringing subsided in her ears, Robin could distinguish the roar of rapidly approaching aircraft. Helicopters, from the *throp-throp* of rotors. And not Ares Solutions aircraft since their three charter helicopters were already on-site.

New enemies?

Or was it possible the cavalry had actually arrived?

Then they swept into view over the Quonset hut. Three Sikorsky helicopters and two Black Hawks. All bearing sky-blue and white markings. One by one, the Sikorskys hovered down to the far side of the storage shed and slurry pits from the Ares Solutions aircraft. The Black Hawks settled into a leisurely orbit low enough one couldn't miss massive machine guns thrusting from side doors, missiles under their bellies.

At the storage shed, Trevor Mulroney had relinquished the RPG launcher to watch with narrowed eyes as helicopter runners touched dirt. The Ares Solutions team seemed as uncertain of their next move as the villagers jostling tightly around Robin.

But even deep in the rainforest, the significance of that sky-blue and white color combination was familiar. As the first blue helmets poured from a Sikorsky, a cheer rose around Robin.

Robin was not so sanguine, because she'd spotted familiar broad features and huge, powerful frame in a medal-bedazzled uniform stepping down among the UN troops. Governor Wamba strode their direction, a detail of his own militia at his back. Keeping stride with him was a Caucasian male with gray hair and weathered features, his suit and tie clashing sartorially with a wide-brimmed Stetson hat and cowboy boots.

Robin had never seen Mulroney disconcerted. Never thought he could be. But the Earth Resources CEO looked stunned as he stepped forward from the storage shed. "Marshall? What are you doing here?"

Then his glance fell furiously on a second Caucasian male trailing

Wamba's security detail. "Jensen, is this your doing? Consider yourself fired!"

"No, consider *yourself* fired!" The man Mulroney had referenced as Marshall turned to the huddle of Ares Solutions operatives now emerging from the storage shed. "Pieter Krueger, right? Haven't seen you since Angola in '97. And Ernie Miller, you were one of ours. So you're running ops with Ares Solutions these days? Well, I'm here to tell you this op's over. In fact, as of—" the new arrival checked a Rolex watch— "three hours ago, Ares Solutions is under new management. Marshall Corp has bought out your company. That goes for Earth Resources, too. All terms of your current contracts will remain the same. But I want your team packed up and ready to roll out of here within twenty-four hours. Consider this a not-so-hostile takeover. Wamba?"

At a snap of Wamba's fingers, the governor's own security detail hurried forward. "Samuel Makuga and Trevor Mulroney, you are both under arrest for crimes against the Democratic Republic of the Congo."

A blue helmet stepped away from one of the helicopters. "Just a minute. We've got at least two embassies registering charges against Mr. Mulroney here. We've been ordered to take him into custody." The sight of uniforms swarming around Mulroney and Makuga was as incredible to Robin as the compliant retreat of her Ares Solutions teammates.

But even as she grappled to make sense of it, Michael was striding forward to greet another newcomer heading toward them from a Sikorsky. "Alan Birenge! I don't know what's more welcome medicine for sore eyes—you or that UN contingent! How did you pull this off?"

Matching the BBC journalist's slim, café au lait features and wire-rimmed glasses with his Skype profile photo, Robin at last allowed tension to drain freely from her body. Then she wasn't just latching on to hope. It really was over.

Somehow beyond all probability, all expectation, decked in the most beautiful wrapping of sky blue and white, a miracle had arrived!

> > >

"No need to panic. What I've gathered from both our embassies, you can count on extradition before too many nights in a Bunia prison cell."

"A British one should make me feel better?" Trevor Mulroney was still clinging to the hope that he was caught somewhere in a dream. Or a nightmare. "Why are you interfering here, Howard? Didn't I tell you I had everything under control? I can still turn this around."

"No, you can't." The Texan drawl held as much regret as certainty. Howard Marshall held up an iPad. Among bold headlines, the words *rhenium, Ituri, Congo,* and *Earth Resources* jumped out at Mulroney.

"The story hit wires stateside in time for our evening news. As we speak, it's hitting morning papers in Singapore, Japan, Hong Kong. Your countrymen will be watching it with their breakfast tea in another hour. Speaking of which, you might have gotten away with something as stupid as going after a BBC journalist if Alan Birenge hadn't already contacted your embassy and mine. Your goons walked right into an ambush. They've been singing like canaries. Turns out a certain corrupt police commander in Kampala happens to be a half brother to Ares Solutions' local field commander, a Samuel Makuga."

Trevor Mulroney clenched fists white-knuckle with rage. "Don't tell me you wouldn't have made the same call! As for that police commander, he's also cousin to Governor Wamba. Those were Wamba's contacts in Kampala. His goons back when he was playing patsy with the Ugandans, selling them conflict minerals before the peace settlement. Everything that's happened here Wamba's been part of, up to his big, dirty neck. And what do you mean, you're taking over Ares Solutions and Earth Resources? You've got no authority—"

"On the contrary," Howard Marshall interrupted smoothly. "Once photo evidence made your collusion with a war criminal like Samuel Makuga undeniable, I had no choice but to call an emergency board session for Earth Resources. As top shareholder outside yourself, I was a logical stand-in for CEO. And since Ares Solutions is part of the Earth Resources pie—"

The American tycoon's gesture indicated Mulroney's handpicked field team, currently striding toward the Mi-17s without a backward glance. And why not? Despite long years of mutual acquaintance and combat with Mulroney, these were mercenaries, fighting for whoever paid their contracts. Which would now appear to be Howard Marshall.

"As to Wamba," Marshall went on, "the governor is of course appalled at the excesses to which his subordinate has stooped while contracted to handle security for a *mzungu* mining corporation. Wamba and his own superiors in Kinshasa are even more appalled to discover this same *mzungu* conspired to cheat the Congolese people of their latest national treasure trove."

A few meters away, Makuga's bared teeth and Swahili curses gave voice to Mulroney's own fury as Wamba's security detail stripped the Congolese field commander of weapons and bound arms and wrists behind his back. Between his own bared teeth, Mulroney gritted, "I should have known. Wamba's your man too, isn't he? Let me guess, he was on your intelligence payroll even back when he was still running around the rainforest. No wonder he ended up with the biggest goody bag at the peace settlement. Like Saddam Hussein and Manuel Noriega in their day. And now after all I've done over the years for you and your government, you're going to give Wamba a pass and hang me out to dry!"

"Yes, we've certainly had a long and profitable relationship." The American's shrug held genuine regret. "Believe me, Mulroney, I'd have preferred to continue working with you. Okay, so you lied about my original investment here. I'd have done the same. And it was to my government's benefit as well as yours to keep under wraps what's really in those rocks. If you'd pulled this off, we'd be having a different conversation. But with the cat out of the bag, I've got to do what's best for Marshall Corp and my own country. We need that rhenium. And frankly, you're just plain too dirty now to touch.

"Thankfully, I'd started digging with your first request for more funds last week. Flew to Kinshasa to meet with my own people the moment I got a whiff of trouble on the horizon. And thanks to my nephew Carl's tip-off, I was able to get a jump on negotiations before this hit headlines. In truth, while I personally would have preferred our prior and highly profitable arrangement, my own government is not completely averse to the bottom dropping out of the rhenium market. If nothing else, it'll make future concessions here a lot cheaper. And with ample and low-cost product, there'll be less incentive for the competition to get frisky in the zone. Especially since those negotiations include a generous budget for Governor Wamba's forces to be trained and armed under American oversight to bring a genuine peace and end to the Ituri conflict."

You mean, to guarantee a safe flow of product, Mulroney corrected sourly even as the American confirmed.

"My government's leaving no wriggle room for the Chinese or anyone else to slip into this zone. Nor will your own shareholders be raising any complaints since the settlement includes a complete payoff of Earth Resources debt by Marshall Corp. A win-win for everyone, wouldn't you say?"

Marshall turned away. "And now if you'll excuse me, I need to chat with your Ares Solutions mission team. Since this op's already in-country, Marshall Corp's got an issue with a local warlord down in our Katanga copper concession they might as well deal with while they're still under contract."

As the wide-brimmed Stetson headed toward the Mi-17s, Governor Wamba's security detail closed in around the former CEO of Earth Resources and Ares Solutions.

A win-win, definitely. For everyone, that was, except Trevor Mulroney.

CHAPTER FORTY-SIX

"I was praying you'd find some powers that be who could give Trevor Mulroney a call and order him to stand down." Michael was pounding Alan Birenge on the back and being abused in return, as strong men do when showing affection. "But all this? How did you pull this off? And at such short notice!"

"You think I'd leave my daughter's physician to the chance aid of the powers that be? No, sending hooligans into my Kampala hotel was the final nail in Mulroney's coffin. If Ms. Duncan's evidence and Wamba's earlier shenanigans hadn't already prompted me to contact my embassy, we'd be writing a different story right now. They'd just sent a security escort when a certain off-duty police unit showed up. Believe me, the moment my family was evacuated to a safe house, I started calling in every favor in my arsenal. It helped that my story had already hit the wires, so there was no turning back, even when my embassy found out who was involved."

"Yes, I was concerned that even if you got the story out, Mulroney might be considered untouchable as far as rousting any action out this way in time. What still gets me is how easily Mulroney managed all this. He didn't need confederates or some big conspiracy. The only intel it took was his word and a crooked local partner like Wamba for the authorities, the international press, even his hired private army to accept that Joseph was the bad guy and launching a war here was a good thing."

"Yeah, well, it's not a first. And it won't be the last. Nothing stopping the next multinational from bringing in their own firepower. No restrictions, no international accountability . . . Hey!" Alan Birenge's intelligent gaze suddenly lit up behind the lenses. "I think I've got my next big story! Thanks for the idea."

"Story or crusade," Michael responded dryly.

Even as the two men conversed, Michael's glance had marked Robin's approach, swept her slim frame up and down, with evident relief that she was in one piece and uninjured. As though by natural right, he held out his hand. When Robin placed her hand in his, he pulled her forward. "Alan, you haven't yet met in person a very special friend, Lt. Christina Robin Duncan."

The journalist shook Robin's hand vigorously. "Ah, yes, we wouldn't be standing here right now were it not for your courageous action. When I heard Mulroney bursting in on you—well, let's just say it added to the urgency. Though it wasn't my doing that scrambled a whole fleet of blue helmets by the time an embassy chopper delivered me to Bunia. When I mentioned American citizens were at risk, my embassy called yours. Seems one of their intelligence bigwigs already had an inkling something was going on and was flying in from Kinshasa. He insisted on hopping a ride here with the UN team."

The journalist nodded toward the Stetson hat now leaving the storage shed. "Marshall is a big name in the mining industry. I haven't quite figured out yet just how this particular clan member ties into this whole story, but from what I've gathered, it was Howard Marshall who got Wamba to turncoat on Mulroney, so I guess he's got a right to be here. I'm beginning to think there's a lot more to this story than I've pieced together so far. And speaking of stories—" Alan Birenge looked from Michael to Robin—"I've got a follow-up to file within the hour. Any chance of getting you two on record? And on camera?"

Robin was already shaking her head. Deeply grateful though she was for this man's arrival, the last thing she wanted was to find her face splashed across the world's news cameras. "Look, I'm sorry, but if there's any way you can do it, I'd prefer keeping my name out of this altogether. I just want to go back to my normal life, my family, and forget all this."

"I have to agree, Birenge," Michael put in firmly. "My sister and her family will still be in the zone when this is all over. And so will Governor Wamba. Things will be a lot safer if any involvement of the Stewart clan or Taraja is kept out of this. But if you want a story, there's a young man who deserves to have his name cleared before the world. He's the real story here. Joseph?"

The massed villagers had begun to break up, some drifting toward the destroyed brush corral, parents gradually releasing children to run free. Joseph's own priorities were clear as he headed instead to cut wires and fuses, lifting away explosives that still offered a threat. He waved off Ernie and the French Algerian as both started instantly toward him. "No, please, I know what I have done, so I can more quickly remove the danger alone. But please keep all away."

He had snipped free the last bundle and was stepping back when Michael and Robin led Alan Birenge over. There was still such a dazed, shaken look in Joseph's eyes that Robin exclaimed, "Are you okay, Joseph? How do you feel?"

"I am okay. It is just—when I heard the explosion—" a shudder went through Joseph's body as he laid the disarmed explosives down on a fuel drum—"I believed I was dead. I did not dare dream to find myself still among the living. As to how I feel?" He paused to survey the dispersed villagers, Samuel Makuga and Trevor Mulroney being led toward a Sikorsky. A broad smile banished the dazed look. "I feel . . . forgiven."

"Hey, that's a great line! Can I quote it? And you speak English. Mind if I get you on record?" As Alan Birenge pushed his way forward, Robin discreetly withdrew. Joseph would be okay. And vindicated at last.

She turned suddenly back. "Mr. Birenge. Would you happen to have a phone on you? I need to let some people know I'm okay."

"Of course." The journalist was already focused completely on his new interview subject as he handed Robin a latest model iPhone. "It's the BBC's tab, so call anywhere you like as long as you want. You've earned that much if you won't let me feature you."

Robin pulled up the Skype app before remembering one other matter she needed to take care of first. Ernie Miller and his teammates had drifted to the Mi-17s. Walking up to the Vietnam vet, Robin said quietly, "Thank you for intervening back there."

Ernie raised shaggy, gray eyebrows. "Nothing to thank. On the contrary, it was a well-needed reminder there are limits beyond which no contract is worth it. I'm beginning to think it's time for me to hang up my hat and get out of this business."

Robin said nothing further because a wide-brimmed Stetson was advancing purposefully toward the group, and she'd just caught sight of Carl Jensen loitering a few meters away. Robin finished going through the Skype activation steps as she hurried over. "Carl, I'm not even going to discuss your part in all this since everything's turned out okay. All I'm asking is that you rustle up some of your communication gear to find out if Ephraim and Miriam and the others in Taraja are okay. Especially since, thanks to you, their own communication system is blown to bits."

The reconnaissance technician's shrug conveyed no contrition. "A security patrol we left at Taraja has hand radios. But if you're worried about that Congolese doctor Makuga shot, last report is he's just fine other than a hole in his leg."

"Shot?" Striding up behind Robin, Michael demanded sharply, "Are you saying Makuga shot Ephraim? . . . No, I couldn't give a rip what your report says. You get me Taraja on the line right now."

The beep of a Skype link coming online pulled Robin away from Michael and a suddenly much less apathetic Carl Jensen. It was past midnight in South Carolina, so it was with scant hope that Robin attempted the call. But as Robin headed past a Sikorsky in search of a spot far enough from people and noise to offer both quiet and privacy, Kelli appeared on the small screen. Pale, tired features were devoid of their usual careful makeup, red-gold hair caught in a casual ponytail.

"Kristi?" Robin demanded urgently.

"Kristi's fine. Wonderful, in fact. She's out of intensive care now. And Brian . . . Kristi's pediatrician says everything looks good. Do you know what that means, Robin? Kristi is going to live! To be a normal little girl. To grow up, marry, have kids of her own."

As her sister's voice broke, Robin cut in. "But . . . you're saying she's already had the operation? That's why you were at the hospital? But I never got you the money."

"It was Brian's doing. He fought with the insurance company. Made them back down and agree to pay for it. He didn't let me know ahead of time because he didn't want to get my hopes up. Because of the urgency, he scheduled the operation as soon as approval came through. The specialist who performs the experimental procedure is an old friend. There's something else, Robin."

A glow lighting blue-green eyes so like Robin's, the soft curve of an unpainted mouth were more beautiful than Kelli's normal glossy perfection. "Brian asked me to marry him tonight. I said yes."

Robin must have managed some noise of congratulation because Kelli was chattering on. "Of course we'll wait until you can come home for the wedding. Just so it's not too long. Brian's got his own house in a great neighborhood with good schools. Oh, and he wants to adopt Kristi too. It's going to be wonderful. And not just for me and Kristi. You've worked so hard, Robin. I can't tell you how much it means to know you'll finally be free to do what you want for a change."

Robin didn't stay much longer on the line. Filling Kelli in on her own less savory activities over the last twenty-four hours would simply spoil her sister's rejoicing, and it would be hours before she could speak to Kristi herself. She'd met Kristi's current pediatrician, a tall, gangly blond in his midthirties, only a handful of times. But her impression of Brian Peters had been a man both kindly and firm, passionately committed to his small patients, and Robin could not be more delighted in her sister's choice of husband or father for Kristi.

Even better was Kelli's other news. Robin could only shake her head in wonder and disbelief. All her worrying and scrabbling for funds, and her niece's Creator and heavenly Father already had in place all the time his own vastly superior plan for Kristi's salvation and future!

And yet intermingled with joy as Robin cut off the Skype connection was an unexpected sensation of lostness. As Kelli had pointed out, for the first time in five years, Robin was free.

But to do what?

> > >

"Wow, this is really good! Got a problem if I run this one?"

Joseph was less impressed with the digital photo Alan Birenge was displaying on his camera. If not for the surroundings, he wouldn't have recognized the man standing beside piled fuel barrels and explosives in tattered shorts and bare feet, dried mud and red clay camouflaging features and body, vine and twig harness still decorating biceps and torso.

Taking his silence as acquiescence, the journalist swept on. "You studied at London's School of Mines, worked in a lab there. I'm just trying to picture you in suit and tie. Of course once charges are dismissed, there's no reason you couldn't return to your studies, even another overseas job. And your people—obviously they can't rebuild here since the mine will still be going forward. You're their leader. Have you given any thought to what comes next?"

To what comes next? For so long, Joseph had not expected there to ever be a *next*; he'd given the future little thought at all. But he did so now as the journalist thrust a digital recorder at him.

"You are right that we cannot rebuild here. But in Taraja there is still much land not yet reclaimed. They have opened their doors to those left homeless by conflict. We will begin by going there. And some may wish to remain here at the mine, working as free men for wages if it is placed under just administration. As for me—" Joseph shook his head. "I cannot leave yet. If the outside world is to come into the Ituri, my people need someone here who understands that world. Who knows not only of such things as geology, but of fair wages and labor practices. Of protecting our rainforest while harvesting its treasures. And if the new administrators of this treasure prove as evil and corrupt as the last, they will discover that Jini, the ghost, is still able to rise up and fight. Not just for my village, but for all the Ituri people. Perhaps when all is settled, when I can be sure those I leave behind are safe, I can go abroad again to pursue my own dreams."

But even as he spoke, Joseph had a sudden conviction that he would not leave the Ituri again. The thought brought no rebellion, but peace, even contentment. Youngest of siblings or not, the events of the last months, his own gifts and education, had made him a leader.

Like his father.

And like his father, it was his destiny to make this place his own. However beautiful, the Ituri was no paradise. Nor would it ever be the paradise he'd dreamed of making it. Not so long as human beings remained sinners, capable of evil and greed and violence. And there were things he would miss if he stayed here. Libraries, travel, technology, all the offerings of a vast outside world.

But this rainforest was where he belonged. Where he'd been called by the Almighty to raise a light in the darkness. To use the education and training his Creator had afforded him for the benefit of its people. To prepare its next generation to make a difference in the future of their country and world.

A call from one of the blue helmets drew away the journalist. Carrying the disarmed explosives into the Quonset hut, Joseph took note of villagers dragging blackened cooking pots from the smoldering embers of the brush kraal. Others had heaped wood to start a fire, the first flames now rising to compete with the growing smudge of orange and red streaking the eastern horizon above the rainforest canopy. A file of women and girls threaded their way toward the river with water jars. Two men had unearthed a canoe and were now pushing off the riverbank to add some fish to breakfast preparations.

"*Jambo*, Joseph." The greeting came from one of the village's young women, Adia; she'd been a child of seven when he'd left to study in Taraja. She held out a green coconut with the top sliced off. "You look tired and thirsty. I brought you refreshment."

Though her expression was demure, a smile dancing in wide-spaced, black eyes, tugging at a full, beautiful mouth was a reminder of why his father had been content to build his life in this Ituri Rainforest.

The thin, white liquid of the green coconut was cool, refreshing as its imported counterparts, tea and coffee, would never be. Joseph drained the coconut in a single, long draught. Returned Adia's smile.

He was home.

CHAPTER FORTY-SEVEN

Robin slid the borrowed phone into her knapsack pocket. But she did not head immediately back toward the others. Her wanderings while talking to Kelli had led through the mine diggings to the base of the rocky knoll marking the encampment's far perimeter. With a brightening sky overhead, Robin could now make out the zigzag of a footpath leading upward where blasting had not yet disturbed the rock formation.

On impulse Robin headed up the path, not slowing until she emerged on top of the ridge. Below, the militia army had melted back into the rainforest, leaving empty the muddy field outside chain-link fencing. An Mi-17 had risen from the ground and was angling over the rainforest toward the Taraja base. The dismantling of the Ares Solutions op had begun.

As the second Mi-17 hovered skyward, Robin scrambled over a

pile of boulders to the crest, where she could look out in the opposite direction of the mining encampment. Here she could no longer see the ugly gray gash where the rock outcropping had been blasted away for molybdenum ore or the barren clearing that had once been thatched homes, fruit trees, and crop beds of a village.

Instead, she looked across a vista so perfect her throat tightened with its beauty. A sea of tossing green billows melted unbroken into the much paler green of approaching dawn. A single bright star still marked the horizon between rainforest and sky.

The morning star.

Spreading out at a slightly northeast slant to Robin's right was an archipelago of rock outcroppings. Daybreak's paintbrush had transmuted the rock formations into a fantastic blend of shadows trimmed in copper, bronze, and gold, so that the overall impression was of some ancient lost city swallowed up by rainforest.

Even knowing now the treasure they contained, Robin found the rock formations a bizarre anomaly to stumble upon among thousands of square kilometers of unbroken rainforest canopy, their odd geometric contours more some modern art project than happenstance. Not such a fanciful thought. Was not the Creator of the universe just such an Artist who'd filled these rocks with rare treasure and placed them in the Ituri Rainforest to be discovered at this precise point on the planet's time line?

Robin had climbed high enough now that rounded treetops lapped at a ledge just below her, easily fifty meters from the rainforest floor. When she'd flown over this jungle by helicopter, those trees had appeared a uniform bed of giant broccoli, any sights, sounds, smells of life they might have cradled eclipsed by the roar and diesel fumes and sheer distance of the helicopter.

When she'd run and walked and fled beneath that same canopy, those treetops had been so high overhead, she'd glimpsed only brown and black tree bark and shadows and the muck beneath her feet.

But here at such close range, Robin was at once above and

intimately drawn into the rainforest canopy. A breeze had set the treetops to swaying in stately rhythm, filling Robin's ears with the rush of waves crashing upon a beach. As leaves tossed in a wild dance of their own, she could see that what had appeared a uniform green was indeed countless hues of that color.

Rich, dark greens.

Emerald-green leaves so shiny they sparkled in the light.

An almost silvery-gray olive green that was the undersides of leaves as the wind lifted them.

Yellow-greens of palm fronds.

Bright greens of lianas looping from bough to bough.

Other hues were brightening into full color in the growing light. Flowering trees dotted the canopy with mustard yellow, flame red, white, and the palest of pink. A cascade of orchids spilled from a tree bough, creamy petals tapering through shades of lilac toward the heart of each blossom, a deep, rich lavender. A silvery ribbon far to Robin's right was a waterfall spilling down the side of one of the most distant outcroppings.

Robin felt as alone in this beautiful scene as Adam when his Creator awoke him to life. Until a loud chitter below was followed by a furry black-and-white face thrusting itself from among the leaves. Another joined the first, then another and another, as though called together to gawk at this strange intruder into their world.

The troop of colobus monkeys scattered as a neon-green rope Robin had assumed to be a liana released its grip on a nearby branch to slither away. A reminder that the original Paradise had not been without its dangers. But Robin didn't allow the viper to spoil her mood. Until this moment, if by her own choice as she could admit now, Robin had seen only the darkness of this vast equatorial kingdom.

Today she saw its beauty.

Its myriad, incalculable variety of tree and blossom and fruit.

The lavishness of life it held.

As she slid and scrambled down to the ledge to better relish that exquisite panorama, a truth hit Robin like a dousing of cool spring-water in the heat and thirst and exhaustion of the forced desert march her life had so often seemed of late. All this splendor and magnifi-cence. The sheer vastness of it. The wealth and variety of color and sound, plant and animal. The music of water and wind and bird-song. Even the gorgeous hidden shimmer of jewels and metals placed within the earth itself for discovery as though in some over-the-top extravagance of gift giving.

All this could have been birthed of nothing but similarly extrava-gant and measureless love. Love of an almighty Creator for his cre-ation. Love of a heavenly Father for his children.

Suddenly, spontaneously, Robin flung her arms wide as though in a fruitless attempt to embrace all she could see. *I love you, Father God. And I know now without any shadow of doubt just how much you love me. How much you must love every human being whose body, mind, and soul you've knit together with such care. You created such a beauti-ful playpen for your children. You didn't need to make it so beautiful. So many colors. So much variety. All to surprise and delight us the way I love surprising Kristi with something special when I come home from a trip. Except a love that could create all this is as far above my love for Kristi as your amazing creation is beyond my homecoming gifts.*

And you gave us this world so we could enjoy it and each other. But children can't grow up if they can't make their own mistakes—and learn from them. And we're the ones who've made such a mess of your beautiful world. If it hurts me to see what a mess we've made, how we've grabbed and kicked and punched for ourselves instead of working together, how much must it hurt you! You had every right to leave us wallowing in the consequences of our own bad choices.

But you didn't. You sent a Light into the world to show us the way back to you. Yesu, nuru ya ulimwengu. *Jesus, Light of the World. I could still wish there was some way for you to carry out what you're doing without ever giving us the choice to do wrong. That people could be strong, true shining lights for you without ever going through fires of suffering. But I'm finally ready to admit in my stubborn, limited brain and heart that you know what you're doing. You can and will bring forth the beauty of pure, refined gold from the ugly dross we've made of the earth.*

"You look happy."

At the quiet baritone, Robin whirled around with such precarious haste her boots scrabbled on the edge of the rock shelf. A strong hand shot out to grasp her wrist, pulling her to a safer distance from its precipitous green drop-off. Which only brought her up close to a trim, muscled frame.

"Michael! What—what are you doing here?"

Robin had made that same startled, breathless exclamation less than a week ago. But this time the emotions behind it were totally different. She smiled as widely as she'd flung out her arms.

"I *am* happy! This world is still full of darkness. The war is still raging. The end of human evil and human suffering is not yet. But on this day at least, light won out and goodness prevailed. *God* prevailed. Whatever happens next, for Joseph and his people, for the Congo, for me, I can now trust that God is love, even when I don't completely understand. His purposes will not be thwarted. However badly we humans behave, God will turn it ultimately to good."

Robin broke off, reminded to ask, "Speaking of which, did you get through to your sister? Is Ephraim okay?"

"Yes, I did." Michael released Robin's wrist. "A flesh wound, no fracture. He's already insisting on getting back to his patients, Miriam says. I thought you'd want to know. Saw you heading up this way and followed. I hope you don't mind. And your sister and niece? I assumed that's who you wanted to call."

"Oh no, of course I don't mind. And Kristi and Kelli are good. Better than good." As Robin filled him in, Michael lowered himself to the ledge, leaning against the rock face. Robin settled herself beside him. They should both be getting back to the encampment. People would be looking for them. But for this brief interlude, to be alone in this glorious place with Michael was another gift she would simply savor.

"It's funny. For so long I've had to be there for Kelli, take care of her and Kristi. But now—all she's been through with Kristi, especially this recent crisis, has really changed her. Made her stronger. More beautiful than she ever was as the family homecoming queen. She's finally ready to be Kristi's mother without me tagging along. And a good man's wife.

"Your sister was so right about everything. I'd have done anything to keep Kelli from going through these last horrible five years. But then I'd have held her back too from developing all that character, perseverance, and other things in the verses Miriam quoted." Robin's pleasure trailed into regret. "Maybe I did hold her back when I always insisted on stepping in to save the day every time there was a problem."

"Hey, you can't beat yourself up over past mistakes. If they were mistakes. In any case, your sister was hardly the only one going through a fiery furnace these last years. Or coming out as pure gold!" A vibration in Michael's voice pulled Robin's gaze from the sunrise. Beside her, a strong-boned profile was tilted skyward, long lashes narrowed thoughtfully on a dissipating orange and purple streamer as though it held every mystery of the universe.

"Jini, you mean? Joseph? Yes, even to the very end there, when I knew the truth of his story, I wondered if he'd choose to follow the kind of path Makuga and Wamba have done. He was angry enough. And he certainly had every excuse—some might even say every right—to want revenge. To become as much the monster as Trevor Mulroney made him out to be. Instead he chose to offer up his own life to try to save the others. Just as Miriam hoped and prayed for that sweet little boy she used to know, Joseph chose to follow the Light, to become a light in the darkness."

"Yes, he did. But I wasn't thinking of Joseph." The long frame leaning against the stone shifted position so that Michael was no longer studying the sky but Robin's face.

"I was thinking of you, Christina Robin Duncan. Do you realize what you did out there today? You didn't just manage to bring Birenge and his people here in the nick of time. You stepped—no, rushed into danger to face down one of the most powerful men on earth. To place your own body as a human shield to protect Joseph and his people—and me! We'd have all been dead when the cavalry finally arrived if not for your intervention."

Something Robin read in the glow of his gaze, the approval of his tone, was making her heart race. But she could not let him believe a falsehood. "That wasn't really me. I didn't really plan anything. I didn't even think about it. I just . . . reacted."

"Yes, you just reacted. And it's how you reacted that shows the person you are. The person you've become. The Lt. Chris R. Duncan I knew in Afghanistan was a girl. Beautiful. Maddening. Chock-full of ambition. Determined to show up every male member of her family tree. A girl who stole my heart so completely that five years later I still haven't found it again."

Michael reached to take Robin's left hand in both his own, smoothing her palm flat with a thumb before intertwining strong fingers through her own. "But the Robin I ran into at that Uganda-Congo border crossing had grown into so much more. A woman who gave up her lifetime dream for the well-being of her sister and niece. A woman with so much compassion for the hurting and destitute, even while she's tried to convince herself and others she doesn't care. Who didn't hesitate to lay her own life on the line when push came to shove.

"I know the risk it took to send that evidence once you knew Mulroney was on to you. Not just for you, but Kelli and Kristi. You could have walked away. Made the excuse you were only obeying orders. Standing up to Mulroney took more courage and steel than any Marine platoon heading into combat. Every Duncan on your family tree should be proud of the woman, daughter, Marine you've proved yourself to be."

Robin kept her gaze on those entwined fingers as she admitted shakily, "Mulroney told me he'd pay everything for Kristi if I'd just walk away. But even if I'd believed him, there were kids in that prison mine. Families who loved their children as much as I do Kristi. I couldn't trade Kristi's life for theirs. That's when I realized it wasn't up to me to save Kristi or anyone else. Their life paths are in God's hands, not mine. Nor could I try to read the future, to make the right choice, so everything would turn out the way I wanted. All I could do was the right thing in front of me."

Michael's grasp had relaxed enough for Robin to tug free, pushing to her feet. "In any case, it's all over. *Really* over now that Kelli and Kristi are taken care of. I can't even begin to think where I'll go from here. After this op, I'm done with private contracting. And though I ways love the Marines, somehow I don't think a female Duncan al is anywhere on the horizon. I guess I'd better start writing some résumés. There's got to be something out there worth doing with the rest of my life."

Robin halted as she realized how her words might be read.

Misread.

Hastily, she added, "Of course I'm sure I'll find something soon. And since I've got a wedding to help plan, it'll be good to have some free time. Meanwhile, we'd better be getting back before a search party comes looking."

"Robin, stop!"

One boot was already on the path when Michael cut through Robin's babble. She turned straight into a tall, lean frame. This time when Michael took possession of both her hands, there was no pulling away. He flattened her palms under his own against a hard torso. Through spread-out fingertips, Robin could feel his heartbeat, its rapid rhythm belying his easy, relaxed stance. Michael stepped closer so that only their entangled hands were between them. His breath stirred a loose strand of red-gold hair.

"Christina Robin Duncan, do you really think I'm going to let you just walk off into the sunrise again after all this? You told me down there when we were about to get blown up that you should have come after me five years ago. Well, that goes both ways! When I came out of that coma, even when I heard that voice message from your sister and believed it was you, that you didn't want to have anything further to do with me, that you blamed me for your brother, I should still have hunted you down. Made you say what you had to say to my face.

"Instead I've wasted five years. Okay, maybe they weren't really wasted. Maybe this was all part of God's plan for our life journeys from the beginning. But I'm not leaving this ledge without finishing what was interrupted on the bank of that Band-e Amir lake five years ago. Robin, I love you. And I know beyond every shadow of doubt that you love me."

Across the restless treetops from the ledge, a shiver of light had now become a distinct curve above the horizon, burning away the last streamers of red and orange. Somewhere in the far recesses of Robin's consciousness, beyond the ridge, down in the mine encampment, a sharp staccato was growing too loud to be ignored any longer. Lengths of wood, empty fuel drums, metal barrels converted into an impromptu percussion section. Then voices joined in. Freed prisoners singing in celebration of an unexpected new day.

But Robin had ears only for the warmth in the deep baritone voice that was no longer gentle but shaken with fervent, passionate conviction. The flame in tawny eyes blazing into hers was sunshine burning away the mist of a cool jungle morning. Dancing on the brown, tranquil swells of a Congo tributary. Melting the last frozen crevices of Robin's heart.

"Back there in Afghanistan when we were interrupted, I had nothing to offer you. I was leaving. I couldn't even ask you to go with me. You'd barely started your deployment. All I could do was share my heart. Hope you cared enough to wait a year or two until we could work something out. I never thought it would be five years. Or that

God would give me—us—a second chance. But he's brought us back together for a reason. I've been sure of that since I walked into that border hut and thought I had to be hallucinating. And now there's nothing left separating us. No reason to wait. I'll be leaving stateside in a week or so. We could go together, see what your sister has in mind. Or . . . Ephraim is a minister. He and Miriam would be happy to—"

Robin was free to move only because one of Michael's hands had released hers to slide around her waist, the other rising to push back that windblown strand of red-gold hair. Her hand over his mouth interrupted the flow of speech. Arms slid around his neck as Robin stood on tiptoes to brush lips against a strong jawline.

"Michael Stewart, I love you more than I can ever wrap into words, more than life itself. And if what you're trying to say with all of this history lesson is what I think you're trying to say, the answer is a very definite yes."

Michael's arms around her tightened so that her rib cage creaked ominously. Robin hardly even noticed. Then his head came down, warm breath against her own, until there was no longer breath for further speech. Beyond the ridge, a staccato of sticks against metal and wood picked up pace. The rejoicing of freed prisoners swelled in volume. Took on those unbelievably rich, complex harmonies that were the Swahili people's gift to the rest of the world.

"Yesu, nuru ya ulimwengu."

"Jesus, Light of the World."

Unnoticed by the mute couple standing motionless as one on the ledge, the curve of yellow light above the far green horizon became a half circle. Then a sphere of molten gold resting on a bed of jungle foliage.

Dawn rose over the Congo.

ABOUT THE AUTHOR

As a child of missionary parents, award-winning author Jeanette Windle grew up in the rural villages, jungles, and mountains of Colombia, now guerrilla hot zones. Currently living in Lancaster, Pennsylvania, Jeanette spent sixteen years as a missionary in Bolivia and now travels as a missions journalist and mentor to Christian writers in many countries, most recently Afghanistan. She has more than a dozen books in print, including *Betrayed*, *Veiled Freedom*, and *Freedom's Stand*, as well as the Parker Twins series and the political suspense bestseller *CrossFire*.

Visit the author's website at www.jeanettewindle.com for further information and a list of recommended reading.

DISCUSSION QUESTIONS

1. Robin is no humanitarian—she's just in the Congo to earn her "fair market price" to pay for her niece's surgery. Does the fact that she needs the money for an altruistic purpose make it any less grievous that she's taking part in a mission that exploits the Congolese?

2. Michael Stewart has compassion on the border guards demanding bribes before the Ares Solutions team can enter the Congo, since he knows their own government isn't providing a decent living for them. Do they deserve this compassion? Has there been a time when you've needed to exercise exceptional negotiating skills?

3. Robin would've given anything to be initiated into her family's male sphere of gun ranges and exercise grounds. Is there any role that you long for? How should you respond when you find yourself in a dissatisfying role?

4. Colonel Duncan, Robin's father, had very unrealistic expectations about the right of a parent to dictate career choices for his children. Do you have any unfair expectations of the people in your life? What steps could you take to surrender them?

5. Robin has learned to survive among suffering people by keeping her focus on her own job, heart, survival, and family. She believes the Congolese do the same. Is there another option for any of them? Do you see any of the characters in *Congo Dawn* living by a different set of priorities?

6. In chapter 8, Carl attempts to help the mother and her "blind" child at the airport fence by giving them money. Does offering a temporary fix to people in difficult circumstances help them in the long term? Why or why not? Name other options.

7. In chapter 12, Trevor Mulroney states, "But if there's one thing those early multinationals knew, it's that sometimes you've got to make war to make peace." Is that ever true? If so, when?

8. Michael says to Robin in chapter 14, "How can you even be certain who are the good guys and the bad? And believe me, the line between the two around here isn't as clear cut as you want to think." In a complicated world like ours, how do you determine who is good and who is bad? Why do you think this is so challenging sometimes?

9. What situations in *Congo Dawn* require forgiveness? How does the lack of forgiveness damage countries, people groups, and relationships? What can end a perpetual cycle of revenge? Give examples of revenge in the story and examples of characters who choose to seek alternatives to revenge.

10. Ephraim tells Robin of a Congolese saying in chapter 17: "Our Christianity is as wide as the Congo River at flood season, but also as shallow as a puddle under a hot sun in dry season." What does he mean? Describe how this problem can also be seen in the Western church. What steps can the church take to promote a faith that is both wide and deep?

11. Ephraim also says that he doesn't pray for an end to the fighting, hunger, and death besetting the Congo, but that "God would use these evils to purify us as a people. To purify us as a church." How can this prayer also apply to the United States? Do you think it is a difficult prayer to pray? Why or why not?

12. In chapter 21, Michael recalls injustices in Europe's history (aristocrats mistreating peasants, torture at the Tower of London) that changed only when Christians began practicing Christ's teachings "to the point where their societies were turned upside down." What practices could Christians follow today to impact our culture and turn society upside down? What practices could you implement in your own life?

13. At first, Robin believes that the Ares Solutions operation will impact the Ituri Rainforest for the better. She tells Michael in chapter 21, "Once we can secure stability and open transportation, Earth Resources will be able to bring in some heavy-duty mining gear. Make this place a model for mining here in the Congo. Offer a chance for a real life to the locals." Michael responds, "They have a real life." Do we sometimes think technological advancements automatically lead to better lives? Can you think of an example where technology has done more harm than good?

14. According to Miriam in chapter 26, human suffering is "God's equivalent of tough love." What does she mean by that? Have you ever bailed someone out of trouble, even though they needed to feel the consequences of their sin?

15. Later in the chapter, Miriam says, "Darkness, suffering, [and] injustice are the very things that show the measure of a person's true character as peace and comfort never can." Has this been true in your own spiritual walk? Give an example.

16. As the story begins, Robin, Joseph, Wamba, and Mulroney all use the darkness around them as an excuse to turn from the light. In the end, how are Robin and Joseph different from Wamba and Mulroney?

17. When you discover Joseph's motives for carrying out violent acts (blowing up the mine, etc.), can you overlook his methods?

18. Robin collects "hazard pay" to accept the contract work in the Congo. What type of hazard pay would you require to do a dangerous job? What would that job be?

Fires smolder endlessly below the dangerous surface of Guatemala City's municipal dump.

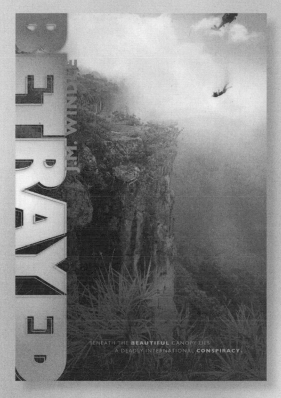

A politically relevant tale of international intrigue and God's redemptive beauty and hope.

TYNDALE
FICTION

www.tyndalefiction.com

Available now at bookstores and online!

CP0323

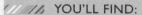